DRAGONS

Ty Drago

eBooks
Pennsville, NJ

PUBLISHED BY
eSpec Books LLC
Danielle McPhail, Publisher
PO Box 242,
Pennsville, New Jersey 08070
www.especbooks.com

ISBN: 978-1-949691-45-0
ISBN (eBook): 978-1-949691-44-3

Copyediting: Greg Schauer
Interior Design: Danielle McPhail
Cover Art and Design: Mike McPhail, McP Digital Graphics

Interior Illustrations: Ed Coutts
360 degree Europa Surface © Jurik Peter, www.shutterstock.com
CG models by Daz3D
Jupiter and Ganymede image courtesy of NASA

For my kids, who live
within these pages.

PART ONE
THE PRISONER

I wake up with a start, thinking three things in rapid succession.

First: This is a weird dream.

Second: Wait a sec. This doesn't feel like a weird dream!

Third: Oh… furk.

My mom wouldn't approve of that last one.

With a gasp, I sit up on the mattress.

I'm wearing an orange jumpsuit. On my feet are these little white gum-soled canvas pull-ons, without a doubt the ugliest shoes I've ever seen. Don't ask me why, but it's those pull-ons that tip me from "confused" to "scared." But when I look around, "scared" ratchets up to "terrified," and my stomach tries to crawl right up my throat.

I'm in some kind of futurey-looking cube, maybe twelve feet to a side.

Glowing squares in the ceiling cast an artificial light that makes the flat gray walls look, if possible, even flatter and grayer. Nearly every inch of every surface, ceiling and floor included, is made up of featureless metal tiles.

There's no door, no windows, and no furniture. In fact, the only things in the room, besides the foam mattress, are a square pedestal sink and a somewhat shorter, square toilet. No soap, no towel. Both the sink and john look like they're made of the same gray tiles as the walls.

I climb to my feet, half-expecting something bad to happen when I do.

When nothing does, I try the sink faucets. The water's cold. I cup some in my palms and drink. It tastes clean. In fact, it tastes almost *too* clean. Sterile. That doesn't make a lot of sense to me, but it's the impression I get.

The toilet works — well, like a toilet. No answers there. With no towel in evidence, I dry my hands on the legs of my jumpsuit.

Above the sink is a small mirror. Except it's not *really a* mirror, just a rectangular grouping of those same square tiles. Only these are *polished* somehow so that they give me back my own reflection.

More futurey weirdness.

My complexion's sallow, the way I get when I spend too much time playing vid games. If this was home, my mom would be all over me with epithets like, "You're not getting enough rest!" and "You're not getting enough sun!" I once considered asking her if she wanted me to take long afternoon naps in the backyard.

But, as I recall, I kept that particular snark to myself.

Where are *my folks?*

Do they know I'm missing? They *must*, and are probably crazy with worry, even crazier than most parents would be in such circumstances, given—everything.

My heart's hammering and the sweat on my face and hands has nothing to do with the temperature. Trust me on that one. A part of me wants to lay back down on the palette, curl up into a ball, and—well—hide.

Instead, I say aloud, trying not to sound scared, "Okay, what's the deal?"

I don't expect an answer.

Which is probably why a shock shoots up my spine when I get one.

"You're in no danger."

I don't scream. Honestly, I don't.

But I *do* whirl around, searching for the source of the voice. It sounds mechanical, disguised. That *could* be a good thing. If my captors don't want me to be able to ID them, then maybe they don't intend to murder me after they get the ransom.

You know… the ransom my folks can't afford to pay.

Except a ransom motive is only the *best-case* scenario.

Questions tumble through my mind, lots of them. I pick the most obvious. "Where am I?"

The reply is both immediate and unhelpful. *"Safe."*

"Great," I say. The voice seems to come from everywhere at once. I can't even tell if the speaker's male or female. "Not what I asked, though."

"All your questions will be answered eventually. Are you hungry?"

"No." Though I am.

"Thirsty? We can do better than tap water."

"No." Though I am.

"Then what are you?"

"Pissed off."

"This must all be very confusing."

"Confusing? You furking kidnapped me!"

No immediate response. So, I wait, trying to ignore the twist in my gut.

"All this is for the greater good. Soon, everything will be explained to you."

"Why not now? Doesn't look like I'm going anywhere."

"Not quite yet."

"Listen, if you're looking for a ransom, you snatched the wrong kid."

"We know exactly who we 'snatched.' You're Anthony 'Andy' Brand, eighteen-year-old senior at Haddonfield High School in New Jersey, Class of 2099."

My mouth goes dry. "If you know all that, then you know that my folks aren't anything like rich!"

"We're not interested in money, Andy. But we'll address that later. For now, I'd like you to do something for me."

Here it is. The big ask. Will they demand that I strip naked? Could all this be some kind of perv party? I can't spot a vidcam, but they know I just used the sink, so they must be able to see me. Besides, they changed me into this jumpsuit, which means they've already seen my junk.

Unfortunately, bad as a sexual angle would be, there are worse possibilities.

"What kind of something?" I ask, trying to sound more impatient than scared.

I hear a gentle *swoosh* from above. I glance up in time to see something drop out of a square hole in the ceiling and land at my feet. A moment later, a tile slides over the hole and blends in with the rest, indistinguishable.

Do all *these tiles move?*

Warily, I look down at a crumpled piece of paper.

I reach for it.

"Don't bother. It's blank."

"Then what's it for?" I ask, though I know. Of course, I know.

"I want you to burn it."

My stomach lurches.

"What?"

"I want you to burn the paper," the voice repeats tonelessly, as if reciting the time of day.

"I… don't understand."

"You understand perfectly, Andy. I'm aware of the rules of your people, but these are extraordinary circumstances. As far as any potential damage goes, these walls have an extremely high heat tolerance. Believe me when I say that there's zero risk."

"Believe *me* when I say that I don't care."

"I can appreciate that. However, we do need to see it."

"See what?"

"See you burn that wad of paper."

"Okay. Fine. Whatever. But you're going to have to give me a lighter."

Silence.

"Or, I don't know, a match?"

"I was really hoping you wouldn't play this game."

I look balefully around, struggling to seem genuinely confused. "I don't know what you want from me!" I whine. It's a good whine, one of my all-time best. "How am I supposed to start a fire without even a lousy match?"

"I'm disappointed, though I suppose I shouldn't be surprised."

I do a dance of exasperation. I scowl. I huff. I throw up my hands, putting all the *"What the furk do you expect me to do?"* into it as I can.

"Burn the paper, Andy."

"How?"

"Burn it."

"I can't!"

"Of course, you can, and we both know it."

With a frustrated cry that I *think* sounds genuine, I kick the wad of paper into a corner of my cell. "I don't know who you are, but you're a lunatic!"

"All right. Obviously, this was too much too soon. Let's try again later."

"What? Furk later! I want to go home!"

"The fastest way for that to happen is for you to cooperate."

"How can I cooperate when what you're asking doesn't make any sense?"

"Why don't you get some rest? I suggest you lay down on the pallet. I don't want you to get hurt when the vector takes effect."

"The what?"

"Lay down. For your own sake."

"I'm not doing anything for you! I don't know what any of this is about, but I want nothing to do with it!"

"Your call, I suppose."

A moment later, the world starts spinning. Alarmed, I try to steady myself. I can't. Whatever's happening to me happens *fast*. Darkness closes in. As it does, a single horrific understanding wracks my already overtaxed brain.

They know! My God… they know what I am!

Then I hit the floor hard and stay there.

TWO – Days 1-2

Conceal and Protect.

Those words, always capitalized in my mind, were drilled into my head from toddlerhood — so much so that I, as Tony and Bonnie Brand's son, grew up thinking of it as our family motto. Back when I was in fourth grade, I learned about familial coats of arms. Afterward, totally jazzed, I drew one for *my* family. It depicted a fire-breathing dragon shooting flames out over a charred and blackened field. I even wrote the words "Conceal and Protect," very carefully, above it in big block letters.

Eight-years-old and largely friendless, I showed this "masterwork" to my mom, who immediately paled.

"It's beautiful, sweetheart." My father was at work, and we were alone in the house. Even so, I remember the way my mother looked furtively around as if worried that someone might see. "You'll be a great artist someday if that's what you want. But… this isn't something that you can ever show to anybody."

I was crest-fallen, pun intended. "But… I thought we could put it above the fireplace!"

Without warning, Mom pulled me into a desperate hug. "I wish we could, Andy. Your father and I would be so proud to have it there. But it's too dangerous. We've talked about this."

I squirmed and pulled away. "Dad says we shouldn't be ashamed of what we are."

"And he's right," Mom replied tearfully. "But we're not the only ones in danger."

"Why do we have to hide? If we're not supposed to be ashamed, then why are we always hiding? I'm so sick of hiding!"

She looked at me, stricken, and suddenly my newly found, pre-pre-adolescent fury vanished like smoke.

"Sorry," I mumbled.

"No, *I'm* sorry," she said. "I know you want to be like the other children. But you're not. Our family is Kind, and we need to remember how few we are and how many *they* are. Andy, human beings scare so easily, and they always strike out at what scares them. This means that to live among them, we have to try to *appear* human... even though we never will be. But it's not about shame. It's never about shame."

Now, alone in this strange cell, my mother's words echo. That day's conversation was a pivotal one, grimly transformative, and I never forgot a word of it.

We have to try to appear human... even though we never will be.

This, of course, is how my captors must see me.

Inhuman.

When I wake up after being "vectored," whatever that means, I'm stretched out on the tile floor where I fell. The room is unchanged. I have no idea how long I've been asleep. Hours, certainly. Maybe longer. Without a clock or window, time's a bit of a mystery.

What isn't a mystery is how hungry I am.

"Hello, Andy."

The Voice—yeah, I'm capitalizing it now—makes me jump a little. I try to hide the reaction and don't reply.

"You must be hungry."

This time, not replying's harder. My stomach growls.

"No? Well, let's skip breakfast then."

"Wait!" I call, jumping to my feet. "Yes, I'm hungry."

I immediately hear a scraping sound, and another wad of paper lands on the floor in front of me.

"Breakfast is waiting. All we ask in return is a little cooperation."

My stomach growls louder. "What do you want me to do?"

"You know the answer to that question."

"So... what? You're not going to feed me unless I obey?"

"Cooperate," the Voice corrects patiently.

I glare down at the new wad of paper. Then I kick it into the corner with the first one.

"No hurry, Andy. When you're hungry enough, just say so. I'll keep your food warm."

The Voice goes silent.

I wait, but it doesn't return.

Time passes furking slowly. The growling in my stomach deepens. I struggle to ignore it. Drinking water helps. Every so often, I go to the sink and fill my belly from its tap. But the feeling doesn't last and, before long, I have to pee like a racehorse. After a while, I get into a torturous rhythm. I wait until my stomach's too empty to bear, and then I drink myself full and, later, pee myself silly.

Rinse and repeat.

It makes for a brutal day. I keep expecting the Voice to return, maybe to tempt me, first with lunch, then dinner. But it doesn't. They're letting me, as my mother sometimes likes to say when I'm being a snot, "stew in my own juices."

It frankly sucks.

But they want me to break Conceal and Protect.

And. That. I. Will. Not. Do.

Eventually, and without warning, the lights dim. They don't go out completely. If they did, I'd be in pitch darkness in this windowless room. But they drop low enough that I sense this is supposed to be "nighttime," that I made it through a full day without eating. I wish I could call it a win, but every second of the ordeal feels like a minute and each minute like an hour. And I have no reason to think the night's going to be any easier.

I do my best to sleep. Cramps twist my guts, forcing me to lay curled up in a tight ball.

I'll never know how, but eventually, sleep finds me.

In the "morning," after a fitful night of pain and terrible dreams that left me sobbing in the dark, I awake to find a big bowl of oatmeal waiting for me.

I run to it and eat greedily, shoveling the food into my mouth with the included spoon.

As I do, the Voice says, *"You're a stubborn young man."*

I don't reply as I lick the bowl clean. I half-expect to vomit, but I don't. The stuff tasted like paste, thick and sticky but easily digestible. Maybe *they* don't want me puking either.

Nice of them.

"This would all go so much easier if you'd just cooperate."

"How?" I ask.

"You know how."

"What I *know* is that you want me to somehow start a fire without a match. If you're expecting me to use my heat vision, then I suggest you try a big guy in a cape and with a red "S" on his chest."

The Voice says nothing more.

Sometime later and without ceremony, my lunch arrives.

THREE – Days 2-4

My cell has no shower, though I'm not sure I'd use it if it did. After all, I know they're watching me.

No vids. No books. Not even a furking deck of cards. Just lots and lots of empty hours.

I spend them thinking.

I begin with a few observations. One, this cell isn't just clean; it's *immaculate*—not a speck of dust to be found. It's what my science teacher would call "hermetically sealed."

So then how does the air get in?

Since that seems a relevant question, I start exploring, examining every tile within reach. They're all about four inches square, and so tightly packed that I can't even get a thumbnail into the seams. Each is identical, except for the reflective-mirror ones above the sink and glowing-lamp ones in the ceiling.

Eventually, I find it.

A vent.

It's just a grouping of six tiles at floor level in one corner. Each has a gridwork of pinprick holes drilled through them. And, when I put my hand against them, I can feel a steady, gentle airflow.

Well, at least they aren't going to suffocate me.

Time passes.

The lights dim, so I sleep. I wake up when the light returns. Then I sit and wait. Food comes. I eat. Then I sit and wait some more.

The Voice doesn't speak.

Sound boring? You have no idea.

Finally, four days after first waking up in that cell and two days after finding the vent, everything changes.

Day Five starts like all the rest. Breakfast is due. Oatmeal with cinnamon. *Always* oatmeal with cinnamon. In the meantime, I've taken to sitting beside the vent, liking the air on my face while I wait for the feeding tiles to slide open.

"Hello?"

I gasp.

It isn't the Voice. No, this is soft and faint, with nothing tinny or electronic about it.

For several seconds, I don't dare move.

The whisper comes again, "Hello?"

The vent.

I slide down closer and peer intently into the gridwork of pinpricks, looking for light. But it's as black as always.

Once more, the whisperer speaks, "Is anybody there?"

Gathering myself, I say, "Hello." It comes out as a dry croak.

"Oh, my God… I *did* hear someone!"

Distrust and hope war between my ears. Hope wins, for now. "Who are you?"

"My name's Miranda. Are you… a prisoner, too?"

I process that question. There's a lot of information in it. "Yeah," I finally say. "I'm Andy. Um… how long have you been here, Miranda?"

"I'm not sure. A week, maybe? I count the times they lower the lights."

I smile at that. "Me, too. I think this is my fourth or fifth day." I swallow. My heart's pounding, though I'm not sure why. "Do you know what they want?"

"No. You?"

"No," I lie, which makes me wonder if she's lying too. "Um… what's your last name?"

"What?"

It's a stupid question, but too late to backpedal now. "Your last name. What is it?"

"Fiero, why?"

Fiero is Spanish. It means wild, brazen. *Fiery.* Having it means she might be Kind.

Maybe.

"You still there?" Miranda asks, sounding a little frantic.

"Yeah. I'm here."

"Don't go away, okay? I've been all alone. I kind of... need somebody to talk to."

"I won't go anywhere," I promise, meaning it. "I'll just lay here and talk to you for as long as you want."

"I'm going to move my pallet over," she tells me. "That way, I'll be more comfortable."

"Good idea. Me, too. Hold on."

I stand up, my thoughts churning as I drag my pallet across the tile floor and stretch out on it. "Still there?"

No reply.

"Miranda?"

Still nothing.

My heart, which has slowed, starts hammering again.

"Miranda!"

"I'm here!" she exclaims. "Sorry. It took longer to drag my stuff over than I thought."

The depth of my relief surprises me. "Oh... good."

"So... Andy. What should we talk about?" She sounds nervous but hopeful. "This doesn't feel like a 'small talk' situation. Besides, I couldn't tell you what the weather's like if you asked. I haven't been out of this room since I got here, and there's not exactly a view."

"Yeah," I reply, smiling like an idiot. "I say we stick to common ground. You tell me how you got here, and I'll tell you how I got here."

"Um... aren't you worried they might be listening?"

"I *know* they're listening. I just don't care."

She giggles. It's a sweet sound. "You're right. Furk 'em!"

At that, we both laugh, the sudden camaraderie pleasantly natural.

"How'd they get you?" I ask.

"Uh, uh. You first."

I hedge, but only briefly. "I was walking home from school in the rain. There was nobody but me on the street. All of a sudden, this van pulls up. At first, I thought it was just parking. Then three guys in black jump out. They don't say a word. They just grab me and press something over my face."

"Like chloroform?" she asks.

"Fancier. It felt like a gas mask. But it did the same thing. I took a breath, and that was it. The next thing I knew, I woke up here, and this voice was talking to me."

I wait, but Miranda says nothing. Maybe *she's* hedging, too.

Finally, she says, "I got taken right out of my bed in the middle of the night. I live with my father. I woke up just in time to feel them grab me and put a cloth over my face… in my case, definitely chloroform."

"Did they hurt your father?"

"They say they didn't."

"Good." I'm relieved, though I'm not sure why. It's not as if I think our captors are paragons of truthfulness or anything.

"How old are you?" Miranda asks.

"Eighteen," I say, a little tentatively.

"Me, too. Where do you live?"

"Haddonfield, New Jersey. It's near Philadelphia. You?"

"Carmel," she replies. "California."

Two kids taken — well, at least two — one from each U.S. coast. Too far apart to be random, but I figured *that* out the moment the first wadded piece of paper dropped out of the ceiling.

Did they test Miranda, too? Very probably they did, *if* she's Kind.

But I'd never ask. Doing so would be the same as admitting to the Voice that they're right about me.

Conceal and Protect.

"What do they want from us, Andy?"

"I don't know."

"Have they hurt you?"

"Yes," I say.

"They have? How?"

"They're keeping me in a cage against my will," I reply. "That hurts me."

"But they haven't… tortured you, or anything."

"They didn't feed me during my second day. But that's stopped. Now I get meals pretty regularly."

As if on cue, I hear the feeding tiles slide open, followed by the now-familiar scrape of a tray being pushed through. I don't bother looking up.

"My breakfast's here," she says.

"Mine too."

"Want to eat with me?"

"Sure," I say.

FOUR - Day 5-9

Over the next few days, my "girl next door" and I huddle in the corners of our respective cells. We talk about everything and anything, passing long hours in the comfort of each other's company.

Miranda was born in Arizona. Her mother died in childbirth, and her father moved them—she and her brother—to California before she turned one. Her father's a capital investor, whatever that is. She's eager to talk about her childhood, for the most part. But, when I ask about her brother, Miranda's attitude changes, becoming more subdued.

"His name was Charlie," she says.

"Um… was?"

"He died."

"Oh. I'm sorry."

"It happened a while ago. A sudden heart attack. Some kind of congenital problem that nobody knew about."

"That sucks, Miranda."

When she answers, her tone is unusually self-possessed, deliberate. "Charlie was always my father's golden boy, his heir apparent. He'd been home for the summer from Oxford when he just… collapsed. My father was devastated." Then, after a pause, she adds, "So was I."

I have no idea what to say.

"Andy? You there?"

"I'm here. Sorry, Miranda. For your loss, I mean. Ugh. I'm not good at this kind of thing."

"Don't worry about it."

I feel like a moron.

"Andy?"

"I'm here."

"Don't stop talking to me, okay?"

I'm quietly relieved. "Okay."

We swap theories about the Voice. As a calculated risk, I tell her about the wads of paper and the Voice's demand that I somehow burn them. When I'm done, I ask carefully, "So… are they going after you for anything crazy like that?"

"No. They pretty much just leave me alone."

"Pretty much?"

"Well, the Voice sometimes grills me about my dad and me: where we go on vacation; what religion we belong to; even what restaurants we like."

"That's way different from me," I say, perplexed. Either she's not Kind, or she is, but she's cagier than I am. Either way, I'm stymied.

I'm bothered a little that Miranda seems more willing than I am to cooperate with our captors. She insists that she answers their every question truthfully and completely, which means she's never been badgered or starved. It seems—I don't know—*collaborative*. But the more we talk, the more I get that she's as scared as I am. The difference is that I've channeled my fear into defiance. She's gone the other way, hoping that cooperation will get her home.

I wonder which of us is right.

What if we're both wrong?

Then, eventually, she gets around to asking what I look like.

"Pretty ordinary, I guess," I reply.

"You mean you've got two eyes, two ears, and a nose, just like everybody else?"

"Sure."

"Kind of plain-looking? Sort of… meh?"

"Yeah… Wait! No!"

She laughs. "Then how about specifics? Pretend you're looking in a mirror. What do you see?"

I sigh. "I'm tall and kind of skinny."

"What color's your hair?"

"Brown."

"Long or short."

"Short."

"Straight or curly?"

"Totally straight."

"Eyes?"

"Brown."

"Skin color?"

"White, I guess."

"Pimples?"

"Shut up."

She giggles.

"Fine," I say, pretending to be annoyed. "Your turn. Hair?"

"Blonde."

"Details. Honey blonde? Strawberry blonde? Or are you a bleached blonde like my sixty-year-old neighbor?"

"Cute. I guess you'd call it dirty blonde."

"Long? Short? Curly? Straight?"

"Wavy, I suppose."

"Skin color?"

"My father calls it olive-skinned… except for my teardrop."

"Your what?"

"Never mind."

"Come on. What teardrop?"

"I'm not sure why I mentioned it. It's… embarrassing."

"You know about my pimples."

"Yeah, but everybody gets those. This is more… permanent."

"Well, now you *have* to tell me."

"Promise you won't laugh?"

"Swear to God."

She says, "I've got this birthmark under my right eye. It's what they call a port-wine stain, except mine is shaped like a teardrop. It's almost perfect, so much so that most people assume it's a tattoo."

"That sounds really cool," I say, meaning it.

"It's awful. I've tried to get it removed, but it's so close to my eye that the doctors won't touch it."

"So? From what you're describing, it sounds…"

"Sounds what?"

I take the chance. "Beautiful."

When she doesn't reply, I worry I've gone too far. Then she says, with a smile in her voice, "Thanks."

"You're welcome. But we're not done. What color are your eyes?"

"I think I liked it better when *I* was interrogating *you*."

Now it's my turn to laugh. It feels good to laugh. "Blue?" I ask. "Green? Hazel?"

"Sort of gray, I guess."

"Gray? I don't think I've ever met anyone with gray eyes."

"Well, now you have."

"Not yet. Not until we're face to face. How tall are you?"

"About five-five. You? You said you're tall."

"Six-four."

"Jeez. You're a giant!"

I smile. "Only among lesser mortals." It's something my dad likes to say—sardonic for a number of reasons.

"Wow!" Miranda exclaims. "If… I mean, *when*… we do meet, I'm going to break my neck looking up at—" She suddenly stops talking. I wait, straining to hear. Seconds tick by.

"Miranda?" I ask.

Do I hear voices? If so, they're faint. Over the past few days, we've figured out that sound doesn't carry between our cells unless it originates right beside the vents. Once, as an experiment, I tried standing across the room and shouting, but Miranda reported afterward that she couldn't hear a thing.

Just like I can't hear anything now.

So, I wait. But Miranda doesn't come back.

I try calling. Nothing. I try again. The same. Eventually, I lay back on my pallet, which is now permanently stationed beside the vent. There, I stay, leaving only to drink from the tap, pee in the toilet, or fetch first one meal, and then another from the slot across the room.

She doesn't return.

Eventually, the lights dim. But I can't sleep. No way.

Sometime later, as I lie on my back in the dark, a single word slips through the vent. "Andy?"

"Miranda!" I exclaim. "You okay?"

"Shhh! I don't want them to hear this part."

"What? What part?"

"They told me not to tell you."

"Tell me what?"

"Some guys came in. They were wearing uniforms with a weird insignia. Corporate, I think."

Corporate? That makes no sense. "What kind of insignia?"

"It was an embroidered Planet Earth, or one hemisphere of it, with missiles or rockets blasting off it."

With a start, I realize that I know that logo.

"Did the uniforms have the letters CSE anywhere?" I ask.

"Yes!" Miranda whispers sharply. "On both shoulders. Do you know what it means?"

"Yeah, but it's nuts."

"Tell me!"

"It stands for Coffin Solar Exploration. It's part of Coffin Industries. You know… Charles Coffin."

"The billionaire?"

"That's him."

"How do you know?"

"I'm kind of a science nerd, and you can't swipe through ten pages of any tech journal without Coffin Industries getting a shout-out. They're in everything from biotech to global communications, and CSE practically *owns* space travel. I don't think there's a colony in the Solar System that Charles Coffin doesn't either own or run, and his security forces have been contracted by the U.N. to serve as an off-world police force."

"You think those guys in the black uniforms are… cops?"

"Corporate cops, yeah."

"So, we've been kidnapped by a… billionaire?"

"Or somebody working for him. What did they want from you?"

"They didn't say at first. They just showed up and grabbed me without a word. Then they took me down a hallway to this other room. Inside was a chair and a doctor. The doctor ran tests on me. It took forever, and it *hurt*. I kept asking her what she was testing me for, but she told me I wasn't allowed to know yet."

"Yet?" I say. "What's that supposed to mean?"

"No clue. When she was finally done, the doctor had me brought back here. She made a point of saying that they know you and I are talking and, for the most part, they don't care. But I wasn't supposed to mention what had happened to me, not a word of it. Or else."

"Or else what?"

"She didn't say. You don't think they'd… I don't know… separate us or something, do you?"

The very idea sends a jolt of panic through me. "No way," I tell her.

"Good."

"Um… I don't suppose this doctor mentioned anything about me?"

"No. Sorry. Except for not talking to you about any of this, your name didn't come up at all."

"Figures. Anything about when they're going to let us go?"

"I asked. But she wouldn't say." I hear her yawn. "Listen, Andy. I couldn't wait to get back here and tell you what happened, no matter what they said. But… now that I have, I'm *really* tired. You mind if I go to sleep?"

"Of course not," I tell her. "I'm pretty beat, too. I haven't slept either."

"You haven't?"

"Been too worried about *you*."

"That's really sweet," she says with another smile in her voice. Hearing it puts ants in my stomach. But in a good way.

"Thanks," I say.

"For what?"

"For telling me what happened. For not listening to them."

"Andy," she replies. "All we have is each other."

FIVE – Day 10

They come for me after breakfast the next morning.

Miranda's been telling me about this dream she had last night. In it, she was stuck inside a tight little box, unable to move or breathe. Completely trapped. Seriously, you don't need to be Freud to figure that one out, and I almost say so. But then a big section of the wall across from me *opens*, a hundred tiles sliding aside all at once. It's the first time I've seen it happen on this scale, and it might have been cool under different circumstances. Beyond the newly created archway, I see only a featureless corridor.

Two stone-faced men enter. They are both wearing black uniforms, though I notice that the insignia Miranda described is conspicuously absent.

Interesting.

"Come with us," one of them commands.

"Where?" I ask, sitting on my pallet in the corner.

"No questions," he says.

"No promises," I say.

"Come on," the other one tells me. "Don't make this hard."

"Where am I?" I ask.

Instead of replying, they cross my cell and yank me to my feet. Then, each gripping an upper arm, they march me out into an empty hallway. There are no visible doors, which I suppose makes sense. Who needs doors when the walls themselves are *malleable*?

I've even heard of such tech. Last year, during a field trip to the Franklin Institute, I saw an exposition of "new architectural sciences." They had a demo of something like this.

What did they call the stuff? Some trendy, catchy name…

Liquid Bricks. That was it.

And guess what corporation sponsored the exhibition.

My guards haul me along the corridor, ignoring my questions. Their treatment isn't rough exactly, just hurried, as if I might be contagious.

Or flammable.

As we approach the hallway's blank end, another doorway appears, the tiles sliding aside all but soundlessly. It's a cool effect, and I almost say so. Before I have the chance, I'm ushered into this new room. It's at least twice the size of my cell and filled with sophisticated medical equipment. In the center stands what looks like a dentist's chair, except it's surrounded by gadgets that I've never seen in any dentist's office.

"That looks scary," I remark.

"Nothing to worry about," one of the men replies.

"Have a seat," adds the other.

I have a seat. The chair's well-cushioned and nicely ergonomic. Frankly, it's the most physically comfortable I've been since waking up a captive. Seeing me properly settled, my guards take up posts beside the newly formed doorway.

Moments later, a woman enters. She's tall, slender, and very dark-skinned, with short-cropped hair and a cold, almost regal beauty. She's wearing a green jumpsuit with white piping that, for some reason, *screams* "doctor" at me. Nodding to the guards, she approaches the chair and offers me a thin, professional smile.

"Good morning, Mister Brand."

"Hi," I say.

"I'm Doctor Afua Okeke, and I'm going to be running some tests this morning."

"That's nice. Where am I, Afua?"

She eyes me. "Frankly, if you were more cooperative, you'd know by now. As it is, you'll just have to live with the mystery until you decide to behave more like an adult than a petulant child."

I gape at her. When I made my demand, I expected silence, maybe even threats, not a lecture.

Unfortunately, as my parents can testify, I suck at being lectured. "Oh, I get it. I've been kidnapped, drugged, starved, and imprisoned… and now I'm supposed to be a "grown-up" and shrug it off? Is that what you're saying?"

Okeke looks taken aback. "Mister Brand—"

"Furk you," I say. "Your 'disapproval' of my behavior means exactly zilch. Cooperation goes both ways. You want mine? How about starting with some answers? What is this place, and why am I here?"

The uniformed guys step forward menacingly. I ignore them. Meanwhile, Okeke studies me with new eyes—not respect so much as "renewed fascination," as if I'm a lab rat that's just presented her with some unexpected data.

Finally, she says, "I'm not authorized to provide those answers. However, if you'll allow me to run my tests, I'll speak to the… person in charge. Perhaps we *should* adjust our attitude toward you."

"Adjust your attitude," I mutter, parsing the promise.

"Quite so. Now then, can we get to work?"

I agree because, let's face it, what choice do I really have? "Okay."

"Good. Now sit back. I'd like to start with a few basic health questions."

What comes next frustrates both of us. No, I don't know my blood type. No, I don't know if there's any history of cancer, heart disease, stroke, diabetes, typhoid, cholera, swine flu, or Rocky Mountain spotted fever in my family's history. I'm not sure what my mother's parents died of, nor my father's. I've got no idea if I might be anemic, and I'm honestly not even sure what hyperthyroidism *is*.

Okeke records my unhelpful responses on some kind of gadget she wears on her wrist. Then the physical stuff begins. Over the next few hours, she tests my vision, hearing, breathing, heart rate, blood pressure, body fat percentage, and something she dubs my "synaptic efficiency." She takes a blood sample (painful), a urine sample (embarrassing), and even a stool sample (totally disgusting). For the record, those last two are collected by yours truly in a nearby alcove with a toilet.

Finally, she tapes something to my forehead and says, "This is the last test. You've been very patient. Thank you."

Does she expect a "You're welcome?" If so, she'll be disappointed.

But apparently, she doesn't.

"I'm going to ask you a series of important questions. I want you to answer quickly and honestly. Will you do that?"

"Whatever," I tell her.

"Absolute honesty is required here."

"Sure." I don't mean it, of course. I wasn't taught honesty when I was a kid, at least not where 'important questions' are concerned. Quite the opposite, in fact.

Looking me hard in the face, she says, "You grew up in New Jersey?"

Okay, *that* one I can answer honestly enough. "Yeah."

"And your parents' names are Anthony and Bonnie?"

"That's right."

"And your last name is Brand?"

"Yeah."

"That's Swedish for fire, isn't it?"

I pause, just for a second, but she pounces on it like a hungry lion.

"Quickly!" she snaps.

"Um… I guess so."

"You guess?"

"I'm not sure."

"You're not sure what your last name means?"

"Not really. Are *you* sure what *yours* means?"

"What happened to the Roman city of Pompeii in 79 A.D."

I blink. "What?"

"Quickly and honestly!"

I know what she wants. I also know she's not going to get it. "Um… a volcano, right?"

"What *really* happened?"

I shrug.

"Quickly and honestly!"

"That's as quick and honest as I get."

"In Chinese legend, who is Lady Huǒ?"

"Who?"

"Quickly and honestly!" she says, her tone sharp. "Comply!"

"I… don't know." That one's good. I almost believe it myself.

"Is it true that the American government only dropped one atomic bomb on Japan in 1945?"

Again, I hesitate. These rapid-fire subject changes are jarring and, I suppose, meant to be. *Furk, these people know way too much!*

"That's not what they taught me in history," I manage to reply.

"What happened in Nagasaki on August 9th of that year?"

Despite myself, I feel my throat close a little. Involuntarily, I swallow. I tell myself it's a reaction any of the Kind would have.

Nagasaki, like Pompeii, weighs heavily on us—as a people, I mean. Hard-learned object lessons.

"A bomb blew it up," I say.

"Honestly," she reminds me.

Again, I shrug.

She studies me, looking exasperated. Then, after so long a pause that I begin to hope this furking interview is over, she says, "Tell me about Miranda."

"Miranda?"

"We know you two have been talking. Please tell me everything the two of you have said to one another."

"Why?"

"That doesn't matter. Comply." The woman's face is expressionless, though her eyes shine with an unsettling intensity. Obviously, this is another test, though I don't get the point of it.

"No," I say.

"No? Why not?"

"Because it's none of your business."

To my surprise, that morsel of defiance almost earns me a smile. "An interesting argument for a prisoner to make to his captors."

I say nothing.

"Unless you comply, you won't be eating for the rest of the day."

The threat makes my insides tighten. The memory of that long second day is too fresh. Suddenly, hunger feels like a dog at my heels, although I just had breakfast. Nevertheless, I continue saying nothing.

"Then, how about Miranda?" Okeke asks.

"How about her?"

"Comply, or Miranda doesn't eat today."

"What? You can't do that!"

"Of course, we can. We could cut off her water too. She gets no food or drink for twenty-four hours."

My already tightening insides turn into boa constrictors. "Don't," I say, my anger rising.

"Then comply."

She sounds like the Voice. I wonder if she is.

Tucked away deep inside of me, my dragon stirs. Alarm bells go off in my head. I ignore them. "You leave Miranda out of this!" I tell Okeke, not quite screaming—but not quite *not* screaming, either. "Do you hear me?"

"All right," she replies, her hands up in a placating gesture. "I'm sorry if I upset you. We'll drop the whole thing."

Blinking, I notice that both guards now flank me. They're trying to look tough, but I can almost smell their nervousness.

And hers.

With some effort, I calm myself, calling back my dragon.

Gradually, the tension in the room eases. I settle back into the chair, and the guards relax. So does Okeke, blowing out a long sigh. Then she peels the something off my forehead, the same something that I completely forgot she put there.

"Gentlemen," the doctor says. "Please escort Mister Brand back to his cell. Mister Brand, it's been a pleasure. I think you can expect a better than typical lunch today."

"Thanks, loads," I mutter. I've got the feeling I just did something very, very stupid. "Can I ask a question?"

She regards me, expressionlessly. "You can ask, but I can't promise to answer."

"What was the point of all those tests?"

Doctor Okeke hesitates, considering. Then she holds up the slip of tape that she'd stuck to my forehead. "Beyond the general state of your health," she replies. "The point was *this*."

I swallow dryly.

I was afraid of that.

SIX - Days 10-13

When I get back, I tell Miranda everything—well, everything I can tell her without breaking Conceal and Protect.

I detail Okeke's tests, only leaving out the last, the purpose of which is now crystal clear to me. The sticky thing was a dermal thermometer. Okeke wanted to see how much my temperature changed when I got pissed off.

And, like an idiot, I let it happen.

Looking back, however, I can't imagine reacting any differently.

She threatened Miranda.The upshot of the whole mess is that, over the next three days, we're left inexplicably alone, without even any interruptions by the Voice. We spend the time talking together, eating together, and even sleeping together—though, of course, with several

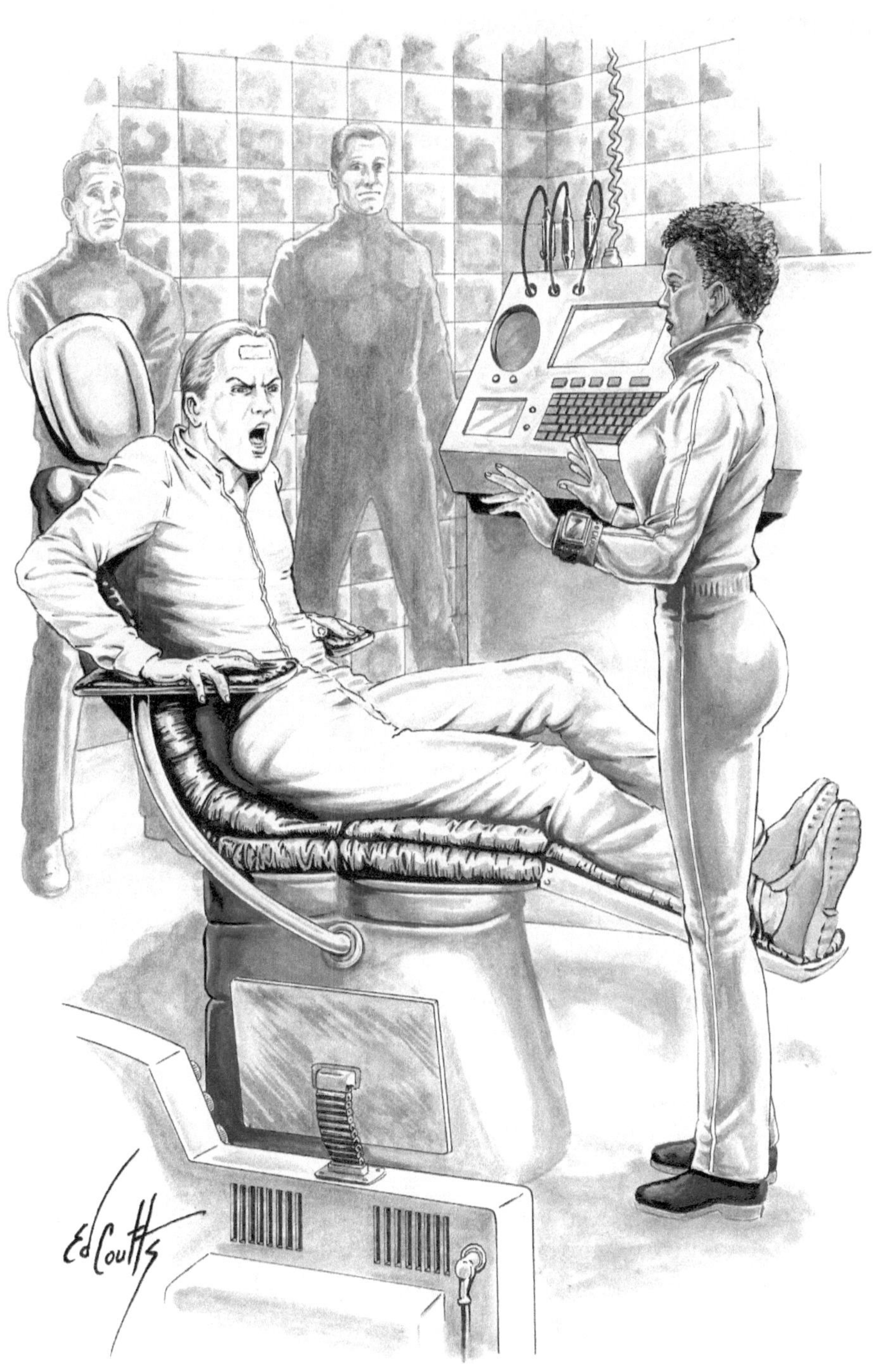

inches of Liquid Brick between us. By now, I've formed a very clear picture in my mind of Miranda Fiero.

She gave me the basics: height, hair, eyes, general shape. But the rest I've cooked up between my ears. Her hair's disheveled from captivity, and locks of it keep falling across her face. Absently, she pushes them away, the gesture both unconscious and sweetly graceful. Her lips are full, her cheekbones high. Her nose is small and slightly pointed. And on her right cheek, just below her eye, sits her port-wine birthmark. A perfect teardrop.

In a word: beautiful.

I wonder… worry really, if she's formed an equally vivid picture of *me*. And, if so, just how disappointed will she be when we finally meet face to face?

If we ever do.

That's part of our connection, a shared uncertainty. Neither of us knows what will happen tomorrow. And, while we make it a point never to speak of it, that tenuousness makes each hour we share precious.

Yeah, I know. It's sappy.

And, of course, the big downer is that, sooner or later, the last hour *does* come.

This happens on the eleventh day of my captivity, the eighth since meeting Miranda, and three mornings after my visit with Okeke. Everything starts routinely, with a shared oatmeal breakfast and a heated discussion about our varied tastes in vids. I like the action variety, preferably American made. Miranda's into foreign romances, most of which I've never heard of. I'm talking zero common ground. Yet, after vigorously debating the merits of each genre, Miranda finally, begrudgingly admits that some of my thrillers and superhero epics sound pretty cool.

I don't feel the same about her stuff. But I don't tell *her* that.

"Okay. I guess some of these chick flicks of yours don't sound *too* bad."

She giggles. "Liar! You'd hate *Les Emotifs anonymes*!"

"Maybe not! You don't know!"

"Listen, Andy Brand, I think I know you well enough by now to guess—" Her words cut off suddenly, and I hear her draw a startled breath.

"You okay?" I ask.

"What do you want?"

"You okay?" I ask again, more urgently this time.

"Let me go!"

Heavy footsteps follow. A scuffle.

"Miranda!"

She cries out in pain.

"Leave her alone!" I scream into the vent, pressing myself as close as possible. I'd squeeze right through the pinholes if I could.

"*Miranda disobeyed.*"

The Voice. It's back for the first time in days.

"How?" I demand, jumping to my feet. "What did she do?"

"*She told you about her tests, which was strictly forbidden. Though we noticed that, while she told you everything, you held some things back, didn't you, Andy?*"

"She's got nothing to do with any of this!"

I hear another cry, this one loud enough to reach me even though I'm no longer right beside the vent. "What are you doing to her?"

"*She's not your problem anymore.*"

"What's *that* supposed to mean?" I exclaim. I can feel my dragon stirring. I know it's wrong—and a part of me also knows it's exactly what they want, that this has been carefully orchestrated so I'll react just this way.

But, right now, I don't care.

"*It means you won't be speaking with Miranda anymore.*"

The statement shakes me to my core, hitting me even harder than I imagined.

"What? Why not?"

No reply.

I pound on the wall between my cell and Miranda's. "Answer me, you bastard!"

Nothing.

I stagger back, my chest heaving and my breath coming in ragged gasps. They've got Miranda in there! They're hurting her.

And it's *my* fault.

As it did in Okeke's chair, my temperature rises. I know I should stop it, contain it, exert the iron control that my parents drilled into me since I was old enough to walk.

Conceal and Protect.

But... Miranda.

Suddenly, the thought of never seeing her, of never again hearing her voice, hits me like a kick in the nuts.

And they've taken her.

Like Hell.

I call my dragon.

It emerges from my every pore like sweat, far hotter than any flame. It bubbles and sizzles along my skin, not burning my jumpsuit but *vaporizing* it, until nothing remains but a few red embers of fabric that ride the thermal updrafts all the way to the ceiling. Simultaneously, my hair stands straight up, as if trying to escape the heat radiating off my scalp — only to be trapped, anchored by its own follicles. An instant later, it melts and boils away to nothing. The same thing happens to my eyebrows, lashes, and every other hair on my body.

There isn't any pain. Not even discomfort.

Instead, it feels good. It feels right.

It feels like — *me.*

I start grinning, exactly as I did in the woods with my dad on my seventh birthday — when he showed me what I am.

For long seconds, I simply stand there, my naked skin glowing first red and then white. Above me, assaulted by wave after wave of blistering thermal energy, the ceiling begins to drip molten metal. Dollops of it swell and fall, only to sizzle away to nothing before they land. Below me, the floor buckles as the Liquid Bricks soften. My feet, bare now, the ugly pull-ons cooked into non-existence, sink a couple of inches into a super-heated quagmire.

I take a step forward, then another, the air seething around me.

In the far corner, two forgotten wads of paper burst into flame and burn away in a millisecond. A moment after that, my now-familiar pallet shrivels and disappears. Even the smoke left behind is consumed by the heat. Meanwhile, the nearby sink and toilet bubble, soften, and sag, their bricks drooping like something in a Salvador Dali painting.

My cell has become an unrecognizable inferno.

I take another step forward, my every movement driven by a single, overarching thought.

Miranda!

I raise my hands, the radiant heat rippling the air and blurring their features. Reaching out, I place them flat against the wall where they instantly sink in, as if the metal has turned to hot butter. Then, twisting my wrists and spreading my arms, I part them like heavy drapes. The Liquid Bricks, now truly liquid, ooze aside, dribbling down beside me as I step through the newly formed gap my dragon has forged.

And, just like that, I'm in the next room.

Miranda's cell.

But it's empty.

I'm too late! They've taken her!

I turn in an agitated circle, sending out waves of radiating heat, trying to decide which of the remaining three walls I should penetrate next. On the furthest of them, the Liquid Bricks suddenly slide apart, revealing a man-sized opening.

I study the new exit suspiciously.

Someone — the Voice presumably — wants me to go that way.

I'm being led into a trap, with Miranda as the bait at the end.

But it doesn't matter.

I move through the opening, the archway melting around me. The hallway in both directions stands empty. No people. No openings.

"Andy, where are you going?"

I notice with grim satisfaction how the Voice's words crackle and break. Apparently, the hidden speaker's suffering a bad case of heatstroke.

"Where's Miranda?" I demand, my voice sounding alien as it moves through the curtain of rippling air.

"This way."

Another opening appears at the far end of the hall. They've made the doorway bigger this time, probably hoping to limit the damage I do.

So, heading through it, I purposely let out more of my dragon, until my footfalls leave impressions in the floor and the new archway drips and sizzles like a lavafall.

Inside, I find Okeke's testing room, devoid now of medical equipment. Even the "dentist's chair" is gone. There's no sign of anybody.

Another opening appears in the side wall.

What's their plan? Do they think if they lead me around by the nose for a while, I'll give up? Not a chance. I'll burn this whole place to the ground, if necessary. Or maybe they're hoping my dragon will get tired?

If so, then they know *nothing* about the Kind.

Or perhaps they're goading me forward in the hope of stopping me. Containing me.

Well, let them. Just let them *try*.

SEVEN – Day 13

I'm led into another room, then another. I force myself to go slowly, melting away the walls more carefully and deliberately than I really have to. The last thing I want is to stumble into a small room with people in it, with Miranda in it, while my dragon is in full flame.

Finally, I find myself in a large, oblong chamber, empty as the rest. No doors. No windows. No furniture. No nothing. In the nearly two weeks that I've been a prisoner in this place, I've seen exactly one chair and no tables at all.

Even prisons have furniture. Don't they?

Deeply weird.

For a moment, I study the barren room through a haze of blistering thermal energy. My stomach feels like a hard knot, twisted tight with anger, desperation, and no small amount of shame. I keep telling myself that I'm betraying nothing, that my kidnappers knew from the beginning what I am. However, my parents' warnings aren't as easy to abandon as their teachings were. But Mom and Dad aren't here. I don't even know where *here* is, though I suppose if I burn through enough walls, I'll find out.

The bottom line is that I'm alone.

With surprisingly little effort, I push away my guilt and focus instead on Miranda. I can't hear her screams anymore, but somehow, somewhere, I *know* she's screaming. And that certainty keeps me going. I'm going to find her. And I'm going to make them stop.

"Well?" I call. "Is this the end of the cattle chute? Maybe I'll just start burning through every wall I see until this whole place comes down."

I wait.

No response.

"Last chance!" I exclaim. Then I spread my arms, ready to summon still more of my dragon.

Immediately, a section of the opposite wall slides open, and a girl steps through.

I lower my arms.

"Hello, Andy," Miranda says.

At the sound of her voice, relief washes over me. But then I realize two things in rapid succession.

One is that Miranda's now seeing me for the first time.

And the other is that what she's seeing — isn't human.

What can possibly be going through her mind as she finds herself confronted with my bald, naked, burning form? Terror can't begin to describe it. Except she doesn't look terrified. She doesn't even seem particularly surprised.

Then I realize a third thing.

Miranda Fiero's different than I imagined. She may be eighteen, like she said, but her manner and bearing make her seem older. Also, her hair does *not* hang loose around her face, tangled and coquettishly rumpled from her captivity. Instead, it's tightly braided, with the plaits wrapped into a knot atop her head. Also, her face is longer than I pictured, her lips less full.

She's still beautiful, but a little — severe.

She's also wearing a black uniform, like the guards, and not an orange jumpsuit like the one I have... or *used* to have.

In fact, I might wonder if it's even her, if not for the teardrop birthmark below her right eye.

This *is* Miranda. Maybe not as I pictured her, but definitely Miranda.

And that's enough.

I pull back my dragon.

Doing so makes my skin tingle, and my very bones vibrate with unspent energy. It doesn't hurt, exactly. It's more like a fullness in my chest and head, a feeling of containment, confining and uncomfortable. The feeling makes me long to loosen my grip again, release the dragon once more. But I exert more control and, with a final effort, manage to corral it in its metaphorical cage, slam the metaphorical door shut, and throw its metaphorical deadbolt.

There.

I stand rooted in place, breathing hard.

And look at her.

She looks back at me, her face impassive.

"Let me get you some clothes, Andy," she says. "And something to eat. After expending all that energy, you must be famished."

With that, I finally recognize the lie.

It falls over me like a bucket of ice water, chilling me to my core. In the space of a few terrible moments, the knot of worry in my gut twists into something else.

Something much, much worse.

"Who…" I gasp. Then I swallow, regroup, and try again. "Who *are* you?"

"You sure you don't want something to eat, maybe some rest before we get into all of that?"

"*Who are you?*" I scream. For an instant, I sense my dragon rise anew. I suppress it.

She replies calmly, "My name is Miranda Coffin."

"Coffin… as in Charles Coffin?"

"His daughter," she says. "And, for the purposes of this mission, his adjunct."

His daughter. She's Coffin's daughter.

And she was put in the cell beside mine deliberately.

Of course, she was.

"Was anything you told me… real?"

"Some of it."

"Why?" I demand. "Why did you do this to me?"

"Because we needed to break down your cultural barriers, to convince you to put aside Conceal and Protect."

"You know about that?"

"We know quite a lot about your people and about you in particular."

So, my folks were right. All their warnings, all their teachings, were smack-dab on the money. The Kind were *known*. The Kind were watched.

The Kind were feared.

"We're not dangerous," I say, which is ridiculous, given what I've just displayed.

"Of course, you are," she replies easily. "But that was never the point. We're not going to harm you, Andy. The fact is, we need your help."

"My help? With what?"

"There are a lot of people… human people… in desperate trouble," Miranda tells me. "And only a Dragon can save them."

PART TWO
THE CREWMAN

Miranda touches something on her wrist.

A moment later, new openings appear in the room's side walls, and a dozen soldiers come rushing in. They're black-clad, like Miranda. They all have CSE patches on their shoulders and serious-looking rifles in their hands. Wordlessly, they take up protective positions around the girl, all of them eyeing me with wary menace, their weapons at the ready but carefully lowered.

Through their ranks emerges another uniformed soldier. He's short, stocky, has a military haircut, and carries himself with obvious authority. He stops directly in front of me, eyeing me up the way I might eye up a rattlesnake.

From behind him, surrounded by her guards, Miranda says, "Andy, this is Lyle Spencer. He's the Head of Security for Coffin Solar Exploration."

"Hello, Mister Brand," Spencer says. He's got a ridiculously deep voice, like thunder.

"Hi," I mutter.

Spencer nods to one of his underlings, who steps up with a bundle in his arms.

"Put this on," Spencer says to me. "Nobody wants to talk to you while you're naked as a newborn."

I wordlessly accept the bundle. It's a uniform like theirs. Black long-sleeve shirt, black pants, black boots. Even the socks and underwear are black. "You want me to get dressed right here?"

"It's a little late for modesty," Spencer replies.

Fair point.

So, I dress, feeling all their eyes on me. No one speaks. No one even moves. After lacing up the last boot, I straighten and ask Spencer, "Now what?"

Miranda replies before he does. "Now, food and rest."

Spencer defers to Miranda. Apparently, she outranks him, which is interesting, given she's a teenager and he's maybe forty.

"No," I tell them both. "Now, *answers.*"

Miranda considers for a moment. Around us, a lot of people with guns wait. "All right. Go ahead, Andy."

"Where the furk am I?"

"Are you sure you're ready to know?"

That seems an odd response, and it gives me pause. But I nod apprehensively.

Miranda taps her wrist again. "You might want to prepare yourself."

"For what?"

On the wall behind her, the tiles suddenly vanish. No, that isn't quite right. I can still see their outlines, like a ghostly grid work floating in mid-air. Instead, they've somehow been repurposed into a large, single video monitor, ten feet to a side. Despite everything, there's no denying it's amazing tech.

"This is a real-time projection," Miranda explains matter-of-factly.

I almost ask, "A real-time projection of what?" but then the words catch in my throat.

Stars.

A universe of them. Thousands of pinpricks — millions — scattered across more emptiness than my mind can really fathom. And, in the center of this lighted tapestry, itself glowing in the surrounding darkness, is a visage that no science nerd worth his nerdhood could ever fail to recognize.

Bands of colors, broken only by a single, large red vortex.

As unmistakable as a fingerprint.

"Is this a joke?" I demand, though I know it's not. There's nothing funny about any of this. I suppose it could be another trick. But, if so, what would be the point?

Jupiter.

I'm looking at the planet Jupiter.

My eyes find Miranda's. "I... don't understand..."

Her reply is like a punch to the gut. "You're aboard the *CSES Conquest*, and we're three days out from Jovian orbit."

"But... that's crazy!" I exclaim.

She doesn't reply.

I stammer, "Doesn't it take... like... *two years* to reach Jupiter from Earth?"

My gaze draws back to the wall-size monitor. There sits the largest planet in the Solar System. To be this close to it is breathtaking—and absolutely, bone-jarringly, stomach-churningly terrifying at the same time.

"*Conquest* is the fastest spacecraft ever built," Miranda replies, again matter-of-factly but with obvious pride. "This is her maiden voyage, and we're about to set a stunning new record. When we arrive, we'll have made the trip in just eighteen days."

"What?" I exclaim. "That's impossible!"

"Not for this ship."

I try to process everything. It isn't easy. I've been away from home for weeks. My folks must be out of their minds. But, right now, that kind of pales beside the idea of being in space—deep space—on my way to Jupiter of all places. The unreality of it is dizzying. And the worst of it by far is that *Miranda* did this to me.

I start toward her, though not in anger. I'm still too shocked to be properly angry. I just want—*need*—to face her down without all of these uniformed strangers between us.

But Spencer steps into my path, his expression grim.

"Get out of my way." I tell him.

"Take it easy."

I meet his eyes. They're hard as stone and just as unyielding. I suppose I should be intimidated. But today, I summoned my dragon after a lifetime of careful abstinence. Today, I confirmed something that I suppose I always *knew*, though only on a vague, theoretical level.

I am dangerous.

"You want me to 'take it easy?' You people *kidnapped* me, ripped me away from my home and family, my furking *planet*, and you expect me to just roll with it? What happened to my parents?"

"They're fine," Miranda says gently.

"They must think I'm dead or something!"

"My father sent someone to see them. They were told that you're in no danger, but that you're needed for an important task. We've promised to return you to them."

"Is that right?" I say bitterly. "Gee, that's nice of you! You steal me from my life, but that's okay because you'll bring me back when you're done with me!"

"Calm down, Brand," Spencer growls.

"Or what? You'll shoot me?" I ask him, my jaw clenched.

"Your family's fine," Miranda says again. "They're being well taken care of… financially. We know this is all a terrible hardship for them, and we wouldn't be doing it if it wasn't absolutely necessary." She comes forward then, bypassing the intervening guards to stand at Spencer's shoulder. "Andy, I'm sorry for what we've had to do to you and to them. But everything that's happened has been for a noble purpose. Please, let's all continue this somewhere more comfortable. I promise we'll answer all your questions and tell you exactly what it is we need from you."

"What if I don't care what you need from me?" I demand.

"I'm betting that, once you understand the situation, you'll agree to help. But, if you don't, then you have my word that we'll turn this ship around and get you home as quickly as we're able."

"Adjunct!" Spencer exclaims.

"It's all right," she tells him. "I know Andy. It's going to be fine."

Outwardly, I glare at her.

Inwardly, my mind hums and my nerves sizzle. *She knows me*, I muse bitterly. And I suppose she does. I spent the last week pouring my heart out to her back when I *thought* we were friends, maybe more than friends.

"Yeah," I say. "I thought I knew *you*, too."

Her eyes lower.

I look from her to Spencer, to Jupiter, and back again. I'm pissed, sure. I'm also scared and almost physically sick from betrayal.

But I'm curious, too.

And ravenous. Miranda's right about that much. Doing what I just did has left me starved.

"Fine," I tell her. "I'll listen."

TWO – Day 13

"Okay," I say. "Start talking."

They've led me to a conference room of sorts, really just another chamber with a table and chairs as the only furniture — all Liquid Bricks. Apparently, the stuff can make more than sinks and toilets.

This room's located on the same floor — or is it deck? — as my cell. Over Spencer's protests, Miranda has ordered the guards to wait outside.

Along with Miranda and Spencer, Okeke's in attendance. There's also the captain of the *CSES Conquest*, a grouchy-looking Asian guy named Wei Li. Of them all, he seems the most hostile, scowling as if I'm a skid mark on his kid's underpants. Okeke regards me with undisguised fascination. Beside her, Spencer eyes me warily.

That leaves Miranda.

But I'm having a harder time reading *her*.

She played me like a fiddle, got me to betray my parents and the Kind. She claims to have done it for a "noble cause." But given all the lies she already told me, why should I believe her now?

For like the hundredth time, I think, in rapid succession:

I've been taken.

I've been imprisoned.

I've been starved.

I've been poked and prodded.

I've been manipulated.

I've been betrayed.

And I'm in outer friggin' space!

Despite everything, I can't help geeking out. I mean, Jupiter's out there. Freaking *Jupiter*! The Kind don't travel unless we have to, so I'd long ago given up on any idea of becoming an astronaut. Yet, here I am, traveling through space in the fastest ship ever built!

Then, inwardly, I shake myself.

I'm also a kidnap victim.

Yeah, I know; all of this isn't hitting me as hard as maybe it should. But give me a break. I'm still processing. Two weeks ago, I was a high-school senior. My biggest worry was applying to M.I.T to study, of all things, interplanetary engineering. And I was also working up the courage to ask Lauren Feller to the prom.

I had a life.

And now? Now I don't know *what* I have.

Miranda says, "Why don't you eat?"

I look down at the simple fare that was awaiting us when we arrived. Burgers and hot dogs. Mentally, I'm too pissed to eat. But, try as it might, my outrage can't overcome my hunger. So, I grab a hotdog and bite into it, not even bothering with mustard.

"Talk," I say around a mouthful of food.

"Watch your tone, Brand," Spencer warns me.

"Drop dead," I reply.

He glowers. He seems good at glowering.

"Please, Mister Spencer," Miranda remarks. "After everything we've put him through, his anger is justified. Andy deserves some answers."

Spencer says nothing. His eyes remain fixed on me.

I down the rest of the hotdog and start in on a burger. As I do, I look expectantly at Miranda.

She says, "Sixty-three days ago, a CSE mining colony was seized by terrorists. We need someone with your particular capabilities to help us affect their rescue."

Chewing, I say, "I don't give a furk."

Spencer barks, "Brand!"

"Andy–" Miranda begins.

"No," I say flatly.

"No, what?"

"No, I won't do it."

"Lives are at stake."

"Then, *you* do it."

"I can't."

"And I won't."

"Why not?" Miranda's tone remains measured and calm.

"Because we aren't superheroes," I reply. "We don't wear capes and go around saving people with our magical fire. With great power does *not* come great responsibility. We are under no obligation to help anyone do anything, period."

"Andy, please."

"No! You ripped me away from my family, and now you want my help? Who the hell do you think you are? Who do you think *I* am? I don't know those people, and I don't care about them any more than they care about me. Now, take me home."

"I can't do that."

"You promised to take me home if I said no. Well, I'm *saying* no. Now, take me home."

Spencer jumps to his feet and declares darkly, "Give me five minutes with him."

I laugh. It sounds bitter even to my own ears. "And you'll *what*? Beat me into submission? You've already stripped me of my dignity and coerced me into breaking the Kind's most sacred rule. What makes you think I won't just turn you to *ash*?"

Spencer looks ready to explode. But I notice he doesn't say another word.

"Sit down, Mister Spencer," Miranda says.

Looking furiously frustrated, he complies.

Miranda turns to me. "Andy, we're talking about more than a hundred innocent men and women who will likely die if we can't get to them. And that's assuming they're not dead already. Will you at least hear us out?"

"Why should I?"

"Because I'm asking you."

"Who is? You or Miranda Fiero?"

She has the decency to flush at that. "I'm sorry for the deception. I'm sorry for all of it. But we're desperate."

"I don't care." Except I do, a little. A hundred's a lot of people, and all the outrage in the world isn't enough for me to completely turn my back. Reluctantly, I ask, "A mining colony?"

"Yes."

"Which one?"

"You haven't heard of it. Its very existence is proprietary. We call it simply Mining Colony 13. MC-13 for short."

"MC-13?"

"Yes."

"And this… MC-13 is on Europa?"

Spencer blanches. "How the hell did you know that?"

I ignore him. Meanwhile, Miranda grins at me. "Yes."

"Wait a minute!" Spencer exclaims. "I want to know who told him that!"

"Nobody," Miranda replies before I can. "He figured it out."

"Yeah? How?"

I swallow down the last of the burger. With a sigh, I sit back and reach for a handy glass of water. "Where else could it be?"

Spencer asks, "What?"

"Miranda already told me we're heading for Jupiter. Since nobody's landing on that big-ass gas giant, we must be going to one of the moons… the Galilean moons, since they're the largest and most stable. There's only four of them, right? Calisto, Ganymede, Io, and Europa. Calisto and Ganymede are airless rocks. Io's volcanic. But Europa's covered with ice."

"So?" he demands.

"So, I'm Kind. Where else out here would you need me?"

Spencer considers. Scowling, he says, "You're quite the little scientist, aren't you?"

"A genuine nerd," I tell him.

"Very good, Andy," Miranda says.

"Uh-huh. But none of the *rest* of this makes any sense. Zero!"

"How so?" she asks.

"First, why kidnap me at all? Why not *ask* me to help?"

"And what would you have said? What would your parents have said?"

I start to reply, then stop. I know exactly what my parents would have said: "No." Moreover, they'd have denied that they even *could* help. They'd have gone to their graves before betraying Conceal and Protect. Any of the Kind would.

Any but me, apparently.

When I don't answer, Miranda simply nods as if she's scored a point, which I suppose she has. "Next concern?"

"Second, some colony sitting on the surface of Europa doesn't need me to get to it. Unless…" I blink, making connections between my ears.

"Unless?" Miranda prompts.

"It's not *on* the ice," I say. "It's *under* it."

Again, she nods. Even Okeke looks impressed, though Spencer and Wei continue glaring. Miranda explains, "MC-13 is attached to the underside of Europa's permanent ice shelf, beneath twenty miles of rock hard, ancient ice."

The idea is more than a little mind-blowing. CSE's put a colony… with *people* in it… under twenty miles of ice on a Jovian moon! That kind of news would have lit up every science convention on Earth. Except it hadn't. Somehow, word of MC-13 never reached any of the media outlets. How the furk had Coffin and his people—?

"What else, Andy?"

"Huh?" I ask stupidly.

"What other concerns do you have?"

I drag my thoughts away from the ultra-furking-cool bomb she's just dropped. Steeling myself, I say, "Third. I'm not going to kill anybody. Not for you, not for anyone. No Kind would."

Doctor Okeke says, "Now, Mister Brand, we both know that isn't true."

I feel my face redden. "What do you know about it?"

"Why, quite a bit."

"Is that a fact? You're not Kind. I know that because, if you were, then I wouldn't need to be here."

"No, obviously I'm not… Kind. But I've been studying your race my entire career."

"No kidding."

Okeke either misses my sarcasm or ignores it as she clears her throat and says primly, "If I may?"

Miranda sighs but nods.

"*Homo sapien draconus*," Okeke announces. "That's the traditional trinomial nomenclature for your sub-species, Mister Brand." Then she rises, looking all tall and scholarly. "The term, of course, appears in no textbook and is never discussed, at least not openly, at even the most academic anthropological conferences. As far as all but .001 percent of the scientific world is concerned, Dragons, to use the colloquial epithet, don't exist. I assume you know why this is?"

I just look stonily at her. I'm good at looking stonily. Just ask my mom.

Undeterred, the good doctor plows forward. "It's because of a centuries-old agreement, one that originated in Europe and moved, first east into Asia, and then west to the New World. Since around 1700, it has been quietly embraced by every nation on Earth. No one discusses it, and there are no written records of it. But, in certain circles, it's recognized as the first global non-proliferation treaty ever created. It doesn't have an official name, of course. But every U.S. president since Jefferson has called it the "Draconian Accord.""

"Just the Accord," I correct flatly.

"What?" Okeke asks.

"We just call it the Accord."

"Oh. I didn't know that."

"No, you didn't."

But my snark finds no target; this woman's on a roll. "Of course, the nature of the… Accord… isn't public knowledge. If humanity at large knew that Mister Brand's people lived among us, the results would be… catastrophic. Put simply, the Accord states that the governments of Earth will leave the Dragons in peace, letting them live where they want and how they want. And, in return, the Dragons will remain hidden under the blanket of humanity, revealing neither their existence nor their power. This is for everyone's mutual safety."

"I'll bet," Spencer mutters.

Okeke says, "Did you have a question, Mister Spencer?"

"Yeah. If these… things… are so dangerous, why don't we just wipe them out?" He's looking right at me as he asks this, challenge in his eyes.

I say nothing.

Miranda exclaims, "For God's sake, Spencer!"

"It's a question of survival, Adjunct," the security chief replies. "These… creatures could blow up the world, or most of it. Why have they been allowed to live? Why hasn't somebody rounded them up and headshot every last one of them?"

Deep inside me, my dragon rumbles.

Okeke clears her throat. "It's been tried."

Everyone looks at her.

"In 1864, Confederate President Jefferson Davis ordered all Dragons then identified to be living in the South to be arrested and detained in Fulton County Jail in Atlanta, Georgia. He told them this was for their protection, but his secret writings indicate he had… darker motives. Once he 'had them all' as he put it, he would offer them beer laced with enough hydrogen cyanide to 'send them all to Hell in a single draught.' Apparently, it didn't work. We don't know exactly what happened, but the Dragons escaped… and much of Atlanta burned to the ground."

"Sherman did that!" Spencer protests. "Sherman burned Atlanta!"

He's wrong, but I don't say so.

However, Okeke does. "General Sherman took credit for it. As it turned out, the loss of life was minimal since most of the city had already been evacuated ahead of the Union army's invasion." She looks questioningly at me. "Looking back, one wonders if the captured Dragons *anticipated* that. There could have been much more destruction than there was."

I say flatly, "We prefer to be left alone."

She nods as if I've confirmed her suspicion. It annoys me.

To Spencer, she says, "Regardless, the Union was very much pro-Accord at the time. There are secret communiqués suggesting that Sherman helped the captured Dragons resettle in the northern states. To this day, most American Dragons live in New England, the Mid-Atlantic states, or the northern Midwest."

Spencer utters a derisive snort. "But if their existence is supposed to be such a big secret, then why do they all have last names that have something to do with fire?" Spencer points at me. "Didn't you say 'Brand" is just Swedish for fire?"

Okeke says, "That's more of a cultural norm than an aspect of the Accord. Wouldn't you agree, Mister Brand?"

This time I *do* reply to her, though I keep my eyes on Spencer. I'm not sure why. Challenge? Stubborn bravado? Or maybe I'm just idling on pissed off. "We settle ourselves where we can. We find jobs. Go to school. Make friends. We try to live quiet lives. But if something happens. If one of us slips up and shows even a glimpse of our dragon, then we bug out, leave in the middle of the night, abandon everything. No good-byes. No forwarding address. We just… disappear."

"Great," Spencer mutters. "But what's that got to do with—"

"And we pick a new last name, one that's linked to our dragon. We do it partly because it helps other Kind recognize us, since we don't exactly meet up at the local Dragon Lodge. And we do it because it lets… authorities… know we're around. That piece of it is for the Accord."

Spencer grins viciously. "Like your own little Megan's Law, huh?"

"No. Not like that."

"Interesting," Okeke says, seemingly oblivious to the tension.

"Your dragon," Miranda remarks in an attempt to change the subject. "That's what you call your ability?"

I nod.

"So, Dragons have dragons?" she asks with a slight smile.

"We don't like being called that."

Her smile withers. "Oh. Why not?"

"Because we're *people*, not giant scaly lizards. 'Dragon' is the name we've given to a particular organ in our body, the only one we have that you don't. It's the organ that lets us do what we can do, and every Kind spends their life learning not to use it. But how would you like to be called 'spleen' just because you have one?"

"Except you *did* use it," Spencer says snidely. "Didn't you?"

"Yeah, I did." I keep looking at Miranda as I say this.

This time she doesn't flush.

Okeke clears her throat again. "The first historical reference to Mister Brand's people comes from the Greek scholar Pliny the Elder and refers to a tiny percentage of the population that demonstrated an ability to create and manipulate heat. These he dubbed *salamandra*, referring to a nature spirit attuned to fire, which was back then considered one of the four basic elements of the universe. The term "Dragon" doesn't appear in literature for a few more centuries. But when it does, it pops up in virtually every culture on Earth."

"So, he's a fire elemental?" Wei asks. It's the first time the captain has spoken.

"Of course not!" Miranda replies, and the sharpness in her tone surprises me.

But Okeke says, "Not so fast, Adjunct. The captain has a point. The ancients credited fire elementals with holding sway over what we today call thermal energy. Now, there are four methods of generating thermal energy: friction; electromagnetic radiation, specifically in the infrared and microwave wavelengths; nuclear fusion; and nuclear fission. Of these, all but nuclear fission exists in nature, which may be why it's the only mechanism that has never been linked to Dragons."

Both Miranda and Wei fall silent.

Okeke, big surprise, does not. "There's evidence to suggest that a *homo sapien draconus* was responsible for the volcanic eruption that destroyed Pompeii in 70 A.D. One may even infer from certain accounts that the city's destruction was deliberate. Pompeii was a politically powerful port, one that had possibly earned the ire of Rome. Mention has been made in some arcane texts of a 'demi-god wearing the shape of a man' who ignited the fires of Mt. Vesuvius at Emperor Vespasian's command.

"But the earliest documented official acknowledgment is found in imperial records from the Tang Dynasty of China, during the reign of Emperor Xuangzong in the 8th century. Certain passages imply the presence in Xuangzong's court of a woman called Lady Huŏ, a prized councilor to the emperor. Her reported exploits in defeating his enemies are so outlandish that she's been dismissed by most scholars as a myth. But I'm convinced she was a Dragon, and that she used her talents to forward Xuangzong's agenda. Huŏ, as I suspect you're aware, Mister Brand, is one of the Chinese words for 'fire' or 'flame' and—"

Okay. Enough.

Loudly, I exclaim, "Do you all want to know what I'm *'aware'* of?"

They all stare at me.

"Show some respect," Spencer growls.

"Furk you."

His face reddens.

When I stand up, both Wei and Spencer jump to their feet as well. At the end of the table, her lecture interrupted, Okeke looks alarmed. Only Miranda remains calm. She watches me from her seat with those amazing eyes of hers, even deeper and more penetrating than they'd been in my imagination—back when I thought we were friends.

I push all that away, or try to. Then I face Okeke and, actively ignoring the others, say, "You've spent a lot of time studying us. Good for you. But that doesn't mean you *get* us."

Okeke looks flustered, Wei wary, Spencer pissed.

I keep on addressing the doctor. "Now, normally, I wouldn't tell you a damned thing. Conceal and Protect. But you people ripped that away from me along with everything else. So… you want to know us? Fine. Here goes."

I abandon my seat and start circling the table, gripped by sudden, nervous energy. They all follow me with their eyes, clearly unnerved, as if I'm a tiger out of its cage. "I know the stories about Lady Huǒ. Every Kind does. My folks hold her up as a shining example of what *not* to do. Because of her, news of our existence spread like crazy… which caused the rest of us to be hunted by every warlord who wanted a pet firestarter.

"And while we're on the topic of Pompeii… here's what *really* happened. A slave named Flavius, one of the Kind, escaped from his psycho jerk of a master and fled to the mountain. Then, when his owner's thugs chased him there and one of them gut-stabbed him, his dragon came out and ignited the eruption. The whole city… something like two thousand people… ended up dead. Rome had nothing to do with it.

"How do I know? From *him*. Flavius survived the eruption and, much later, ended up writing it all down for the Kind, to keep others from making the same mistake. It was the first of what we call the Chronicles, a secret collection of… object lessons, I guess… compiled for millennia and from all over the world. My folks started teaching them to me when I was four. And you know what the Chronicles' most important lesson is?

"Hide.

"Because every time we step out of the shadows, something terrible happens. With the possible… and I mean possible… exception of Lady Huǒ, we never start trouble. Instead, trouble finds us, and, more often than not, a lot of innocent people get killed because of it.

"So, we created Conceal and Protect, and you know what? For the last few centuries, it's worked… for the most part. You leave us alone, and we leave you alone. We *never* break that truce. Unfortunately, every once in awhile, one of you *does*. Every Kind knows a simple truth about humanity. There will always be powerful humans who think the rules don't apply to them. The fact that I'm standing here feels like pretty solid proof of that to me."

At this, Miranda at least has the decency to look uncomfortable.

Spencer doesn't. "That's crazy! I refuse to believe that none of you *ever* uses this dragon of yours!"

"When it's fight or flight," I tell him. "We *always* choose flight. The only time our dragons come out is when we get suddenly, badly, mortally hurt… or, on very rare occasions, when someone we care about is in danger." I lock eyes with Miranda. "There's no way I can explain what it cost me to do what I did today. What I did for *you*."

"I'm sorry, Andy," she whispers.

"Mister Brand…" Okeke begins, but I raise a hand to shush her.

"I did what I did, and I have to live with it." I finally stop back at my chair and, with an aggravated grunt that would have made my mom roll her eyes, settle into it again. "By the way, I'd really appreciate it if you'd stop calling us 'Dragons.'"

Silence falls over the table.

All of them still look anxious, if somewhat relieved now that I'm no longer orbiting the room. All except Miranda, who's watching me without any apprehension at all. In fact, a funny little smile plays on her lips.

After several pregnant moments, Okeke asks, "Adjunct, should I… continue?"

Miranda replies, "Not right now, Doctor. It's been a difficult day for everyone. Let's break here. Captain Wei, can we assign Andy quarters of his own? Proper quarters, not a cell."

"Yes, Adjunct," Wei replies, though he doesn't look happy about it. "Just around the corner from here."

"I'll have my men escort him," Spencer suggests.

Miranda shakes her head. "Enough guns. Captain, please summon a crewman to show Andy to his quarters and issue him an e-man." She smiles at me. It seems a sincere smile. "Andy, you're no longer anybody's prisoner. Go where you want, when you want. I know you don't trust us, and I don't blame you. Earning your trust means giving you ours. So, you have full-access to *Conquest*, stem to stern… private quarters and command-level restricted areas excluded, of course."

I don't say a word.

But Wei does. "Adjunct, I have to protest!"

"Then protest," Miranda tells him. "But that's my decision."

Everyone stands. Everyone but me. "So, that's it?" I ask.

"That's it," Miranda replies.

"Are you going to turn the ship around?"

She looks pointedly at me. "Do you still want me to?"

"I… don't know."

"Then sleep on it, and we'll talk again tomorrow. And since no one has seen fit to say it before now, allow me to formally welcome you aboard."

THREE – Glimpse

"Miranda."

"Hello, Father."

"I've been receiving some troubling reports from your mission colleagues."

"Don't you mean subordinates, Father?"

"That kind of thinking is unprofessional."

"You gave me command of the mission."

"Yes. Exactly. The mission. But Wei commands the ship and Spencer the security force. Your primary role as Adjunct is to serve as my eyes and ears and to speak for me."

"I've been doing that."

"Have you?"

"The mission objectives are being efficiently met."

"I'm not sure I'd call the incineration of an entire deck of the ship, efficient."

"It wasn't an entire deck. There were no injuries, the damage is repairable, and, as a result, we've secured the subject's cooperation."

"From what I've heard, he's an angry, petulant, loose cannon."

"And which of my 'colleagues' told you that? Spencer, Okeke, or Wei?"

"All three."

"Naturally."

"It's not funny, Miranda."

"No, it's not. Let me guess what they each recommended. Spencer wants to vector him until we reach the landing site, Okeke wants to vector him so we can study him, and Wei wants to vector him so he can blast him out an airlock."

"One hundred percent correct… on all counts."

"Now who's laughing?"

"Seriously, Miranda. Is it wise to give this… creature… full freedom of movement aboard Conquest*?"*

"This 'creature,' Father, is proving himself to be more perceptive than anyone anticipated, me included."

"Yet, he fell for your ruse."

"That was naivety, not stupidity. Besides, he's powerful, more so than Okeke estimated. I don't think we could contain him at this point if we tried. Yes, we could put him back to sleep, but eventually, we'd need to wake him and deal with him all over again. I'm simply suggesting that we turn a hostile potential resource into a cooperative asset."

"Does he know what we want of him, yet?"

"I plan to detail things for him tomorrow."

"How much of the truth will you reveal?"

"Exactly as much as he needs to know."

"That's my girl."

"I'm your adjunct, Father. Not your girl."

"No need for that. You've always been my daughter, while your tenure as my adjunct began with this mission. But your point is taken. You have my full, professional support."

"Thank you."

"Miranda, are you taking your medication?"

"Yes."

"Are you?"

"Father, we both know Okeke's monitoring that. I'm sure she's already given you a positive report."

"She has. I just worry."

"About me or the mission?"

"Both."

"Well, don't. I'm in complete control. I'll get this done."

"Glad to hear it. Make contact again once you have the 'perceptive' creature safely on the team."

"I will. Good night, Father."
"Good night, Miranda."

FOUR – Days 13–14

The quarters they give me are on the same deck as both my cell and the conference room, though in a section well removed from the one my dragon turned to slag. This makes me wonder just how big this ship *is*, and if it even *has* any other decks, or if we're aboard some kind of giant Frisbee.

At first glance, these new digs look a lot like my old ones. There's no furniture, not even a sleeping palette. There *is*, at least, a separate room with a shower and toilet.

I glance back at my escort, the first non-military crewmen I've met. He's a young-looking, dark-haired guy dressed in a blue jumpsuit with the ship's insignia—not CSE's, though they own the ship—on its breast pocket. Unlike the security people, there's no hint of bravado. At best, he seems nervous. At worst, scared.

It makes me wonder how much he knows.

"Where's the bed?" I ask him as I step tentatively into my new "digs."

"Anywhere you want," he replies. Then he points at a bundle of linens, tightly folded, that are stacked up in one corner of the room.

I scowl. "Does everybody on this ship sleep on the floor?"

Something about my irritated tone makes him visibly swallow.

Oh, yeah. He knows all right.

He hands me a strip of black composite plastic. It's about two inches wide and has the kind of magnetic clasp that's gotten real popular with watches in the last few years.

"What's this?" I ask.

He holds up his own wrist; he's wearing one just like it. "It's an environment manipulator, or 'e-man' for short."

I fit the gadget around my left wrist. "How's it work?"

He shows me.

Wow. I mean, *wow.*

With this "e-man," I can basically command the Liquid Bricks to make whatever furniture I want, from tables and chairs to a bed, dresser, and even a full-length mirror. I can open doorways and create video monitors. I can even add chair cushions and a thick bed mattress since the Liquid Bricks offer flexible density.

It's incredible, and I'd be lying if I said my inner geek wasn't inwardly geeking.

The tiles, my escort explains, run ten deep in every wall and twenty deep between decks, and so are redundant enough for just about anything to be conjured into existence. The only thing the Liquid Bricks can't do is make food or fabric, which is why all crew and passenger quarters come with sheets, blankets, towels, and a pillow.

The tutorial complete, my escort, still looking nervous, leaves me alone — to play.

I don't.

For a while, I sit on the floor and stare at nothing. Then, after my butt starts aching, I fiddle with the e-man until a chair rises out of the floor in a flurry of shifting tiles. Then I sit on *that* and stare at nothing, noting with vague interest that the cushion really is soft, just as advertised.

I might even be enjoying this if it didn't suck so damn much.

Checking the bathroom, I find soap, shampoo, and towels. So, moving in a fog of melancholy, I take my first shower in — well — more than two weeks, I suppose.

Afterward, I dress in some pajamas that were provided along with the towels. Then, just to see if I can, I go to my "exit wall" and use the e-man to summon an opening. I half-expect it to fail, indicating that I'm still a prisoner, despite all of Miranda's talk about "trust."

But it works just fine.

Peeking out, I look both ways, but there's no one. No other open doors either, though it seems a fair bet that there are more rooms like mine lining both sides of the hallway.

I wonder how many people are on this ship.

Stepping back inside, I dismiss the opening and create a vid monitor — a nice big one. Then I select the option for an external view and allow myself my first good look at "real live" outer space.

By all rights, the view should thrill me.

It doesn't.

From the current angle, I can only see a small part of the ship, though I can tell it's big — several hundred feet long, at least. The hull curves gently above and below me, and, as far as I can see, my room is somewhere near the front.

Definitely *not* a flying Frisbee. More like a soup can.

Jupiter dominates the visible starscape. It looks big and scary and cold, but maybe that's just my mood. I can't spot any of the moons. Nevertheless, I know they're out there.

Europa.

Feeling about a thousand things, I use the e-man to make a bed—king-size because, why not? —and climb up onto it. After more than a week on a floor pallet, it feels pretty good. After a while, I rise, fetch the linens from the corner, and make it up properly. Unlike most kids my age, I kind of like a made bed.

Sometime later, the lights dim. "Low-Lights," Miranda called it. Apparently, it's a ship-wide practice and not just for prisoners. It helps the crew maintain a regular sleep rhythm, insofar as space travel will allow.

I'm a space traveler.

Lucky me.

I worry about my folks, guilt gnawing at my guts. What will they say when they find out what I did today? True, I was manipulated into abandoning Conceal and Protect, but that changes nothing. I know with rock-hard certainty that either of my parents would have died before they showed their dragons to humans.

But would they have let someone else *die?*

I have no idea. It's not something that's ever come up. It's not something we've ever discussed.

It's not something the Kind—well—do.

As I settle myself between the sheets on my new bed in my new room, I don't expect to sleep. There's just too much stuff bouncing around inside my head. But it does feel good to lie here, warm and relaxed. Maybe I'll just rest a bit, then—

The next thing I remember is a dream.

I'm running through the streets of a foreign, but somehow familiar, city. I know I should know where I am, but I can't quite remember. All I do know is that I'm terrified—and that something awful is about to happen.

People crowd every road and alley, glaring impatiently as I push past them. They aren't scared, though they should be. But they don't know about the men who hunt me, men who are, themselves, oblivious of what I am but who will kill me if I let them.

I cannot let them.

Not here.

I turn corner after corner, trying to lose myself amidst the tightly packed wooden buildings, two or three stories high. But wherever I go, I'm awash in a sea of innocent people — all of them struggling to survive in this war-torn city. These are simple folk, the families of young men sent off to fight, many never to return. These people don't pretend to understand the reasons for the conflict. They know only that their divine emperor needed troops, and so their husbands and sons have gone forth to die for vague reasons like "glory" and "honor."

It's the summer of 1945, and the whole world is at war.

Panting, I shove through a final line of passers-by and find myself in an open square. It's still crowded, but at least I have room to maneuver, room to breathe.

Then I see them.

Hard-looking men appear on the far side of the square, armed with long knives. Their predatory eyes fix on me. I try to double-back, only to find three more behind me.

I've been trapped.

Desperately, I run for a nearby baker's shop. I have some half-formed plan of hiding amidst ramshackle rows of shelves and wares.

But before I get three steps, I feel the cold steel of a thrown knife between my shoulder blades. Crippling pain tears through me, and, without realizing it, I drop to my knees.

From deep within me, my dragon awakens.

No. Please…

As the hard men close in, innocents flee the square. But it's already too late. They can't possibly flee far enough.

One of the murderers says something in a language I should know but don't. He sounds both angry and triumphant. He's a fool. They all are.

And so am I.

My dragon emerges. Normally, I can contain it. But now, my ability to do so is draining out of the wound in my back.

Forgive me, ancestors.

The hard men don't even have time to be astonished. In an instant, the square is gone, its buildings obliterated by the wall of fire that moves out from me in all directions. The surrounding streets are consumed; the people turned to ash in a single instant.

My dragon reaches further, losing little of its power as the city is consumed. Five blocks out. Ten. Twenty. Fifty. Nothing survives. No people, no animals, not a single plant. In the city center, the buildings are higher, stronger, and I pray they will withstand the onslaught. But they don't. When the dragon strikes them, they're swept aside as if by a god's unseen arm. More die. Many, many more.

Everything succumbs to the terrible fire.

My dragon continues until nothing is left but shattered rubble, the groans of the dying —

— and the dead.

I see it all. I don't know how, but I do. I stop trying to count the bodies. There are too many, far more than my poor conscience can bear. I try to look away, but I can't. I have no head to turn, no eyes to close.

I am spirit now.

My body lies in what remains of the square. The knife is gone from my back, melted to nothing along with the rags I wore. But the wound it left behind is mortal.

I feel no pain. Only shame, which is so much worse.

Today, I have killed thousands. Tens of thousands.

Forgive me…

I still don't remember my name and, now that I'm dead, I don't suppose it matters. But I do finally recall the name of the city that my dragon has just consumed. It's a name that, as the last of my life leaves me, finds its way onto my tortured lips.

"Nagasaki…"

My eyes snap open.

I'm back in my bed aboard *Conquest*. A sound comes from somewhere in the room, but right now, I barely notice it. My heart pounds, and I'm trembling head to toe.

I've just had my first memory dream.

It's a Kind thing, though rare even amongst my people—a racial memory phenomenon that manifests only at extreme moments. This realization shakes me badly, mostly because I know what brought it on.

I broke Conceal and Protect.

I bury my face in my hands, the dream images—all that destruction and death—still burning behind my lids.

The weird sound returns, not shrill but insistent. Like a chime.

Looking blearily around, I notice that one of the tiles against the far wall—the *exit* wall—is blinking.

Is that supposed to be a doorbell?

I rise and pad over there, tapping my e-man. The Liquid Bricks obediently slide apart, revealing my very first house guest.

"Good morning," Miranda says.

She's not dressed in a CSE security uniform this time. Instead, she's got on a green dress, long-sleeved and form-fitting. I try not to look too hard.

"Hi," I say.

"Did I wake you?"

I almost ask, "Don't you know?" Because I figure, for all their talk of trust, they *have* to still be watching me. But I hold back, though I'm not sure why. "It's okay."

"Can I come in?"

I hesitate, my thoughts a jumble. The memory dream and its implications are still too fresh. But that's only part of it. The other part is Miranda herself. She sounds so much like the girl I knew back in my cell, the girl who never existed. Furk good intentions. What she did to me sucked. It sucked big time.

But, somehow, that doesn't stop my insides from flip-flopping when I look at her.

"Sure," I say.

Smiling, she enters. "Happy with the quarters?"

"It's better than a cell."

"I wanted to ask if you'd join me for breakfast on the Observation Deck. We have a lot to talk about."

Her whole "Sorry I Used You But Let's Be Friends Anyhow Thing" should be pissing me off. And it is, sort of.

But I *do* want answers.

"Okay," I say. "But I need to get dressed. Can I meet you there?"

"It's a big ship," she replies. "How about if I wait, and then we go together?"

"Whatever."

I march into the bathroom, using the e-man to shut the opening behind me. Then I march back out because I forgot my black CSE uniform, the only clothes I have. Miranda smiles at me but says nothing.

Smooth.

I dress and brush my teeth with a toothbrush I find by the sink. All the while, I'm keenly aware that she's out there—waiting for me. Close. So close.

I'm an idiot.

When I go back out, Miranda's standing by the viewport I made last night, gazing at Jupiter.

"This is my first trip into deep space," she says, sounding wistful.

"Mine, too," I reply dryly.

She glances at me. "I know I've been saying this a lot, but I really am sorry about that."

"Uh-huh."

"Shall we go?"

"Can I ask a question first?"

She smiles. Damn, she's got a great smile. "Dazzling" isn't too strong a word. "Andy, you can ask as many questions as you want."

"Where does the gravity come from?"

Miranda laughs, looking genuinely surprised. It's nothing like Miranda Fiero's girlish giggles but the more melodic chuckle of a self-possessed, adult woman. The distinction makes my stomach hurt. Honestly, a lot of things about her make my stomach hurt.

"With everything that's going on," she remarks, "*that's* the first thing you want to know?"

"Figured I'd start with an easy one. I know you're not using centrifugal force; otherwise, the stars out there would be spinning, and the wall with the porthole, instead of the floor, would be "down.""

"You're one hundred percent correct," Miranda says. "We're using linear acceleration."

I blink. "Seriously?"

"Seriously."

I've read enough to understand the concept, sort of. Linear acceleration creates artificial gravity by steadily increasing speed and using the constant acceleration—and Newton's First Law—to pull everything "down" toward the rear of the spacecraft. In theory, you can reach 1G, full Earth gravity, as well as go places at unbelievable speeds. In practice, however, it requires an insane amount of fuel, way too much to be practical.

"I didn't think anyone had gotten it to work," I say.

"*Conquest* is the first," she replies with pride. "I think you'll find it's a ship of 'firsts.'"

"I read somewhere you'd need something like a moon-sized fuel tank."

"Not for us. *Conquest* represents a revolutionary leap in fission propulsion technology."

She sounds like a sales pamphlet, but I don't say so.

"And this leap of yours is going to get us to Europa in sixteen days?"

"Eighteen," she corrects.

I count backward. "But you said we're three days out from Europa. And I woke up in my cell thirteen days ago."

"We launched from Earth orbit two days before we woke you."

"Oh."

"I'm sorry, Andy."

But I'm not in the mood for another apology. So, I return to my original thought. "That's crazy fast, way faster than anyone has ever gone before."

"By an order of magnitude. This is the most expensive and advanced ship ever built. It's been years in the planning and construction and wasn't supposed to be officially launched for another year. But the situation on Europa is so dire that my father agreed to launch her early. Now, come on. Let's get some breakfast in you, and I'll tell you the rest."

FIVE – Day 14

Miranda leads me out of my room and along the empty corridor — which, without visible doors, looks more like a tunnel than a hallway. Along the way, I ask, "Did you pick 'Fiero' because you were hoping I'd think you were Kind?"

She hesitates for only a moment before replying, "Yes."

Honest and direct. Okay, she gets points for that. "Did your mom really die in childbirth?"

"Yes."

"And did you really have a brother?"

This time her hesitation is a beat longer and her answer, when it comes, is a little abrupt. "Yes. That part of what I told you was true. Stop right here."

We've reached the end of the hallway with only a blank gray tile wall in front of us.

"Now what?" I ask.

She touches her e-man. A moment later, I jump as posts made of Liquid Bricks rise to form a waist-high railing that frames us on all four sides. Right after that, the three-foot square of tiles below our feet, railings included, begins to descend into the floor.

"Whoa!" I exclaim.

"Relax," she tells me with a distracted smile. "The Observation Deck's two decks below us. This is how we get there."

As we clear the floor, I peek over the lip of the platform to see what's lowering it. Except nothing *is* lowering it. As we glide, vertically and noiselessly, down through the hallway of this new deck, there isn't anything between us and the floor but empty air.

"Magnetic fields," Miranda explains.

"How's it work?"

"That's a question for the engineers. It's expensive. I can tell you that."

"It's so furking cool," I admit, and it is. "Genuine, real-world levitation."

"A ship of firsts."

The deck just below my own seems to be populated by black-clad CSE guys. Two of them eye me warily but relax when Miranda nods to them. No one speaks while yet another opening appears below us to allow passage.

"How many people on the ship?" I ask as we leave the armed men behind.

I half expect her to waffle. She doesn't.

"Captain Wei's crew numbers twenty-two. Mister Spencer's security detail adds another forty. Include Doctor Okeke and myself, and the full complement is sixty-four. You make it sixty-five. The truth is we're only at about one-third capacity. *Conquest* can comfortably carry up to two hundred passengers. But since this is a rescue mission and not a business or public relations trip, all three passenger decks are vacant."

"Is mine one of those decks?"

She hesitates. "No. You're up on Deck 1."

"By myself?"

"Yes."

"Because nobody wants to be around me."

She shifts uncomfortably. "It was… a concession to Captain Wei. People fear what they don't understand."

"Is that a fact?" I reply with full snark.

We enter a tube of sorts, well-lit but barely wider than our platform.

Meanwhile, Miranda rallies. With another smile, she assures me, "It's just temporary. Before long, you'll be seeing plenty of people."

"Is that right?"

She nods, still smiling.

"Even though they're all afraid of me?"

She doesn't reply to that. Her smile falters.

So, I push it. "Like Captain Wei."

After a pause, she says, "Yes." Now her smile is gone completely. Despite myself, I find I miss it.

"And Spencer," I say.

"Him, too."

"What about you?"

"Me?"

"Aren't you… afraid of me?"

"No," she replies.

"Why not? You know what I can do."

"I also know what kind of person you are. What you did yesterday… what we *made* you do… was an act of kindness, not violence."

For some crazy reason, my throat tightens up. "I thought they were hurting you."

"I know."

"And I thought it was because of me."

"I know that, too."

"Miranda?"

"Yes, Andy?"

"Were you the Voice?"

She doesn't respond right away.

So, I add, "The Voice never talked to me when you and I were… together."

"Occasionally, it was Okeke," she finally replies. "But most of the time, me. I'm so sorry, Andy."

Another apology. "Are you?"

"Yes, I really am. When this mission started, and you were brought on board asleep, it was easy to think of you as just a part of the plan. But later, talking to you for all those hours and days… well, it wasn't all a lie. The caring about you part wasn't a lie."

And, God help me, I find I *want* to believe that.

Miranda says, "Here we are."

The platform halts, becoming instantly indistinguishable from the bottom of the tube. A moment later, the railing recedes just as an opening appears, tiles moving aside as though living things. The chamber beyond is unexpectedly dark.

"This is the Observation Deck?" I ask a little apprehensively.

"Step inside."

So, tentatively, I do.

The first thing that hits me—and it hits me hard enough to take my breath away—is the starscape. It fills the entire sky, from horizon to horizon, a panorama of bright pinpricks with, as its crowning jewel, the enormous colorful visage of Jupiter. At first, I just gape up at it, my admittedly over-taxed mind struggling to make sense of what my eyes are telling it. I mean, we're *inside* a spaceship, two decks below the one on which I slept last night.

How can this be over our heads?

Then the tiny corner of my brain that isn't all "swept away with wonder" whispers, *Because it's another projection, dumb-ass.*

Well, of course, it is.

Slowly, my eyes and thoughts adjust, and I take in the rest of the room. It's very big, seeming to fill the entire deck. What's more, the circular space is nearly empty, with only a small island of furniture in the center. Like most everything I've seen aboard *Conquest*, these are made of Liquid Bricks, though I can already tell that lots of expertise went into their creation. The seats, backs, and even the armrests are cushioned and color-coordinated. I didn't know changing tile color was an option. There are even cushioned footrests.

From behind me, Miranda says, "Sorry if it's a bit much. I wanted to impress you."

"Mission accomplished," I mutter, looking skyward again—well, ceiling-ward, I guess. The ceiling's obviously higher than on my deck, twice as high at least. And now that I'm looking closely, I can see it's curved, like the inside of a dome. With a gasp, I exclaim, "This is a planetarium!"

"Yes, it is."

"Why on Earth would you put a planetarium on a spaceship?"

To my surprise, Miranda bursts out laughing. "Well, when you say it like that, it sounds ridiculous." Then, coming up beside me, she says, "The plan has always been to use this deck for special events. Fancy dinners. Official functions. The sort of events intended to dazzle dignitaries, VIPs, and the like. But, since there's no need for any of that on this mission, it's totally unused, which means we have it to ourselves. Food's over there, by the way."

I look where she's pointing. Atop a table in the room's center, a small buffet's been laid out.

Seeing it makes my stomach growl.

Miranda says, "Make a plate and pick a chair. Then we'll talk."

Feeling hyperaware of the captivating starscape overhead, I join her in the relatively mundane task of building a mound of eggs and bacon. Afterward, Miranda settles gracefully onto an armchair, while I—somewhat less gracefully—take the other, balancing both plate and coffee mug.

"How are we seeing this?" I ask, nodding upward.

"The same way we see anything. *Conquest* has almost no windows or viewports, not even on the bridge, which is actually several decks below us. We don't need them. All along the outer hull, scanners provide a full, real-time, three-hundred-and-sixty-degree view. Since this deck is completely open and the ceiling's so high, it makes for a nice display."

"It's pretty cool," I admit. "Though I'm guessing that's not the reason you brought me down here."

"Actually, there is a practical purpose. But we'll get to that. Why don't you eat first?"

"You sound like my mom."

She laughs again. I like it when she laughs. "God forbid!"

I scoop a forkful of eggs into my mouth. "There," I tell her snarkily. "I'm eating. What purpose?"

She grins. Then, with a few taps on her e-man, the stellar landscape above us zooms in, displaying a shining white moon that, science geek that I am, I recognize at once. From this distance, the surface of Europa looks nearly as smooth as glass, but with grayish, crisscrossing striations—more scratched cue-ball than planet.

Miranda asks, "Beautiful, isn't it?"

And it is, in a cold and uncompromising sort of way.

She taps her wrist again, and we zoom closer. I can see now that the striations, which I thought to be cracks or even canyons in the ice, seem to be as smooth as the rest of the weird world.

"The dark lines are sea salt," Miranda says. "Turned brown by radioactive bombardment. It's not as beautiful close up. But then, few things are."

The image zooms again. We're *very* close this time, the view maybe only a mile across. I can now tell that the ice isn't really all *that* smooth.

There are fissures and jagged areas where plates of the stuff, some the size of city blocks, have been shoved against and even atop one another, probably by tidal activity. Below all that ice, twenty miles of it, Europa has a massive global saltwater ocean. That's where the sea salt comes from, pulled to the surface over time by Jupiter's insane gravity, only to get cooked by the cosmic rays.

Miranda asks pointedly, "See it?"

"See what?"

"Keep looking."

Haven't I taken enough furking tests?

I make a show of looking a little longer. "Nope," I say finally.

She touches her e-man yet again, and a single dark spot zooms into prominence. It's square metal, clearly man-made, and maybe a hundred feet across.

"What's that?" I ask.

"The only evidence that anyone lives here. It's a cargo lift that runs from the surface down to Mining Colony 13. It's how they get their supplies. It's also how they deliver the ore they mine to the surface for pickup."

"A twenty-mile elevator?"

"Yes."

"Jeez. How often does it get used?"

"A CSE freighter stops by every three months. It delivers food, medicine, repair parts, and other necessities. It also picks up the quota of ore. Since its inception, everything has proceeded like clockwork. Not a single hiccup. Shelton runs a tight ship down there."

"Shelton?"

"Mike Shelton is the owner and proprietor of Shelton Metals. They're a small mining concern and not exactly famous, but over the last ten years, they've earned a reputation for being the most productive off-world mining company in the Solar System. CSE partnered with them to mine tantalum. Are you familiar with tantalum?"

"It's a rare metal, isn't it?"

"The rarest. Or, at least the rarest *stable* metal. It's conductive, dense, hard, and has a high melting point. Up until about fifty years ago, it was primarily used in electronics and... believe it or not... dental tools. But in the last half-century, it's become *very* useful in the space industry, particularly in ship manufacture. Unfortunately, on Earth, there just isn't very much of it. However, about five years ago,

CSE probes identified veins running through the Europan mantle, below the floor of the moon's global ocean. *Big* veins… ten thousand times the entire supply currently in human possession.

"So, the problem became… how to *get* it? That's where Shelton and his company came in. Mike Shelton designed a one-of-a-kind, solar-powered, orbital laser capable of generating more than a petawatt of concentrated heat. He's been using it to mine asteroids, which is where they do most of their business. Our end of the partnership involved transporting the laser to Europa and providing a power source, since the sun is so much further away out here. It took about twelve standard hours of continual operation, but we eventually melted a hole through Europa's ice shelf deep enough and wide enough to accommodate the colony."

I try to picture some big ray gun orbiting low over Europa and blasting a heat beam straight down, like something out of a sci-fi movie.

"Okay…" I say. "But didn't the ice… reform?"

"It did, but we had time to install and establish MC13 before that happened. The entire colony is modular, so it wasn't a matter of construction, per se. We used a crane to lower the components, which were then assembled in place. The hardest part was dealing with Jupiter. Its gravity well and ridiculously big magnetic field played havoc with our crane operations. But, in the end, we pulled it off. All this was a little over two years ago." She regards me for several moments, and then remarks, "You're not eating."

I shovel some more egg in my mouth. Then I look pointedly at her.

She taps her wrist again.

A man's face appears above us: thirties with short-cropped red hair and a tightly trimmed beard. "This is Michael Shelton. In addition to being owner of the company, he's also the on-sight administrator of MC13. His job is to keep the tantalum flowing, sifting trace amounts of it out of the ocean water, like large-scale panning for gold. The colonists then process it, package it, and send it up in the lift, where quarter-annual cargo ships pick it up. In the twenty-seven months since they started mining, the amount of usable tantalum delivered has been incredible. MC13 is, by far, the most productive mining concern in the System, and the results speak for themselves."

"Speak for themselves?" I ask.

"Oh, I didn't mention that. *Conquest* is constructed almost entirely of tantalum."

"The Liquid Bricks?"

"That's one of the trade names, yes," she replies. "The metal is wonderfully versatile. As I said, this ship is a prototype, but CSE intends to make more like it and use their unprecedented speed to open up the Solar System in ways never before imagined. Right now, Jupiter is as far as mankind has been able to reach. In the near future, we may visit Saturn, Uranus. Maybe further."

It's impressive. No doubt about that.

Miranda says, "Then, around two months ago, we received a communication from MC13 declaring that no further deliveries would be made. All tantalum production had been halted."

"Terrorists?" I ask.

"Terrorists," she says.

SIX – Day 14

"They call themselves Orpheus and Eurydice," Miranda explains.

"Sounds Greek," I say.

"You know the story?"

"I'm a science nerd. I don't do Greek mythology. It just *sounds* Greek."

"It is. Orpheus and Eurydice were doomed lovers. Orpheus, a demi-god, fell hard for and married Eurydice, a beautiful mortal girl, only to have her get bitten by a snake and die. The story goes that he went down into Hell and rescued her."

"Okay…" I remark thoughtfully. "Seems a weird choice of handles for a couple of terrorists."

"We thought the same thing. Anyway, the first communication arrived as a written message, transmitted from Europa to one of the supply ships and forwarded to us via CSE's proprietary satellite network. It was… succinct." Miranda taps another control, and words begin scrolling beside Michael Shelton's photo.

"We are Orpheus and Eurydice. We have full control of Mining Colony 13. We demand that Coffin Solar Exploration relinquish all ownership and authority over Europa and publicly declare her a free and independent world. Until this happens, no further tantalum will be delivered to the surface for pick-up. Any attempt to invade the colony via the lift will force us to detonate

charges planted in the shaft, effectively sealing us off from the rest of the Solar System. Do not test us."

Now, I don't have a lot of experience parsing terrorist threats.

But this one seems — thin.

"I don't get it," I say. "They're not threatening any of the colonists."

"Not explicitly, no. But the implicit threat is obvious. MC-13 isn't self-sustaining. They need regular supplies. If these terrorists seal the lift shaft, the colonists will starve."

"Wouldn't that kill them too, though?" I ask. "This Orpheus and Eurydice, I mean… plus any soldiers or whatever they have with them?"

"A suicidal mentality isn't exactly unknown among their class of people."

That seems a weird way to put it — though, I suppose, pretty accurate.

"Even so, you decided not to do it?"

"Do it?" she asks.

"Publicly declare Europa to be free and independent. You didn't do that. If you had, it would have been all over the news."

"Andy, we *can't* acquiesce to these people. CSE has been administrating the Solar System for almost thirty years! The infrastructure we provide keeps supply lines moving, without which hundreds of thousands of people on worlds, moons, and asteroids can't survive. Our security force keeps the peace. It's a responsibility that my father took on long before either of us was born. If we were to allow ourselves to be blackmailed into declaring any particular colony free, the resulting chaos would tear down the entire network. The loss of life would be… incalculable."

She paints a scary picture and, from what I've seen on the news vids, she might be right. Since I've always lived on Earth, I don't exactly have a lot of firsthand knowledge to draw from. But this much I do know: most, if not all, of the off-world media outlets are owned by Coffin Industries.

"All that happened sixty days ago?" I say.

"Sixty-four," she corrects.

"Whatever. What's gone down since then?"

"Quite a bit. First, my father ordered a media blackout. The *last* thing we need is for this to get out to the System at large. The second thing he did was respond to Orpheus and Eurydice."

"How?"

"He kept the supply ship in orbit and had them act as a relay."

"What did he say to them?"

She touches her e-man again, and the overhead image switches to another communication, this one bearing the CSE logo. *"Our first concern is the safety of the colonists. I require proof of life that Michael Shelton and his complement are unharmed. No demands will be considered until I have that."*

"Short and sweet," I remarked.

"My father isn't one to waste words," Miranda said.

"Did the terrorists respond?"

"They did, but not for two days. By then, things had gotten tense. The supply ship didn't have the fuel to stay in Jovian orbit much longer. They kept monitoring the surface for signs of movement but reported nothing."

"Did they see a ship?" I asked.

"What?"

"The terrorists got there somehow, right? If the only way down to MC-13 is by using the lift, wouldn't there be a ship sitting on the ice nearby?"

"Very good, Andy. No, there was no ship. However these terrorists got to the moon, their transportation evidently left them there. Anyway, we finally got another communication. This one, interestingly enough, was audio."

At her command, a recorded voice fills the empty air around us, delivered by an unseen sound system.

"This is Orpheus and Eurydice. The terms are non-negotiable. You will receive no further communication from us until the public announcement of Europa's free and independent status is made."

The voice sounds male but is so electronically disguised that I can't be sure.

Miranda says, "We tried analyzing the recording but got nowhere. Whatever tech they're using to hide their identity is very advanced."

"Nothing's mentioned about the health of the miners," I say.

"Nothing."

"Did your father try again?"

"He did. And again. And again. No reply. Then, after a week passed without any further progress, a new, radical proposal was put on the table."

"What proposal?"

"To launch *Conquest* on a rescue mission."

"And whose idea was that?" I ask.

Miranda's expression is inscrutable. "Mine, actually. The ship had been completed the previous month and needed only a little final preparation to get her space-ready."

"So, your father launched it with Wei as captain and you as 'Adjunct.'"

"Yes."

"What exactly does an adjunct do?"

"Wei commands the ship, but I command the mission. I speak for my father and have his full authority to act as I see fit."

"Wow," I say. "Not bad for an eighteen-year-old."

She doesn't reply.

"You *are* eighteen, right?" I ask.

"I'll be nineteen next month," she says, which strikes me as a very "eighteen" thing to say. This is a teenage girl. Smart, sure. Brilliant, probably. But still too young to drink. Yet, here she is in charge of a mission to Europa in the most furking cool spaceship ever made.

It makes me wonder what kind of childhood she had. But I decide not to go there.

"So… what's the plan?" I ask. "I mean, it's great that we can get to Europa so lickety-split and all, but if you try to go down the lift to reach the colony, they'll blow it."

"Presumably."

"That means you need another way to get down there."

"Yes."

"What about the laser?"

"The supply ship reported it destroyed. We don't know how, but Orpheus and Eurydice apparently overloaded it, and it exploded. A wreckage cloud was identified in a loose orbit around Europa. By now, most, if not all of it, has been sucked down to Jupiter. Rebuilding it would take years, even if we had the means to reverse engineer Shelton's proprietary tech."

"Which leaves you with no way to get through twenty miles of ice."

She nods.

"And whose idea was it to steal *me*?"

"My father's. He's always been fascinated by Dragons. Oh, I'm sorry. You said you don't like to be called that."

"Would *you*?"

"I suppose not. Anyway, my father called a meeting. I was there. So were Spencer and Okeke. Others, too. Scientific advisors. He called it a brainstorming session, but between you and me, he knew what he intended from the get-go. Otherwise, Okeke wouldn't have been invited. She's a medical doctor, but her passion is the study of…"

"The Kind," I offer. "When we talk about ourselves at all, we just say 'the Kind.'"

"The Kind," she echoes before continuing. "While my father's always had an interest in your people, Okeke's frankly obsessed. You're mankind's most interesting secret, kept for millennia, yet openly known by pretty much everyone with the right sort of influence, wealth, or political clout."

"And Charles Coffin's got all three," I remark, not bothering to hide my bitterness. "So, your dad decided to send *Conquest* out here with someone aboard who could take the place of Shelton's ice-melting laser and get Spencer's guys down to the colony."

"Yes."

"And why'd you pick me?"

"We didn't. A profiling protocol did. The asset chosen had to be healthy enough to handle the rigors of space travel and Europa's harsh environment. They also needed to be deemed psychologically… flexible… enough to forgo your people's cultural taboo against revealing themselves. And, finally, they had to be capable of generating enough thermal energy to do the job." Then, after a hesitant pause, she adds, "Not all Drag—Kind are as strong as others."

I absorb this.

I don't like it.

"Psychologically flexible? You mean, willing to turn traitor."

"You haven't betrayed anybody, Andy."

"I abandoned Conceal and Protect," I tell her. "And you made me do it."

Miranda looks away, seeming genuinely upset. "I'm not proud of it. But we had to test you."

"That's crap!" I exclaim, feeling my anger rise. "You wouldn't have launched into space for two days and something like… what, twenty million miles in this speedster… if you weren't 100% sure that I could call up enough of my dragon to do the job!"

She replies in a feather-soft voice, "You've got it wrong. We weren't testing to see if you had the power. We were testing what it would take to make you… *show* that power."

"What about that game Okeke played? The one where she asked me all those questions about Pompeii and Nagasaki. Then, when that didn't get a rise out of me, she threatened you… all while taking my temperature?"

"That was to see if you could be… motivated… into displaying some sign of your true nature."

"More mind games. Well, did it work? How high was my fever?"

Miranda smiles thinly. "Okeke wasn't sure. Her custom-made dermal thermometer only went up to one-hundred-and-twelve, and you burned right past that. I've never seen her so excited.

"Great," I mutter, crossing my arms. My mom always hates it when I do that. She says it closes me off. Well, right now, I *feel* closed off. "And you found out that I was willing to dump my entire belief system… for you."

"This mission doesn't call for a 'heat machine,'" Miranda tells me. "We don't need a cowed prisoner who'll get us down to the colony based on fear or threats." She pauses, then adds, "What we need… is a hero."

Almost unconsciously, I uncross my arms.

SEVEN – Glimpse

"Good morning, Miranda."

"Evening here, Father."

"Good evening, then. How is our… special guest… doing?"

"He's been briefed on the situation and has agreed to help."

"Is he capable of helping?"

"You know he is."

"I don't mean as a Dragon. Does he understand the… realities… of what we have to do?"

"Insofar as he needs to."

"Miranda, you need to be careful with this creature. You betrayed him once, and he nearly destroyed the ship!"

"That's an overstatement."

"Not according to Spencer's report."

"Spencer, with all due respect, worries about things he doesn't need to."

"I pay him to worry about things he doesn't need to. And, I have to say, your cavalier attitude concerns me."

"Not cavalier. Simply not alarmist. Andy's a person, not a 'creature.' And he's certainly not a monster. He's intelligent and perceptive."

"So, you've said. I'm concerned you're getting too attached to him."

"That won't happen, Father."

"Good. Because, after his task is complete, it may be necessary to remove him."

"I don't agree. Once things are made clear, he'll recognize the wisdom in it."

"And you think this because he… admires you?"

"Partly."

"A schoolboy crush is useful, to a point. But when the truth comes out, his attitude might change. He's already demonstrated a concerning temper."

"Only in defense of others. Oh. Yes, I see your point."

"I'm glad."

"Don't worry, Father. I won't fail you."

"If you think mission failure is my only concern, then you misunderstand. The most precious thing on that ship, my daughter, is you. And he could kill you in a heartbeat."

"So could Spencer or any of his men. Andy simply wields a different weapon."

"Spencer and his staff are in my employ and loyal to me. This… person… is an outsider, one who has every reason to resent us. Even hate us."

"I think he's moving past that. As I said, I've won his full cooperation, with three conditions."

"Conditions?"

"He doesn't want to be caged anymore. Free access to the ship."

"Something you've already granted him, much to Spencer's chagrin. What else?"

"He wants us to stop calling him 'Dragon.' Apparently, his people consider it a derogatory term."

"Simple enough. I'll have Wei and Spencer issue such orders."

"I've already done so."

"It may be more… effective, coming from me."

"If you say so, Father."

"And his last condition?"

"He wants to speak to his parents."

"I see."

"What do you want to do, Father?"

"What we've been doing, Miranda. I want to manage him carefully. Where is the Drag… Mister Brand, now?"

"In the Mess, getting dinner."

"With Wei's crew?"

"Yes."

"I'd keep an eye on that, too. The crew knows what he is. While they've all been screened, they're spacers, not CSE soldiers… and lack both the discipline and loyalty of Spencer's security personnel. One of them might say something untoward, especially concerning the current political climate. We don't want to spark a confrontation, no pun intended."

"No, we don't."

EIGHT – Day 14

"You're that Dragon, right?"

I look up from my lunch. Tuna salad and baked beans. Not great, but I'm making it a point to enjoy it while I can. Miranda has warned me that, starting tomorrow, the gravity's going to begin to lessen as *Conquest* decelerates on its approach to Europa. Over the next two days, we'll go from 1G, Earth gravity, to zero-G. After that, eating's going to become—problematic. Tubes instead of plates. Dried meat instead of cooked.

Honestly, though, I'm kind of looking forward to it. I've never been in space before. And, so far, this experience hasn't really felt like "space," despite what the Observation Deck and the viewscreen in my room have shown me.

Maybe floating around like a *real* astronaut will change that.

But these thoughts get knocked right out of my head when a stranger drops onto the bench across from me, a look of challenge in his eyes. He's young, my age or a little older. He's also crew instead of security—which is interesting since he's the first blue uniform to speak to me since the escort who showed me to my room yesterday. And *that* guy was terrified.

"Huh?" I ask, taken by surprise.

His dark hair is cut short, though not in the military skull-croppy way the security guys all seem to like, and he sports one of those wispy high-school mustaches. "I said you're that Dragon."

"Am I?"

"Aren't you?"

"Do I *look* like a giant lizard?"

"Not so much."

"There you go."

"But you *are* the Dragon."

"I'm not big on being called that."

"Called what, 'Dragon'?"

"Yeah."

He grins like I've said something funny. "Then what *do* you like being called?"

"Andy usually works."

A small crowd has gathered, some holding trays of food like mine. Most look like teenagers, and all wear both blue uniforms and bemused looks.

"Okay, then… Andy," Mustache says.

"He doesn't *look* like a freak," one of the other kids remarks.

"Shut it, you asshat!" Mustache snaps.

I gaze uncomfortably down at my tray, my appetite squelched.

One of the crewmen crumples a napkin in his fist and tosses it over to the tabletop's far end, right up against the tile wall. There it sits, looking forlorn and familiar. "Let's see you burn that," he says.

I look up at him and, with a little start, realize he's my fidgety escort from yesterday. Apparently, the group has lent him courage. Mob mentality. I've seen it before.

Furk, this ship's just like high school.

"No," I reply.

He scowls. "Why not?"

I almost tell him because I don't *want* to, but Mustache beats me to the punch, and with a better line. "Because the man ain't a trained monkey."

"He ain't a man either," my escort says. "Besides, if he won't prove it, how do we know he can even do it?"

Mustache eyes him pityingly. "We've spent the last few shifts rebuilding half of Deck 1. Trust me, he's got nothing to prove… leastwise to *you*, Skirter."

"I'm getting bored," a third crewman says. "If there's no show, I'm going back to my lunch."

"Oh, there'll be a furking show," Skirter says. He's glaring back at Mustache now, all peer-driven bravado. In a low voice, he says, "Sounds to me like Greenjeans here's the one with something to prove."

Suddenly the tension's thick, and I find myself wondering if I shouldn't burn the stupid napkin just to defuse this ridiculous schoolyard nonsense.

Then someone else in the Mess calls, "Stow it!"

Mustache instantly jumps to his feet. All of them snap to attention.

A new guy stalks over to us. He wears the same blue uniform, but this time with shoulder epaulets. He's also older than the others, as old as my dad, and wears a scowl so deep that it looks permanently etched into his face.

"Leave it alone," he says, growls really. He's got a big, square head and jet-black hair that's fronted by a widow's peak so sharp it would have made Dracula jealous.

I'm guessing I'm the "it."

"Sorry, Chief," Skirter says. "We were just curious."

Mustache—Greenjeans?—says nothing.

The chief eyes them impatiently. "Curious, huh? Well, this morning I was inspecting Deck 1, or what's left of it." He points a finger at me. "*It* did that. So, there's no need for you to make it prove itself with a furking napkin!"

"He," I say.

"What?" the chief barks, looking at me for the first time.

"I'm a 'he.' Not an 'it.'"

His scowl gets even deeper; I wouldn't have thought it possible. This guy looks like his cheeks would crack if he tried to smile.

"Chief," I add with a phony grin.

Turning away from me, he tells the kids, "Finish your meals and get back on duty. Now."

"Aye, Chief," Skirter says.

"Aye, Chief," Mustache says.

The man-in-charge hammers me with one more glare before stalking off toward the exit. After a moment, the kids follow, looking cowed—all but Mustache, who hangs back. Then, when he's sure the rest are out of earshot, he leans close and meets my eye.

"I think I like you, Draco," he says. "I'm Eric Halabura, Engineer's Apprentice First Class."

Then he offers me his hand.

Draco? Seriously?

"Andy Brand," I say, shaking the offered hand and putting special emphasis on my last name.

Speaking in a low voice, he asks, "Seen much of the ship yet, Andy Brand?"

I shake my head. "Just here, the Observation Deck, and Deck 1, where my room is."

There's an odd look in his eye. For a long moment, he considers. Then, glancing furtively around, he says, "Want a quick tour of Engineering?"

I study him, not sure how much I trust this guy. He seems okay, I guess. But I know the crew's afraid of me. Hell, everybody's afraid of me. Still, something in his expression seems earnest and more serious than his light tone of voice suggests.

"You serious?"

As I watch, he makes another careful assessment of the room. The blue uniforms, Widow's Peak included, have all left, taking their lunches with them. Besides Moustache and me, the only people in the mess are Spencer's security guys, and they seem to be ignoring us. Apparently, having reached the same conclusion, Moustache—Halabura—sits down again. "Sure, I'm serious. You up for it, Draco?"

With a sigh, I ask, "What's this 'Draco' thing?" I know, of course, that the word is simply Latin for dragon, though I'm a little surprised that Halabura knows it, too.

"I've decided that's your handle."

"My what?"

"Your handle. Everybody's got to have a handle."

"Why?"

"It's a spacer thing."

I recognize the term, of course. Any science nerd would. A spacer is a cultural label describing someone who lives and works entirely Off-Earth, especially in and around Mars and the asteroid belt.

"You're a spacer?" I say.

"All of the crew are."

"You were born in space?"

He nods. "Yep. On a Martian orbital. I've never even set foot on *terra firma.*"

I try to wrap my head around that. I'm talking to a real spacer. Back home, spacers have developed a kind of folk-hero status. Not rebels, exactly, but more like fierce individualists. Spacers are the frontiersmen who man the colonies and work the mines, and they're often known to push back against authority, which out here means CSE. I guess I shouldn't be surprised to find them this far out. But aboard a Coffin ship?

"Everybody on board is a spacer?" I ask, incredulous.

"Just the crew. Not the blackbirds."

"Blackbirds?"

He gestures sneakily at the table nearest the Mess door. It's crowded with Spencer's troopers. "Blackbirds. CSE thugs. Definitely *not* spacers. In fact, they're kind of the opposite."

"Oh," I say. It's all I can think of.

"Anyway, despite the blackbird garb they're making you wear, I figure you for a spacer, too."

He means my black uniform, the same as Spencer's, and the rest of his security force.

"I was born on Earth," I tell him.

"It ain't your point of origin that matters. It's where you decide to *go* that tags you as one of us. And here you are."

"I didn't 'decide' this."

"Exactly! Coffin furked you just like he furks the rest of us every day. In my book, that makes you a spacer, which means you need a handle. Every spacer's got one. What's more, they tend to stick with you. I know guys who've gone by their handles for so long that they're not even known by their birth names on manifests anymore! I'm not there yet, but it'll happen."

"You've got a handle?"

"I'm Greenjeans."

"What does that even *mean*?"

"On my first ship, I managed to crack open a canister of solvent and get myself soaked in it. It didn't hurt me, but it dyed my face, hands, and clothing all green. Took a week to get it off. One of the old-timers aboard started calling me Greenjeans right away, and it stuck."

"How old were you?" I asked.

"Twelve."

"Jeez."

"Yeah. It really pissed me off at first. I even got into a few fights over it. But eventually, I got used to it. So now, pretty much wherever I go, I'm Greenjeans. It's some reference to an old 20th-century kids show… I think."

"Never heard of it," I tell him.

"Yeah, me neither. Anyway, from now on, you're Draco."

"I don't like it."

"You're not supposed to. Part of a spacer handle is that, when you get one, it annoys you. Maybe it even pisses you off. It's how you know it's legit."

"That's nuts."

He grins. "So's flying around the wrong side of Mars in a vacuum."

He has a point, sort of. I make a sour face and look at him. "Draco?"

"Draco. Hey, it's better than Greenjeans."

Okay, maybe it is.

Greenjeans remarks, "You must be pretty lonely, huh?"

"What?"

"Strange people. Strange ship. A bunch of million miles from home. Lonely."

I feel a shudder run through me, totally involuntary. "That's one word for it, I guess. The crew's afraid of me."

"I'm not." Then, when I eye him skeptically, he adds, "It's true, Draco."

"I could destroy this ship," I tell him, maybe a little peevishly.

"So, could I," he replies. "So could any other engineer onboard. Close the 'right' port and reroute the power the 'right' way, and we'd all be blown to dust faster than you can say Schrödinger's Cat."

It's an angle I've never considered.

He continues, "Of course we *don't*, no matter how much the blackbirds piss us off. And why not? Because we're not homicidal maniacs with suicidal tendencies. Trust me on that one. Most of us have been *tested*."

It takes me a second to realize it's a joke. Then, despite myself, I laugh.

"Why does the crew get so pissed off at the… blackbirds?" I ask, trying out the unfamiliar term. "From what I can tell, you and they pretty much just stay out of each other's way."

"True enough, I guess," he admits. "But there's a lot of history between blackbirds and spacers… and the Solar System's a whole lot bigger than just this ship."

"What's that mean?"

"You want the Spacer 101 course?" he asks, leaning forward and adding a new edge to his voice. "The *real* story? Not the one you get from the newsvids on Earth?"

When I nod, he gives the room yet another once-over and says, "Can do, but not here. My offer stands. Want to see Engineering?"

"Am I allowed?"

"Furk, no. That's what makes it worth doing."

I regard him thoughtfully.

I've suddenly got the feeling that I'm getting pulled into something—or, more to the point, something *else*. The smart thing to do would be to stay put and finish my lunch.

So, naturally, I reply, "Sure. Why not?"

NINE – Day 14

I follow him out of the crowded Mess and down the hall to the nearest lift. "I hate these things," he remarks as the rails rise and we drop through the floor. "Too much fancy tech on this boat. I like it better when you use ladders, or just bob from floor to floor in zero-G."

"So, you've always been a spacer?" I ask.

"Yep. My pop captained an ore tug out of Ceres. After my mom died when I was five, he used to take me on his runs. I guess you could say I grew up in deep space. Didn't learn how to read until I was almost ten. But I could fix a leaky fuel line and reroute a plasma buffer when I was six."

"Wow," I say.

He shrugs. "Took it all for granted back then. Landed my first apprenticeship at twelve. Told you about that already. Been touring the System ever since."

These days, close to a million people work Off-Earth. But the idea of spending your whole life breathing recycled air and never seeing rain or snow—well, it kind of challenges my perspective. And imagine starting out that young! Eric Halabura has been 'Apprentice Greenjeans' since I was in seventh grade.

"I think maybe I envy you," I admit.

He grins. "Who wouldn't? But that's a pretty big compliment coming from somebody with your… skill set."

"It's not a skill set."

"Then what is it?"

"How we're made. Part of our nature." How weird it is to be talking so freely about the Kind. Completely forbidden. Yet here I am, doing it anyway. "We're born with it, and we spend our lives learning to control it, hide it."

"Gotcha," he replies. "Here's 14. You want to check out the landers?"

"I saw them earlier. Two shuttles."

"Not shuttles, Draco. Landers."

"What's the difference?"

"Shuttles can maneuver in atmosphere. Landers can't. They're designed to go down to the surface and then straight back up again. It's the best way to handle situations like Europa."

"Can't the entire ship just land?"

"*Conquest* ain't designed to land anywhere. Each deck is an individual module built on Earth and shot into orbit for assembly. All the new, big ships are like that."

"Oh."

"Ta-da! Here we are!"

As the lift stops on Deck 15: Engineering, Eric steps off and marches confidently down the hallway. I follow. Along the walls, lighted signs and arrows point us toward "Engine Room" and "Maintenance" and something called simply "The Workshop." At the end of the hall stands an open archway, the room within well-lit and, from the look of it, crowded. As my tour guide leads me inside, the "crowd" turns out to be machine parts, tons of them. These fill the big chamber from floor to ceiling — terminals, piping, and gadgets of all shapes and sizes, the purposes of which I can't begin to guess.

"*This* is the Engine Room?" I ask.

"Not hardly. This is the Workshop, where the stuff that breaks goes to get fixed, assuming it's transportable."

"Some of these things look pretty furking heavy." A few pieces are bigger than I am.

"Not in zero-G."

"Oh. Right."

"Now, can I ask *you* a question?"

I shrug. "Sure." I'm expecting something about fire and Dragons and not being human.

But Eric surprises me, "Where are you quartered?"

"What?"

"Where's your room? Where did they put you?"

"Oh, I'm all the way up on Deck 1."

"Yeah," he says, his manner suddenly reserved. "That's what I thought."

"Why?"

The two of us have stopped in the middle of the otherwise unoccupied Workshop, surrounded by spare spaceship parts. "Remember I told you this ship got constructed modularly?"

"Yeah."

"Each deck was made individually on Earth, then put together in orbit."

"I've read how it works."

"Good for you, Draco. But do you know why the Detention Deck is Deck 1?"

No, I don't. In fact, now that I consider it, it's weird. I mean, this ship has a furking planetarium. Wouldn't it have made more sense to stick the Observation Deck on the nose of the ship, so that the view could be—I don't know—*real*?

"Why?" I ask Greenjeans.

His gaze is steady, his tone serious. "It's a call they made last minute. Before this mission, *Conquest* was still in pieces. Coffin, himself, specified in what order to assemble the modules. And he put Deck 1 at the ship's forefront so, if necessary, it can be jettisoned."

"Jettisoned?"

"The Detention deck's got space for a hundred 'guests,' Draco. That's enough to make it more like a prison than a brig, wouldn't you say?"

"That's why all the CSE guys... blackbirds... are on the deck below," I remark.

"Deck 2, the Security Deck. They're the first line of defense in case something on Deck 1 gets... out of hand. But, if they fail, then the entire prison can just be fired off into space."

"You're telling me they've got me there so that they can jettison me if they decide to?"

"That's what I'm telling you."

I try to absorb this. "That's something she never mentioned."

"Who?"

"Miranda."

"So, you're on a first-name basis with the Ice Queen?"

I feel my face flush and turn away from him.

"She's playing you, Draco."

Of course, she is. She has been since the beginning. But, for all that, she's also kind to me. Patient.

And I'm—alone.

When I look back at Eric, he dishes up a smile. "Ain't none of my business. I just figured you had a right to know. Come on. I promised to show you where the magic happens."

He heads toward the exit at the far end of the Workshop. Slowly, as if moving through a dream, my mind still reeling, I follow him into a small empty antechamber with a broad archway on the left.

Together, we step through it and into what has to be the Engine Room.

It fills one entire hemisphere of the deck, a big half-moon with a high ceiling and a long, gently curving wall that traces *Conquest's* outer hull. This wall features a half-dozen enormous viewports through which stars glisten like icy jewels in a black sea. In-line with these big windows, equidistant from one another, are six white cylinders. Each is at least ten feet in diameter and more than twice that high, with jungles of pipes, tubes, and cables tethering it to a central monitoring station.

"Cutting-edge fission reactors," Greenjeans announces, sounding almost proud of the fact. "Totally state of the art. Six of them power all of the ship's functions. That includes the two big argon thrusters in our tail. *Those* bad boys are capable of delivering enough meganewtons to blow your mind!"

The place is crowded with men and women in blue uniforms, all of whom move from station to station like they really, really know what they're doing.

"And these folks are *all* spacers?" I ask.

"More or less."

A few notice us and stare, but, for the most part, we're ignored. So, I ignore them back, heading straight to the nearest viewport. I expect it to be a projection, like the planetarium. However, as I get close to it, I realize that I can see the ghost of my own reflection. Tentatively, I touch the smooth, transparent surface. This is no collection of repurposed

Liquid Bricks, but instead some kind of clear polymer, maybe a foot thick and room-temperature to the touch. A genuine window.

And beyond it waits the blackness of space. Real space.

"Pretty amazing, isn't it?" Greenjeans asks, coming to stand at my shoulder.

"Yeah."

"Is it worth it?"

"Worth what?"

"Is being here and seeing this worth all the crap they put you through?"

"How much do you know about the crap they put me through?"

He shrugs. "You were brought aboard asleep. They waited until we were solidly at 1G before using the vectors to wake you. They didn't want low or no gravity to tip you off to where you were, not right away. Mind games."

"What *are* vectors?"

"Nobody's told you about vectors? It's short for 'aerosol vector.' Liquid Bricks have a lot of different templates. One of them allows for rapid directional chemical disbursement."

"Directional chemical *what*?"

"Picture chloroform, fired at you in a tight, concentrated burst from six or more feet away. Knocks you out almost instantly. And they've got tiles like that spread all through *Conquest*. No way to distinguish them from the rest, not even with an e-man. Nobody talks about them… but they could be used to put people to sleep… or wake them up, depending on which drug they pick." He looks pointedly at me. "Like they did to you."

Vector.

I've never heard the term. Or maybe I have. I seem to recall the Voice using that word, just once, the first time I woke up in my cell. And didn't I get knocked unconscious immediately after — right off my feet, in fact?

It's another thing Miranda never mentioned.

The list is getting long.

"Why are there windows down here but nowhere else on the ship?"

Eric motions to the floor at my feet. I notice, for the first time, parallel tracks that run along the floor from the window to the nearest reactor. Similar tracks connect each of the other reactors to their respective viewports.

"What are they?" I ask.

"An emergency protocol. Our fission reactors are as safe as they can be. But, in the event something bad happens… I mean the catastrophic kind of bad… and one of them threatens to go, well, nuclear, then it gets rolled along this evacuation rail and right through this polymer viewport. The ports are made to pop open on command."

"Wouldn't that depressurize the whole engine room and kill everybody?"

"In theory, we'd have all been evacuated by then."

"In theory," I say.

"So?" Eric asks.

"So what?"

"You never answered my question. Is it worth it?"

Looking out over the starscape once more, I take a moment to weigh — really weigh — the pros and cons. Finally, I reply as honestly as I can. "I… don't know."

He nods as if this is exactly the answer he expected. Then he asks, "Ready for that Spacer 101?"

"Okay."

"Let's make this quick," he says, looking around. More of the crew are watching us now. The active engine room becomes less active by the second. "The chief's off-deck at the moment. This time of day, he's usually with the captain, giving a status report. But he could be back any minute. So… there are two kinds of folks out here. Spacers and corporates, right? Corporates are, on paper at least, in charge. They own most of the mines and *all* of the colonies."

"Like CSE," I say.

"CSE, the blackbirds, and their on-site management. Some of the colonies on Mars and the asteroids have thousands or tens of thousands of spacers living on them full-time. Thing is, Earth news vids describe life out here as all frontier-ish, but it's not. There aren't any homesteaders eking out individual livings. Everybody works for the corporates, be they docs, nurses, schoolmarms, or bartenders… and the corporates, in particular Coffin, own the media. So, the truth gets… spun. Follow?"

I nod.

"That's been the way for the last twenty years, and the corporates are determined to make sure it don't change. Spacers, in the meantime, keep clamoring for more rights, self-rule. But we're not getting it, and we won't. That's what makes this mission to Europa so important to Coffin and his daughter."

I blink. "You just lost me. What—"

"Greenjeans!"

We both whirl around as Chief Widow's Peak approaches. I still don't know his name, but there's no mistaking his expression. Pissed. In fact, something tells me this guy wakes up pissed every morning, and his mood only gets worse as the day wears on.

"What the hell are you doing, bringing *him* down here?" he barks so loudly that everyone in the Engine Room who hasn't already done so stops and stares. Widow's Peak towers over Greenjeans, though my new friend—if that's what we are—looks more bemused than intimidated.

"No problem, Chief," Eric begins. "I was only—"

"You were only *what?* Trying to get us all killed? Bad enough to have this thing on board in the first place. But to actually bring him into my Engine Room—"

Well, at least he's got the pronoun right.

Widow's Peak plows on. "Do you have any idea what would happen if he got hurt?"

"Chief—" Eric begins.

"I warned you not to get chummy with this… thing. But, like always, *you* went off on your own, didn't you? Listen to me. You're just six months away from full journeyman, right? Well, get back in line or, swear to God, I'll get your apprenticeship revoked. You'll end up shoveling ore on a scow or pit-mining some asteroid!"

"Enough!" I yell.

They *both* look at me. Eric has gone pale, while Widow's Peak is beat red.

"I'm not a thing," I say.

Widow's Peak sneers. "Well, you're damn sure not a man!" Then he points a fat finger in my face. "I want you out of my Engine Room. Hell, I want you off the ship, but that's not my call. Now get gone!"

Almost without thinking, I let a little of my dragon out.

This is *way* over the top, and I know it. My display with Miranda was one thing. That came out of desperation, the need to save someone I cared about. But this is just me being pissed off. My folks would be ashamed of me.

But they're both millions of miles away.

Chief Widow's Peak screams and snatches his hand back. The finger that he was shoving in my face is already blistering badly, as if he pressed it to a hot stove and left it there. It's a second-degree burn, not third; I'm not *that* far gone. But it's bad enough.

"See what it did to me!" he exclaims. He turns in a circle, giving everyone a look at his scorched finger. The blister I've made is getting bigger and bigger. It needs to be lanced, and then the whole hand bandaged. But he probably won't require skin grafts.

Probably.

He continues, "See what the corporates let on board! Do you all know what would happen if he got injured? Do you have any idea what he would *do*?"

Greenjeans gapes at me.

This was no napkin.

Without a word, I turn and, feeling dozens of eyes drill into me, head for the exit. I half expect someone to come after me, but they don't. Of course, they don't.

I'm dangerous.

I'm a monster.

A thing.

A dragon.

TEN – Day 14

I go straight to my quarters and throw myself facedown onto my bed, the way I do back home whenever I'm in trouble and get banished to my room. For a long time, I just lay there, replaying the events in Engineering and feeling a little sick to my stomach.

I just burned somebody. It was something I'd never done even accidentally, much less deliberately.

In the last twenty-four hours, I've managed to throw away pretty much everything my parents ever taught me. Next thing, I'll forget how to tie my shoes; apparently, that's how bad I am at retaining important life lessons. When I tell them—and, yes, I'll *have* to tell them—the looks on their faces are going to crush me flat.

Conceal and Protect.

Until this moment, I don't think I truly grasped the brutal practicality behind that philosophy. My mom's right; she always has been.

Human beings fear what they can't control. It's something to keep clearly in mind, though mental clarity hasn't exactly been my personal motto lately.

"I'm sorry, Mom and Dad," I whisper.

My wrist chirps or, more accurately, my e-man does. Startled, I raise my head from the mattress of Liquid Bricks and stare at it for several seconds before I realize it's an incoming call.

I didn't even know this thing had a radio.

Rolling over onto my back, I touch a pulsing control, raise the gadget to my face and say tentatively, "Hello?"

"Andy, it's Miranda."

"Oh. Hi."

"Have you eaten?"

I consider the meal I abandoned down in the Mess when Greenjeans convinced me to follow him into trouble. Does Miranda know about the "incident" in Engineering? If she doesn't, she will soon. That Widow's Peak guy looked like a born snitch. "Close enough," I reply.

Then she says something that turns my black mood right around. *"Good. Ready to talk to your parents?"*

"What? Yes!"

"Do you know where the Comms Room is?"

"No."

"Deck 8. Just follow the signs. I'll be waiting."

The pulsing light goes out.

I all but run out of my quarters and down to the portside lift.

The Comms Room turns out to be smaller than I would have thought, just a cubical space with a lighted circular platform and waist-high control console in the center.

Miranda stands on the lighted platform, looking as amazing as she did this morning.

"Hello, Andy!" she says, beaming. "Come on in!"

I step inside. "This… isn't what I expected."

"No? What *did* you expect?"

"A bunch of communications workstations, I guess. Keyboards and screens."

"We're much higher tech than that."

"How does it work?"

"You talk."

"Out loud?"

She laughs. "That usually works best."

"How long does it take a message to reach Earth?"

Her smile widens. "Virtually instantaneous."

I blink. "What?"

"I told you this was a ship of firsts. Liquid Bricks and linear acceleration are only two of them. This one, I think, might be the most impressive." She gestures at the futurey pedestal that stands at the edge of the lighted circle. "I give you… the Casimir Radio."

I approach and examine the pedestal's controls. A numbered keypad and a few unmarked buttons. That's it. But the name Casimir is vaguely familiar. Something I read.

I say, "But doesn't it take radiowaves something like a half-hour to travel from Earth to Jupiter?"

"Thirty-three minutes," she corrects. "And only when the two planets are at their closest. Then again, that's assuming we're transmitting through normal space."

"Normal space?" Then I remember. "Casimir. Like in the Casimir Effect?"

She positively beams at me. "Ha! I knew you'd get it!"

And I do get it. I just don't quite believe it.

The Casimir Effect describes a type of negative energy generated by restricting the amount of electromagnetic radiation in a vacuum. It's named for a long-dead Dutch physicist named Henrik Casimir. From what I've read, Casimir Energy might be able to help stabilize a wormhole, creating a shortcut through spacetime that would allow people to travel ridiculous distances really quickly. Except nobody's ever come close to getting it to work. While tiny, brief wormholes have been created in controlled lab experiments, none of them ever had enough size or stability to allow even small bits of matter to pass through them.

But—

"You've found a way to create a wormhole stable enough to transmit radio waves through!" I exclaim, suddenly in total geek-mode.

"We have, indeed! Instant communication to and from anywhere, and the speed of light be damned."

I gape at the sleek, elegant gadget in front of me. Am I really going to be talking to my parents through a genuine *wormhole*?

"How's it work?" I ask.

"Heavens, Andy, how should I know? I'm an MBA, not an astrophysicist. All I can tell you is that it does. I do know that it requires the use of a dedicated CSE satellite in Earth orbit. It's the satellite that creates and maintains the wormhole. All the Casimir Radio does is reach out to it. That part *does* require a standard radio signal to be sent, which I already did… about forty minutes ago. The satellite then opens the wormhole through uberspace, linking it to here."

Uberspace? Seriously?

But this doesn't feel like the right time to be editorializing.

"How do you know when the connection's made?" I ask.

"The circle lights up."

"It's lit up now," I point out.

Miranda nods. "Which means the link has been established with the satellite and we can dial whenever we're ready. *Are* you ready, Andy?"

I nod. For some reason, my throat is dry.

"Then go ahead and call your parents. The transmission beam is very narrow, so the speaker has to stay inside the circle."

Nodding, I eagerly tap in my mom's mobile number.

An AI's disembodied voice announces, *"Your call is commencing now."*

A light appears on the wall behind the console, directly at eye level.

"That's the vidcam," Miranda explains, stepping out of the circle. "Your parents, if they accept the video part of the link, will appear in front of you as a big holographic projection. It can be a little startling. Fair warning."

"Thanks."

I hear the familiar digital ring of a call being made. The sound, so ordinary, seems incongruous considering where I'm standing.

Three rings go by. Four. Five.

My palms are sweaty.

"You've reached Bonnie Brand. I'm afraid I'm not available to talk just now. Please leave a message."

Mom's voice sounds both cheerful and a little rushed. Very *her*.

"Can I try my dad?" I ask.

"Sure. Just hit the red button to end the call and reset."

The dialing process restarts. This time I enter my father's mobile phone number. Mom's pretty notorious for leaving her phone around the house but Dad's obsessive about keeping his close at hand. Looking back, I should have called him first.

But then, after some more digital rings, I hear, *"This is Tony Brand. Leave me a message."* Business-like, almost abrupt. Very *him*.

The line chirps, indicating it's ready for my vidmail.

I feel a stab of alarm.

"Leave a vidmail," Miranda suggests. She sounds almost as disappointed as I am.

I throw what has to be a death's head smile on my face, and croak, "Dad? It's me. Andy. I just want to let you both know that I'm okay. I… God, I have so much to tell you. I guess maybe…" I look at Miranda. "Can they call me back?"

She shakes her head.

So, I face forward and add, "I'll try again a little later. I'm… sorry this happened. But I'm okay. I really am." That's when words fail me. My smile, such as it is, collapses. Tears sting my eyes.

An unhappy silence ensues. Finally, mercifully, the AI reads my long pause as completion. *"Your call has ended."*

"I'm sorry, Andy," Miranda assures me. "Just bad timing, I guess. I'm sure—"

Abruptly, a gigantic face fills half the room, and a voice booms, *"Good evening, Mister Brand."*

I almost jump out of my shoes.

Nearby, Miranda stiffens. She doesn't look happy.

"I apologize if I startled you," the Great and Powerful Wizard of Oz tells me. *"I'm Charles Coffin."*

A lot flashes through my mind when I hear that name. This is a man I've admired most of my life. Well, I've admired his accomplishments. About the man himself, I don't really know very much. For example, I never knew he had kids named Charlie and Miranda, one of whom died young. Even so, being addressed by Charles Coffin himself is both intimidating and, yes, a major honor for a nerd like me. This is the man who privatized space travel. If he isn't the richest person on Earth, he's certainly in the top five, and his name is synonymous with space-age advancement.

In short, Charles Coffin is a living legend.

"I'm sorry to come at you this way. I know you were calling your parents."

I stammer, "I… left a… vidmail."

"Ah. Well, you're welcome to try again later. As often as you like, in fact, which is a privilege that very few of your shipmates enjoy. But Miranda and I want you to feel, not merely at home aboard Conquest, *but welcome. Because you are welcome, gratefully so."*

I muster my courage and push through my star-struck stupidity long enough to reply, "That'd mean a lot more if I hadn't been kidnapped and dragged out here against my will."

Peripherally, I see Miranda pale. Sassing the great Charles Coffin is an apparent no-no.

"I appreciate your frankness. Here's some in return. There are currently about seven hundred Dragons living on Earth, and we modeled the majority of them, those we could find, looking for the best candidate for this mission based on a wide range of parameters. Those models produced one name as the likeliest to possess both the power and inclination to aid us. You. So, given your admission to my daughter that you wouldn't have capitulated of your own free will, what choice did we really have but to… borrow… you? As Miranda explained, there are lives at stake."

You've got to admit, it's a sweet piece of logical rationalization. *Your free will got in the way of what we want, so we took it away from you. No big deal, right?*

"Do you understand what I'm saying to you, Andy? May I call you Andy?"

"I think I like Mister Brand better."

There's a pause. The giant head looks disconcerted, as if he can't quite grasp that I haven't collapsed under the weight of his reason. *"Well, regardless, I'm glad to have you on our team."*

I don't offer a reply.

The Wizard of Oz vanishes a few moments later.

The lighted platform goes dark.

Miranda clears her throat and says, "The wormhole's been collapsed."

"I figured."

"Andy, my father… he's used to getting his own way."

"Uh-huh."

"I know you don't believe it," she says. "But what he told you just now was kind of an apology. A Charles Coffin Apology."

"You're right," I reply. "I don't believe it."

ELEVEN – Day 16

The next two days aren't good ones. In fact, they suck, even by "kidnap victim on a spaceship" standards.

During that time, I revisit the Comms Room and try to call my folks again, and again, and again. The result is always the same. Voicemail. At one point, Miranda asks if there's anyone else I might reach out to. A relative. A neighbor. But there isn't. The Kind live scattered lives. Both my parents, like me, are only children, and of the handful of distant cousins, aunts, and uncles I know about, none are close enough for "reaching out." As far as neighbors go, I've lived in Haddonfield, New Jersey my entire life, and couldn't have named anyone else on our block. We keep to ourselves. I've never even been trick-or-treating.

Miranda keeps telling me there's an explanation; we just don't know it yet. But I'm not buying it. In my gut, I know something's wrong.

Now I'm headed down there yet again, and I'd be lying if I said I held out any hope. As any science geek will tell you, Einstein believed the definition of insanity was doing the same thing over and over and expecting a different result. So, either I'm bat-furk crazy—or old Albert never found himself shanghaied in space and trying desperately to phone home.

Over the last forty-eight hours, *Conquest* has now gradually transitioned to zero-G. This has brought with it a number of changes, and not the least of them is that the only way to get around is by pulling one's weightless body through the corridors. The lifts are offline, replaced with person-sized openings in the floor and ceiling through which to float between decks. For ease of use, Liquid Brick-based handholds have been strategically added. These are a godsend since the reality of weighing nothing means that, if you push off the wrong way, you can crash *hard* into the opposite wall, ceiling, or floor—and break a bone.

In fact, Spencer and Captain Wei have become so concerned for my "safety" that yesterday they petitioned Miranda to confine me to quarters, maybe even strap me to my bed. Miranda described to me a heated discussion, which apparently included Okeke assuring the senior staff that a "dragon's fight-or-flight" reflex can't be triggered by something as mundane as a broken bone—that a more catastrophic injury is required.

And that's true, I think.

But apparently, they didn't buy it.

Miranda ended up pulling rank, even going so far as having them all adjourn to the Comms Room so that Charles Coffin himself could deliver the edict.

Bottom line: I'm *not* to be made a prisoner again aboard *Conquest*.

Of course, this doesn't explain why I'm still on the Detention Deck.

So yesterday evening, I worked up the courage to ask Miranda about that.

"It's another compromise," she told me. "I know it's unnecessary, even insulting, but Spencer's less open-minded than I am, at least where you're concerned."

"And I'm sure none of this has anything to do with what happened down in Engineering the other day," I remarked sourly.

She shrugged. Miranda already knew all about the incident, of course. As I figured, Widow's Peak ratted me out, big time. Within hours, the whole ship got the skinny, and, since then, the crew's been even more standoffish than usual. Spencer and his blackbirds, on the other hand, pay me more attention than ever—the kind of attention usually reserved for ticking time bombs.

"And who decides if I get jettisoned into deep space?" I asked at the time, trying not to sound as unnerved as I felt.

"That won't happen."

"Who decides?"

"I do. And I promise you that it won't happen."

They're good, reassuring words. So why don't I feel any better?

Anyway, this morning, being in a first-class funk, I hold off heading straight down to the Comms Room and Miranda for yet another round of "Disappoint the Hostage," Instead, I decide to indulge in a little exploring. So, by-passing the port "pass-thru," as the lift-less openings are now called, I spend some time randomly wandering the Deck 1 corridors.

After floating down a half-dozen of these and turning a bunch of corners, all without finding anything of interest, a voice suddenly says, "Hey, Draco! How do you like flying?"

Looking to my right, I spot Greenjeans, whom I haven't seen since that stupidity with his boss down in Engineering. Eric's tethered to the floor and is repairing a section of tile using a screwdriver-like tool. He offers me a grin.

"Sucks," I reply.

"Yeah, well, get used to it. This is what *real* space travel feels like!"

"What're you doing?" I ask.

He laughs. "Fixing what's left of your handiwork."

That's when I realize where I am. This is the part of the deck that I—well, melted—when my dragon came out, back when I thought

Miranda Coffin was Miranda Fiero. Most of it looks to have been repaired, the Liquid Bricks I destroyed, hundreds of them surely, replaced.

"Sorry," I mutter, though I'm not.

"It's just grunt work. The tiles are supposed to be aligned in a specific matrix; otherwise, they don't do what they're told. It's all very proprietary, and, usually, it works great. But newly installed ones can be tetchy. So, Tuttle's got me running around testing and fixing them."

"Who's Tuttle?"

Eric looks surprised. "Chief Tuttle! You remember him. He's the guy you flash-fried the other day."

So, that's *his name.*

I feel my face redden.

"And this is… what? A punishment?"

"More or less. I get the crap jobs when I'm on duty, and I'm confined to my bunk when I'm not."

"For how long?"

"Until the chief decides otherwise."

"Sorry," I tell him, and this time I mean it.

He gives a dismissive wave. "Life of an apprentice. Don't sweat it. I get in trouble a lot. I got a big mouth. Ask anybody. You never *did* answer my question, by the way."

"What question?"

"Down in Engineering, before the crap hit the turbines, I asked you if it was worth it."

"I told you I don't know."

"Yeah. But now that you've had a couple more days to think it over, I'm guessing that answer might have changed."

I frown. "Not really. It's… complicated."

He regards me. "You got yanked right out of your life and sent into space on a ship populated by blackbirds who are all, let's face it, afraid of you."

"Right. Complicated."

"Except I saw your face at the Engine Room viewport. You were looking out at the Big Black like a man in love."

Despite everything, I can't help smiling—a little. "Maybe."

"Honesty. I like it. So… *was* it worth it or wasn't it?"

"It might be, *if* I can get in touch with my folks."

"More honesty!" He grins.

"I have to get to the Comms Room," I say.

"Phoning home?"

"Yeah. But, so far, no one's been picking up."

His expression darkens, though not with anger. It's more like I've touched on a tender subject. "Well, better get to it then. I've got another fifteen of these little bastards to replace before lunch. We'll catch up later."

A few minutes after that, Miranda and I meet in the Comms Room and try yet again.

And, again, we fail. Just like the last half-dozen attempts. Voicemail.

I feel empty, sick to my soul. But I leave another message, this time including a special telephone number that Miranda gave me, a line to her father's private office.

Then, as I end the call and am about to step out of the circle, the Wizard of Oz appears again. *"I know how frustrating this must be for you,"* he says in his booming, electronic voice.

I don't reply. I don't even look at him. Out of the corner of my eye, I see Miranda. She's gone pale.

Charles Coffin asks, *"Knowing the culture of your people, mightn't your parents have relocated? Changed their names? Isn't that the protocol in the event of discovery?"*

"They wouldn't have left without me," I reply with rock-hard certainty. I'm still not looking at him.

"Then, we'll find them, surely."

Again, I don't reply.

A moment later, the big head vanishes, and the Casimir Radio goes dark. From the shadows, Miranda whispers, "I'm so sorry, Andy."

At least *her* eyes I'm able to meet. Miserably, I hear myself ask, "What's happened to them?"

"I don't know. I really don't. But we can try again later."

But I barely hear her.

Could Coffin be right? Could my folks have—run?

It *is* something the Kind do, though I'm not sure I'd label it a "protocol." If something happens in a particular place, something that threatens to expose our true nature, my people just pull up stakes and start over somewhere new. My family has never done it in my lifetime. However, I know for a fact that my mom and dad once *did* it, having lived in Michigan under another name before I was born. But if something similar went down in Haddonfield, then my folks might be anywhere by now, with my only clue being an assumed surname with a vague reference to fire.

But would my parents really have done such a thing, given my circumstances?

If the threat to Conceal and Protect was dire enough… maybe, they would.

Which means I really am completely alone.

Miranda takes my hand.

At first, this startles me. I guess I'm not used to being touched. But when I try to pull away, she holds firm and, when I meet her eyes — her incredible eyes, she gazes back at me with compassion.

"Andy," she says softly.

I swallow and mumble, "What?"

Smooth.

"I want you to be mine."

Suddenly, it's warmer than usual in the Comms Room. "What?" I mumble again.

Smoother.

She kisses me.

I realize it's coming a half-second before it happens, which doesn't give me much time to prepare. I try to remember if I brushed my teeth. Then I run through my limited breakfast menu. Since zero-G started, all food comes in tubes. What tube did I pick up this morning in the Mess? Cinnamon raisin? If so, then that's probably all right.

Oh God, what if I picked the ham and onion omelet?

Then our lips touch, and it no longer matters. Abandoning worry, I just kind of lean into the kiss. By then, we've both given up our grips on the rail, and our bodies begin to react to our shared motion by moving us upward, toward the ceiling. As we rise, I momentarily feel myself starting to drift away from her, and, instinctively, I wrap both my arms around her waist. At the same time, her hands cup my face, keeping it close to hers, the kiss deepening.

It's *electric*, and it goes on for a long time.

Finally, she pulls back and looks at me. I immediately get lost in her eyes, my heart thudding behind my ears and my breath coming in little gasps.

She whispers, "Will you be mine?"

"Yes," I gasp. "Yes, I will."

She smiles magnificently. "Then come with me."

"Where?"

But, instead of answering, she takes my hand.

Navigating the ship linked in this way isn't particularly easy in zero-G. It requires floating precariously along corridors, around sharp corners, and down pass-thrus between levels, all while holding hands. But we're motivated, and we manage it.

Miranda's private quarters are on Deck 7, the Officers Deck.

Enough said.

TWELVE – Day 16

That afternoon, it happens.

Conquest is on its final approach to Europa—though, according to Eric, we can't really orbit the moon. Very little in the Jovian system is that simple.

"See, we've got this ridiculously big planet looming over everything," he explains as we eat lunch together in the Mess, strapped to our seats and sucking our respective tubes of weirdly flavored space grub. So far, he's still the only crewperson willing to spend time with me, except for Miranda. But the adjunct has a ship to run, and she warned me that I probably wouldn't see her again until this evening.

But I can't deny that what we did in her private quarters this morning has distracted me from my problems. To be honest, I'm having a hard time thinking about anything else.

"I mean, look at all the factors," Greenjeans continues, blissfully unaware that I'm only half-listening to him. "Europa orbits this gigantic planet every three days. Meanwhile, the gigantic planet revolves on its axis every ten hours. Now add into the mix the fact that Jupiter's magnetic field is the biggest in the Solar System, besides Sol, itself, and what have you got?"

"A planet with a gravity well so deep that it'll suck down any ship that tries to establish a stable orbit around Europa?" I venture.

Science nerd, remember?

"Well, yeah," he says, looking momentarily nonplussed. "Exactly that. So, instead, *Conquest* will settle into an orbit around Jupiter that allows for close Europan fly-bys every eleven hours or so. As it does, the ship will slow its speed to match the moon's, giving us a window of time to transport stuff down to the surface and back again."

"How big a 'window?'" I ask.

"Maybe an hour. Doesn't leave a lot of room for screw-ups." He grins. "Fortunately, spacers don't make many."

"Good to know."

Suddenly, he leans forward and asks, "So, how is she?"

Just as suddenly, I'm *fully* listening. "How's... who?"

"Don't play innocent with me, Draco. You know exactly *who* I'm talking about. The Ice Queen! You were *seen* going into her quarters this morning. This is a big ship, but it ain't *that* big, and the news hit the grapevine inside of ten minutes. By now, everybody knows you two made the nasty."

The nasty? Seriously?

I groan. "*Everybody* knows?"

His grin widens. "Well, not everybody. I doubt any of the spacers told any of the blackbirds. But, face it, it's juicy gossip! She's the "king's" daughter, and you're... well... you. You gotta figure on *some* talk!"

All I can do is mutter, "Oh."

"Hey, listen," Greenjeans goes on — ever on. "I'm not dissing you. I'd be lying if I said she hasn't made the top of my spank list. So, believe me, my hat is off."

I almost ask what a "spank list" is but decide I don't want to know.

He gives me a lascivious wink. "So, I gotta ask. Are you in the 'don't kiss and tell' column or the 'got nothing to compare her to' column?" Then, when I offer no reply, he nods. "Gotcha. The 'got nothing to compare her to' column, it is!"

"No!" I exclaim too quickly.

Eric chuckles, though there's no mockery in it. "*My* first time was a girl on Mars. She worked in a commissary, and we met when she served me lumpy oatmeal. We were both sixteen, and neither of us knew what we were doing. I got it kind of all wrong, and, looking back, I don't think either of us had much fun. We just felt like it... needed doing." He meets my eyes. "I hope you represented our dumb-ass gender better with the Ice Queen."

When I was eleven, my father explained the "facts of life" to me. As it turned out, he'd made up some computer slides to help "clarify" things.

He really had.

Yet, as uncomfortable as *that* conversation was, this is worse.

"Um..." I begin.

Then a new voice says, "May I join you?"

We both look up to find Doctor Okeke hand-railing her way over to us. She's clutching one of the netted pouches that pass for cafeteria trays in zero-G. In it is a tube of the "Vegetarian Cuisine" flavor Eric warned me to avoid at all costs, as well as a squeeze bottle of water.

"Sure!" I say instantly and without thinking, my only goal to escape Greenjean's grilling.

Across from me, Eric smirks.

Okeke nods gratefully and eases her weightless body down onto one of the benches, anchoring herself with the Velcro straps, same as us. Here's a tip if you ever find yourself in zero-G: it's much easier to do anything if you're firmly anchored. That's because the barest hand movement can send you flying off in unwanted directions, frequently out of control.

It makes sex—complicated.

Furking Newton.

"So," the doctor says as she opens her lunch net. "I do hope this isn't awkward, but I couldn't help overhearing some of your conversation and, frankly, I have some questions."

Oh, you've got to be kidding me!

Across the table, Greenjeans fights the giggles.

"Look," I say quickly. "I'm not going to talk about anything Miranda and I—"

Okeke holds up a hand. "I'm sorry. I didn't make myself clear. I've no interest in any specifics where you and the adjunct are concerned. You're both consenting adults. No, Mister Brand, my questions are about Dragon procreation in general."

Please, God. Kill me now.

The look of comedic rapture on Greenjeans' face makes me want to punch him.

"For example," the doctor goes on. "It's my understanding that Dragons tend to live in isolated family groups hidden in the midst of small human communities, and that these family groups have little, if any, contact with each other. Is that correct?"

I try to think of something snarky. Finally, I just nod.

"Then I'm very curious about mating practices," Okeke says.

Oh, my God…

On the other side of the table, Greenjeans loses his fight. He turns away, vomiting laughter.

Okeke says, "Perhaps I framed that too… clinically."

"Ya think?" I mutter.

"What I meant to ask, Mister Brand, is how did your parents meet?"

Okay. At least *that* question doesn't make me feel like a bunny in a cosmetics testing lab. Besides, what's the point of Conceal and Protect now?

I reply, "On the dark web."

Eric's laughter fades, and he perks up. Apparently, this topic is interesting.

"The dark web," Okeke echoes. "I'm not sure what you mean."

"Really?" I ask her, a smidge condescendingly. "You know all about the Kind, but you've never heard of the dark web?"

"I have," Eric remarks unhelpfully.

So, I explain. "It's a part of the internet that most people never access. Secret sites that don't advertise on search engines."

Greenjeans leans forward. "So, there's a Dragon dating *site*?"

"Something like that."

"What's it look like?" he presses.

"Pretty basic. It just lists those Kind, both male and female, who are interested in meeting each other."

"Pictures?" he asks eagerly.

"Text only. Short little ads… kind of like the "personals" columns in old print newspapers."

"Oh," he replies, looking a little crestfallen.

Okeke says, her eyes *shining* with interest, "I'll need the IP address."

I meet her gaze. "No."

"What?"

"I said, no. I won't tell you how to find the site."

She looks aghast. "Why ever not?"

"Because humans aren't invited to participate, and we sure as hell don't want them 'lurking.'"

"I'm a scientist, Mister Brand. I don't lurk. I… observe."

"We don't want to be observed."

Okeke's eyes quit shining. "I see," she says, and now it's her turn to look crestfallen. "Well, let's put that aside for now, shall we? Perhaps a different topic?"

"Good idea."

"There's very little understanding of Draconian procreative habits."

"Draconian *what?*"

Eric starts laughing again.

Okeke is unfazed. "The general consensus amongst those few 'in the know' is that mated Dragons usually bear no more than two children and often only one, which is the key reason for their low population. You would seem evidentiary in this regard, having no siblings."

I say nothing, but I say it as loudly as I can.

"Do you know of any other members of your species who grew up in a household with more than two children?"

"No," I reply.

"And how often do family units socialize with extended family or the broader community?"

"Rarely."

"How rarely? Specifics, please."

"*Really* rarely."

"Mister Brand, you're not being very forthcoming."

From my perspective, I'm being forthcoming as all get out. My parents would be screaming if they could hear me.

I say nothing.

Undaunted, Okeke tries a juicier tangent. "It's my understanding that unions between humans and Dragons are always barren?"

Again, I say nothing — though Okeke's not completely right. Kind *do* sometimes marry humans, though it's frowned on, and most of these couples are never able to have kids.

But my mom told me about some rare cases.

They're called "Splits," half-human and half-Kind, and their lives are often — difficult. I've never met one. But I think maybe Mom did, or at least heard of one. "Date anyone you like, Andy," she once told me. "But don't marry a human girl. Nothing but misery will come of it. Besides, there are so few of us already, and whenever one of us marries outside the Kind, we lose potential babies."

I remember listening, but not really promising to follow through.

You see, I had a thing for a human girl named Becky Cooper in my ninth-grade class at the time.

Okeke droned on. "…with an estimated global population of barely seven hundred, Dragons are an endangered species. Perhaps someone should institute a regimented breeding program, if only to keep the numbers from trending downward."

"Would *you* do that?" I ask.

"Do what?"

"Participate in a 'regimented breeding program.'" I glare at her. "And how would it work? Would my mom be tied to a bed and fed intravenously so that the 'males of my species' can impregnate her? Or would we all get tranq-ed and tagged like bears, with GPS chips under our skin to monitor our… mating rituals and procreative habits?"

She blinks, clearly confused by my reaction. "I'm not trying to offend you, Mister Brand."

"We're *people*!" I tell her, hotly. "Not animals! We don't have 'mating practices.' We have families!"

She recoils, her face ashen. Only her seat strap keeps her from bouncing off the ceiling—but not with embarrassment.

With fear.

Because Dragons aren't allowed to get mad.

Which only makes me madder.

"What's with the flinching?" I demand. "You afraid I'm going to go the Kind-version of rabid and let my dragon 'bite' you?"

"Of course… not!" she stammers. Across from me, Eric's smug smile is gone, replaced with a look of what I guess I'll label social discomfort.

Everyone else in the Mess has gone quiet. The blackbirds are fingering their sidearms.

I ignore all of it.

"Then get this," I tell Okeke, jabbing my finger at her, Chief Tuttle-style. "Furk your scientific curiosity. I'm not your lab rat, and I'm not answering any more questions. Ever. Got it?"

"Really, Mister Brand!" Okeke exclaims, struggling to compose herself. "There's no need to be rude!"

"Drop dead," I tell her.

An instant later, she does.

Something shoots through the wall at Okeke's back with enough force to shatter one Liquid Brick and send four others whipping out into the zero-G like throwing stars. Two jab the ceiling and stick there. One slashes the table beside my hand, leaving an inch-deep groove. The last careens off the serving table and catches one of Spencer's men in the thigh. Marble-sized blood droplets bubble weightlessly through the air while the guy who owns them curses.

Meanwhile, the original projectile catches Okeke in the back of her skull and emerges through the center of her forehead, killing her instantly. But instead of crumpling, the zero-G bounces her head off the table but then keeps her mainly upright, her limp arms bobbing weirdly, like an underwater marionette.

It's all so *fast*, so utterly without warning, that I can't speak, can't breathe. I'm not even sure I'm *thinking*.

I hear Eric exclaim, "Dust cloud!"

At the same instant, an alarm sounds, and tiles on the wall near the ceiling start flashing red.

Suddenly, everyone in the Mess Hall is in motion.

With some effort, I manage to croak out, "Dust cloud?"

But Eric ignores me. Untethering himself, he launches with practiced ease toward the Mess's exit, joining with his fellow crewmen. The blackbirds, in the meantime, are tending to their wounded, all but one.

Spencer's pointing a finger at me.

I hadn't even known the security chief was in the room.

"You!" he calls. "Get back to your quarters. *Now!*"

I just stare at him, Okeke's corpse floating not a foot away from me.

"Move it, Dragon!" Spencer barks. Then, grabbing a random blackbird, he orders, "Escort Brand to Deck 1. Do it!"

The soldier looks almost as stunned by the goings-on as I feel. But he nods and motions for me to follow.

Reluctantly, I do.

THIRTEEN – Day 16

We're in the hallway when the first *hard* shake hits.

As the blackbird escorts me toward the port pass-thru, both of us pulling ourselves along using Liquid Brick rails, the deck suddenly trembles so violently that we'd have both been slammed to the ground if not for the zero-G.

"What was that?" I gasp, clutching the railing more tightly.

"How should I know?" my escort exclaims. He looks almost as green as I feel.

"Where's Miranda… Ms. Coffin?"

"Someplace safe, I'm sure. Keep going."

But instead of following him, I let go of the rail just long enough to tap my wrist. "Miranda? It's Andy."

Always before, when I've done this, she's answered immediately. It's something I've come to count on over the past few days. But this time, there's no reply.

"She's in trouble," I say.

"Not my problem," the blackbird insists. "My orders are to get you to your cell."

He called it a "cell."

But this barely registers as a blip on my screen as I try Miranda again. And, again, my e-man refuses to even confirm the connection.

Around us, the shuddering continues.

"We have to go, Brand!" my escort barks. "I'm sure Ms. Coffin's fine. Maybe her e-man is just switched off."

"She wouldn't do that!" I snap back. "She runs the ship, and the ship's in trouble!"

"Then she's too busy to answer you. Get over it."

"I need to make sure she's all right!"

"You can make another attempt from your quarters."

"I'm going to go find her."

The blackbird draws his gun. "I've got my orders." He's trying to sound tough, but I can tell he's as scared as I am.

"You know what could happen if you shoot me, right?"

"You *have* to come with me!"

Conquest shakes again, even more violently this time.

I hold the soldier's eyes. Neither of us speaks. It's a tense moment.

But then my wrist says something.

"Andy? Where are you?"

I raise the e-man, my heart leaping into hyperdrive. "On Deck 11. Where are *you*?"

"Engineering. Listen, I need you to go to the Comms Room and stay there!"

"The Comms Room?"

"It's in the middle of the ship. You'll be safest there."

Nearby, my escort lowers his gun, his face going pale.

"What's happened?" I ask her.

"We've hit a dust cloud. Usually, the sensors pick them up in time to avoid them, but this one slipped through."

Another shudder hammers the ship, the worst one yet. It makes my teeth clatter.

"Please, Andy! Go!"

"Spencer wants me on Deck 1."

"No!" she says sharply. *"Comms Room. Tell him that's an order!"*

"Okay. I'll go to the Comms Room. Be careful."

"I will." I hear relief in her voice. *"There's been a little damage to the outer hull, but it's not too bad. I'm working with Chief Tuttle now, and he thinks—"*

In the background, I hear a tinny, metallic-sounding crash. Miranda gasps.

Then nothing. The link's been broken.

Furk!

"What happened?" the blackbird demands.

"Don't know," I tell him, staring stupidly at my wrist.

And before you say anything, *yes*, if I get killed, my dragon could come out just like in my Nagasaki memory dream. Unless it happens instantly, like with Okeke, in which case *Conquest* would be fine. Or if I just get wounded—a broken arm or leg, for example—in which case I can contain it.

But if I bleed out with enough time to allow my dragon to realize what's happening, well—

The smart thing would be to do what Miranda says.

Except something bad just happened in Engineering—and Miranda's down there.

I say to the blackbird, "What's your name?"

"My… name?"

"Yeah, your name."

"Exler. Corporal Ray Exler."

"Well, Corporal Exler. We both know you're not going to shoot me, which means you've got a choice. You can come with me to Engineering, or you can stay here. I don't care which."

"I've got my orders," he says again, but this time there's zilch behind it, not even false bravado.

"I get that. I just don't care."

The ship shakes again, rattling dangerously as if we're bouncing through space in a coffee can filled with pebbles. As it does, Exler and I stare each other down.

I'm still scared, but not as scared as I was. Weird.

Finally, he holsters his gun. "I'll go with you."

With *Conquest* shuddering and creaking around us, we head for the pass-thru. From here, it's a wide-open path four decks down to Engineering—simple enough, though the way the ship's getting jostled makes it look like a chute in a 3D pinball game.

"You sure about this?" Exler asks me as if *I* would know.

"Absolutely," I reply as if it's true.

I take the lead, launching myself downward headfirst and using the grips along the wall to clear the lower deck, and then the one below that, and the one below that.

It's slow going, but we get there.

Deck 15 shakes worse than the upper floors, and portions of the wall have buckled as if this entire part of the ship's been gripped in a giant's fist and squeezed. Ahead is the same corridor that Greenjeans showed me two days ago, the one leading to the Workshop.

Exler and I head that way.

The workroom's a wreck. The hull damage is bad here, and most of the bins are either torn open or so bent that their contents escaped. Machine parts of all shapes and sizes now float in mid-air, weightless but still dangerous thanks to their mass.

From the far side of the long room, I can make out voices, loud and urgent.

I'm not sure, but one of them sounds like Miranda.

"Which way?" the blackbird asks. "I've never been down here before."

"I have," I tell him. Then I push off the threshold and start slowly, carefully, navigating the room. At one point, a big metal *something* bounces off a lateral wall and hurtles toward me. I fight the instinct to block it with my arm, having read enough to know that, in zero-G, the flotsam will either break my arm or send me careening off into something else.

So instead, I yell, "Watch it!" Then I duck.

The *something* passes harmlessly over my head.

I blow out a sigh.

But then the *something* ricochets off the archway and slams into Corporal Exler's left shoulder blade from behind.

He cries out, his arms flailing. The *something*—a hunk of machinery that I can't identify—has skewered him with one jagged point. Blood envelopes us both in a curtain of undulating red orbs.

Panicking, Exler slams into me. This sends us both hurtling out of control, carried along by the *something's* momentum, which has now been transferred to *us* in the zero-G. The physics of the whole fiasco flash uselessly through my mind as I scramble for a handhold that might break our inertia.

My fingers brush an open cabinet door. It's a sturdy steel panel with an embedded handle that I grab onto for all I'm worth.

I jerk to a stop in mid-air, wrenching my shoulder. Stabbing pain jolts me from my wrist to my neck. Gritting my teeth, I hold on as Exler, his eyes glazed with shock, nearly tumbles past.

At the last second, I manage to grab his ankle with my free hand.

Another jerk hits me harder than the first. Now *both* my arms are alive with pain.

Exler screams again as the *something*—it kind of looks like a car manifold, but what do I know?—tears itself out of his shoulder and continues toward the Workshop exit. The blackbird flails reflexively, kicking me in the face. I gasp, tasting blood, but continue to hold on, my upper body stretched taut as a guitar string between the cabinet and the injured man.

With the *something* finally gone, our momentum bleeds away.

Slowly, tentatively, I let go of both Exler and the cabinet.

We float, stationary, our inertia spent.

I take a breath.

"You okay?" I ask him.

Globs of blood are still dancing around us. But something tells me that, if the manifold cut one of the guy's major arteries, there'd be a lot more of it. Exler's eyes look half-wild, but he manages a pained nod.

"I've got to keep going," I tell him. "You stay here. Put… I don't know… pressure on the wound or something. I'll get help."

He nods again. Apparently, the whole "orders" thing is ancient history now that his arm has nearly been ripped off.

I don't blame him.

I push away from the cabinet and float gingerly to the antechamber at the rear of the Workshop. The *something* is already there, having slammed into the wall hard enough to get lodged in the Liquid Bricks.

A chill kisses my spine.

If we'd still been between it and that wall, we'd have been crushed to paste.

I push away that disturbing mental image before turning and entering the Engine Room.

The first thing I see is the six fission reactors and the spacers managing them. Everyone is sporting a short flexible tether, which they use to anchor themselves to a workstation. Then, once they've done their task, they unhook the tether, launch themselves to the next location, and re-tether again. Very efficient. Very professional.

Nevertheless, their urgency—make that barely managed desperation—crackles through the air like electricity.

I spot Eric among the crewmen, his face awash in nervous sweat as he navigates the big room with practiced ease. I'm vaguely jealous of how well he moves without gravity.

Then I spy Miranda.

She's high above me, gripping a maintenance rail that circles the top of Reactor Two, her ponytail dancing around her head in the weightless air. Her face is slick with sweat, but she's in control, barking orders to the spacers. "Keep shouting out hull integrity! If it drops below twenty, we evacuate! Chief Tuttle, any word from the bridge? Are we through the cloud yet?"

Replies get called back to her. Hull Integrity is at forty percent. No word from the Bridge.

Meanwhile, I wave at Miranda, trying to get her attention.

And just like that—I mean *click*—it dawns on me how pathetic I'm being.

This is *Miranda's* ship. True, she's not its captain, but it's still *hers*, and not just because her father owns it and she's his "adjunct." No, it's hers because of who she is. Young and brilliant, sometimes a little cold, but a capable and natural leader. A commander down to her toes.

And here I am, playing the half-baked knight-in-shining-armor. Except the sad truth is that I'm an idiot schoolboy who disobeyed her request—her order—to go somewhere safe, and not just so *I'd* be safe, but rather so I wouldn't endanger the ship and its crew.

Her ship.

Her crew.

For several painful seconds, I find myself hoping she won't notice me floating down here in the Workshop archway. Maybe I can just slink away and go where she sent me, injured Exler, or no injured Exler.

But then our eyes lock.

"Andy!" she exclaims in alarm. "What are you—"

That's as far as she gets before the entire ship *buckles*, the impact slamming me painfully against the threshold. Somewhere behind me, Exler cries out.

I watch with dumbstruck fascination as a ripple runs along the floor, walls, and ceiling—rolling forward, like a wave on the ocean. Instinctively, I grip the edge of the threshold, bracing myself as, around me, metal groans and tears. The sound's so loud that it almost drowns out the screams of the crewmen being whipped at the ends of their tethers. A few, those unlucky enough to have been untethered when the shock hit, are bouncing around like ping pong balls.

Somehow Miranda manages to maintain her grip around the railing atop Reactor Two.

I still have no real idea what's happened. More dust maybe, or have we somehow hit something bigger? Whatever the cause, the result is a sudden and drastic reduction of *Conquest's* inertia, dropping its speed way more quickly than I'm willing to bet the owner's manual allows for.

Someone yells, "We're losing One and Two!"

The bolts securing Reactor Two to the floor snap like rifle shots, and the entire construct, all ten by twenty feet of it, rises off the floor, tilting sharply. The only thing holding it in place now is the huge pipes feeding into it from above—and these start groaning, as if in physical pain.

Miranda gasps in alarm but, with no other recourse, keeps her grip on the now nearly vertical railing.

Somewhere I hear Eric exclaim, "Reactor One's going critical! Jettison protocol's been triggered!"

"Out!" Tuttle cries. "Everybody out!"

That's when Reactor One, the reactor closest to me, detaches from its pipes and moorings and rides the floor track toward the big viewport, moving faster than I would have thought possible given its size. The moment it hits the polymer, the entire viewport pops and hisses before detaching from the surrounding bulkhead.

And, just like that, the Engine Room is exposed to open space.

Somebody screams; I'm pretty sure it isn't me.

Pretty sure.

Both the viewport and the reactor disappear into the void—taking the atmosphere in the room with it.

Instinctively, I grip a nearby guide bar and good thing too, because, in the *next* instant, my body is sucked toward the open window with enough force to pull the boots off my feet.

Gritting my teeth and squeezing my eyes shut, I hear Tuttle yell, "We're venting atmosphere!"

No kidding.

"Adjunct!" someone else calls.

I crane my neck toward Reactor Two.

Miranda is still clutching the reactor's top railing, except now her body has gone as horizontal as my own, fighting the hurricane screaming past us.

"Why aren't the bulkhead doors sealing?" Tuttle demands.

"System failure!" someone calls back.

"Then hit the manual override!"

"No!" someone else exclaims.

"Do it, or we'll lose the whole ship!"

"You'll kill us!"

"We're already dead, son!"

I listen to this exchange, struggling to hold onto the guide bar.

Are we dead?

"Give me a sec!" I yell, wondering if anybody will hear me over this decompressive rush. In my mind's eye, I can picture the air, the precious life-affirming air, getting sucked out of the ship, level by level, via the pass-thrus, as if a gargantuan monster has jammed a gargantuan straw into *Conquest* and is sucking it like a milkshake.

"Damn it!" Tuttle exclaims. "What's that freak doing here?"

Freak this…

I call my dragon.

In the first instant, my CSE uniform vaporizes, and what little hair I've managed to grow back since last time sizzles away. In the second instant, the guide bar softens, and, for a horrible second, I'm sure it's going to liquefy and send me shooting across the Engine Room and out into the Big Fat Nothing.

But before that happens — maybe *just* before it happens — I release one hand and point it backward, directing heat, *my* heat, toward the open viewport.

What *is* heat?

Sorry. I don't want to turn this into an Okeke-esque lecture right in the middle of the action. So, let me just explain it the way my dad explained it to me, one day deep in the New Jersey Pine Barrens. It was just the two of us, and we'd found ourselves a remote spot in Wharton State Forest, miles from anyone. We *needed* such a secluded place because these camping trips were about more than S'mores and fishing.

They were about learning.

"Heat," my father said, "is the transfer of kinetic energy from Point A to Point B."

It was deep winter with four inches of snow blanketing the ground. However, even though we'd made no fire, we weren't cold.

The Kind are *rarely* cold.

"Son, your 'dragon' isn't fire at all. Fire is just combustion… a chemical reaction involving oxygen and fuel. What we produce is 'thermal radiation,' and some of us are capable of making quite a lot of it and for an extended period of time.

"But what I want to show you now is a little different."

With that, he raised his hand and did what I'm trying to do now. Except my father pulled it off without cooking himself bald and naked. Clearly, I'm not there yet.

Still precariously gripping the melting archway threshold, I throw as much thermal energy as I can backward, aiming it, directing it, so that the charged air shimmers between me and the open window. I don't hit the breach itself. That would accomplish nothing beyond warming a minuscule corner of local space.

Instead, I aim for the floor right below the viewport, putting as much of my dragon as possible into the thermal stream my body is generating, keeping it tight and laser-focused and counting on tantalum's high melting point.

Within seconds, an entire section of floor goes from red-hot to white-hot.

"That's step one, son," my father told me back in the woods. "Thermal energy focused on the spot you want to affect until it begins to melt. Then, and this is the tricky part…"

Gritting my teeth, I lower my dragon's frequency. This isn't easy, but I manage it, using nothing but my internal thermostat to know just where "it" is.

Microwaves.

These hit the white-hot blistering tantalum an instant later, sending its already excited atoms into a full-blown particle orgy.

An instant after that, the firewall goes up.

A physicist or aerospace engineer would probably call it a plasma shield. A Sci-Fi nerd might gleefully dub it a force field. Both would be kind of right and kind of wrong. Overall, I don't suppose it matters.

It works; *that's* what matters.

The wall of low-frequency energy rises, as heat does, from floor to ceiling, completely sealing off the broken viewport from the rest of the engine room. The air rushing past me and venting out into open space suddenly stops with a sigh that almost sounds disappointed.

To my left and overhead, Reactor Two ceases straining and floats benignly in the zero-G, still fastened to the ceiling, if just barely, by the twisted wreckage of its piping system.

Miranda, her face the color of chalk, finally releases her hold on the reactor's railing as two of Tuttle's guys zip up to help her.

Chief Widow's Peak himself, however, is staring at me.

I meet his eyes, my teeth still gritted.

"How…?" he stammers. Floating beside him, I see that Greenjeans is grinning ear to ear.

"You got some way to plug that hole?" I gasp breathlessly.

"W… what?"

Keeping my dragon's fire under control, if just barely, I say, "This isn't… as easy… as it looks."

The chief blinks. Then he nods. "You heard the man!" he barks at Greenjeans and the others. "Let's get that breach sealed!"

FOURTEEN – Glimpse

"Miranda."

"Yes, Father."

"Who's with you?"

"Spencer and Captain Wei."

"Good morning, gentlemen."

"Good morning, sir."

"Good morning, Mister Coffin."

"Captain Wei, what's Conquest's *status?"*

"We're currently in an elliptical orbit around Jupiter that brings us close to Europa every ten hours fifty-three minutes. Thus far, no landings on the moon have been attempted, pending repairs."

"Casualties?"

"Only one fatality."

"Doctor Okeke."

"Yes, sir."

"A tragedy. How many injured?"

"Eleven, Mister Coffin. Nine crew and two security. A couple of concussions, plenty of bruises and lacerations, and one broken collar bone."

"Captain Wei, why wasn't the dust cloud detected in time to course-correct around it?"

"Because it wasn't a dust cloud, Mister Coffin. It was a debris field… the remains of the orbital laser. Gravitational forces apparently pulled it away from Europa since its location and trajectory were mapped by the supply ship. The larger, heavier pieces fell into Jupiter, while the lighter ones formed the cloud that we encountered. We didn't see them because we frankly weren't looking for them, and the sensors weren't calibrated for their lower density."

"I see. But if these pieces were so light, how did they do so much damage?"

"When combined velocities are high enough, it doesn't take much mass to turn even the smallest bit of refuse into a threat. As it was, our velocity met with that of the debris, causing the hull ruptures and impact tremors we experienced."

"But it could have been worse, Father."

"The adjunct is quite correct, Mister Coffin. The damage we experienced could have crippled or even destroyed the ship."

"And would have, Father, if Andy hadn't stepped in."

"Is that so? Spencer."

"Yes, sir?"

"You're awfully quiet. Do you agree with my adjunct's assessment?"

"The Dragon ignored orders to evacuate. Instead, he risked the lives of everyone by disobeying his assigned escort and charging down to Engineering in some romantic attempt to aid your daughter."

"If he hadn't, Father, we'd all be dead. He saved the ship."

"Did he, Wei?"

"Possibly, Mister Coffin. His actions certainly saved the lives of everyone in the Engine Room, including the adjunct. I've debriefed each of the crewmen present, and there's a clear consensus. At the time of Brand's intervention, one reactor had been ejected, another was cycling toward overload, and the ship was venting atmosphere at an alarming rate. Best case, we would have had to seal off the entire deck, thereby dooming every soul on it. Worst case, attempts to get the emergency protocols back online would have failed, and most of the ship would have vented into space."

"Sir!"

"Yes, Spencer?"

"The Dragon *still* disobeyed orders, sir! If he'd been injured while on his way to Deck 15, which could easily have happened, then all his so-called heroics wouldn't have meant a thing!"

"Father, only a mortal wound would have done that. Mister Spencer is overstating the risk."

"The hell I am!"

"Enough, both of you. Miranda, have you spoken with our guest?"

"Yes, Father."

"What does he have to say for himself?"

"Exactly what you'd imagine. Andy disobeyed orders because he was worried about my safety. It was an admittedly dangerous gamble."

"But one that paid off."

"Yes, Father."

"It demonstrates more courage than his race is generally credited with."

"Andy's rather unique, even among the Kind. That's why we chose him."

"Nevertheless, it's a lesson about the Dragon that we need to remember. But, for now, let's move on. Captain Wei, what's the repair estimate?"

"We've effectively lost two of our six fission reactors. The others are nominally functional, but I won't risk our return trip to Earth until they're back up to acceptable levels. That, by itself, will take a week. Then there's the hull damage. The worst of it is in the Engine Room. Fortunately, with Brand's... help... we were able to apply a gel sealant across the breach. A dozen other, smaller breaches, including the one that killed Doctor Okeke, have been located and sealed as well. However, such repairs are only stop-gaps. Replacing these seals with permanent hull plating will require another week's effort."

"So, two weeks in Jovian orbit?"

"At an estimate, Mister Coffin."

"Time enough to do what you're there to do. Wouldn't you say so, Miranda?"

"I would, Father. We've initiated landfall protocols."

"Good. I want this part of the mission to go smoothly. No 'debris clouds,' if you take my meaning."

"I do, Father."

"Spencer?"

"Yes, sir?"

"Make sure a healthy contingent of your men accompany the adjunct and our guest to the Europan surface. Have them armed and ready to use force if they encounter any resistance… but only if absolutely necessary."

"I understand, sir."

"Good. Now, Mister Spencer and Captain Wei, I need some time alone with my adjunct. You have your respective tasks."

"Yes, sir."

"Very good, Mister Coffin."

A pause.

"Are we alone, Miranda?"

"Yes, Father."

"I have to ask this, given the doctor's unexpected loss. Are you taking your medication?"

"Of course, I am."

"Our agreement was that you remain on that medication, at the recommended dosage, for the duration of the mission."

"I remember."

"Good. I've put my faith in you, Miranda. The last thing I need is backsliding."

"That won't happen. I promise. Can we drop it now?"

"Very well. Let's talk about the Dragon, then."

"Andy? What more is there to say?"

"Is he in love with you?"

Another pause.

"I believe so, Father."

"I suppose you've slept with him?"

A third pause.

"Miranda?"

"Oh, I have. I'm trying to think of how to summarize it. He's… enthusiastic, if a bit clumsy. That's to be expected, of course, since I'm his first. Basically, Andy wants to please me."

"I see. Well, you know my feelings about this fraternization. However, given the way the Dragon behaved during this crisis, I must admit that I now see the wisdom of it."

"Father?"

"Yes, Miranda?"

"Why is it so hard for you to use his name?"

"Listen to me, daughter. Do what you must to earn this creature's trust and cooperation. But don't humanize him. As far as I'm concerned, he's

ordinance, like a pistol or explosive. Necessary, even vital. But nothing more than that."

"But—"

"It's important that you understand this fact, especially given the tragedy with his parents."

A fourth pause.

"Of course, Father."

PART THREE
THE ASTRONAUT

Today, we'll be landing on Europa.

According to Miranda, I won't be in the first lander and probably not in the second. Those will be used to ferry the supplies, equipment, and people necessary to secure the landing site and prepare the "coring unit." Only once this is completed will they bring me down and set me up to—do my thing.

Nevertheless, soon I'm going to be wearing a spacesuit and standing on the surface of one of Jupiter's moons. Despite my uncertainty regarding my folks, I'm geeking out about it.

Since the Engine Room yesterday, the attitude on the ship has changed, at least toward me. The spacers are all smiles now. The "Draco" handle has really caught on, and wherever I go, somebody in a blue uniform greets me using it. Even the blackbirds have warmed somewhat, except for Spencer. The soldiers don't glare as much. A few, like Exler, looking a little the worse for wear after his injury in the Workshop, have openly thanked me.

Last night, Captain Wei himself even shook my hand and welcomed me to his crew.

Suddenly, I'm a hero instead of a freak. It's an angle to Conceal and Protect that my parents never told me about.

And it doesn't suck.

Greenjeans has become my self-appointed publicist. He's told the story of the hull breach a dozen times, with each retelling painting me as a little braver, a little more selfless—and *way* more powerful.

I'm currently seated in the Mess with yet another tube of flavored protein and surrounded by rapt crewmen. Across from me, Eric's reciting the "adventure" yet again. Of course, my body is once more completely hairless. No eyelashes or eyebrows. Not even nose hair.

But I don't mind.

"So, Draco here raises his hand at the hull breach and shouts, 'By the power of Grayskull!' and shoots a heat beam from his fingertips that forms a wall of shimmering energy that plugs the leak up tight!"

I just smile.

Don't judge me. It's been a rough ride.

"Does it hurt?" another of the apprentices asks me. Her name, stenciled on her breast pocket, is *Hubert*. But more than once, I've heard people call her "Wrench"—her spacer handle, though I have no idea why.

I respond, "Does what hurt?"

"Doing… what you do," she presses, gazing at me with keen interest. "I mean, it burns off your clothes and all your hair, right?"

"Um…"

"Right," Greenjeans replies.

Wrench says, "So, does it *hurt*?"

"No," I tell her.

"Then what *does* it feel like?"

I realize that *all* of them are looking at me, the dozen spacers at my table, as well as at the neighboring tables. Even the blackbirds on hand, Exler among them, have gone silent and attentive.

The spotlight.

I flounder. How do I explain what it feels like to call my dragon? It's not something my parents ever prepared me for. Quite the opposite, in fact.

Seconds tick by.

Finally, I ask, "How many of you have ever seen snow?"

They exchange confused looks. Even Greenjeans seems taken aback. Then, gradually, some hands raise. Maybe half of them. The rest, I suppose, either grew up in a tropical climate on Earth—or off-world.

"Okay," I say, nodding. "So, those of you who *have* seen snow… try describing it to the ones who haven't."

"Cold, white, lumpy rain," one of the hand-raisers offers.

"What?" Wrench asks. Her hand *isn't* raised.

"Snow," the guy explains. "It's like rain. But instead of soaking the ground, it piles up in cold white… piles." Then, noting her expression, he says to me, "Yeah, I get your point."

"Except we all know what snow *is*," a third crewman points out. "I mean, I've seen pictures of it. But you're…" His words trail off.

I hold up my open palm and summon my dragon—just a little. It rises from my skin, heating up the air above my hand and making it ripple.

Around me, the crewmen gasp. The nearest of them, Eric included, draw back instinctively.

"It feels like… being myself," I tell them. "All our lives, my people hide this. We're taught that any display of power frightens the humans we have to live with and puts all of the Kind in danger. That's what we call ourselves, by the way, not Dragons." I say this pointedly, but without sounding angry. Because I'm honestly not angry. For some reason, I don't mind the dog-and-pony show. Maybe it's because these people are simply curious.

And curiosity beats fear any day.

After thirty seconds, I pull back my dragon and let the heat dissipate.

For about thirty seconds after *that*, nobody says a word.

Finally, Wrench remarks, "I like your new uniform, Draco."

Eric replies before I can. "I know, right? Our man here burned off his blackbird uniform and demanded spacer clothes!"

A few of them actually applaud at that, weirdly even a few of the blackbirds.

"Well, fellow travelers," Greenjeans declares. "Our hero needs to eat. What's say we all give him some room?"

The crewmen disperse, most of them smiling. A few, like Wrench, seem reluctant to go.

"Wrench likes you," Eric says once we're alone.

I have no idea how to respond to that.

He adds, "Of course, she *knows* you and the Ice Queen are… interfacing. That's probably part of the appeal. Don't get me wrong, Draco. She's definitely hot for you… no pun intended. But the boss lady isn't exactly popular. So, tempting you away from her would boost her rep, even if it did end up getting her fired. She's a lifelong spacer. It's how we roll."

"I don't think I'm tempted."

"Your call."

"Grayskull? Seriously?" I say, eyeing him.

Greenjeans shrugs. "It's something my pop used to say whenever he managed to fix something. I think he got it from his old man. Don't ask me what it means, but it sounds good, don't it?"

"I guess."

"Now… um… can I ask you a question?"

His tone surprises me. It's less cocky than usual, more circumspect.

"Sure," I say.

"Had you ever done… what you did… before yesterday?"

"Just in practice, out in the woods during camping trips."

"You set up walls of fire in the woods on Earth?"

"Yeah."

"Couldn't you start a forest fire or something?"

"We were careful."

"But why learn how to do something when your whole culture centers around never doing it?"

"Because the key to controlling something is understanding it, right? My folks taught me how to use my dragon so that I'd know how *not* to use it. Does that make sense?"

"I guess so," he replies. Then, brightening, he changes the subject. "Okay, then… ready? It's moonfall today!"

"Not for me," I reply. "Miranda says I'm stuck up here until they have the coring unit ready."

"Oh. Right. Well, for what it's worth, Europa's no great shakes."

"You've been here before?" I ask, surprised.

He makes a dismissive gesture. "A half-dozen times. I've even visited MC-13."

"You have?"

"I was there when CSE drilled the hole in the ice and dropped the modules down. Some of us went down with the colonists to help fit the pieces together."

"Yeah?"

"Yep. Watched the Shelton Laser fire from orbit. For that one, a bunch of us suited up and went spacewalking for a better view. It was… *stellar!* I mean, I've seen space lasers discharge a pulse or two over the years. But nothing like this. The furking thing had to run for half a standard day before the shaft was made." He eyes me suddenly. "Do you figure you'll be quicker or slower than the laser was?"

He's asking me if, being Kind, I can burn through that much ice as fast as a state-of-the-art industrial laser.

He really is.

And the crazy thing is, I honestly don't *know*.

"I guess we'll see," I reply.

After lunch, I head up to the Comms Room, hoping to talk to Charles Coffin about my parents. I've given up leaving them voicemails. My only hope now is that the billionaire's bottomless resources will somehow track them down. Given that I saved his daughter's life yesterday, he promised me daily updates on the search.

I just wish I trusted him to follow through.

Such thoughts churn through my head as I navigate the now-familiar corridor between the pass-thru and the Comms Room. Ahead, the doorway stands open and, as I guide myself inside, I expect to find Miranda waiting for me, as usual.

But she's not there.

Spencer is.

For a moment, the two of us eye each other in silence. I haven't spoken to him since before the Engine Room incident and frankly haven't missed his sparkling personality. Right now, for example, he's looking at me as if I'm something he spotted in a public toilet.

"Hi," I say lamely.

He doesn't reply.

"Um… I was expecting Miranda to be here."

"She's not," he says. "I am."

"Yeah, I kind of picked up on that."

He lets go of the guide bar he's holding and floats smoothly over to me, clutching the door frame to steady himself. This guy's at least twice my age, and authority radiates off him. "You may have the rest of the ship fooled," he growls. "But not me."

Okay, I admit it. He intimidates me, just a little.

I try for snark but manage only a hasty, "Huh?"

"You're not a man. You're not even a boy. You're a *thing*."

It's an old song and hearing it shores up my defenses. "Whatever." I turn, ready to pull myself out of the Comms Room.

An iron fist clamps down around my upper arm. "You'll go when I *say* you can go."

I look back at him. "Get your hand off me."

Spencer sneers. "Or what, Dragon? You'll burn me? Go ahead. Let's see how Mister Coffin reacts when you cook one of his senior staff. Not even your precious Miranda will be able to protect you then."

I don't reply, wondering if he's right. Besides, something tells me Spencer *wants* me to react that way. He *wants* to prove that I can't handle confrontation without falling back on fight or flight.

Animals rely on instinct and natural defenses.

Thinking beings… well, *think.*

So, I pick my words. "I'll leave whenever I want. But if you have something to say to me that doesn't involve lobbing insults, I guess I'll listen."

My answer, delivered as calmly as I can manage, seems to disconcert him. His sneer becomes a scowl. At last, he releases me and says, "You're going down to the moon's surface tomorrow."

"I know."

"Yeah, well, what you don't know is that, while you're down there, the adjunct isn't in charge. I am. That means you'll do everything I tell you to do… without complaint or hesitation. You got that?"

I almost tell him to go furk himself—except, again, I get the feeling he wants me to defy him. I suddenly wonder if we're alone. Oh, the Comms Room is empty except for the two of us. The corridor outside, too. But that doesn't mean we're alone.

There are Liquid Bricks all around us, after all.

"I got it," I say.

"And if you do anything to jeopardize our mission, if you step just a little bit out of line, I'll end you."

"Okay."

"I mean it, Dragon. I'll put a bullet in your brain and take what comes before I let you screw up our objectives. Are you completely clear on that?"

"I'm completely clear on it." Then I smile, putting all my "wholesome boy-next-store" mojo into it.

My acquiescence seems to disappoint him. "Good," he grumbles. "Now get out of here."

"I've got a call scheduled with Mister Coffin to discuss my parents."

"Mister Coffin's got better things to do than chase after your freak family."

I raise my e-man. "Let's see if Miranda feels the same way."

"Fine! Make your call. Just remember what I told you."

Then he pushes past me, gliding smoothly down the corridor and around the corner.

I float my way over to the green-lit circle and activate the pedestal. At once, the AI requests a phone number.

I recite it from memory. Charles Coffin's personal line.

Yeah, I'm a big shot now.

It rings. It rings. It rings.

Then it disconnects.

I try again. Same result. I try a third time. Nothing. Not even vidmail.

Without knowing why, I'm suddenly certain that Coffin's talk of finding my folks was all crap—fodder to keep the pet Dragon happy.

Just one more lie.

TWO – Day 18

For what seems like the hundredth time, Miranda tells me not to worry.

She first said this to me yesterday, when we met in the Observatory for dinner. She repeated it later when we were in her quarters. Then she told me again over breakfast this morning.

And now she's telling me as we strap ourselves into our seats aboard one of *Conquest's* landers.

But I'm not buying it.

"Something's happened to them," I say. I've been thinking that dark thought for days, but this is the first time I've said it aloud.

"I'm sure they're fine," she replies.

"Would you just stop saying that!" I tell her and, yes, it comes off harsher than it probably had to. I see this in her face when she looks at me, a flash of anger that turns into hurt. I immediately feel bad. She's just trying to reassure me, after all. And my parent's ghost-act isn't *her* fault. Right?

Right?

"Sorry," I mutter.

Around us, the lander's alive with activity. Twenty-four blackbirds, Spencer and Corporal Exler included, are noisily strapping in, while two spacers, one a pilot and the other an engineer, run pre-flight checks in the cockpit.

The lander is forty feet long and half that wide, all sharp angles and smooth gray titanium. No Liquid Bricks here. Aside from small thrusters for making minor trajectory adjustments, it has no horizontal engines—just a vertical one for a controlled descent and a quicker ascent.

"It's okay," she mutters back.

I blow out a sigh. "Things aren't right. I don't know how I know that, but I do. I keep telling myself that something happened that forced them to relocate. New town. New last name. New lives. If so, then when I get home, I can find them. They'll have left word for me on the Kind's "personals" site on the dark web. But, in my gut, I know they didn't. Somehow, I *know* something's wrong."

"I didn't know about the dark web," she says. "I don't think my father does either."

It's true. I mentioned it to Greenjeans and Okeke a couple of days back, but I've never told Miranda. I probably would have eventually. But that was one secret about the Kind that I guess I wanted to keep out of CSE's hands.

So, why did I do it just now?

Because I'm scared.

Miranda says out of the blue, "It's my fault."

I stare at her. "What?"

"Well, not mine, exactly. Ours. Coffin Industries'. After we took you, I wanted to visit them myself, tell them everything that's happening on Europa, make them understand. I even suggested bringing them along with us, keep you all together. But both my father and Okeke were against it." She meets my eyes. "I... should have fought harder for it. I'm sorry, Andy."

I look into her face, at the teardrop birthmark — I don't know why, but it draws my gaze — and feel better. Not a lot better as my stomach's still in knots. But a little.

"It's okay," I tell her. "This isn't your fault." Though, of course, in at least a small part, it is.

"How about this?" she suggests. "Getting on the public internet is tough this far out. But, if you want, you can give me the IP address for this personals site, and my father's people can try to locate your parents."

I don't know how I feel about that idea. On the one hand, it might work, and at least I could sleep at night knowing my folks are okay. On the other, it would break yet another of the rules of Conceal and Protect and give me one more reason for shame.

"Maybe," I say with a shrug.

"Think it over, and let's talk about it again once you're finished on the surface."

Finished on the surface.

She means after I melt a hole through twenty miles of rock-hard, primordial ice. Over the last two days, I've spent hours with Miranda and some of Wei's science guys, going over the methodology. Like everything else about this mission, it's innovative to the point of bleeding edge. But I guess it'll work, not that I have a ton of experience to draw from. I mean, who does? But, from what I can tell, they've devised a solid way for me to get Spencer's troops down into the depths of Europa to rescue a hundred miners from God-knows-how-many terrorists.

Or at least two, I suppose. Orpheus and Eurydice.

"None of this makes sense," I mutter to myself.

"What doesn't?" Miranda asks.

"The terrorists," I say.

"What about them?"

I look at her. "Where'd they come from?"

"We don't know."

"Wei's people scanned the surface when we arrived, right?"

"Of course."

"Did they find any terrorist ship?"

"No, but I told you. Their ship probably dropped them off and then left again, much like we're doing now."

"What ship? From where?"

"It could be hidden behind Jupiter, undetectable. Europan orbits are complicated. It's easy to hide."

I guess that makes *some* sense. "And how did they get down to MC-13?"

"The freight lift, obviously," she says. She doesn't seem remotely concerned about my questions. We could be discussing the plot of a vid-show.

"The one you told me needs to be activated from the colony. It can't be called from the surface, right?"

"Right."

"So… the terrorists land on Europa and… what? Knock on the door and say, 'Let us in. You don't know us, and we're not supposed to be here, but open up?'"

"I don't know."

"You'd think the miners would have shut down the lift and told them 'not by the hair of our chinny-chin-chins,' wouldn't you?"

"We don't have all the facts, Andy. We're going on supposition and frankly open guesswork based on what few clues are available."

I hesitate. "I think this *has* to be an inside job."

She regards me passively, her expression unreadable. "What makes you say so?"

"The Law of Parsimony."

"The Law of Parsimony?"

"Sure. You *have* to know it. It's a problem-solving technique that's sometimes called Occam's Razor. It says that the simplest solution is usually the correct one. Well, if you apply it here, then it goes like this… Question: Where did Orpheus and Eurydice come from? Answer: Nowhere, they were already on MC-13."

"That hypothesis was considered, of course," Miranda replies. "But all colony personnel were fully vetted. I've reviewed the psych evals, myself. There were no markers to even suggest a tendency toward extreme anti-social behavior."

"Markers?"

"Psychological red flags. These aren't the nonsense evaluations that the DOD or NSA do. Coffin Industries uses cutting-edge techniques. We don't need to formally interview or even meet the subject. In fact, we prefer not to. Instead, we monitor from afar, watching the subject in their 'natural habitat.' It takes longer, days or even weeks instead of hours. But eventually, we end up with a more accurate predictive model."

"Is that what you did with me?" I ask, a little bitterly. "Watch me in my 'natural habitat?'"

Her slightly smug smile withers. "I'm sorry, Andy."

Which, of course, is a yes.

"But it's not the whole story," she adds hastily. "Psych evals on the Kind are more complicated. Your cultural and sociological contexts are very different. That's why…" Her words trail off.

"Why my psych eval wasn't enough," I finish. "So, you had to do all that stuff to me in my cell."

"Yes."

With everyone settled in, the lander's door clatters closed with an unnerving finality. Suddenly, it feels very close in here, and not just because of the two dozen blackbirds who are crammed in with us. In moments, we're going to be leaving *Conquest*, with these thin walls the only thing between us and the cold vacuum of space.

As the craft comes to life, humming with power, the pilot addresses us. She's a blue-uniformed crewman, a capable-looking woman in her forties. I don't know her, not her name or her spacer handle, but I like her calm, professional demeanor. It's comforting, given the circumstances.

"You've all been briefed," she says through the ship's internal comms. "But since there's a difference between knowing and experiencing, a little more prep won't hurt anyone. In sixty seconds, we're going to drop out of the lander bay. This will deliver some g's. Not a lot, but enough to be a shock when you're used to zero gravity. We won't be flying so much as falling, straight down, to the surface of Europa, using only minor thruster adjustments to keep us plum. Then, when we're two miles from the surface, I'll fire the main engine to slow our descent. Sounds rough, I know, but it's the safest approach."

Around me, the blackbirds murmur, sounding almost as nervous as I feel. And I'm just enough of a science geek to understand why.

Landing and taking off from Jovian moons is tricky because you always have Jupiter's gravity to deal with. If our assent or descent is too gradual, Jupiter could conceivably yank us off course, or even irretrievably away from Europa altogether. So, crazy as it might sound, dropping straight down, hard and fast, is the surest way to keep us alive.

The pilot starts counting down from ten.

"Andy," Miranda whispers, her words meant only for me. She *is* in charge, after all. "I'm scared." Then, as I look at her, she takes my hand.

Rich or poor. Human or Kind. Fear is the great equalizer.

Looking into her eyes, I almost miss it when the pilot's countdown reaches zero.

The lander *drops*.

I hear a number of the blackbirds whoop, only to have Spencer shut them down, as my body gets slammed against my shoulder straps. For the next few minutes, the entire craft shudders as we hurtle earthward—or, more accurately, moonward—in what's basically a barely controlled freefall. Through it all, Miranda squeezes my hand like a vice. I don't mind. Right now, it feels like my stomach and my heart are racing to see which one can climb up my throat first. I'm suddenly grateful that the lander has no windows. It wouldn't do me a bit of good to see what's going on out there now. For the moment, at least, being an astronaut isn't as "cool" as it was an hour ago.

I'm on a spaceship about to land on a Jovian moon.

I try to recapture the wonder I've been feeling lately. But that's gone, at least for the moment, replaced by an awful sense of being completely, utterly, laughably out of my element. I mean, a fire creature on an ice moon. Does it get any more 'fish out of water' than that?

The main engine ignites, and I feel the ship's descent begin to slow. *What happens if we don't stop in time?*

Okay, that last thought's a little bit alarmist. But sitting here, feeling like a raw egg in a clothes dryer—well, you'd get a little alarmed, too.

It suddenly occurs to me, maybe for the first time, how easily I could die on this "mission."

And, so far, I haven't been able to so much as talk to my mom and dad, let alone say good-bye.

Then, as I chew on that miserable idea, we land.

There's no sense of impact. Instead, the engine just suddenly goes quiet, letting me hear the blackbirds' nervous chatter around me. A few of them celebrate a little with laughs or cheers, though Spencer shuts them down once again.

Miranda and I trade looks. There's sweat on her brow, and her usually perfect braids are a bit disheveled. But, for all that, she's still breathtakingly beautiful. And her hand is still in mine.

Smiling, she remarks, "Welcome to Europa, Andy Brand."

A few minutes later, with the lander's compliment having recovered from the drop, the pilot issues everyone a spacesuit.

Okay, now *that's* cool.

Each is color-coded. The security guys all get black, except Spencer, who wears green. This is apparently so his underlings can spot him at a distance. Miranda's suit is bright yellow, for the same reason.

Mine is red. Fire red. Coincidence?

I think not.

Maybe a little bitterly, I remark, "I thought spacesuits were always white."

"Not on Europa," Miranda explains as she dons her helmet. It's big and bulbous and makes her entire head visible behind thick, transparent polymer. "In orbit or on rocky moons, where everything's black, white reflects light. But on Europa, where everything's icy, color works best."

Logical, as always. That's my girl.

The suit's bulky, but not uncomfortable. I'm told the air supply is good for nine hours, that it's heated or cooled based on an internal thermostat, and that any urine and waste I produce is collected, filtered, and disposed of by being ejected out of the suit. Spacers call them 'astrofarts.' Cute.

"Stay close," Miranda warns. "Don't wander off. The coring unit that you'll be working inside is already in place. With luck, you won't be on the surface for more than the few minutes it takes to walk to it, and then again when we walk back. Nothing to it."

I manage a nod.

At last, Spencer starts sending everybody through the lander's airlock, two at a time. Not surprisingly, the blackbirds go first to "secure the site."

I glance at Miranda. She doesn't look scared, exactly—just apprehensive. I get it. Now that I'm in line to step out into a deadly, frozen vacuum, I'm pretty apprehensive, too. I do my best to smile reassuringly at her.

"It's going to be fine," I say, trying to sound braver than I feel.

She smiles back. *"Of course, it is."* Her voice sounds tinny through the comm unit in my helmet.

Our turn comes.

We go second to last, with two more blackbirds bringing up the rear. As the airlock door slides shut behind us, Miranda takes my hand as she did during the lander drop. This time, of course, we're both wearing spacesuit gloves as thick as catcher's mitts. But it still feels pretty good to have her so close.

She says, sounding almost embarrassed about it, *"I've... never set foot on another planet before."*

I almost remind her that Europa is a moon, not a planet. But right now, science-geek mansplaining doesn't seem like the way to go. So instead, I reply, "Me, neither."

"I know."

Of course, she knows.

Miranda says, *"We'll do this together."*

And we do.

It's the last thing we *ever* do together.

THREE – Day 18

Ice.

Lots of ice.

A whole lot of furking ice.

Europa, at least the little bit I can see, is surprisingly free of craters, especially considering all the meteors that Jupiter's gravity must pull in and throw at it. Most astronomers think that the vast ocean beneath the ice, warmed by the moon's molten core, gradually filters up just enough heat for Europa to soften and smooth its surface over time, erasing blemishes.

I'm currently looking at more ice than I can wrap my head around. I suppose there are places on Earth, Antarctica maybe, where the ice fields extend to the horizon. But Earth is much bigger and its horizon much further. On Europa, the horizon almost seems like a short stroll away, an effect made all the more—affecting—by the unbroken whiteness between here and there.

Well, not unbroken exactly.

And not all white, at least not pure white.

Some of the ice is so white that it almost glows. In other places it's darker, clouded by minerals washed up from the moon's deep mantle. And instead of being smooth, the landscape's rippled. Or maybe "rumpled" would be a better word. Seen from ground level, Europa reminds me of nothing so much as an unmade bed, the sheets still bearing wrinkles and rolls left by the person who slept on them.

It's also much brighter than I expected. And, looking up, it's easy to see why.

Jupiter fills half the sky.

It's huge and heavy and almost looks like a cresting wave that's about to crash down and crush us flat. It's so unnerving that I have to look away. Nevertheless, the huge planet glows with reflected sunlight, and that defused illumination floods the Europan sky. On top of that, the icy moon is, itself, the most reflective object in the Solar System, which means that a lot of the light comes from surface reflection. The result is a sky devoid of stars, not black but sort of a dull, unhappy gray, and lorded over by its boss-planet.

"Oh… *my*," Miranda mutters.

"Yeah," I reply, the word coming out as a dry croak.

The surface is another surprise. Instead of smooth, slippery ice, it has a rough, dimpled texture that's fairly easy to walk on. Also, a thin layer of finely ground dust covers everything—freeze-dried water, pulverized by Jupiter's gravity.

Speaking of gravity, there isn't much of it, slightly more than a tenth of a G. The blackbirds that went out before us have already kicked up enough ice dust to make a weirdly iridescent curtain that's slowly settling to the ground.

I've been told that my suit is designed to move "easily" across the Europan terrain, and I feel that tech kick in now. With every footfall, hundreds of tiny filaments in my boot soles *grab* the rough surface and hold on, like Super-Velcro. It requires a slight, deliberate effort to pull my foot up again, but it's smooth enough. As Miranda warned me, I'm mindful to keep at least one foot firmly planted at all times. Bouncing around the Europan surface like an errant ping-pong ball is *not* a good idea.

Once everyone's left the lander, Spencer lines us up. He moves along our ranks, eyeing each of us in turn, nodding approval or making some comment before moving on. When he gets to me, his face darkens. His voice, steeped in warning, fills my helmet. Since I couldn't hear what he said to the others, I assume this is a private comms channel. *"Don't forget what I told you, Dragon."*

"Drop dead," I reply with a smile.

I expect him to get pissed off. Instead, he just grins. It's a scary, knowing kind of grin, and I don't like it one bit.

"Here's the protocol," he says, addressing everyone. *"The coring unit's a hundred yards away, on the far side of the lander. Team Two stays here and secures the landing site. Teams Three, Four, and Five form a perimeter around the freight lift. If that thing so much as twitches, I want to know about it immediately.*

"The adjunct and I, as Team One, will escort Brand to the CU. Maintain open comms channels. No chatter, not so much as a sigh or cough. You all know what's at stake. Distractions won't be tolerated.

"One last thing. Europa receives continuous, highly radioactive bombard-ment from Jupiter's magnetosphere. While your suits have state-of-the-art shielding, each is also equipped with an automated rad sensor. Should your suit register a spike, it'll light up like a Christmas tree. If that happens, you drop what you're doing and head back to the lander immediately… unless

we're in combat. In combat, I expect each of you to stay on post. I don't care if you're cooking like a microwave dinner. Questions?"

There are none.

"Move out!"

We "move out" at a silly, lurching march around the lander, which sits like a big, gray lump on a relatively flat bit of ice.

Beyond it stand two man-made structures.

One is a broad, low platform of gray metal, big enough to swallow our lander whole. It's raised three feet above the surrounding ice and has a tight seam that bisects its perfectly horizontal surface. This *has* to be MC-13's freight lift, the only operable route from the surface down to the colony.

"Do you think they know we're here?" I ask Miranda on Team One's private channel. Spencer'll be pissed at the breach of protocol, but that's just a happy bonus.

"Doubtful. Careful sweeps were conducted from orbit. Any surface scanners or vid cams powerful enough to transmit through all that ice would show up in the RF band. None did."

"But you're not sure?"

"Not completely."

"And if you're wrong, won't the terrorists respond by killing hostages?"

"It's a risk," she admits. *"But so is inaction. Sometimes, Andy, like it or not, there's no 'safe' solution. All you can do is weigh your options, make the call, and hope for the best."*

"Is that what you and your father did? Weigh your options and make the call?"

"We both know how to make the hard decisions. There's the CU."

The term "coring unit" hints at a kind of drill, except the only "drill" involved in this business is me. What I'm looking at is a cone-shaped structure standing about fifty yards from the lift hatch. Even from this distance, I can tell it's made of Liquid Bricks—maybe thirty feet wide at its base, with sides that taper to a point fifteen feet above the surface.

"It's bigger than I thought it would be," I remark. "I mean, considering I'm the only one going into it."

"Its size determines the diameter of the shaft," Miranda replies. *"Both need to be big enough to accommodate a rescue team once the shaft is made and we bring you back up."*

Without warning, the bulk of the blackbirds peel away, forming a perimeter around the lift hatch. Their departure leaves Spencer, Miranda, and me to walk alone the rest of the way to the CU's curved, gently sloping outer wall.

Beside me, Spencer fiddles with his suit's e-man. A moment later, the Liquid Bricks slide dutifully apart, silent in the vacuum, leaving behind a perfect Andy-sized opening.

"Can my e-man do that, too?" I ask, already guessing the answer.

"No," he replies. I guessed right.

"What? Don't you trust me?"

Spencer scowls. He looks about to say something, and probably not a nice something, but Miranda cuts him off. "We'll handle the technical requirements, Andy. You focus on… your part of it."

I move past Spencer and peer through the newly created doorway. Inside is a narrow, slightly curved room, no more than six feet deep. The ceiling is peppered with lighted tiles.

"Go in," Spencer orders me.

Miranda adds in a gentler tone, *"Give yourself a moment to get settled. For obvious reasons, we can't go in with you. Once the airlock cycle completes, remove your spacesuit… well, remove everything… and stow them in the locker you'll find inside. These Liquid Bricks are specially made for this purpose and have a much higher melting point than their counterparts up on* Conquest. *We've run the numbers, and they'll handle the heat you put out."*

"Good to know," I mutter nervously.

"It's safe enough!" Spencer barks. *"Safer than you are out here in that little suit."*

Miranda adds, *"We estimate that you'll reach the bottom of the ice mantle in sixty-nine minutes. That's if you stick to the protocols and do everything the way you've been briefed. Once you reach the convection layer, I'll notify you to stop generating heat immediately, and you'll be brought back up through the shaft you've just created."*

All this, I know. Yet I appreciate her reminding me. It's — centering.

"Coming up will take longer, right?" I ask.

"Right," she says. *"About twice as long. But you won't have to do a thing at that point. We know you'll be pretty spent."*

"Yeah. Probably."

"You okay, Andy?"

I nod.

Except, suddenly, I'm not okay.

Suddenly, I do *not* want to do this.

Miranda steps up and takes my heavily gloved hand in hers. *"We've got this calculated down to the joule, Andy. It'll work, and you'll be perfectly safe. There's nothing to worry about. I know we've put you through hell, and no matter how many times I tell you I'm sorry, it'll never be enough."*

As she says this, I glance at Spencer, who doesn't look sorry at all.

She continues, "But *this*, right here, is what it's all been for. Just get us down there, and Spencer's men will do the rest. Then we can take you home. I know it's been an awful sacrifice."

I almost say *It hasn't been any kind of sacrifice. A sacrifice demands full consent of free will.*

This is slavery.

But her eyes—

"Okay," I tell her. Lame, I know, but it's the best I can manage.

I let go of her hands, turn away, and step into the airlock.

The tiles close behind me.

This small, curved room, like the rest of the CU, is all Liquid Bricks. The only features are a bench against one side wall with an obvious cabinet above it.

It takes about a minute for the chamber to fill with atmosphere.

Once it does, Miranda's voice speaks in my ear. *"Strip down. Put everything in the locker and make sure it's securely closed. You don't want any of it to get heat damaged, especially not your spacesuit."*

I take the spacesuit off.

This requires about ten minutes; spacesuits are complicated. Underneath, I'm wearing my blue uniform. As I start to remove that, I hesitate.

"Miranda?"

"Yes, Andy?"

"Are you guys... watching me? I'm kind of sick of being publicly naked."

"We're monitoring your vitals. But no, we're not watching you."

I wonder if I should believe her. After all, any of the hundreds of surrounding tiles could be vid-capable.

But even if they *are*, what can I do about it?

Feeling helpless and exposed, I remove my jumpsuit. Then I leave everything inside the locker, the door to which is fully four inches thick. Heat shielding to protect my space gear from my dragon, I suppose.

I hope it works.

When I'm done, I step back—butt-naked—and wait. Nothing happens. I wait some more. More nothing happens. Finally, I say aloud, "I'm ready!"

Moments later, a new doorway opens in the interior wall.

Okay, so maybe they *aren't* watching me after all. Either that or they're too smart to show their hand.

I sigh and step into the CU proper.

Miranda spent hours over the last two days briefing me about this.

Designed specifically for this mission, the coring unit isn't a ship, in that there's no engine or even much in the way of moving parts. It's just a single round room if you don't count the airlock, with smooth, heat-resistant walls that taper upward, finally ending at a round, two-foot opening, an "oculus," at the very top. This opening is sealed over with the same space-age gel they used to seal the hull breach in Engineering. Its job is to help bleed off excess heat—well, that and keep the atmosphere inside so I don't, you know, die.

In the room's center is a single chair of Liquid Bricks, flanked by two raised pylons, each with a fist-sized hole fitted into the top. Miranda dubbed this contraption simply the "conduit." Apparently, these pylons connect to twin rods of pure tungsten, a heat-conductive metal with one of the highest melting points known to science. These, in turn, are fastened to a thick plate of the same rare metal that covers the bottom of the CU's outer hull.

"I'm inside," I say aloud.

Miranda's voice fills the room. *"Good, Andy. Have a seat. We're running through a final check."*

"Sure," I say.

My stomach feels like a block of ice, which seems darkly ironic.

I pad across the room on bare feet—the Liquid Bricks feel neither hot nor cold—and settle onto the chair. It is utilitarian, but not uncomfortable. For several seconds, I just sit there, feeling as exposed as a live wire and as scrutinized as an ant under a microscope, despite Miranda's assurances that I'm not being visually monitored.

"Andy? You ready?"

No.

"Yes," I say.

"So, are we."

I take a slow, deliberate breath. Then, as I've been instructed, I slide both my hands into the pylons, reaching down until I feel matching tungsten grips. My fists close around them.

"Excellent. We're getting telemetry. Your heart rate's a little high. You all right?"

I nod. Then, feeling stupid, I say aloud, "I'm fine. Let's do this."

"Okay. Good luck!"

Luck? What's luck got to do with it? If such a thing even exists, I sure as furk don't have any. Look at where I am and what I'm doing.

What I'm being *forced* to do.

I remind myself that there are miners down there, innocent people who need rescuing.

It's a noble cause.

So, why does all this feel so *wrong*?

I take another slow, deliberate breath.

Then I call my dragon.

FOUR – Day 18

"Father?"

"I'm here, Miranda. I can't see you."

"The link's being routed down to the lander. Audio only. I'm sorry."

"It'll do. What's your status?"

"Andy and the CU have begun their descent. So far, progress is within expected parameters. At his current rate of twenty-five feet per second, we're expecting him to reach target depth in just over an hour."

"What about the Dragon's frame of mind?"

"Acceptable. He expressed some concerns on the lander, and he seemed a bit preoccupied and even somewhat paranoid once he entered the CU's airlock. At one point, he indicated concern that we're visually monitoring him. But, once I assured him that this is not the case, he willingly complied with the protocols."

"Are you visually monitoring him?"

"Of course, Father."

"Good. Watch him closely, Miranda. If his resolve falters, you'll see it before it manifests in his thermal output. Should that happen, I expect you to re-motivate him."

"I don't think it'll come to that."

"Nevertheless, I know you'll do what has to be done when… if… the time comes."

"Haven't I always?"

"Yes, you have. By now, our presence on Europa has certainly been detected. We're counting on their belief that they're untouchable beneath that barrier of ice. We don't want them realizing they're wrong, not until the trap closes. And the biggest threat to that particular piece of the puzzle is your pet fire lizard's frame of mind."

"Father… please don't."

"It's not my attitude toward him that needs adjusting. Stay on mission."

"I will. I am."

"I'm pleased to hear it. Let me know when the coring unit has reached target depth."

"Of course, Father."

"And Miranda?"

"Yes."

"I love you."

"Oh. Of course. Thank you."

FIVE – Day 18

It feels good.

No, better than good. It feels *great*!

My dragon pours out of me, starting in my chest where it bubbles and churns as if my ribcage is a cauldron, and then surging up through my shoulders and down my arms. Now, with both my hands gripping the pylons, I can almost sense the thermal energy spreading around the coring unit's outer hull, melting the ancient ice below me.

And letting gravity do the rest.

Miranda assured me the descent would be smooth, and she was mostly right. There was a sickening lurch at the very beginning, followed by a weird freefall sensation as the surface ice vaporized, and the CU slipped downward. Immediately after that, things evened out. Now the descent seems as steady as a lift ride, only a *lot* faster.

Around me, the CU's interior is already an oven. Any human passenger would now be ash, which is why I'm alone, descending an icy shaft of my own making, sending what must be a geyser-jet of steam up into Europa's airless nothing. Without much gravity to contain it, the water vapor, crystalized in the absolute zero, will likely escape into open space. Wistfully, I wonder if the jet can be seen by the telescopes on Earth.

I'm grinning like an idiot.

And my dragon keeps breathing its fire.

Directly in front of me, the Liquid Bricks forming the CU's curved interior wall display telemetry. I'm two miles down and going deeper by the second. For a while, I watch the depth meter's reading spin, mesmerized, until the temperature gets *too* high, and even these "heat resistant" tiles soften and stop working.

And still, I keep falling.

"Andy?" Miranda asks. Her voice crackles; the speaker tiles are starting to melt, too. Soon, I might lose contact with the surface. That should scare me, but it doesn't. I feel too good. *"You're approaching the one-quarter mark. Is everything all right?"*

"Yeah," I reply, the word mangled by the super-heated air.

"The CU's internal temperature's getting higher than expected. Can you try to focus more of your thermal energy into the pylons and less into the ambient atmosphere?"

Not knowing why, I feel my grin widen.

But, wordlessly, I do as she asks.

The CU shudders as its outer temp spikes and even more ice turns to steam in a fraction of a second. This steam is then channeled around the outside of the module and sent shooting up toward the surface.

The process is called "sublimation," if you care.

I don't.

"Good," Miranda says. *"Better."*

I still don't care.

It's more dragon than I've ever released before, more than I've ever dreamed of releasing. Imagine your whole life being able to take just small sips of water only to suddenly drink your fill. Trust me, it doesn't just slake your thirst; it makes you question how the furk you ever survived before now. For the first time, I understand, truly understand, that I'm *not* human.

And it's—amazing!

Then I hear my father's voice, a memory so vivid that it startles me. *"Of all the creatures who've ever walked the Earth, the Kind are unique. We, alone, must never surrender to our true nature. Because... without our constant vigilance, people, communities, whole cities, die in flames."*

Good words from a good man.

But how can something that feels so utterly right—be wrong?

I keep falling.

I lose myself in it, the outflow of energy like a drug. Everything recedes. The CU, *Conquest*, Europa, even my concern for my parents, seems far away, carried off by the pulsating heat.

"Andy?"

I keep pouring forth my dragon.

"Andy?"

I open my eyes without having realized I closed them. Around me, the room shimmers as waves of thermal energy rise toward an oculus that must be trying desperately to cope. The place has gone from oven to inferno, and I don't think I've ever felt as "at home" as I do in this instant.

"Andy!"

I gasp. "What?"

Miranda says urgently, *"You're eighteen miles down. Time to dial it back."*

Dial *what* back? I wonder blearily. She can't mean my dragon, because Miranda cares for me, and she'd never want me to give up something so precious, so *real*.

Well, not unless it was absolutely necessary.

I suddenly remember where I am. Pushing through my dragon-induced fog, I envision the ice shelf I've nearly penetrated. Near the bottom is its convection layer, a mile-thick area where the warm ocean water has softened the ancient ice. It would be easy for the CU to slip through that layer and, riding its own weight, tumble into the hundred miles of ocean beneath it. If that happens, it'll sink like a stone with me onboard and zero chance of rescue.

"Under...stood," I stammer.

Then with an effort, a *lot* of effort, I call back my dragon.

"Eighteen Point Five miles. Stop now, Andy. Let the CU do the rest."

I'm trying.

The dragon fights me. I've just shown it freedom beyond anything it's ever known, and it wants more. But, of course, I'm really fighting myself, that part of my psyche that wants to hang onto this feeling, maybe forever.

It's a hard fight.

But I win.

Control.

The dragon grumbles and goes silent.

I let out a shuddering, almost agonized sigh.

The CU continues to fall, burning its way through the ice using residual heat. But that's been accounted for, at least so Miranda said. She told me that the thickness of the convection layer was charted down to the millimeter and that if I stopped with at least a quarter-mile to spare, I'd be safe.

But still, I fall.

Suddenly this isn't fun anymore.

"Miranda?"

"I'm here."

"I haven't stopped yet."

"You will. Your descent is slowing." But isn't that unease in her voice?

My mouth goes dry, and I'm suddenly very, very aware of my nakedness.

And still, I fall.

"Miranda?"

"Stand by, Andy."

"Miranda?"

The coring unit stops.

It happens gradually. No lurch. Not even a shudder. Just the steady easing of inertia as the CU's heat dissipates, and the surrounding ice closes around it like a blanket.

Or a tomb.

Relief trembles through me, making my teeth rattle.

"You're at the target depth!" Miranda reports, sounding triumphant. *"Great work! Stand by. We're engaging the magnetic drive."*

Around me, sounds rise from the walls of the CU. I see no changes, but, from my briefings, I know what's happening.

And it's seriously futurey.

The CU begins to ascend.

Here's how it works: On the way down here, as the super-heated hull melted through miles of ancient, rock-hard ice, the hull's Liquid Bricks—those super-versatile Liquid Bricks—sluffed off specially designed tiles vertically along the circular walls of the newly created shaft. The tiles were programmed to latch into the smooth, adjacent ice, which hardened within seconds of our passing, leaving behind a trail of sorts.

Each of these Liquid Bricks carries a charge, either positive or negative, and by remotely manipulating the strength of these charges and magnetizing the hull, Miranda's people can summon back their only drilling machine—and the CU around me.

That is what's happening now.

It'll be slow. True, gravity's low on Europa, but mass is mass, and lifting something as big as the coring unit twenty miles straight up takes both energy and time. The prediction is two hours.

So, feeling about a million things at once, I settle into the chair. I'm completely spent and very hungry. Unfortunately, leaving me food and water wasn't an option; neither would have survived the heat of the descent. I just have to wait.

"Andy Brand?"

I reply, "Yeah?" automatically before it clicks that the voice, while female, isn't Miranda's.

"Are you hearing me, Andy Brand?"

I sit bolt upright. "I hear you. Who *are* you?"

"For now, call me Eurydice."

A chill that's got nothing to do with Europa's ice shelf slithers down my spine. If this new Voice is telling the truth, and I can't for the life of me imagine why anyone would *pretend* such a thing, then I'm talking to one half of the romantically dubbed terrorist team who's seized MC-13. A criminal. Potentially a murderer.

"What… do you want?" I ask.

"To warn you."

"Warn me?"

"Yes."

"And why should I believe anything you have to say? I know what you've done."

"Andy, you don't know a damned thing. Now shut up and listen. We have a lot to talk about."

"Um… Fine, I'm listening." I mean, what else is there for me to do?

"Good. Everything they've told you… everything she's told you… has been a lie."

"I don't believe you."

"I don't blame you. But I can prove it… if you'll give me a chance."

"Miranda's monitoring me. She might even be listening to us right now."

"She's not, and you know it. The EM field that the magnetic drive generates blocks high-frequency radio signals."

"But it's working for you."

"That's because I'm piggy-backing on a low-frequency telemetry transmission. CSE won't be equipped to communicate with you that way, even if it occurred to them to try. Besides, by now, Miranda Coffin's attention is… elsewhere."

"What's that mean?"

"It means that, right now, I'm in the colony's freight lift, headed for the surface, and they've almost certainly detected me."

I hear this, and, for some reason, I feel a rush of alarm. There are twenty of Spencer's security guys on the surface, all armed for bear. Terrorist or not, Eurydice is heading right for a killing ground.

But before I can decide if I should tell her, she cuts me off. *"I know what's waiting for me. I also know that if I give them the lift, then I just made this amazing shaft you've created kind of pointless."*

That thought pisses me off — though, again, I'm not sure why.

"I'm timing things so that I'll arrive on the surface just a minute or two after you do, and… assuming they don't shoot me on sight… I'm going to surrender immediately."

"That's suicide!" I say before I can catch myself. But I know Spencer.

"Hopefully, not. But it's necessary. You see, we knew this day was coming, though I have to admit your appearance aboard Conquest *came as a pretty big surprise."*

She knows what I am!

Well, maybe some of that knowledge can be explained by the fact that she's talking to a guy who's just burned his way down through twenty miles of ancient, hard-packed ice. That thought makes me wonder if she can see as well as hear me. Instinctively, I cup my hands around the parts that need hiding and demand, "Are you watching me?"

"You sound like someone who's asked that question a lot lately."

"Are you?"

"I couldn't if I wanted to."

"I don't believe you."

"Second time you've said that, and again I don't blame you. Trust has to be earned…. or, in some cases, stolen."

"What's that mean?"

"I'm guessing, deep down, you already know."

I swallow nervously. My head starts pounding. "Tell me about the miners."

"What about them?"

"Are they alive?"

She laughs. *"Of course, we're alive."*

We?

"Are you one of the miners?"

"Well, I'm a member of the colony's staff. But I'm not a miner by trade."

"But I was told the colonists are all... hostages."

"I know. But, we're not. We never have been."

"I don't understand."

"I know that too, Andy. Fortunately, I've got the better part of two hours to make you understand. But, to do that, first I need to show you something."

"Show me something?"

"Yes. And I'm so sorry, but it's something that's going to be very hard to watch. I really wish there was another way."

Moments later, Eurydice somehow projects a vid on the Liquid Bricks in front of me. It looks like security-vid footage, and the damaged tiles struggle to display it. The quality's lousy, and it has no sound, but what it shows me is clear enough.

More than clear enough.

Devastatingly clear.

And, in the span of a thirty-second clip, my life is utterly broken.

SIX – Day 18

Two hours later, I'm still sitting in the pilot's chair. I'm wrung dry, empty, totally spent. I can't even seem to cry anymore. In fact, I feel tremendously guilty that I've *stopped* crying.

Around me, the CU comes to a halt, intact after its thirty-eight-mile roundtrip journey, if somewhat the worse for wear. Much of the interior is misshapen from heat, a good percentage of the Liquid Bricks just hardened puddles on the floor.

I envy them.

"Andy?" The voice is Miranda's this time, so sincere, so full of concern. *"Andy? Are you all right?"*

I don't, can't reply.

"Please, Andy. Answer me."

I croak out a lie. "I'm good."

A relieved sigh comes through the CU's speakers. *"You did an amazing job! Get suited up and come outside when you're ready. Or… do you need help?"*

"No, it's okay. Just… tired. I'm coming."

"When you do, there'll be a couple of Spencer's people waiting. They'll escort you to the lander. There's a… situation developing that demands my attention."

"Situation?" I ask, hoping the fake interest doesn't come off as *too* fake.

"Nothing that concerns you. Just wait for me in the lander."

"Sure," I reply, ever cooperative, ever obedient.

A good little Dragon.

"Thanks. And again, great work, Andy! You've helped save a lot of lives today."

I almost ask, "Is that right?" But Miranda's already broken the link, though not before she opens the airlock door for me.

Suddenly, I'm alone again.

Outside, the freight lift rises with Eurydice aboard.

I've got less than five minutes.

I force myself to stand. My body's stiff, and my arms feel a bit like warm Jell-O after channeling so much dragon through them. Mustering what little strength I have left, I trudge across the CU and enter the airlock. The heat-resistant locker door seems uncooked. Good thing too, since everything that's coming next depends on it.

I quickly get dressed and then don my red spacesuit. As soon as all its seals are set, the airlock somehow detects it and evacuates the atmosphere in a controlled decompression.

Once the airlock reaches full vacuum, the Liquid Bricks slide noiselessly apart, revealing the stark Europan surface. Immediately, two armed blackbirds appear, just silhouettes against the alien brightness.

"Please follow us, Mister Brand," one of them says. It must be a closed comms channel since I can't hear any chatter from among the other twenty-plus people I know are out there. Apparently, either Miranda or Spencer is remotely controlling my suit's comms system.

I approach my two escorts. Their rifles are lowered. After all, I'm an asset, not an enemy. Their orders don't involve shooting me, at least not yet.

Which I guess is why I'm able to step between them—and stiff-arm them both.

In case I haven't made this clear already, I'm not a fighter. By nature, the Kind avoid conflict of any sort, especially violence. So, this bit of half-ass Kung-Fu is way out of my comfort zone and, until I do it, I'm not at all sure I can. Yeah, I've got the element of surprise. But, on Earth, I'd have bounced off these thugs regardless.

Except this isn't Earth, and the low-G turns out to be my friend.

With matching grunts, both guys topple over, their boots momentarily detaching from the moon's surface, and hit the ice. That ice, being especially smooth around the CU, sends both blackbirds half-sliding, half-tumbling away, victims of my mass and their own low weight.

"Sorry," I mutter.

I head for the lift hatch. I don't run. These suits suck at running. But I move quickly, ignoring the angry threats hurled by my down-but-not-out escorts. These guys will be on their feet and after me in moments, no doubt with way more low-G experience to give them an edge.

That means I need a *big* head start.

Fifty yards away stands the lift hatch, except now lights flash at each of its corners, heralding the approaching cargo lift.

Spencer has positioned his remaining blackbirds in a semi-circle, all facing the rising lift. Fortunately, as we're not currently on the same comms channel, they can't hear me approach in the vacuum—which means, so far, nobody's noticed me. But I know that won't last.

And it doesn't.

Right on cue, I see some of the faces, one of them Spencer's, turn in my direction, tipped off via comms by my offended escorts. A second later, I hear one of those escorts declare, *"Brand! Stop, or I'll fire!"*

I know—or *think* I know—it's an empty threat. He would need a perfect headshot; otherwise, my dragon would likely swallow the entire landing site.

So, I don't reply, and I definitely don't stop. Instead, I keep running toward the hatch, toward the armed contingent, and toward Miranda.

I can see her in her yellow spacesuit, standing beside Spencer in his green one. Both are looking at me and, though I'm too far away to read their faces, there's no mistaking the tension in their bearings. They've got somebody coming up in the lift, which is unexpected enough. For all they know, it's a dozen armed miners, not one woman with a myth-ical *nom de plume*. But, on top of that, now their pet Dragon has assaulted two blackbirds and is coming their way at what, on Europa, amounts to a full run.

They're probably arguing between the two of them about what should be done with me.

A moment later, Miranda wins. My comms link crackles, and her voice says urgently, "Andy! What's wrong?"

I don't reply.

I'm halfway there when the hatch begins to slide open, splitting along its central seam. As it does, the tension around it gets — *tenser* as a whole lot of trained soldiers try to split their attention between the lift and me. I can't help noticing that their raised rifles are mostly pointing at the former. Mostly.

I should be scared out of my mind right now. I know it. But what I'm feeling is more complicated and goes a lot deeper than that.

Ahead, Miranda is coming toward me, her gloved hands up in what I suppose is meant to be a calming gesture. At the same time, Spencer and a half-dozen of his men are fanning out, forming a line between me and the lift. That makes seven armed blackbirds in front of me and two behind.

"*Stop right there, Brand!*" Spencer exclaims inside my helmet. "*Not another goddamn step!*"

In desperation, I do the only thing I can think of. It is, without a doubt, the stupidest risk I've ever taken in my short and, in all likelihood, soon to be over life.

Bounding forward one last time, I put both my feet together, broad-jump style, and then, as the blackbirds box me in, I leap skyward.

In vids, low-G jumps are always shown in dramatic slow motion. In real life, they're a *lot* faster. In an instant, I'm ten feet off the ground, clearing the heads of the advancing soldiers. From this higher vantage point, I can see a pair of sliding doors visible on the lift car's facing side. The good news is that, more by luck than deliberate skill, my descent points me straight at them. The bad news is that I'm heading there more quickly than I'd like.

My comms link crackles, and Miranda yells, "*Andy! What are you doing?*"

I don't reply. Instead, I try flapping my arms like a fool, which accomplishes exactly nothing. Then, perhaps more intelligently, I bend my knees in preparation for the approaching impact.

With an instant to spare, I forget myself and yell, "Furk!"

It would make a lousy last word.

I land squarely and immediately drop into a roll, trying to spend my momentum. Even so, for a second, I'm convinced I'm about to puke out my spine. I hit the ground on my hip, bounce, roll, and bounce again. Thankfully, there's no one in my path. I'm in this unofficial kind of "no-man's-land" between the lift car and the vanguard of Spencer's forces, a patch of frozen moon maybe twenty feet across. Pain lances my legs and back, and my head rings as my helmet slams into the ice. At least, the polymer doesn't crack.

Finally, I collide butt-first with the lift's double doors.

The lift car is a half-cube nearly a hundred feet on each side and twenty-five high. It's made of worn titanium and bears no markings, except a stenciled message across its doors that reads:

STAND CLEAR

But before I can even begin to obey, the doors slide silently away only inches from where I'm sprawled.

A figure appears wearing a gray spacesuit. It looks functional, but far less advanced than my own. The helmet, for instance, is opaque except for its visor. Even so, looking up from the ice just outside the open doors, I can see the wearer's face.

A woman.

Eurydice.

She's younger than I expected—around thirty. Her hair, visible only as bangs inside her helmet, is so dark as to be almost black. She's not tall, maybe five-four, and her eyes are a surprisingly pale blue, almost the same color as the ice I'm lying on.

For a few heartbeats, no one moves. No one speaks.

Then Eurydice smiles at me. She mouths words that, of course, I can't hear. But she forms them deliberately so that I can read her lips.

She's saying, "Hello, Andy."

An instant later, out of the corner of my eye, I see Spencer's men, all of them, bringing their weapons to bear.

With a thrill of panic, I jump to my feet. That's easier to do than you might think in a spacesuit, especially in low-G. Then I place myself directly in front of the woman and spread my arms.

"Nobody shoot!" I yell.

SEVEN – Day 18

Nobody shoots.

Miranda speaks into my helmet, *"Get out of the way."*

"Not until you guarantee her safety."

"What are you talking about? This person is a terrorist. Now step aside."

Spencer chimes in. Where Miranda's angry, *he* sounds red-faced with hysteria. *"Do as you're told, Dragon! Or I'll end you!"*

"Then end me!" I shout back with more bravado than I feel. "Let's see how *that* works out for you."

Seconds pass. To call them "tense" is laughable. Finally, Miranda steps forward, waving to the others to lower their guns. Slowly, reluctantly, the blackbirds obey. Even Spencer.

"What is it you want, Andy?" she asks.

Eurydice touches my shoulder to get my attention. With her other gloved hand, she taps her helmet, somewhere near her ear. Her expression's calm, though we both know the razor's edge we're walking on right now.

This is the way we planned it.

Well, except for the last-minute space jump. That was all me.

I say to Miranda, "Switch our comms to 101 hertz."

At first, Charles Coffin's adjunct—right now, it's easier to think of her that way—doesn't reply. I glance nervously at Eurydice, who somehow smiles and winks.

Miranda says, *"Switching."*

My helmet crackles yet again. But the first voice I hear isn't Miranda's.

"Hi, Andy."

"Hi, Kim."

Miranda comes in then, her tone brusque. *"Doctor Shelton, what is it you're after?"*

Kimberly Shelton, aka Eurydice, replies calmly, though I'm not sure *how* given the number of guns pointed at her. Personally, I'm terrified. *"Well, Ms. Coffin. For starters, how about some peaceful parlay. Lose the soldiers, and let's talk."*

Miranda's eyes move between us. I can almost see her making the connections in her head. Whatever else she might be, she's no fool.

"You somehow contacted Andy during his trip back up the coring shaft," she says. A statement, not a question.

"I did," Kim replies.

"How?"

"Does it matter?"

Miranda considers. *"Not right now."*

"Are you willing to sit down and talk peaceably?"

Miranda considers some more. When she glances at me again, I expect to see something there. Anger. Betrayal. But there's only deliberate calculation. She's processing, weighing variables, considering options.

"Andy," she says. *"I'd like to talk to you alone."*

"No," I reply.

Her eyes widen. She looks between Kim and me again. Her hand touches her suit's e-man, and, big surprise, I hear a crackle inside my helmet as the frequency switches. A private channel, I suppose. *"What did she say to you?"*

I don't answer.

"Andy..."

I meet her eyes and try to see the girl—the woman—I thought I knew. That woman was my age, just eighteen, and yet had more self-possession than pretty much anyone I've ever met. True, she could be distant at times. But she could be tender too. And passionate. This Miranda Coffin, however, is all business, authoritative and deliberate. Has she reinvented herself yet again, or am I finally seeing the real thing?

Struggling to keep my tone level, I ask, "What happened in New York?"

I expect—hope, even—to see her flinch. She doesn't. *"What did she tell you?"*

"Miranda... are my parents dead?"

Her eyes remain locked on mine. Awful seconds tick by, during which no one in our little circle of barely contained mayhem dares move.

At last, Miranda replies, *"Yes."*

Suddenly, it's all I can do to breathe. I expected this. I knew it before I stepped off the CU. But hearing it confirmed so matter-of-factly by someone I thought I—

It's like getting punched in the stomach.

For a horrible moment, I'm scared I might vomit inside my helmet. I sway on my feet, desperately fighting for control. If I lose it now, if I give in to the horror and grief, one of Spencer's guys will seize the opportunity and pull me out of the way so they can gun down Eurydice.

I won't let that happen.

But my mom and dad!

A sob chokes me. My gloved hands ball into fists. Sweat stings my brow.

Then someone squeezes my upper arm. I look over, half-expecting to find Miranda there, as always. But no. The adjunct never moved. Instead, Kim Shelton has placed a gloved hand on me. I notice, with some surprise, that there are tears on her cheeks.

She can't hear us. But she can read the pain on my face.

This stranger. This "terrorist."

I glance at Miranda, whose own eyes remain dry. Always dry.

Suddenly, I think maybe I understand the teardrop birthmark.

I say to her, "They've been dead for more than a week."

Miranda watches me. Unmoving. Unmoved. *"Yes."*

"Along with twenty-thousand other people. More than six blocks-worth of downtown New York."

"Andy…" Miranda begins, and this time there seems to be something there. Compassion? Sorrow? Guilt? She's always been so tough to read.

But I cut her off. "The government, the media, and *your* father are all calling it a terrorist attack, the worst ever."

"I'm sorry, Andy."

"And you knew about it. You've known this whole time."

"Yes."

"And you didn't tell me."

"No, I didn't."

"You let me try to call them again and again."

"Yes, I did."

"We had sex… furking *sex*! And you *still* didn't tell me that my parents were dead, killed by your father's thugs, and that they took twenty-thousand lives with them!"

"Andy—"

"Why?" I demand.

"Because we needed you," she tells me with a plea in her voice. *"You know what's at stake."*

"Do I?" I point at Eurydice. "This is no 'terrorist!' This is Kimberly Shelton, wife of Mike Shelton, the owner of Shelton Metals. There are no terrorists on MC-13. There never were. The colony's simply in rebellion."

"She told you that?" Miranda asks accusingly.

"Yeah."

"And you believe her?"

"Yeah, I do."

"Why? Why would you believe her over me?"

"Given all the lies you've told, how can you even ask me that?"

Miranda looks between us again, recalculating. *"But… just her word wouldn't have been enough to convince you. There must have been more. There must* have."

I sense she's talking more to herself than to me. So, I don't reply.

Finally, she says. *"Andy, I really am sorry about your family. If they'd just left it alone, they would have been fine. But they kept pushing, threatening to go to the police, to the press, and Conceal and Protect be damned! My father did his best to reassure them, to make them understand. But they finally showed up at our headquarters in New York, demanding to see him. Things… got out of hand."*

"You kidnapped their *kid*," I tell her. "Of course, they couldn't leave it alone. What parent would? Would *yours?*"

She blinks as if what I've said confuses her, as if the notion of my mom and dad chucking it all to find me goes beyond the scope of her understanding.

"Spencer," Miranda says.

Spencer's voice fills my helmet. Apparently, he's been on the channel all this time. *"Yes, Adjunct."*

"Please take Mister Brand and Doctor Shelton into custody."

"Do you want to bring them back up to Conquest?" he asks.

"No. For now, put them both in the CU."

"Miranda—" I begin, but she cuts me off.

"Doctor Shelton stays alive until we know the best way to retake the colony," she says, still speaking to Spencer.

"And the Dragon?"

The callous way he asks sends a chill down my spine.

"Him, too."

A few minutes later, the blackbirds toss us, none too gently, through the coring unit's still-open airlock. In the low-G, I go tumbling the length of the small room before sliding to a stop against the opposite wall.

An instant later, Kim lands atop me.

The doorway slides closed, and the overhead tiles light up.

For a moment, I lay there. Being still sealed inside my spacesuit, I hear nothing, not even the ever-present crackling hum of an active comms system. My suit's radio has been remotely deactivated.

So has the airlock. While both the inner and outer doors are shut, and the lights are on, there's no sign of atmosphere filling the small space. We're still in vacuum.

Right now, all that's distant and unimportant alongside a terrible truth.

My family's *gone*.

It feels like I'm drowning in mud. Despair wars with denial as I grapple with the idea, cold and heartless, that I'll never see them again. Worse, I'm having trouble remembering the *last* time I *did* see them. Before school on the day I was taken, I suppose. Or was that just my mom, rushing to work and giving me a hasty kiss on the forehead before disappearing out the door? Was Dad already gone by then? When did I last talk to him? The night before, maybe, at dinner? Or had he been working late?

I can't remember.

It's *killing* me that I can't remember!

Eurydice climbs off me, her body light in the low-G, but I don't really register it. Right now, any body aches seem trivial.

I'm all about the *inner* pain.

A hand takes mine, urging me up. Reluctantly, maybe even a bit resentfully, I climb to my feet. Once there, I look at Kim and find her looking back at me.

There's sorrow in her eyes.

Seeing it brings fresh tears. Once again, I sob as I did in the coring unit when, naked and alone, I watched the security feed from Coffin Industries' New York HQ, the one that ends with two dead Brands in a blaze of power. Twenty thousand people perished in that conflagration, which begs a question: Is it selfish of me to be more broken, *much* more broken, by the loss of two people I loved than ten thousand times more whose names I didn't know?

And if it *is* selfish, do I care?

I want to turn away from Kim, from everything. But I can't. She and I made a pact during the long climb up the shaft. In exchange for the terrible truth she showed me, I promised to meet her at the lift car and use what influence I have to keep her alive. The hope was for Miranda and Spencer to lock us both up in the lander, where there would be atmosphere. But here, in the vacuum of the coring unit's airlock, we can't remove our space suits. Worse, with my comms down, we can't even communicate effectively.

Miranda has turned our spacesuits into prison cells. I can only hope she comes back for us before our air runs out. I don't even know how much Kim's suit has.

I look back at Kim, wondering how to communicate that question to her. But, when I do, I find her gesturing for me to turn around. Confused, I do so—and immediately feel her doing something to the control pack fastened between my shoulder blades. This gadget manages all of my suit's functions, including heat, so I don't freeze, and airflow so I don't suffocate. Realizing this, I feel a stab of alarm, but manage to suppress it. What's she *doing* back there?

Then, I hear a crackle inside my helmet, followed by a couple of shrill squawks that make me want to clamp my hands over my ears— which, of course, I can't.

Finally, Kim's voice rings out clearly, *"There, that's got it. Can you hear me, Andy?"*

"Yeah, I can," I say, astonished. "What'd you just do?"

"Bypassed Coffin's comms override and set your frequency back to one-oh-one."

I face her. "And where'd you learn to do that?"

"I'm married to an engineer, and I've been living in a sub-surface colony on an alien moon for two years. I may not be a physical scientist, but you learn a thing or two if you spend enough time around people who are."

"Oh. Okay. Well, at least we can talk."

"At least. So, this is the coring unit?"

"Just the airlock. The real CU is through there." I point at the blank, inside wall.

"Liquid Bricks," she surmises.

I nod.

"You were very brave out there."

"Was I?"

"You put yourself between me and two dozen guns!"

"Only twenty."

"Oh. Well, never mind then."

"I knew they wouldn't shoot me."

"They could have shot you in the head without triggering an involuntary thermal-reactive response, couldn't they?"

A pretty clinical way of putting it, but accurate.

"Well, yeah. Maybe. But I didn't think any of them would risk it."

"Like I said: brave."

I decide on an immediate change of subject. "What about the lift? Haven't you just handed them access down to MC-13?"

"Nope. They'll find the gears frozen and the controls locked. Better yet, the very presence of that big titanium box filling the top of the shaft will keep them from going around it."

"You thought of everything."

"Everything except somebody melting a second shaft." To my surprise, she says this without rancor. *"Even Shelton didn't see that coming, and he's the real brains behind this protest."*

"You call him Shelton?"

"Everybody does. He hates being called Mike."

"Whatever," I tell her. "Miranda has this coring unit. Her plan is to send blackbirds down to the bottom of the new shaft, and then move horizontally across the underside of the ice shelf… twenty yards instead of twenty miles. Then they'll hit the colony that way."

"We figured. Which makes it surprising that she decided to dump us in here. I was sure she'd use the lander."

"What do you think it means?"

"Probably that she wants to talk to us before the invasion, which is good."

"It is?"

Kim nods. *"I've never been anybody's prisoner before. But the way I figure it, I'd rather be a prisoner of value than… not."*

"Well, I *have* been somebody's prisoner," I say. "And I really hope you're right."

EIGHT – Day 18

We spend the next hour much the same way we spent my trip up the coring shaft—by talking, but with two big differences. First, we're now face-to-face, spacesuits notwithstanding. Second, this time there's a lot more trust.

Kim Shelton, I learn, is a Doctor of Psychology and Psychobiology. Psychology, of course, I've heard of. Psychobiology, it seems, is a branch of science dealing with the biological basis for behavior. Her role on MC-13 sounds to me, to borrow a high school term, kind of like that of a "guidance counselor." The colony is basically a hundred-plus people working hard and sharing limited space—and her job is to keep them sane.

In some ways, she's very forthcoming; in others, not so much. For example, she explained back in the coring unit proper that the colonists on MC-13 voted to stage a "passive strike." But, so far, she hasn't been willing to tell me what exactly *made* them do so.

This is all I know for sure:

The Sheltons and their company came to Europa willingly enough, working on contract with Coffin Solar Exploration. Coffin supplied the cash, materials, and most of the labor. For its part, Shelton Metals provided the innovation, including the laser to drill the hole and the designs for both the first permanent colony on a Jovian moon and the orbital crane that delivered it there.

For a while, everyone was happy. The colonists fulfilled their quotas and made their tantalum deliveries without problem or complaint and CSE, in return, kept them well-equipped and well-supplied.

Now, suddenly, they've cut off the flow of ore and are declaring independence—something that, if granted, would mark the first time any off-Earth colony has won its full autonomy.

What changed? What happened to turn Mike and Kim Shelton into Orpheus and Eurydice?

I asked these questions back in the CU, but Kim declined to answer. When I ask again now, she just shakes her head and mouths, "later."

I get what she's saying. She's worried that Miranda and Spencer are listening in, checking up on us despite having overridden my comms. I sure as hell wouldn't put it past them. Up until now, every-thing Kim's told me they already knew, but she's reluctant to divulge anything beyond that. And I really do understand.

But it still irritates me. Maybe that's not fair to her, but I'm just so furking tired of being kept in the dark and lied to. True, Kim hasn't lied to me, at least not so far as I know. But that doesn't stop me from feeling pissed.

Then I wonder if maybe I'm deflecting, trying to distract myself from the real crap that's rained down on me since waking up in that cell, the real pain that's eating me up from the inside.

Yeah. Probably.

So, despite myself, I shut up.

And we wait.

When the Liquid Bricks on the outside wall finally slide open, I expect to see armed blackbirds as escorts. Instead, there's only Spencer and Miranda, wrapped in their respective spacesuits. Spencer's scowling, as usual. Miranda seems more tentative, as if her anger at my defiance has morphed into — something else.

They step inside and let the opening close behind them. Then Spencer taps something on his suit's e-man, and I feel the airlock fill with atmosphere. Kim and I swap apprehensive looks.

When the overhead lights go green, we all remove our helmets.

Miranda says to me, "I tried to reach you on your comms, but my control's been disabled."

When Kim waggles her fingers, Miranda dismisses her with a look of disdain. To me, she says, "You and I have to talk."

"So, talk," I reply.

"Alone," she says.

Then, without waiting for me to respond, she taps her e-man. Liquid Bricks clatter aside as a new opening appears in the airlock's inner wall. "Let's go in there. Just you and me. Spencer will stay out here with Doctor Shelton."

I don't move. "I'm not leaving her alone with him."

Spencer glares. "Your terrorist friend will be fine," he says. "Unlike you, I know how to do what I'm told."

"I promise you she'll be okay," Miranda adds. "Look, I know things got… tense… a while back. That's why I put you in here, to give everyone a chance to cool down."

I figure there *might* be some truth to that, though getting dumped in an airlock without atmosphere seems like a pretty hardcore "timeout."

"And Kim'll still be here when we get back?"

"I guarantee it. Please, Andy."

I look at Kim, who shrugs.

So, reluctantly, I do as Miranda asks. Moments later, the two of us are alone in the coring unit with the Liquid Bricks sealed behind us. For a long moment, we just study each other in uneasy silence. I wonder, almost painfully, if this is what comes from loving somebody.

It's an awful sensation. Emotional nausea.

Miranda finally breaks the spell. "I need to start by saying again how sorry I am about your parents. I can't even imagine what you must be going through." Then she pauses expectantly, maybe waiting for a thank you or something.

She doesn't get one.

So, she asks impatiently, "What did Doctor Shelton tell you?"

"More than you ever did," I reply.

"We needed your help!" she exclaims so vehemently that I'm actually startled, though I can't tell if she's angry, frustrated, or guilt-ridden. "If I *had* told you what happened in New York, would you have come down here willingly?"

Her outburst leaves her pale, the teardrop birthmark standing out more than usual. But she's still gut-wrenchingly beautiful.

I look away.

"I didn't want to believe her," I say. "Kim, I mean. At first, I told her flat out that I *didn't* believe her. But she convinced me."

"How?" Miranda demands as if that matters. Then again, I know what she's after – and I'm not going to cooperate. Not on this. Not on anything. Not ever again.

I'm done.

But, of course, she gets there anyway. "She showed you something, didn't she? What was it? A news vid? No, that wouldn't be enough. Security footage, maybe?"

I say nothing.

Miranda keeps right on going. "How could she have gotten it? No Earth broadcasts, public or private, reach this far out."

I continue saying nothing.

"How did she get them, Andy?" she demands.

"Go to hell," I say, putting as much ice into it as I can.

But instead of taking offense, Miranda's brows knit. "They must have somebody on *Conquest* feeding them intelligence, probably by standard comms… not the Casimir. I suggested as much to Spencer and Wei, but they refused to believe it. Even my father. *He* says our short-range comms protocols are unbreachable."

Once more, I let her eat silence.

I turn and walk several steps away, putting some space between us.

"Andy," she says from behind me. "Yes, we forced you into this situation. Yes, we used you. And, yes, I can't deny that my company bears at least some of the responsibility for the tragedy in New York."

"Some?" I exclaim without turning around. "Some of the responsibility! You shot my parents!"

Miranda visibly swallows. Then she says in a whisper-soft voice, "I can understand why you think that we're monsters… that *I'm* a monster. In your place, I'd probably feel the same way."

She says this so sincerely that, despite myself, I look back at her.

She keeps going. "But consider this. You did your job. We brought you here to drill that shaft down to MC-13, and you completed your task perfectly. We don't need you anymore. But nobody's vectoring you and hauling you back up to *Conquest* to spend the return trip to Earth in an induced sleep. Instead, I'm standing here apologizing and doing my best to explain our logic, as callous and self-serving as it might seem to you."

She approaches me warily, as if she thinks I'm a frightened deer—or an angry bear. I wonder which it is. "Now," she says, coming close enough to take my gloved hand in hers. I'm not sure why I let her, but I do. "Does all that sound like the act of a monster?"

God help me, I almost cave. Remember, I'm millions of miles from home and, just a couple of hours ago, I discovered I'm an orphan. Here stands someone offering me comfort, a beautiful woman whom I still love. Can you really blame me for backsliding?

But then the security footage that Kim showed me flashes through my mind—really just one frame of it. In it, Coffin's thugs have just shot my mother in the head. Her arms are akimbo, and her knees have buckled. Half her skull is gone. And there stands my father beside her, looking on, his horror evident despite the vid's lousy resolution.

I *think* his face is wet with my mother's blood.

I look into Miranda's eyes. They're full of sympathy and regret.

"Yes," I tell her. "You're a monster."

Then, reaching over to her wrist with my free hand, I touch her e-man and open the airlock door.

"Andy!" she says, sounding alarmed. Her grip on my other hand tightens, perhaps reflexively.

I wrench free and turn away, stepping into the airlock.

Spencer and Kim are gone.

And would you believe a part of me is *surprised*?

The outer wall is blank, of course. Whatever exit Spencer created is now closed. Feeling my face redden, I whirl on Miranda. "Open the outer door," I tell her.

"Andy…"

"Open it!" Then, to punctuate the point, I pull my helmet back over my head and set its seals.

"Andy, she's a criminal."

"So's your father! So are *you*! Now open it! Last chance!"

Her expression hardens. "Or you'll what? You can't do anything to the Liquid Bricks while you're trapped in that suit. Or are you threatening me? I'm sorry, Andy, but what's happening *has* to happen. And we both know it's not in you to hurt anybody."

She doesn't add, "Least of all me."

But she might as well have.

Furious, I turn back and glare at the outer wall as if I can melt its tiles by sheer force of will.

Then I hear words in my head, or rather the memory of words. A dead man's words.

"Being Kind, truly Kind, is an exercise in self-discipline. Your dragon does not command you. You command it. And when you command something, it should be a given that it will never do anything that you don't specifically want it to do."

My father said that during one of our camping trips. At the time, I was standing naked in the middle of a clearing, having burned away my clothes for the third time that day while failing to throw up a thermal wall.

Well, up on *Conquest*, I finally managed the shield.

And now, in the wake of my parents' murder, this seems as good a time as any to complete the lesson.

After all, what do I really have to lose?

I raise my left hand, not my right. I'm right-handed and figure if I end up blowing my fingers off, at least I'll still be able to write my name.

How does that line up with not really having anything to lose?

Shut up. That's how.

"Andy?" Miranda says from behind me.

"Stay in the CU and close the inner door," I tell her without turning. "Or at least put your helmet on. It's about to get windy."

"What? No! You can't!"

"Maybe, maybe not. Let's find out."

I call my dragon.

This time, however, I call it differently. Instead of summoning the heat up from deep inside me, like a volcano drawing up magma, I bring it out slowly, a trickle instead of a torrent. And I send it down my left arm to my left hand—to the ends of my fingers.

Mom… Dad…

An instant later, my dragon peeks out through my fingertips.

The tips of my spacesuit's gloves, each at least a half-inch thick, vaporize in an instant as waves of thermal energy, exactly five of them, shoot out and slam into the airlock's outer wall. Almost immediately, the tiles begin to soften and then melt until finger-sized holes, again exactly five, appear in the metal.

The atmosphere in the airlock begins moving—fast.

Too late, I look around for something to grab. But there's nothing. While looking, however, I notice that the airlock's inner door's been closed with Miranda safely on the other side of it.

I can't help but be relieved.

A split second later, I'm yanked off my feet and slammed hard into the newly perforated wall.

Yeah, I really didn't think this through.

Pain jolts one elbow and one knee, making me cry out. Then I feel myself being pressed against the holes I've just made as if it's possible for me to get sucked through that tiny space and out into the Europan vacuum.

Fortunately, it isn't.

Instead, as the limited amount of atmosphere in the small airlock bleeds away, the pressure on my body eases and then vanishes completely.

With a sigh, I push myself away from the wall and bob lightly down to the floor in the low-G.

That's when my hand erupts with agony.

Remember when I said the Kind don't feel cold? Well, that rule means exactly zilch on Europa. What hits me now is hard to describe. Imagine pressing your fingers to a block of ice for a couple of minutes and then bashing them with a hammer.

Nope, still not enough.

Now imagine your entire body turning inside out, starting with your fingertips.

Yeah, that's closer.

As I scream, bouncing off the walls and clutching my hand, I'm enough of a science geek to know what's happening. The tips of my fingers have been exposed to a vacuum, and, as a result, the water in their tissues is vaporizing in the low atmosphere. Basically, my body moisture is boiling away.

And, holy furk, it *hurts!*

So, I do the only thing I can think of: I point my fingers at the outer wall again and send out more dragon. A lot more dragon. Before I realize what's happening, my entire glove is gone, and my hand is fully exposed. But it's also alive with heat, practically glowing. And, somehow, that's keeping the vacuum at bay.

The pain is gone.

A column of thermal energy much wider and hotter than the five-fingered stuff I produced earlier melts through the tiles in seconds, leaving a fist-sized jagged hole. Fortunately, there's no more atmosphere in here to escape.

I keep my dragon going, making circular motions to melt more and more of the wall until there's a space big enough to step through. All around its edges, the Liquid Bricks bubble and drip, as, beyond the threshold, the surface of Europa is awash in gray steam. My heat has already started vaporizing this tiny section of the moon's icy surface.

I give the molten exit a few moments to cool, mindful of what drops of melting Liquid Bricks could do to my spacesuit. I don't dare call my dragon back, however, not completely. Instead, I dial it down slowly, feeling my way along. Then, when the pleasure starts to give way to pain, I stop, keeping the thermal flow steady, and raise my hand in front of my helmet. The skin looks pinkish and glows faintly as fire roils through my veins. The spacesuit material, forming a jagged cuff at my wrist, has melted against my skin, creating what *looks* like an airtight bond. That's good, since all the dragon in the world won't save me if my air supply bleeds away.

But air is only one problem. I'm about to step out onto the surface of an alien moon with one hand exposed to enough radiation from Jupiter's magnetosphere to cook a human being alive. Then again, as has been driven home to me lately, I'm *not* a human being.

I don't know what'll happen to me out there.

Then I remember Kim—and I get moving.

The moment I exit the CU, I find four blackbirds waiting for me. They all have their weapons drawn, and one of them, I see, is Ray Exler.

Ignoring them, I scan the surrounding tundra. Spencer's bright green spacesuit gives him away. He's maybe fifty yards off, clutching Kim by the upper arm as he drags her toward the waiting lander.

No way am I letting Spencer take Kim off this moon.

But before I get two steps, the blackbirds block my path.

I don't speak. Kim's hack has pretty much trashed my suit's comms unit anyhow. Instead, I meet each of the blackbird's hard stares, including Exler's. As I hold up my bare hand, their grips on their rifles tighten. I let out a little more of my dragon. If we weren't on a zero-atmosphere moon, the thermal energy would be creating tiny rippling mirages of super-heated air. But on Europa, my hand simply glows, first yellow and then white—and, of course, waves of heat radiate out from it in all directions.

Wrapped in their spacesuits, Exler and the others can't feel the heat. But their suits' sensors certainly register it, reacting as they would to a sudden pulse of potentially deadly radiation. How did Spencer put it? *"If your suit detects a rad spike, it'll light up like a Christmas tree."*

Well, here's that spike.

Each blackbird startles and looks down at his e-man, all except Exler, who holds my gaze.

I raise my other hand, the one still gloved and not glowing, and motion them aside.

They get the message. Three of them drop their rifles and back off several steps. Again, all but Exler. He lingers a moment, his eyes on mine. Then, with a nod, he lowers his gun and gets out of my path.

I cross the ice after Spencer and Kim, moving as quickly as I'm able.

Spencer doesn't see me coming, and he certainly can't hear my approach, not in the Europan vacuum. So, when he abruptly whirls around, angry surprise behind his visor, I can only assume that Miranda or one of the blackbirds warned him. His hand is still on Kim's arm, forcing her to turn with him.

She looks alarmed.

The security chief's ever-present scowl morphs into a snarl. Unlike his men, he carries no rifle, but instead pulls a pistol and, before I really register what's happening, fires.

At the same instant, Kim shoves him, putting all her mass behind it. And, despite her much smaller size, Europa's low-G turns out to be her friend as well. Spencer staggers sideways, over-balances, and goes down just as his pistol discharges.

The ice at my feet chips. There is, of course, no sound.

Spencer doesn't slide away like his blackbirds did earlier. Instead, he seems stuck on his back like an upended turtle.

I know it won't last, but it gives me time to reach Kim. For a moment, I stare at her. I know full well how close I just came to dying. Spencer was surely aiming for my head, determined to turn me off like a switch without waking my dragon. It's the way my mom was killed, and, to my astonishment, I find that I'm not as ready to join her as I thought.

"*My hero,*" Kim says, giving me a weak, oddly sardonic smile as if she knows something I don't.

Then there's a crackle inside my helmet, followed by a breathless voice calling, "*Andy!*"

I turn and spot Miranda headed toward us. In the meantime, it seems she's gotten around Kim's hack of my suit's comms system.

"*Adjunct,*" another voice says. Deeper. Way more menacing. Apparently, Miranda looped Spencer in as well. Cozy. "*We need to end this.*"

I glance back at the security chief. He's still on his back but is now pointing his gun at me again, this time from a much closer range. I feel my heart skip a beat as his eyes flash dangerously.

"*Don't fire!*" Miranda tells him. "*Andy, don't move!*"

I don't move.

"You're not taking her on that lander," I say to Spencer.

"*Not your call, Dragon.*"

"*Both of you,*" Miranda exclaims, gasping with exertion. "*Stand down!*"

Kim says something, but while I can see her lips moving frantically behind her helmet's visor, no words reach my ears. Miranda's blocked her.

Facing Spencer, I hold up my bare, glowing hand. "Let us go."

"*Or what? You'll burn me, freak? You don't have the guts.*"

He's probably right.

But he doesn't fire—yet.

I do my best to ignore the way my insides have turned to jelly. Instead, I willfully push everything aside and *think.*

And what I think is, *Enough.*

I lower my hand. As I do, Spencer's sneer turns into a triumphant smirk. He thinks he's beaten me.

He's wrong.

I call my dragon.

He doesn't see it, of course. There's no air for the thermal energy to affect as it covers the two or three yards between us. My heat hits right where I aim, not at his suit, which would melt away in an instant and kill him, but instead at the Europan surface *around* where he lies.

In the space of a heartbeat, a huge amount of the ice under his body vaporizes. But instead of dropping into the newly created hole, which was my half-baked plan, a geyser of steam blasts his prone body straight upward so abruptly that Spencer has no time to react. A look of alarm flashes across his face, and then he's airborne, hurled a dozen feet skyward in Europa's low-G.

Kim looks on in silent astonishment.

In my helmet, I hear Miranda draw a shocked breath.

As for me, I don't think I'm breathing at all.

Spencer, limbs flailing, soars higher. For a single, terrible instant, I'm afraid he's going to escape Europa's gravity. But he doesn't.

"Andy!" Miranda screams. *"What did you do?"*

I grab Kim's hand and pull her with me. After just a moment's pause, she follows me across the ice.

Miranda calls my name again, but I ignore her.

I've chosen my side.

NINE – Day 18

The big, box-like steel lift car still fills the top of the shaft, its cargo doors wide open. The interior's unlit, so I can't tell what, if anything, is inside it.

Then, as Kim and I get closer, I find out.

Six blackbirds emerge from inside the box. Maybe they saw us coming, or maybe Spencer comm-ed them. Either way, they fan out, forming a defensive barrier between us and the lift.

Kim and I swap worried looks.

Spencer's voice booms inside my helmet. *"Stop where you are, Brand!"*

I ignore him and keep going. These security guys know full well what'll likely happen if they fire and fail to kill me outright.

Then Spencer adds, *"Stop now, or my men have orders to shoot* her, *not you."*

I slow my pace. The cold knot's back in my gut.

Seeing me falter, Kim looks questioningly at me, still holding my gloved hand.

"Last chance, Dragon!" Spencer sounds pissed. Then again, when doesn't he?

I suddenly wonder if my parents heard a similar ultimatum in New York, right before they died.

I make a decision.

Raising my bare hand, my enflamed hand, I throw my dragon at the frozen ground between the blackbirds and us. The instant the thermal energy hits the ice, a wall of steam erupts into the Europan sky—twenty yards high, at least. I keep at it, aiming alternatively left and then right, until all six security guys are invisible behind twin curtains of explosive water vapor, leaving us a clear path between them.

Kim grins at me.

"Brand!" Spencer roars.

This is followed by Miranda's voice, *"Andy! Wait! Please!"* She sounds desperate.

We start moving again, loping across the frozen surface as fast as our boots will let us.

A silent bullet, fired from behind us, drills into the ground beside Kim's foot, spraying us both with tiny pellets of ancient ice. Kim falters but keeps moving. At the same time, I pull my hand from hers and push her ahead of me, using my own body to shield her from what I assume to be Spencer's aim. Fortunately, the lift's only a few more yards ahead.

Then, without warning, one of the blackbirds stumbles into view right in Kim's path, half-staggering and half-falling through the wall of steam like a clumsy ghoul. He's no one I recognize. His rifle's gone, probably lost to the steam. He reaches for Kim and, from the fury on his face, fully intends to take his frustration out on her.

What happens next will haunt me forever.

Leaping forward, I put myself between Kim and the blackbird. With my right hand, I shove her clear of his reach. It's a purely instinctive action, one born of fear and adrenalin, and a bit harder than was probably necessary. As a result, I knock Kim right off her feet in the low-G and send her tumbling through the lift's open doors. She lands there, steadying herself and looking worriedly back at me.

At the same instant, and just as instinctively, I swear, I try to stiff-arm the blackbird. But he's too close and, instead, I end up pushing my hand against his visor.

My *left* hand.

My dragon hand.

All I wanted to do was stop him, maybe knock him down as I did my escorts earlier and Kim just now, take advantage of Europa's anemic gravity.

Instead, my palm melts through his helmet.

Then, to my eternal horror, it melts right through his face.

I try to pull back at the last second, I really do. But it's way too late. The guy convulses as he reflexively recoils.

Inside my helmet, I hear Miranda gasp.

The blackbird topples onto the frozen ground. His body jerks spasmodically before going suddenly, terribly still.

For a long moment, I stand there, staring at him.

"Damn you!" Spencer screams.

"Spencer!" Miranda yells. *"Don't!"*

Something hits my shoulder blade with what feels like freight-train force. The impact knocks me off my feet and hurls me into the lift. I catch a glimpse of Kim's alarmed expression just before I hit the floor, cracking my head against the inside of my helmet.

My vision swims.

Spencer shot me!

Oddly, there's no pain, not yet. Shock, I suppose.

As I lay in one corner of the lift, I realize it's getting hard to breathe. I taste blood. It's filling my mouth.

"Evacuate!" Spencer screams. *"Everyone on the lander now!"*

"Andy… I'm sorry." That one's from Miranda.

Then silence.

I cough a mouthful of blood against the inside of my visor.

Kim kneels beside me and, behind her, I can blearily see the lift doors closing.

No! She can't be here! My dragon —

—is rising up inside me. Remember that volcano analogy I dished out earlier? Well, this is like that times a thousand. I already know I can't control it. I'll die trying, but when I *do* die, it's going to come out all at once and destroy everything around me.

I can't talk, not with the blood gagging me. So instead, I push at her, pointing at the closing doors. If she leaves and surrenders to Miranda, and if they all get the lander launched quickly, *maybe* I can stay alive long enough to spare them.

Maybe.

But she shakes her head. She doesn't get it. To her eyes, I'm just a teenager with a bullet wound.

As the two halves of the sliding doors meet, there's, of course, no *clank*, not in Europa's airless vacuum. But I imagine that I hear one anyhow. It sounds like a death knell.

I can already feel my control slipping.

Mom…

Dad…

The next thing I know, Kim is hastily unlatching my suit's pressure seals. She's trying to remove my helmet. Her own is already off.

"It's okay," she says as she frees my head. "The lift maintains an atmosphere."

I take as deep a breath as I can manage, only to turn my head and cough a fistful of blood onto the floor beside me.

"Roll over," Kim tells me. "Try to keep your airway clear. The bullet punctured your lung."

"Listen," I gasp. "You've got to open the doors again. Get out and try to reach the lander! I'm—"

She shakes her head. "Not a chance. You've been shot!"

"Please… I'll kill you if you stay!"

"No, you won't."

"You don't understand!"

"I understand plenty. It's going to be fine. But I need to see the bullet wound. Now roll over."

As I obey, pain lancing up my back, I feel the lift begin to move. We're going down.

Twenty miles.

And I think bitterly, *If I can hold off until we're deep enough, then I might only kill* her.

Of course, I'll vaporize the lift car and at least a mile of shaft. But my dragon won't reach all the way down to MC-13.

At least, I don't *think* it will.

This is why my parents kept drumming Conceal and Protect into me. No one should have to go to the afterlife with innocent lives on their conscience—

—the way my father did.

"Andy," Kim says, her tone gentle but clinical. She's been fingering the hole in my shoulder blade. "You're bleeding out. I can't stop it, and we can't wait until we reach the colony. You need to cook it."

I try to turn my head to look at her. "Cook… it?"

"You need to let your dragon out. It might cauterize the wound."

Let my dragon out? Now? With her here? That'll kill her.

Unless—

"Are you Kind?" I ask weakly.

"What?"

"Are you *Kind*?"

Kim laughs off-handedly, looking both amused and deeply concerned at the same time. "Well, I like to think so."

She doesn't know what I'm talking about.

Of course, she doesn't.

Tears fill my eyes. I've already killed one human being, out there on the ice. I didn't do it intentionally. But I did it.

"Please…" I gasp, the word wrapped in agony and desperation. "I don't want to hurt you."

Her reaction stuns me. "Oh, for God's sake!" Then I feel her stick her forefinger through the hole in my suit and deep, deep into the bullet wound underneath.

Agony rips through me, tearing down what little remains of my self-control. To my horror, my dragon emerges. It's not a full-blown eruption; there's still enough of me alive and conscious to prevent that. But it's more than enough to turn everything inside this lift car to ash.

In an instant, my suit vaporizes. Waves of heat explode from my pores, knocking poor Kim away like a rag doll. In seconds, the walls begin to soften. The floor sags as I start melting through it. I hear the lift stop moving as the electronics fry. The lights flicker and go dark.

Meanwhile, more of my dragon tries to get out. Tries *hard*.

But I grasp it with my mind, restraining it. It's strong—terribly strong—and it *wants* to be free. It wants to be unbound so that it can burn and burn and burn everything in sight before it extinguishes itself.

Yet, somehow, I force it back down—down to its place, its prison deep inside me.

And it goes. Reluctantly but obediently, it goes.

It's over.

My pain isn't gone, but it's lessened—a lot.

With a groan, I manage to roll out of the Andy-sized indent my super-heated body has made in the floor. Tentatively, I reach over my shoulder and touch the bullet wound. It's still there, but the bleeding has stopped.

Cauterized?

I didn't even know I could *do* that.

Then I collapse onto my side, utterly exhausted—and, of course, naked again.

That's when I remember Kim.

Gripped by fresh horror, I look toward the far side of the box, but it's pitch dark. Not that it matters. I already know there's nothing to see. My dragon cooked her to ash.

No, not my dragon. Me.

A voice says, "Andy?"

I gasp, convinced I'm hearing things.

"Andy? Answer me!"

"Kim?"

"I'm okay. How are you? Keep talking. Let me find my way over to you."

Moments later, I feel bare hands on me, touching my shoulders, my back. "Damn it, I wish I could see!" she complains. "But I think it worked."

"H… how?" I hear myself stammer.

"The heat your body generated sealed off the artery. Pretty amazing, really."

"No!" I exclaim. Frantically, I reach out in the dark, touching bare flesh.

"Watch it, buster! I'm as naked as you are."

"Oh, furk! Sorry."

She laughs.

"So, you *are* Kind!" I say.

"I don't know what that means."

"Kind!" I repeat as if that'll help. Then, biting the bullet—no pun intended—I add, "A Dragon."

"Oh! No… I'm not." I hear her stand and feel her way around the inside of the huge box. "Damn it, you were thorough. There were blankets and flashlights in a storage bin over here. But now there's just a puddle of metal. I never imagined your thermal discharge could be so powerful!"

That was nothing. If I'd died…

"If you're not a Dragon, like me," I say. "Then how are you still alive?"

"I can't make fire," Kim Shelton, aka Eurydice, replies. "But I can't be burned by it, either." Then after a long pause, she adds, "I guess I'm what you'd call a Split."

TEN – Glimpse

"Miranda, I'm disappointed."

"Yes, Father."

"You let yourself get too close to this creature."

"If you say so."

"I do say so, and I don't appreciate your tone. Do we know yet how Kimberly Shelton was able to contact him while he was aboard the coring unit?"

"We have a working theory. Regular comms channels were blocked during the ascent. But the CU *was* able to receive low-frequency telemetry requests. We think she may have piggy-backed on those."

"Clever."

"The Sheltons have always been innovative. It's one of the reasons we contracted them for the Europa Project."

"I can understand the value to her in turning our Dragon. But why surrender to us?"

"We're not sure. Our intention had been to interrogate her and then use her as leverage against her husband."

"And it didn't occur to you that she would have expected that?"

"Of course, it did. But the situation was what it was. That's why I decided at first to keep both her and Andy in the coring unit while we considered how to proceed."

"You should have separated them."

"In hindsight, maybe so. In any event, we needed time to search the lift and the surrounding landscape to confirm her surrender wasn't simply a diversion."

"And it wasn't?"

"There's no evidence to suggest it. So, I finally decided that I would distract Andy while Spencer escorted Doctor Shelton to the lander."

"But instead, the Dragon... liberated her."

"Yes."

"And killed a man in the process."

"That was an accident. In the panic of the moment, Andy lashed out."

"And then Spencer shot him."

"Against my direct orders."

"You sound angrier about that than about the death of one of our employees. A fellow human."

"Spencer's actions weren't driven by reason. He simply wanted revenge. We're lucky he didn't kill us all."

"And I intend to strongly reprimand Spencer about that. He acted precipitously and in the heat of the moment. Then again, as I understand it, he'd just watched the Dragon murder one of his men."

"Andy didn't mean to do it."

"And his father didn't mean to kill thousands in New York. Destruction is what these creatures are, Miranda."

"Father—"

"Miranda, I think it's time to make... a change... aboard Conquest.*"*

"What's that supposed to mean?"

"The Dragon's role in this mission is over. The new shaft has been successfully completed. You've done well on that score. However, this is now a purely military operation. For that reason, I've assigned Mister Spencer to the role of my adjunct going forward."

"What? No!"

"Miranda, I know you don't want to hear this."

"Father, what happened down on the surface today was—"

"A direct result of your unwise attachment to the Dragon. The fact is that, once he learned of his parents' fate, Mister Spencer should have put him down immediately. You stayed his hand, and, as a result, Doctor Shelton escaped, the mission was jeopardized, and a man was killed. You've known from the beginning what the Dragon's fate was likely to be. Isn't that true?"

"Well... yes. But Father—"

"But what? You were hoping I'd change my mind about that? I suspected as much, and that's why this reorganization of leadership is necessary. Spencer wounded the Dragon, yes? We detected some kind of thermal eruption several

hundred feet down MC-13's lift shaft, suggesting that he destroyed the lift car. While the Dragon may have survived the eruption, Doctor Shelton certainly did not. Do you agree with these statements?"

"Yes, but—"

"Then you'll also agree that we're left at a severe disadvantage. If the Dragon is, indeed, still alive, then his loyalties have been irrevocably flipped, and Mike Shelton has him. If, on the other hand, he's dead, then we can assume Shelton won't take kindly to the loss of his wife. Either way, our only option now is a full assault of MC-13 via the new shaft that the Dragon created. Again, do you agree?"

"I do."

"Then that's Spencer's area of expertise. It's time to end this ugly business, Miranda."

"Father, please listen. I—"

"Once we have regained control of the colony and dispatched the Dragon, the role of adjunct may fall back to you. Until then, you will defer to Spencer. Questions?"

"No. No questions."

"Good. We'll talk soon."

"Father."

"Yes, Miranda?"

"You're making a mistake."

"Good-bye, daughter."

ELEVEN – Glimpse

"Spencer?"

"Yes, Mister Coffin."

"Are you alone?"

"I am, sir."

"I've informed Miranda of the… change in leadership."

"Thank you."

"Spare me your gratitude. That shot you took on the surface today was ill-considered at best. You could easily have killed everyone at the landing site, including my daughter!"

"One of my men was murdered in front of me."

"I understand that, but my orders were to kill the Dragon with a single headshot. Instead, you wounded him."

"I… apologize, Mister Coffin."

"*Spare me your apologies, as well. It was a mistake, and I expect you to learn from it.*"

"Yes, sir."

"*As of now, you're my adjunct. You have full operational command of the mission. I've already notified Wei. I want you to prepare your blackbirds to descend the new shaft. We've lost the element of surprise, so I expect you to adjust your assault plans to compensate.*"

"Understood, Mister Coffin."

"*Let me make this clear: I want the colony taken and the colonists subdued. But this isn't to become another Vesta or Ramses. I don't want any deaths.*"

"I… don't know if I can guarantee that."

"*I'm aware of your feelings on the matter. For what it's worth, my daughter shares them. I concede that the circumstances have become dangerous, even dire. But my decision is final. We need Shelton and his people alive, for no other reason than any alternative outcome will further delay the resumption of tantalum mining efforts.*"

"Of course, sir."

"*But that doesn't mean your men need to be gentle. Make sure the colonists understand who's really in charge down there.*"

"Yes, sir."

PART FOUR
THE COLONIST

Maybe I passed out or something because I don't remember much about the rest of that miserable day. In fact, the next thing I *do* remember clearly is a dream. My second-ever memory dream. And this one sucks even worse than the first.

I'm standing on a busy sidewalk observing the glass frontage of a particular skyscraper on Sixth Avenue in New York. I'm with my wife. Traffic noises surround us. So do people. Neither of us likes crowds and would normally never consider a trip to such a congested city. But today, we have no choice.

The building we're both watching serves as headquarters for the richest man in America — the man whom Bonnie and I have come here to see.

Or maybe "ambush" is a better word.

After hours of loitering, unnoticed on the street, we see his limousine finally pull up. Moments later, five suited guards escort the man himself, looking filthy rich and supremely assured, safely inside his glass-and-steel fortress.

And Bonnie and I follow.

However, by the time we carefully cross the busy street (getting hit by a car while jaywalking is not an option) and enter through one of a half-dozen revolving doors, the billionaire is nowhere in sight. Frustrated, we announce ourselves at the security desk. I let my wife do the talking. She's better with people than I am.

Today, however, Bonnie's legendary charm falls flat. Instead of an audience with Coffin, or even a polite brush-off, the mention of our names triggers some sort of alarm.

Just thirty seconds later, the lobby is filled with suited men like the ones in the limo. Capable, dangerous-looking men.

Armed men.

They draw their guns, and I instinctively step between them and Bonnie, as if that'll help if they open fire. But they won't. If our names are enough to signal such an alert, then these people must know the reason for it.

Mustn't they?

"We don't want trouble," I say. "We just want to speak with Mister Coffin. It's about our son, Andy."

One of the men, a silver-haired fellow with a military bearing, replies flatly. "Mister Coffin isn't here, Mister Brand. Please leave the premises."

"We watched him come in. We know for a fact he's here."

"As we speak, Mister Coffin is boarding a rooftop helicopter and leaving the city."

"What? Why?"

The man smirks, though I notice he's sweating. They all are. "Why do you think?"

"We're not going to hurt anyone!" Bonnie exclaims from behind me. "We just want our son back!"

"The situation's been explained. I should think it would be clear, even to the likes of you."

"Likes of us?" says Bonnie darkly. "What's that supposed to mean?"

"Just leave, before you're forcibly removed. A restraining order is being issued. You won't be able to come within a mile of this building after today. If it were up to me, you wouldn't be able to come within a mile of this city, or any city for that matter."

I feel my anger rise. Dangerous anger. I suppress it, as always. Because, to a point, he's right. The Kind don't belong in cities. We stick to small towns, places where crime is low, and crowds are minimal, places where we don't need to drive much, if at all, and where it's safe to cross the street. Bonnie and I have lived our entire lives by that philosophy.

But philosophy goes right out the window in the face of what's been done to us.

"You kidnapped our son!" I exclaim. "We have the right to demand him back!"

"Then go ahead," the silver-haired man suggests, smirking again. "Swear out a complaint with the NYPD. Sue us in court. Or go to the press and tell them everything."

I feel my mouth snap shut. I'm stymied, and he knows it.

"But you won't," he remarks. "Will you, Brand?"

"We have rights," my wife says bitterly.

"Human beings have rights. You don't. Now, get out before I have you thrown out. From what I understand, you've been well-compensated for your 'sacrifice.'"

"I refused those deposits into our account," I tell him. "We don't want your money."

Bonnie adds, "We want our boy back!"

"Well, that's just too bad. He's gone. So, you'd both better get used to it."

"Gone?" I say with a gasp. "What are you talking about?"

"Little Andy's off on a trip," the silver-haired man says, grinning. "But, never fear. You'll get him back… eventually, though it'll probably be in a body bag."

A few of the others chuckle at this.

I sense it before my wife says a word. We've been together a long time. I know her moods. And I know when her anger gets the better of her.

"Bonnie," I say urgently. "Don't – "

She steps around me so abruptly that the silver-haired man retreats in alarm. "Give me my son, you furking asshole!"

I have time to marvel; Bonnie never curses, and often scolds Andy for doing so. But then I feel the heat radiating off her body.

Her dragon's on the rise.

I grasp her arm. "Stop," I tell her gently but firmly.

The silver-haired man pales. I can almost smell his fear, as real and palpable as Bonnie's heat. He's been taunting us, because – despite his briefings – a part of him doesn't truly believe. Human denial. The Kind rely on it. Humanity's stubborn refusal to accept the unfamiliar is often the best defense we have. But in this case, disbelief has turned into panic.

He raises his gun and, before I can really register what's happening, he shoots my beautiful, beloved Bonnie in the head.

She's gone in an instant, her dragon extinguished.

I watch her fall as if in a trance. My entire body goes cold.

The lobby is graveyard silent.

"Freak," the silver-haired man mutters. Then he turns his gun on me.

I throw myself across Bonnie's lifeless body. Whether I do this to avoid the headshot or simply out of horror and grief, I neither know nor care. I hear the silver-haired man's second shot. It strikes me in the side of my neck. Blood sprays out. Pain sears the point of impact. Hot pain. Very hot.

"The head!" someone yells. "You have to shoot it in the head!"

"I know!" the silver-haired man exclaims. "Let me just – "

My dragon comes out, and it comes out fast.

I think, I love you, Andy.

I snap awake. There are tears on my face.

I'm lying on my back on a bed. There's a needle in the crook of my arm that's plugged into a gadget beside me. It's beeping softly. The room is small, and its every surface is metal. There's one closed door—more of a hatch, really, with a singular wheel instead of a doorknob—and no windows.

The only other furniture in the room is a large chest of drawers and a single straight-back chair. They're metal, like everything else.

Oh, and the chair isn't empty.

"Bonnie?" the man asks.

He looks to be in his mid-thirties and of medium height, though that's hard to judge when somebody's sitting down. He's got a round, intelligent face with a tightly trimmed beard and short-cropped hair.

And he's a ginger. A *serious* ginger.

I'm still a little hazy from the horror I've just experienced. Gradually, as the fog lifts, I understand that I'm me, not my father, and that the memory dream I had showed me exactly how he and my mother died.

My stomach twists painfully.

"Nightmare?" the man asks with what sounds like genuine sympathy.

"Yeah," I gasp, though calling what I had a nightmare is like calling a hurricane a gentle zephyr. Until now, I always thought such visions were racial memories, somehow coded into our DNA. But what I just witnessed happened only days ago, so some other mechanism must be at work. A psychic link, maybe? But, right now, I can't think about it. I'm too busy struggling to regroup. I just watched my mother die, in-person and up-close through my father's eyes. The image has been burned into my mind, and right now, it's all I can do to keep from vomiting. But, for some reason, I don't want to do that here, not in front of this stranger.

With an effort, I manage to croak, "Who… are you?"

"I'm Mike Shelton. But please call me Shelton. Everybody does. Though I guess you might know me by my *nom de plume*, Orpheus."

"Orpheus…" I echo dully.

Shelton nods.

Orpheus and Eurydice.

I can feel my stomach settling.

Then I remember the lift. "Kim!" I yell, trying to sit up. Instantly, my head starts spinning.

"Whoa, friend! Relax. Lay back down."

"Is she okay?"

"She's fine. Frankly, she's a lot finer than you at the moment. You were in surgery this time yesterday, and you've got yourself about forty stitches, some on the inside and some on the outside. So, take it easy!"

I drop back onto the pillow, noticing for the first time how much my back hurts.

"Ouch," I mutter.

"First sensible thing you've said."

"Where am I?"

"You're on Marius. Where else would you be?"

"What's Marius?"

"You probably know it as Mining Colony 13. We rechristened it for Simon Marius, the German astronomer who gave Europa its name."

Who cares?

"How long have I been here?" I ask.

"Since yesterday. We went through a furk's worth of trouble rescuing you two. You managed to fry my cargo lift pretty good with your heat vision."

"It's not heat vision."

"Whatever. My guys had to ride up the service cables and replace a lot of onsite circuitry. Took about six hours. You slept through it, but poor Kim really had to pee by the time you both made it down here. Not to mention the fact you were both butt naked. You and I are going to have words about that, by the way."

"No! Our clothes… they burned off when I—"

"Relax. I'm just furking with you."

"Oh. But… I mean… you know what I am?"

"What you *are*? That's a pretty telling question. I know you're a Cancer, based on your birthday. I know you're in the 98.9 percentile for height and the 52.8 percentile for weight, which makes you pretty skinny. I know you live in New Jersey… or *did*, before Coffin kidnapped you. How am I doing?"

This guy's a wise ass.

"You know what I mean," I tell him sourly.

"And I know you're a Dragon," he finally concedes. "My point is that's not *all* you are. I get the impression you may have lost sight of that fact lately."

"And what are *you*?" I ask, suddenly irritated. "Some kind of shrink?"

"My wife's the shrink. I'm just a miner. But anybody who's spent a lot of time cooped up with a lot of other spacers in a tin can below a twenty-mile ice shelf on an alien moon learns quickly to look past the surface of things. There, I just gave you my life story in a single breath."

"Thanks," I say.

"Bonnie," he says.

"What?"

"Just before you woke up, you shouted 'Bonnie.'"

I feel my walls go up. Despite everything that's happened, Conceal and Protect is still my go-to. "My mom."

"Crap," Shelton replies. "I should have guessed that. Sorry. Do... did... you always call your mother by her first name?"

"Do you always go by your last?"

He bursts out laughing, but it dies quickly when he sees my expression. "Fair point. Okay, I think I've overstayed my welcome. I'll let you rest." He stands.

"Wait!" I exclaim, trying to sit up. The world spins. I lie back down. "What's happening on the surface? Is Miranda... Ms. Coffin... okay?"

He gives me a disbelieving look. "Seriously?"

I nod.

He sighs. "She's fine, as far as we know. Damn it, kid! The woman kidnapped you and has been lying to you non-stop, and you're still worried about her welfare? What did she do, take your virginity?" Then, when I don't reply, he groans and adds, "Oh. Well, jeez, I'm batting a thousand here, aren't I?"

"Forget it," I mutter, feeling my face redden.

"Forgotten," he replies. "Now, I *am* going to let you rest. Later, we have some serious stuff to talk about."

"Wait."

Shelton looks back at me expectantly.

I ask, "Um... is the lift... unusable?"

He nods.

"So, CSE can't get down here?"

"Not that way. The surface doors are shut again. And even if the blackbirds blow them open with explosives, the lift car's now a half-melted slag pile filling the shaft a few hundred feet down, and it's not going anywhere."

"What about the *other* shaft? The one I made."

"That's a problem. Fortunately, we knew what Coffin was planning, and we've been working on possible defenses. But now I've got a question for *you*. Are you asking me this stuff because you're worried about Spencer and his thugs pouring in here and firing every which way, or are you hoping that Miranda Coffin will ride to your 'rescue'?"

Despite my pain and the bitter memory of the New York dream, that remark moves me past irritation and into pissedoffland. "The way I remember it, I was the one who rode to Kim's rescue!"

"Well, yeah," he says. "Except, we weren't really interested in Kim *getting* rescued."

"What?"

"Did you really think Eurydice surrendered to Miranda Coffin… just so you could turn around an hour later, bust her loose, and return her to the lift? We wanted… *needed*… to get her onto that lander."

"She never mentioned that."

"I know."

"Was that because she was afraid someone was listening?"

He nods.

Then I add, "Or because she didn't trust me?"

At that, Shelton merely shrugs.

Annoyed, I point out, "If they'd taken her back up to *Conquest*, you'd probably never have seen her again!"

"If all had gone as planned, that wouldn't have mattered."

"Wouldn't have mattered?"

"Forget about it for now. We'll discuss it as soon as you're feeling better."

"Sure, you will," I mutter skeptically.

"Listen," he says. "I don't make too many promises, but I'm making this one right now: *No one* on Marius will ever lie to you. Now rest, will you? If I know my wife, she'll be in here waiting when you wake up again. It's just bum luck it happened on my watch. Since getting you both out of that lift, she's barely left your side. Seriously, if I know her… and I do… she'll be royally pissed that I was here for this and she wasn't."

Then, before I can reply, he leaves and shuts the metal door with a clang.

TWO – Day 20

When I wake up next, I'm both alone and feeling better.

I sit up, testing my pain level. My back hurts, but less than before. I wonder how long I've slept. Hours, certainly. Maybe a lot of them.

They apparently helped.

I notice for the first time that I'm dressed in one of those hospital smocks that ties in the back. No underwear. No shoes. Just this nursing-home standard. Fortunately, I'm skinny enough that the smock wraps fully around my torso. At least I won't be mooning the moon.

The only exit, the one Shelton used earlier, stands currently closed. I find myself wondering if it's *only* closed—or locked, as well. A locked door would suggest that, despite Shelton's "welcome to Marius" speech, I'm a prisoner again.

It's not a fancy door. No Liquid Bricks here. But it's heavy and tightly sealed, which I guess is no big surprise aboard a submerged colony. Apprehensively, I eye the wheel it has in place of a doorknob.

Do I feel strong enough to try it?

Tentatively, I slide off the bed and place my bare feet on the floor. My back protests, but the pain helps wake me up. Taking slow, measured breaths, I shift my weight and stand.

No dizziness. So far, so good.

Underwater or not, this is still Europa, meaning the gravity's low. But at least it is gravity and, while I wouldn't want to try jumping anytime soon, weighing a lot less does make it easier to support myself on legs that feel a little like overcooked linguine.

I'm still plugged into that futurey IV. Fortunately, the gadget's mounted on a rolling stand. There's even a convenient handle, clearly portable. So, taking hold of it, I hobble weakly over to the door.

With my free hand, I work the wheel. It turns easily and without complaint. Not locked. In fact, it doesn't take much turning before I hear the *clank* of internal bolts sliding aside. With a sigh, I push the door open.

Outside is a corridor, narrow and with a low ceiling. More doors, just like mine, line both sides of it. There's no one in sight. The light comes from a series of simple ceiling lamps. Still no Liquid Bricks. Everything looks utilitarian and unremarkable. Here it seems, unlike aboard *Conquest*, lights are lights and doors are doors.

In one direction, the hallway goes for about thirty feet before ending in some kind of big round chamber. The other way, it continues for maybe half that distance before hitting a wall with a single door. A sign mounted beside it reads: "Breakroom."

My stomach growls. Breakrooms often mean food, and I suddenly can't remember the last time I ate anything.

So, I head that way, rolling my IV pole along with me. My bare feet make almost no noise. But I notice, as I walk, that my hospital smock flutters around me dangerously in the low-G. I find I need to slowly shuffle my feet or risk a mooning event after all.

Fortunately, I encounter no one.

This door opens as easily as the last one did, providing access to a large, well-furnished room. It's got several long tables, a fridge, microwave, and everything else you'd expect from a simple cafeteria. Like the rest of the colony I've seen so far, it's empty.

Leaving the door open, I step deeper inside. Almost immediately, the dim lights get brighter — motion sensor, I suppose — and by this new illumination, I spot a plate of chocolate chip cookies sitting on a nearby counter.

My stomach growls louder.

I pick up a cookie and sniff it. It smells good. I bite into it. It tastes even *better*. It's oddly hard to swallow, which makes me think maybe I'm still a little nauseous. Nevertheless, a moment later, hunger wins, and the cookie vanishes.

I chase it with another.

And a third.

With a contented sigh, I open the refrigerator. There's quite a bit of food inside; most of it organized into plastic containers. Along the fridge door, I find single-serve juice packets. I pick an apple-flavored one.

The juice goes the same way as the cookies.

Somewhat sated, I turn toward the far wall, which seems to be just one big observation window. Beyond it is a world of black liquid.

Curious, I approach the viewport, my eyes scanning the darkness. Suddenly, my science nerd's heart is pounding. Hey, why not? I'm *here*! On Europa! And this is my first glimpse of what hides beneath the moon's almost impenetrable surface ice.

An ancient planetary ocean.

As I reach the window, still dragging my IV pole, outer lights come on—probably another motion sensor reacting to my presence. The lamps are big and jut out from the colony's hull like giant bulky spiders. But they push back the darkness beautifully, revealing a world that I can only describe as, well, alien.

The first thing I notice is the ice shelf. Not surprisingly, it hangs overhead, about ten feet above me, and extends as far as the eye can see. The inverted landscape looks nothing at all like the cracked and uneven Europan surface. Down here, the ice is perfectly level and as smooth as glass, except for an odd concave indentation directly above the colony. In fact, the colony seems to be sitting within that indent, fastened in place by tractor trailer-sized clamps. The weird indent is huge, much bigger than the colony nested inside it, with gradually sloping walls of sheer, dark ice.

It takes me a few moments to figure out what made it.

The water outside the viewport ripples slightly. It's subtle and hard to spot unless you're looking for it, but I've seen too much thermal energy in my life to miss it, even underwater. Somewhere below us, lost in the unlit depths, there's a source of hardcore heat.

The water itself is *very* clear but not blue or green like the waters on Earth. When I say clear, I mean exactly that. It's like looking through empty air. In fact, without the visible distortion caused by the rising column of heat, I might almost have thought there was no water out there at all.

I press my palm tentatively against the glass, expecting to find it cold. This is an ice moon, after all. Instead, warmth, steady and oddly comforting, greets my skin.

Yep. Definitely hardcore heat.

That's when something strikes the viewport.

From the *outside*, I mean.

I don't scream. That's my story, and I'm sticking to it.

But I *do* yank my hand back and retreat a step.

Then I stare—not believing.

A *creature* stares back at me.

A furking alien.

It's not large, maybe the size of a monkey or a big squirrel. It's got a head perched atop narrow shoulders and four arms, two sticking out of each side of a gray-blue torso that's so thin that I could wrap one

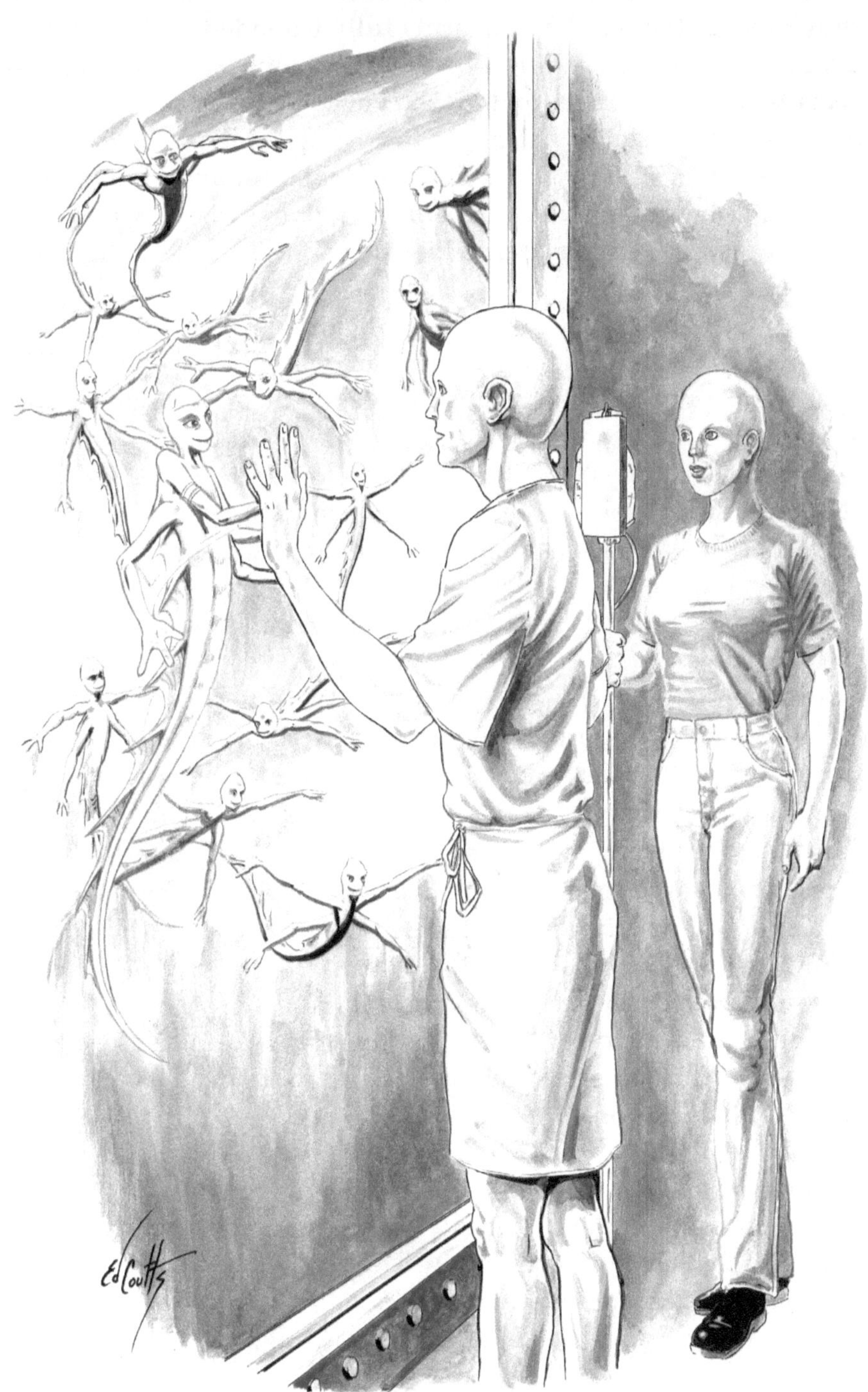

hand all the way around it. Each of its three-fingered hands is pressed firmly against the window, its arms fully extended and forming a kind of "X" with the creature's body as its middle. Thin membranes stretch between the upper and lower arms on each side. Once again, I'm reminded of a squirrel, this time the flying variety.

Instead of legs, the creature has a muscular fin that's longer than the rest of its body combined. There are no gills or scales, just two large eyes that regard me with open curiosity, and a slit of a mouth that's pressed tightly closed.

And it's wearing—something. Not clothing, but jewelry. Two tiny lengths of metal, like rough wire, are wound loosely around its upper right arm. For several moments I study them, wondering what they're for.

Then the creature shifts, its four hands skittering a few feet to the left. Its eyes never leave me, and I get the feeling it's trying to change its perspective—to get a look at me from a different angle.

I turn a little, so it can see my profile.

Its eyes widen slightly. Then it does something that sends a chill down my spine.

It smiles.

The corners of its lipless mouth turn upward, the movement exaggerated so that the smile takes up almost half of its little face. It shows no teeth, if it even has teeth. In fact, it doesn't open its mouth at all. I get the strong and deeply unsettling feeling that this is an expression of appreciation. It wanted a better look at me, and I gave it one, and now it's smiling in gratitude.

A voice says, "That's Ravi."

I whirl around, my heart in my throat.

Kim Shelton stands in the breakroom entrance. She's dressed in jeans and a t-shirt, just as her husband had been. Her head is completely bald, her dark hair gone.

I did that.

Out loud, all I can manage is a stuttering, "W-what?"

"We named him Ravi," she replies, stepping into the brightly lit room. "We think he's the community's leader."

"You mean… there's more of them?"

Kim laughs. Then, her blue eyes sparkling, she nods over my shoulder.

I turn and look.

Ravi's no longer alone.

Suddenly there are dozens of them.

Each is different, though all are clearly of the same species. They practically fill the window, their eyes fixed on me as if I'm the most incredible thing they've ever seen. In their midst, Ravi is still smiling.

For several long seconds, all I can do is gape.

Then Ravi lifts one of his four hands from the glass and, as I watch transfixed, gestures with it. Gestures to *me*.

Coming up behind me, Kim remarks, "He wants you to move closer."

As I do so, Ravi's smile gets even wider. His gestures become more urgent while, around him, the rest of them grow agitated, excited.

I stop within a foot of the viewport. Ravi has shifted again so that he's right in front of me, almost at eye level.

He keeps gesturing.

Nervously, I touch my palm once again to the clear polymer.

Ravi's gesturing hand meets it, his small fingers pressed opposite my own, his tiny palm to my big one, his three digits to my five.

The rest of them all smile. Most are shaking.

"What are they doing?" I ask.

"Not sure," Kim replies. "They do that when they're happy or excited about something."

"What are they excited about? Me?"

"You're the first new person they've seen, and you're interacting with them. They like that. They're incredibly social and welcoming, and they clearly find us as interesting as we find them."

"But… what *are* they?"

Kim hesitates. Then she says, somewhat sheepishly, "We call them dragons."

THREE – Day 20

I moan. "You've got to be kidding me!"

Kim moves up to stand beside me. Instantly, a percentage of the creatures—*dragons*—shift around the window to study her, though I notice that the overwhelming majority stay with me. I suppose that's because they know Kim already.

Well, either that or I'm really fascinating.

"Believe me, nobody appreciates the unintended irony more than I do."

"But why?" I ask, wanting to look at her but unable to pull my eyes away from the viewport. "Why pick *that* name, for God's sake?"

"A first impression, I guess. I was the first to spot one… and with their skinny arms, tails, and fleshy, wing-like membranes, they made me think of dragons."

"*I* thought of squirrels."

She laughs at that. Then, more thoughtfully, she adds, "Besides, we're pretty sure they live inside Smokey."

"Smokey?"

"It's what we call the smoker that's below us. Not very imaginative, I know."

"What's a smoker?"

"The scientific name for it is a hydrothermic vent. They're caused when seawater filters through the oceanic crust and encounters magma. Then it gets heated to seven hundred degrees or so Fahrenheit and comes shooting back up, creating vents of incredibly hot plumes of smoke in the deep ocean. Black smokers form from iron sulfide deposits. White smokers are usually barium or calcium or some other mineral that burns white."

I look past the dragons at the thermal ripples in the water. "But here it's clear," I remark.

"That's because the dragons scrub them clean. As far as we can tell, they live their lives in and around Smokey, feeding off organic molecules and trace minerals spewed out by the moon's molten core. It's an astonishingly simple ecology. Just them and their food. Far less complex than anything on Earth. Our staff biologist can't even make a guess as to how these creatures evolved."

At first, I'm surprised that a mining colony would even *have* a staff biologist. But then I remember that, despite the privatization of space travel, exploration is still considered as important as profit, at least officially. According to international law, even commercial colonies must devote some minimal amount of time and resources to the search for life off-Earth.

And it looks like this one *found* it.

Kim says, "But the mystery's bigger even than that. So far, we've found only one smoker on Europa. It's why we decided to locate Marius here in the first place. And it's a *big* one, orders of magnitude larger than anything like it on Earth. Yet it's also alone. We've launched probes but identified no other smokers and no other communities of dragons living off them. Just here. It's… bizarre."

Sure, but somehow the fact that there aren't *more* aliens seems to pale beside the fact that there are aliens *at all*. The whole thing is almost mind-boggling enough to let me forget what happened to my family.

Almost.

My dad would have been so blown away by this. He is — was — almost as big a science nerd as me.

I clear my throat and ask, "What's… Ravi… wearing around his arm?"

"Noticed that, huh? We think it's a sign of rank. Two bracelets identify Ravi as the leader, chief, community elder, whatever. We don't know how they're fashioning the bracelets. They're obviously made of unprocessed metal, though we can't know what kind since we've never had one for study. Shelton thinks they've found a vein of the stuff in or around the smoker… that *they're* miners, too. We tried sending a probe down into Smokey to find out, but it stopped functioning immediately. The caldera is eighty miles down, and the heat's intense. We know it's there, but, to date, nobody's so much as laid eyes on it, let alone conducted any metallurgic studies. Anyway, as far as I'm concerned, it doesn't matter where the dragons get their jewelry. The bottom line is that *having* it proves they're intelligent."

"Yeah," I say. "I guess it does."

"And self-aware, intensely curious, and quick to learn. They never used to smile. It's a trait they've picked up from us. The waving, too. They have their own language, which they speak using their long single fins. It's vibratory and high-pitched. We've recorded it using underwater mics but, so far, haven't been able to interpret it."

I look back at the dragons, marveling.

Intelligent life.

But there are other things that need talking about. So, with an effort, I tear my eyes away from the miracles outside the viewport and meet Kim's gaze. "Listen," I say tentatively. "I'm… sorry about what happened on the lift."

She rubs her newly bald head and replies with a shrug, "No real harm done."

"So… you're a Split."

She nods.

"I've never met a Split before."

"I've never met a Dragon before."

I almost tell her that we don't like that word. For some reason, I don't. Instead, I ask, "Was it your mom or your dad?"

"My dad. My mom... she died having me."

"Sorry."

"Thanks."

Deaths like that happen a lot with Splits, or so I've heard. Usually, either the mother, baby, or both die due to the high temperatures one or the other generates during labor. That's why Splits are so rare.

"So, you were raised by your dad?"

Kim hesitates. "I... don't usually talk about this. Not even with Shelton."

I get that. I do. But no way am I letting this go. "Since being pulled into all this, I've been dragged halfway across the Solar System, lied to, experimented on, and lost my family. You're the closest thing to Kind I've met since leaving Earth. That means maybe, just *maybe*, I can trust you. But you've got to earn that trust, Kim. You've got to make me believe."

"'Kind,'" she remarks. "I'd never heard that term before two days ago."

"Your father didn't share the Chronicles with you?"

"He wasn't around. I don't remember him at all. I was raised by my mother's sister. She still doesn't know what I am... or, if she does, it's not something we ever talk about. Everything I know about Drag—" She catches herself. "– about *Kind*, I learned on my own. For a long time, I thought I was a freak. It wasn't until I was a teenager, scouring the dark web, that I found my first reference to your people. That's when I started finally... understanding myself."

I glance toward the viewport. There are even more dragons now, perhaps as many as a hundred, all pressed up to the outside of the polymer. Can they hear us? That seems unlikely. Heck, I can't even tell if they have ears. Maybe they just like the way our lips move when we talk.

I say to Kim, "So... you can't be burned?"

"Nope. Well, except for my hair."

I point to my own head. "Been there. Done that."

For some reason, the dragons find this gesture hilarious. All of them start shaking.

Kim, on the other hand, manages only a forced smile. "When I was young, I scared my aunt half to death. I had no fear of flames. Zero. We had a fireplace, and, in the winter, when it was lit, I'd sit in front of it for hours, just... staring. Then, when no one was looking, I'd stick my hand in and just kind of stroke the burning wood. My hand would come back sooty, but that was it."

That computes. From early childhood, Kind are taught never to "display" like that. But Kim wouldn't have gotten that lesson.

"One day, of course, my aunt *did* catch me. Gave me a good scolding and made me promise never to do it again. Then, a couple of years later, I ran through the kitchen playing and tripped her while she was carrying a hot pan full of fried bacon for breakfast. The grease spilled all over my arm and back."

"But no burns," I guess.

"No burns. My aunt told me tearfully that I was 'lucky' and, after that, we never spoke of it. I was only eight at the time, but I got the message. I was a freak."

Sounds like a sucky childhood to me.

I ask, "Where's your aunt now?"

"Back in Philadelphia, on Earth. She loved me like I was her own and put me through college. She's the only parent I've ever had. But this is the one part of myself I've never been able to share with her."

"Does Mike know?"

"Shelton," she corrects me.

"Okay, does *Shelton* know?"

"Of course. But I didn't tell him right away, not until well after I joined Shelton Metals and he and I started... dating. After a while, it got serious, and I figured he had a right to know who, or what, he said he wanted to marry."

"How about the crew here on Marius? Do they know?"

"I've never formally announced it, but pretty much everyone knows. Shelton and I aren't big on lying, especially to our friends."

"That's... refreshing."

"Besides, there have been times when my... unique nature... came in handy around here."

"On an ice moon?"

"You'd be surprised."

"Kim, I can't remember the last time I *wasn't* surprised."

"Fair enough. My turn. You're not the only one with questions. Before you came along, I'd never met a… Kind. What little I've managed to research is all second- or third-hand. You people aren't big on written records."

"Just the Chronicle."

"You mentioned that before. What is it?"

"It's a big collection of memoirs and other stuff. You know about the Jewish Talmud? It's kind of like that. No single author. It's been collected over time and eventually got put up on the dark web."

"I never found it," she remarks wistfully.

"It's not easy to find."

"I guess not. And I suppose Kind don't keep a lot of diaries."

"Sure, we do. Sometimes. In fact, keeping personal journals is kind of encouraged."

"Really?"

"Absolutely. Except you never, ever mention the Kind. It's…" I struggle with how to describe it.

"…one more method of camouflage," Kim finishes for me. "You're literally encouraged to write a fake diary so that if anyone finds it, it'll throw them off the scent."

"Yeah. We call it Conceal and Protect. Capital letters."

"That has to have been tough. Never being able to confide in anybody outside your family."

"It's all I ever knew."

"Were there other Kind around?"

"In Haddonfield, New Jersey? No. Once a year or so, we'd visit my mother's relatives up in New York. But, even as a kid, it was uncomfortable. My cousins and I were all trained never to discuss our dragons, not even with each other. It put up this… wall… between us. It's hard to explain."

"No, I get it. Splits like me are even rarer than Dragons. Oh! Sorry." I shrug.

"Is it considered a bad thing?" she asks.

"You mean calling us Dragons? Honestly, I'm kind of getting used to it."

"No. I mean being a Split. In some cultures, half-breeds are…" Her words trail off.

"I've never met any other Splits, but I certainly don't have a problem with you being one. Mating with humans is discouraged.

But that's more about practicality than prejudice. It makes for risky pregnancies."

"Yeah, I read that…"

"Here's how it is," I tell her. "In our culture, all Kind are brother and sister to all other Kind. We may not talk about it, but that's the way it works. So, I guess, by that reckoning, you're my half-sister."

"Oh," she says, brightening. "I like that."

"Me too."

"I went by your room looking for you just now and discovered you'd decided to take a walk. Probably not a great idea, but you seem to be doing okay."

"Yeah. Low-G helps."

"Just mind the ceiling. Don't jump too high on Marius. You'll clunk your head."

"Good tip. Thanks. Um… could I get something to wear? This smock keeps… floating up. It's kind of drafty."

She laughs. "Sure. Those things aren't meant to be walked around in, at least not on Europa. Don't worry. We'll hook you up. But, for now, how about getting back to bed? You still need rest."

"I've had enough rest. I want to see more of the colony."

"This isn't *Conquest*," Kim tells me. "We don't have Liquid Bricks that float up between levels. We have stairs and ladders."

"Oh."

"Give it until tomorrow. Okay, Andy?"

"I guess."

"Good. Then you, me, and Shelton can discuss what comes next."

I nod, a little reluctantly — though, truth be told, I can feel myself starting to wear out. "But before I do the 'good patient' thing, can I ask one more question?"

"Sure."

I swallow nervously. "Um… did I… kill someone up on the surface?"

"Andy, it was an accident."

"But did I?"

She doesn't hesitate. Well, not much. "I'm afraid so. But it wasn't your fault."

"Wasn't it?"

"I was there. I saw what happened."

I nod, though I'm unconvinced. Almost absently, my eyes return to the viewport. The dragons are still there, and this time all their attention seems fixed on me. Their smiles are gone. Instead, their huge eyes seem full of—what? Sympathy? But that's ridiculous. They can't hear us and, even if they could, they wouldn't grasp what happened, what I *did*.

Would they?

"Why am I here?" I mutter.

"What?" Kim asks.

I meet her gaze. "I said... why am I here? Coffin kidnapped me to use me to get through the surface ice so that Spencer and his blackbirds could reach you all. But they only did that because Shelton and you, Orpheus and Eurydice, sent those comms to CSE, declaring Europa's independence. Why'd you do that?"

At first, Kim doesn't reply. Finally, she nods toward the viewport. "Because of them."

"Them? The dragons?"

"Yes. We found out that our tantalum mining was killing them."

FOUR – Glimpse

"How's our patient?"

"Back in his room. He wandered into the Breakroom, med cart in tow."

"Did he? Kid's tougher than he looks."

"When I found him, he was interacting with the dragons."

"Yeah? Well, so much for easing him into things slowly. Just so long as you didn't tell him about the tantalum."

"Um..."

"Kim!"

"Shelton, he and I had a really good talk. We can trust him!"

"Is that right? And, during your 'good talk,' did he happen to mention that he lost his virginity to Miranda Coffin?"

"*What?*"

"Yeah, I was going to tell you before, but you were on shift."

"Seriously?"

"Do you think I'd make a thing like that up?"

"Damn."

"It changes things."

"Not necessarily. I saw the way he treated her up on the surface. Whatever the two of them had going is over."

"Is that your professional opinion or just something you want to be true?"

"Both, wise ass."

"Did you take the samples?"

"Darcy's got them. They're viable, but she says it'll be at least a day or two before we know anything even halfway definite."

"Are you going to tell him you took them?"

"Eventually. I don't want to freak him out while he's healing."

"Nice rationalization, Kim."

"I know…"

"Well, tell him or don't. It's your call. Just don't spill anything else about our situation. At least, not yet."

"Didn't you promise we wouldn't lie to him?"

"Yeah, but that's not the same as telling him everything."

"It's not like he can run back to the surface and give away all our secrets."

"It's not him 'running back to the surface' that worries me, and you know it."

"He's a person, not a bomb."

"Kim, he's a person who can *become* a bomb. Look what happened in the lift, and you told me yourself that was him trying to hold it back."

"Andy's not the bad guy here."

"Maybe not. But until I know for sure whose side he's on, I want to play our cards close to the chest. Okay?"

"Hmm."

"Kim. *Okay?*"

"Okay, *boss.*"

"Kim, you're the only person I've ever met who can make 'boss' sound like 'furkhead.'"

"If you say so, boss."

FIVE – Day 21

I killed somebody.

Kim dubbed it an accident, and I suppose it was. But that doesn't make the guy any less dead or me any less responsible. It's every Kind's most primal fear. We have the power. Humans have the numbers. The inevitable result of an inter-species war would be mutual destruction. So, a long time ago, my people declared an edict—unspoken like all the rest—but universal.

Kind don't kill.

Yet I did.

I'm a killer. Maybe not a murderer, *per se*, but *"per se"* feels paper-thin right now.

So, lying alone in my small room, I don't sleep.

Until, finally, I do. This time there are no Memory Dreams.

Just nightmares.

When I next open my eyes, Kim is standing at my bedside, checking my pulse. She's wearing a different jeans and t-shirt combo than in the Breakroom, so I guess I slept through whatever passes for "night" down here.

Meeting my bleary eyes, she smiles and asks, "How are you feeling?"

I run a quick internal diagnostic. My shoulder blade still hurts, but it seems to have hit a low baseline. Whatever painkiller's in that IV, it's doing its job and doesn't seem to be making me loopy.

"Not bad," I reply. And that's true if I discount the fact that, every time I close my eyes, I see either my mother getting headshot or my burning palm melting into that blackbird's face.

"Glad to hear it," she says. "Mind if I ask a personal question?"

"You mean *another* one?"

She sticks her tongue out at me. It's a silly gesture, but one I might appreciate if I wasn't so furking depressed.

I reply, "Why not? I seem to be out of secrets."

"Have you ever been hurt like that before?"

"You mean *shot?*"

"I mean any kind of serious injury. Ever break a bone, for example?"

"No. A few bruises and skinned knees. I wasn't what you'd call a rough-and-tumble kid."

"Would you say that's a cultural thing or particular to you?"

My hackles rise. "You're starting to sound like Okeke."

I expect her to ask me who Okeke is, but she doesn't. "Sorry. Like I said, you're the first of my father's people I've ever met."

My hackles lower, a little. As excuses for prying go, that one's—reasonable. "It might be a trait of the Kind. I don't think the Chronicles specifically mention it. But we naturally try to avoid getting seriously hurt because of the risk of..."

She remarks, "It's just that you're healing awfully fast."

"Am I?"

"Are you in any pain?"

"A little sore, maybe. But I figured the painkillers—"

"Andy, we're not giving you any painkillers. We don't know your physiology well enough to safely prescribe them. That drip is just to keep you hydrated."

I look from her to the IV, then back to her.

"My stitches..."

"Are still there. But I checked them when I came in just now. They look ten days old, not three. The internal ones have probably been absorbed already, and the external ones seem ready to come out."

I flashback to something my dad once said. Were we in the woods or the living room? I don't suppose it matters. "If you ever *do* get hurt, son, the first thing to do is stay calm, not just for your own sake but for the sake of any humans around you. The second thing to remember is that your dragon is *not* your enemy. It's there to protect you. It isn't something separate or apart from you. It *is* you."

But does my dragon protecting me extend to fast healing? If so, neither of my parents ever said as much.

And now they never will.

I push that thought away. Between guilt and grief, I'll fall to pieces if I'm not careful.

Swallowing dryly, I say, "I didn't know about that."

"I've never read about it either," Kim replies. "And I've been researching... Kind... all my life. So, there's nothing in the Chronicles?"

"I don't think so. But I haven't read *all* of it."

"You haven't?"

"Well, there's a *lot* there. Something like twenty thousand pages, and only about two-thirds were ever translated into English."

Kim smiles ruefully. "That wouldn't stop me. I'd read it with a pocket dictionary if I had to."

I don't tell her that, when my parents ordered me to study the Chronicles, I often surfed the web instead.

As if sensing my discomfort, Kim raises a hand. "Forget it. I have to remind myself that you grew up knowing this stuff. For a Split like me, who's been chasing her heritage forever, a font of knowledge like that would be gold."

I almost apologize but catch myself. Apologize for *what*, exactly?

An awkward moment passes between us. I think it's our first.

Finally, Kim asks, "Um… do you want me to take the stitches out?"

"You know how to do that?"

"Well, normally our staff biologist does it. She's our medic. But she's on shift right now down in the labs. Don't worry, though. I've got first-aid training, including applying and removing sutures. Who do you think sewed you up in the first place?"

"Oh."

"I'll spray on a local anesthetic. You won't feel a thing."

"Okay," I say.

Kim goes to work, and, aside from a weird pulling sensation, she's as good as her word. For the first couple of minutes, neither of us says anything. Then Kim suddenly remarks, "I never thanked you."

"For what?"

"For coming to my rescue up on the surface."

"Yeah? Your husband… Shelton… told me I shouldn't have done that, that you'd surrendered yourself for a reason."

"I did, and he's right, you shouldn't have. But it was still brave."

"What *was* the plan, anyway?" I ask as she pulls the last stitch. "Why just turn yourself in?"

"Well, part of it was so that you and I could connect in person."

"I get that. Now, how about telling me the rest, and I hope this isn't going to be another 'we'll get to that later' thing."

"Not from me, brother."

"You wouldn't talk to me about it up on the surface."

"I didn't know you then like I do now. Besides, I was afraid your girlfriend was listening."

"She's not my girlfriend!"

"*Was* she?"

I frown. "I guess so."

"Did you formally break up with her?"

"We were done the minute I found out how much she's been lying to me."

"And you're sure she *knows* that?"

I have no reply. The fact is I've never broken up with anyone. I'm not sure I know how to do it—formally.

Kim nods. "That's what I thought."

"Shelton thinks I'm still hung up on her. That's why he doesn't trust me. "

"He's not as good a judge of character as I am. People get into their 'trust zone' at different paces."

"That's a shrink thing to say."

She shrugs.

"So?" I ask. "What *was* the gambit on the surface all about?"

"My environment suit had a small, short-range device built into it. Once I was inside the lander, it would have automatically hacked into the onboard comms, interfaced with *Conquest* and, from there, the Casimir Radio."

"The Casimir Radio?" Then the seemingly ever airborne penny drops. "You wanted to send a transmission to Earth!"

"It's bigger than 'want.' It's pretty much the only hope we have and, perhaps more importantly, the only hope *they* have."

"They?"

"The dragons."

"Oh." Did I really almost forget about the native Europans? Kim told me in the Breakroom that the tantalum mining was killing them but never explained how.

But that can wait. Other things are percolating between my ears. "So, you can't get any transmissions to Earth?"

"Nope. Even if we had the means to launch one, communication satellites don't last long around here. Nothing can orbit Europa, not with Jupiter so close by. And nothing electronic can withstand that big bastard's magnetic field. Since we've been here, the only way to send a message to Earth has been via the supply ship. But, naturally, since Orpheus and Eurydice debuted, CSE has made damned sure that our declarations are kept strictly in-house."

"Does Charles Coffin know about the… dragons?" Furk, even when I'm not talking about myself, I don't particularly like that word.

"Of course."

"And Miranda? Does she know?"

"Yep."

I shouldn't be surprised *or* disappointed, but I'm both.

I say, "She played me an audio clip of either you or Shelton.... the voice was disguised... declaring that no more tantalum would be delivered until Coffin Industries publicly acknowledged Europa's independence. She must have faked it to get me to play along."

"No. That was us. Well, Shelton actually."

"But it didn't mention any native lifeforms."

"It also wasn't the first communication. Listen, this is going to be a long story, and I'd like Shelton to be in on it. I've got some clothes for you. What say you get dressed and we go down to Ops?"

"Sure. Um… can I have a minute to change?"

"Why so shy?" she asks. "We've already been naked together." Then, before my discomfort can turn into full-blown horror, she bursts out laughing. "Sorry, couldn't resist. I'll be in the hall."

Everybody's a comedian.

SIX – Day 21

It turns out that Marius isn't anything like *Conquest.*

Where CSE's prototype ship is long and sleek with many levels, Marius is squat and drab and has only three decks. My room and the Breakroom are on the Ice Deck, called that because it's the one closest to the ice shelf's underside. This is the residential deck, Kim tells me — which is why, during mid-shifts, it tends to be empty. Everybody's either sleeping or working below.

Kim explains, "Nobody's room is any bigger than anybody else's on Marius. It's a fairness thing… part of Shelton's all-for-one management style. It makes things tight for the married couples, like Shelton and me, but we get by."

I wonder what "getting by" means. Then I decide I don't really want to know.

The Ice Deck is designed with corridors branching out from a central hub, like wheel spokes, each with its own shared bathrooms. "Showers are communal and co-ed," Kim explains. "So, I'm sure you'll feel right at home."

I swallow back a sarcastic response.

At the hub of the "wheel" is a large round room with a wide, central, spiral staircase that winds downward. As we approach, a handful of locals appear at the top of it, chatting amongst themselves—the first people I've met on Marius who aren't Orpheus or Eurydice.

Four of them are adults in their thirties, but the other two are young—around my age. All wear the same jeans and t-shirt combo that Kim and I have on. This seems to be the Marius "uniform." Each of their shirts is uniquely adorned with a picture, slogan, or complex, abstract design.

Noticing Kim first, the six of them nod greetings.

Then they all see me—and freeze.

Queue the spotlight.

"Hi," I say into the weighty silence.

"This is Andy," Kim announces pleasantly. "Andy, these are—" She rattles off names that I forget as soon as she says them.

After several mile-long seconds, one of the women shakes my hand. That gets the rest of them to follow suit. A short bald guy with a mustache that almost looks like it's eating his face actually hugs me. "I hear we have you to thank for bringing Kim back to us. When she took the lift up to meet you, most of us figured we might never see her again."

"Um… sure," I stammer.

"We're heading down to Ops to see Shelton," Kim says, looking a bit uncomfortable herself. Whatever decision was reached and by whom to send her up the surface to "surrender" had clearly been a tough one.

"He's there," one of the women reports. "So's Francis."

"Great. I thought he was on night shift this week."

"He is, but you know how he gets during a crisis."

"Sadly, I do."

"Who's Francis?" I ask.

"Francis Swift. Head of Ops," Carnivorous Mustache replies. "But, around here, everyone calls him Saint Francis the Objector."

"Why?"

"You'll find out," another guy remarks. "Wouldn't want to color your opinion."

"Enough," Kim says, not unkindly. "You all up here for lunch?"

They are.

"Then get to it. Breaks are liable to get few and far between once things start heating up around here."

"No pun intended," I add before I can stop myself.

They all look at me. Their smiles falter, even Kim's.

Apparently, everybody's a comedian… but me.

"Got it," I say uncomfortably. "No fire jokes."

"I like him," the first woman announces, grinning. She looks the closest to my age — short, petite, and with close-cropped hair died a deep purple. "Welcome to paradise under the ice."

"Thanks," I say. She's wearing a black t-shirt printed with the words "No boyfriend, no problem."

I suddenly wish I could remember her name.

"Well, enjoy, guys," Kim says. "We've got business downstairs."

"Sure thing," Carnivorous Mustache says. "See you around, Andy. And a quick piece of advice. Keep the gallows humor to yourself. Down here, life's a little too precarious for that."

"Okay," I mutter. "Right."

Kim leads me down the spiral staircase. As we pass the second floor, identified as the Lab Deck, and continue down toward what I presume is Ops, my escort remarks, "Darcy."

"What?"

"Darcy. That's her name."

"Who?"

"The purple-haired girl who smiled at you. Darcy Piatkowski. She's a biologist and our resident medic."

"*She's* your doctor?"

"A medic, not a doctor. She was apprenticed to our last one."

"You have apprentices?" I ask.

"We're spacers, Andy. Apprenticeship is how spacers, most of them anyway, learn a trade. Darcy joined us when the colony was first founded. She was fifteen at the time. She's seventeen now. When she got here, she was a gawky girl, though stone-cold brilliant. Well, she's still brilliant, but the last two years have blossomed her, wouldn't you say?"

"Sure," I mutter uncomfortably.

Kim smiles but says nothing more.

At the bottom of the staircase, a large round viewport is built into the floor. It looks down into the depths of Europa's planetary ocean, and, when we reach it, I stop for a moment and stare. What strikes me most is how clear the polymer seems, almost as if it isn't there.

Then, with a gasp, I realize it *isn't* there.

"We call it the moon pool," Kim tells me. "Get it?"

I get it.

Crouching down, I reach a tentative hand toward the smooth surface. I half-expect Kim to stop me, but she doesn't. I take this as permission.

My fingers slip into water that's unexpectedly warm and feels like — well — water.

I pull my hand out and sniff my fingertips.

"It's… fresh."

"Yes, it is," Kim replies.

"I thought Europa's ocean was supposed to be salty."

"Oh, there's *some* salt. It's basically rich, complex mineral water, not too dissimilar from what you'd find in the Great Lakes back on Earth. Different trace elements, though."

"Like tantalum."

"Lots of tantalum," she says. "There's also some cadmium and chromium, all sorts of organic molecules, and even surprisingly high concentrations of deuterium. That's a hydrogen isotope. Also, some oceanic regions are saltier than others. I know that doesn't really fit with the rules of salinity, but water behaves more peculiarly in low-G than anyone suspected. Depending on temperature and currents, the salinity of Europa's ocean varies wildly. Here, most of the time, it's low."

"Is it drinkable?"

"In a pinch, but we tend to filter it thoroughly before we use it. Even so, it means we don't have to recycle moisture, the way they do on mining colonies in the asteroid belt."

"Do the dragons ever come into the… moon pool?"

"Occasionally. They don't breathe air but do seem to enjoy poking their heads up and looking around. A few have even tried climbing out of the pool. But they always go right back in again. Our air pressure is probably uncomfortable for them. We *think* they need oxygen the same way fish do on Earth, but we're not sure. They don't have any visible gills." Then she adds, almost out of the blue, "We swim with them."

"What?"

"During our off-hours, some of us get into the pool and swim with them. There's a safety cylinder that extends down about fifty feet, as wide as the pool itself. It's there to block any currents so that the moon pool doesn't flood the Ops Deck, and it's always calm. The temp's a steady 84 degrees Fahrenheit, so it's like bathwater."

"People swim with the dragons?"

"Yep."

"Have you ever done it?"

"Sure! It's…" Her expression turns wistful. "…amazing."

"Wow," I say.

I mean… swimming with aliens. Seriously?

When I finally straighten, my head swims a little. I tell myself it's because I stood up too fast, but I know better. It's just all a lot to process.

A *lot* of a lot.

"You okay?" Kim asks.

"Should I be?" I reply, a little wearily.

"No, I guess you shouldn't. Listen, Andy, we can hold off on this. You're entitled to the answers you want. But they're complicated, and they can wait. Shelton and I will completely understand if you need a little more downtime."

It occurs to me that if Miranda were to make that offer, I'd wonder if I was being played. From Kim, it seems genuine. I just wish I knew for certain.

"I'm good," I tell her.

"You sure?"

"I'm sure. Ops. Lead on."

Kim leads on.

The spokes of the Ops Deck "wheel" are wider and fewer. Four corridors jut out from around the pool, each at a ninety-degree angle from its neighbors. We head along one of them, passing doors sensibly labeled to identify what's behind them. Every one of the doors is thick metal with a wheel instead of a knob, just like my room upstairs. In addition, massive vertical hatches bisect the corridor along our path. These all stand open, each looking as sturdy and formidable as a bank vault.

"For flooding," Kim remarks, noting my interest.

"Has that ever happened?" I ask, a little nervously. Like most of the Kind, I don't care much for water.

"Once, early on. When one of the mods was lowered down the lasered shaft, it took some incidental damage that the sensors didn't catch. But a week later, after everyone had moved in, its seals failed, and the ocean started pouring into the Ops Deck. The flood doors closed automatically, saving the colony."

"Did you… lose anybody?"

Kim replies in a faint voice, "Two. It was pretty terrible."

"I guess it was." Lame.

"One was the staff physician we'd gotten from Mars. Darcy's journeyman. That's how she became our medic. True, she's not an M.D., but she knows her way around Sick Bay." Then, shaking her head, she adds, "Honestly, the whole thing was a nightmare. I mean, I've been off-Earth long enough to understand how dangerous it is out here. But, before that day, I'd never lost anybody. It was a rough time for all of us."

"I'm sorry, Kim."

"Thanks. Here we are."

At the corridor's end stands a final closed door. Its sign says simply: "Mining Operations."

Kim opens it and gestures me inside.

The chamber reminds me vaguely of *Conquest's* Engine Room—a half-moon with viewports occupying most of the far wall. Tons of high-tech equipment take up at least half of the floor space with men and women busying themselves at various incomprehensible workstations. Here, however, there are no blue uniforms. Just jeans and t-shirts.

"Welcome to Ops," Kim tells me.

Almost every head turns my way. A few appear nervous, the rest curious. But at least there's none of the hostility I had to contend with on the ship.

Do these people all know what I am?

If so, then they seem less afraid than I've gotten used to.

Mike Shelton's among them, talking to a big guy wearing a grim expression. Looking up, Shelton waves us over, a move that makes the big guy's expression that much grimmer.

"The man of the hour," Shelton announces, offering me his hand and a tight-lipped smile. "Feeling better?"

"Yeah," I say, shaking the hand.

"Better than he should be," Kim says.

"So, you were right," her husband remarks. "He's a fast healer."

"That doesn't begin to say it."

"Lucky."

"That's me," I say snarkily. "Mr. Lucky. Why, I practically crap four-leaf clovers."

To my surprise, Shelton bursts out laughing. Apparently, gallows humor does have a home aboard Marius. After a moment, Kim laughs too.

Mister Grim Expression does not. He reminds me vaguely of Chief Tuttle, though whether that's because of his scowl or his pronounced widow's peak, I'm not sure. "Boss," he says, and his voice is deep like Tuttle's too. Do deep voices come with widow's peaks? Is it a genetic thing? "Impending invasion, remember?"

"Right," Shelton replies. "You've fortified the northern-facing bulkheads?"

"Sure, but they were never designed to withstand controlled explosions. If Coffin's people want in, they'll get in. I figure they'll latch onto the underside of the shelf as soon as they pierce the convection layer. Then, they'll crabwalk their way over here and breach our hull up on Ice Deck. Of course, none of this would be happening—" He motions at me and adds loudly, "—if *that* one hadn't just drilled through twenty miles of solid ice for the blackbirds."

Suddenly, most of Ops goes uncomfortably quiet.

I get the feeling that I've played this scene before.

Except, this time, I don't blame them.

It *is* my fault they're in trouble.

"Ease up, Francis," Kim says, her expression darkening. "Coffin told Andy that we were holding hostages. You know that!"

"Which proves that he's both dangerous *and* naïve. And it doesn't explain why he's here, on Marius, at all!"

Kim steps up to the man. She's much smaller than Francis, but that doesn't stop her from going toe to toe with him, matching him glare for glare. "Bringing him down to Marius was a group decision."

"I seem to remember voting no," Francis rebuts. "In fact, so did a bunch of us."

"And you were out-voted," Shelton remarks.

"Well, maybe a simple majority shouldn't be enough for something like this. Something like that." Then he points a beefy finger in my direction.

"You know," I tell him. "The last time a guy pointed his finger at me like that, he ended up with blisters on it."

"Yeah," Grim replies. "I *do* know."

I almost miss the implications of that comment. Almost.

My irritation fades as I look at Shelton and say, "You've got a spy aboard *Conquest!*"

"Told you he catches on quick," Kim says.

I shake my head. "Miranda... Coffin's daughter... considered it a possibility. But apparently *Conquest's* captain and the security chief kind of dismissed it."

"Good thing, too," Shelton remarks.

"Who is it?" I ask.

Shelton replies, "Let's go talk in private. Francis, how much time have we got before CSE pays us a visit?"

"Hard to be sure. We don't have eyes on the surface, and *Conquest* is behind Jupiter at the moment, so no comms are coming down. But our most recent intel suggests we've got another day before they're ready to hit us. Call it around 1500 hours tomorrow."

"Three PM tomorrow," Shelton acknowledges. "Got it. Let see if we can't find a way to buy ourselves some time."

"How?" Grim asks.

Everyone in Ops is still quiet, attentive.

Shelton says, speaking to them all, "I'm working on it. In the meantime, redirect one of the external vidcams to cover the convection layer directly beneath the new shaft. If nothing else, that'll tell us when they break through."

"Yeah, okay, boss," Francis acknowledges. "Good idea."

Nodding, Shelton turns to Kim and me. "Let's hit the briefing room."

This turns out to be a small windowless chamber adjacent to Ops that consists of a table and about a dozen chairs. It's nothing like the ultra-futurey conference room up on *Conquest*—just gray utilitarian walls and a maze of piping for a ceiling.

The three of us sit.

Once we're settled, I say, "This spy of yours spilled that I was kidnapped, taken aboard *Conquest,* and what Coffin wanted me to do. Am I right?"

Shelton says, "You're right."

"Who is it?"

"Not yet."

"Not yet?"

"I'm not going to tell you that yet."

"Why not?"

"Because I don't trust you."

"Shelton!" Kim exclaims.

"Sorry, Kim, but this is how it has to be. Everything Andy's done, whether well-intentioned or not, has either screwed up our plans or made our situation worse."

"Wait a furking minute…" I begin.

His eyes meet mine. Shelton's good at the stone-eyes thing, but he's no Spencer. "First, you drilled the shaft that Coffin Industries is going to use to invade this colony. Second, you 'rescued' Kim before she could get into the lander and link us with the Casimir Radio. And, third, you destroyed our lift, which basically strands us down here with limited supplies and no way of evacuating in case of an emergency."

I'm surprised to find Kim glaring at him almost as hard as I am.

Shelton raises a placating hand. "Don't get me wrong. I understand *why* you did those things. And none of it means you're not welcome here."

"Francis the Objector seems to disagree," I say.

"Yeah, well, there are more than a hundred people on Marius, and there's no such thing as a hundred people who completely agree on anything. That's just human nature. No offense."

"None taken."

"But Francis isn't in charge," Shelton goes on. "The colony voted to bring you back with us when we rescued Kim from the lift."

"Voted?"

"That's how we make most big decisions around here."

"Very democratic," I remark.

He doesn't reply.

"And if the vote had gone the other way?" I ask. "Would you have left me in the lift to… what? Bleed out?"

Kim says, her tone sheepish, "You wouldn't have bled out. You heal too fast for that."

"Die of thirst then."

Shelton says, "I'm not in the 'what if' business, Andy. The vote *didn't* go against you, and that *didn't* happen."

"Uh-huh. So, I'm welcome here, but not trusted. Is that it?"

"For the time being, let's just say that your welcome comes with… caveats."

"Caveats?" I ask, not bothering to hide my bitterness.

"Addendums? Codicils? Sorry, I'm not a lawyer. You can go any- where you want to on the Ice Deck. But I don't want you wandering around the Lab or Ops decks without an escort."

"I'll be his escort," Kim says.

"You have your own work to do."

"My staff can handle things. Besides, if Francis is right, we've only got to worry about the next... what? Twenty-seven hours?"

Shelton chews on that. "Fine. You get to babysit our guest." Then he turns to me. "I'm sorry, Andy. I know the first time we talked I was all 'Hi, there! Welcome aboard!' And I meant every word of it. But I've got my people to worry about, and they have to come first. I hope you understand."

"I guess so," I tell him.

"It's nothing personal."

"Sure. We're cool."

Except we're not. Shelton can frame it however he likes, but the bottom line is that, once again, I'm a prisoner. The only thing that's changed is the prison. Yeah, I realize things on the surface went south — seriously south. I suddenly flash on the face of the man I killed and just as quickly put the traitorous thought away.

But everything I did up there I did because —

Because *why?*

I guess because Kim opened my eyes to Miranda's manipulations. I'm an orphan on an alien world, with no home, no means of travel, and no real friends. Right now, Earth feels as unreachable as Valhalla, and I'm not sure what I have waiting there for me anyhow. An empty house? An empty life?

"Um... can I get something to eat?" I try not to show them how exhausted I suddenly feel.

"Sure," Kim replies, giving her husband a look with a lot behind it. "Come on, Andy. Let's head back up to the Ice Deck and grab some food."

SEVEN – Day 21

"I didn't know Shelton was going to do that."

Kim and I are back in the Breakroom on the Ice Deck, though this time not alone. Maybe two dozen people are in here with us, having lunch, among them the six spacers we ran into on our way to Ops. They sit together two tables over, and all of them — well, everybody present, if I'm honest — are looking our way.

That includes Darcy, who seems to be looking our way, *my* way, most of all.

How do I know? Because I keep looking *her* way. I can't seem to help it.

Is it crazy to feel a stab of guilt, like I'm cheating on Miranda?

Never mind. I already know the answer to that.

"It's okay," I tell Kim.

"No, it's not. And he and I will be having a *talk* about it later, believe me."

"I get it. He's got a lot on his shoulders."

She doesn't look convinced. In fact, she looks *pissed*—so much so that suddenly I feel a little sorry for Shelton.

The viewport is crowded with dragons. Some have their little hands and faces pressed to the polymer watching the diners, while others keep whizzing through the water, moving close and then away, their bodies like small gray blurs.

Aside from occasional waves and smiles, the colonists ignore them. Kim tells me the dragons are always here at mealtime, that they like to watch us eat. At first, it was fascinating for everyone. But after years of it, it's become routine. "Human beings can get used to anything given enough time."

We're eating scrambled eggs, which is a weird thing to do in low gravity. When you fork some of it into your mouth, there's less weight to it, so that it almost feels like there's nothing there. Except, when you taste it, it tastes right. Then you swallow, and it's somehow tougher to convince the food to go down your esophagus. Imagine trying to swallow something while standing on your head. It was easier with the cookies earlier, though I remember being a little weirded out by the sensation even then.

Kim watches me. "Everyone struggles with it at first. Just relax and take your time."

"I feel like I'm going to throw up," I complain.

"You won't. Your throat muscles just aren't used to having to work so hard. They'll adapt. Didn't you have this problem on Conquest? I thought they dropped the artificial gravity as you approached Jupiter."

"They did. But they switched us over to zero-G food. You know, flavored paste."

Kim makes a sour face, "I hate that stuff."

"Me too," someone adds.

I look up to see Darcy standing beside our table. She smiles down at me and adds, "And don't listen to Kim. A bunch of us *did* throw up at first." Then she offers me a squeeze bottle. "Here. Fire some juice down your gullet after every bite. It helps."

I glance at Kim, who shrugs.

I take the bottle, tilt my head back, and squirt apple juice into my mouth. The force of the little jet overcomes the low-G, and I get what feels like my first "real" swallow.

"Yeah," I say afterward. "That *did* help. Thanks."

"No problem," Darcy replies. "Point-one grav has got its special challenges. But there's a cooler side, too. Watch this!" From a nearby counter, Darcy takes three butter knives and starts juggling them. After a few seconds, she adds a fourth and then a fifth—until finally, a half-dozen of the furking things are buzzing through the air around the girl's purple-haired head like big angry bees.

"Whoa!" I exclaim.

Kim rolls her eyes.

"The trick's in the acceleration," Darcy explains, her hands moving crazy fast. "On Earth, acceleration is 9.8 meters per second squared. Here, it's only a smidge over 1.3. That means stuff accelerates about seventy-five percent more slowly in freefall. That's why you can jump higher here and fall further without getting hurt. You can also juggle well because objects in motion move more slowly through the air than they do on Earth when reacting to the same amount of force and traveling the same circular path."

A minute later, someone else in the cafeteria stands and starts juggling ceramic coffee mugs. Then a third person starts doing it with dinner trays.

Kim groans. "They'd try it with chairs if the ceilings weren't so low. There's nothing more annoying than a spacer who's also an engineer."

"Excuse me!" Darcy complains. "I know this stuff, and *I'm* a biologist!"

I turn to Kim and ask, "Aren't you a spacer, too?"

"Of course. But I'm not an engineer."

"Or a biologist!" Darcy chimes in.

We both ignore her. "And Shelton?" I ask. "Is *he* a spacer, too?"

Darcy says, "We're all spacers on Marius, Andy. No corporate types here. 'Spacers do the work. Corps make the money.' Haven't you heard that phrase?"

"No, but… isn't that kind of the way *all* corporations work?"

Kim considers. "I suppose it is, but things are more extreme out here. Most colonies are more like corporate life in the early twentieth century, before labor unions. Workers are paid poverty wage for sixteen- or even twenty-hour days. Labor's cheap, safety is a low, low priority, and anything even resembling healthcare is nonexistent. Step just a little bit out of line, and you're fired and left to starve at best… or beaten and jailed at worst."

"No," Darcy amends. "There's worse than even that."

"True enough," Kim agrees with a nod.

I say, "On Earth, the… imbalance… out here isn't really public knowledge."

Kim laughs humorlessly. "'Imbalance.' I like that. We know all about the spin Coffin puts on how things work out here."

"Then, why do it?" I ask. Does that sound naïve? What can I say? I'm a newbie.

In answer, Kim points to the viewport. Beyond it, the dragons are watching the jugglers, of whom there are now a half-dozen scattered around the breakroom. The Europans are all smiling and shaking, enjoying the show.

"I can't speak for everyone," Kim says. "But *I* do it for the sight of my friends and fellow spacers spontaneously entertaining the first alien intelligence anyone's ever encountered."

"Bingo!" Darcy declares.

And, with that, I make a decision.

Standing up, I take the fork from my own plate. Given Darcy's explanation of Europan juggling, this is a parlor trick I'd never be able to pull off on Earth—for two reasons. One, the fork would be too heavy. Two, my parents would never permit it.

But my folks are gone, forever gone. And Conceal and Protect can go furk itself.

I toss the fork into the air. Then, holding my upturned palm beneath it, I keep it there.

It's ridiculously easy. All I do is let a tiny bit of my dragon out, just enough to excite the air molecules between my hand and the utensil. Hot air rises, and the fork is light enough that the thermal updraft easily keeps it bobbing in midair about six inches above my palm.

A parlor trick, like a crumpled napkin—only way better.

Kim jumps to her feet, though whether it's in astonishment, alarm, or both, I can't tell. Nearby, Darcy stops juggling, letting the knives drop to the Breakroom floor in a noisy low-G kind of clatter.

The rest of the cafeteria seems to utter a collective gasp.

I smile grimly.

"What's the matter?" I ask. "You all know what I am, right?"

Kim says in a low voice, "Andy, maybe you shouldn't…"

"Why not?" I reply, speaking normally. "I've spent my entire life running from this, pretending to be something I'm not, and look where *that's* gotten me."

Kim glances nervously around. Everyone's staring in silent shock at my little stunt—all but Darcy, who's grinning from ear to ear.

"Is this really what you want?" Kim asks me. "To scare everybody?"

I meet her eyes, ignoring the plea I see there. "What is it they're scared I'll do? Blow up, maybe? Melt a hole through an outer wall and drown us?"

Around us, no one speaks.

Finally, Darcy says, "No."

When Kim and I look at her, she adds, "At least, *I'm* not afraid. Why should I be? Boss, any of us could kill everyone in this room just by walking in here with a gun and shooting out the viewport. Any of us could destroy the colony simply by sneaking into Ops and releasing the docking clamps. Do you ever worry about that?"

"No," Kim admits.

"Then why worry about Andy? I think what he's doing right now is incredibly cool!"

A murmur runs through the cafeteria. Gradually, the miners begin to relax. A few even start chuckling.

For myself, I'm not sure what I feel. I'm not even sure why I'm putting on this little display in the first place. So much has happened to make me feel powerless that I guess I just wanted to remind everyone of the power I *do* have. I know that sounds immature, especially since these spacers haven't done anything to earn my animosity.

But they're *here* and, right now, that seems to be enough.

I call back my dragon and let the fork fall into my hand. The metal's hot to the touch, so hot that it would have scorched a human.

Kim steps up and takes it from me. Naturally, it doesn't burn *her*.

"Any other tricks you'd care to share?" she asks dryly.

I meet her judgmental eyes, still feeling defiant. Then I pick up a spoon and an empty coffee mug.

"Andy..." Kim says.

I don't reply, and I don't stop. Instead, I dangle the spoon over the mug, holding it between thumb and forefinger. I remember what I did back in the coring unit when I'd focused the release of my dragon on one specific spot. It comes to me even easier than I expected.

The heat I release is brief, less than five seconds, but its temperature is so intense that the spoon instantly liquefies. It spills from between my fingers and into the cup, where it almost immediately hardens again, now as an eighth-inch thick puddle of gray metal.

Finally, I turn the cup over with a dramatic flourish and let the thin round disc that had once been a spoon clatter to the floor.

Darcy starts excitedly, clapping.

Within seconds they all are. Except Kim.

Kim looks pissed.

Then someone points at the viewport and exclaims, "Look at the dragons!"

We do.

Instead of being spread out across the width of the wide window, the Europans have all converged in one spot. They're now motionless, bunched together, and staring right at me. No smiles this time. No shaking.

They look — *riveted*.

"I've never seen them do *that* before," Darcy remarks, her whisper conspicuously loud in the quiet Breakroom.

Kim studies them, her annoyance with me forgotten, at least for the moment. "Me, neither."

Someone else says, "I think they're looking at... him."

"Andy," Kim says quietly. "Please cross to the far wall."

"What for?" I ask.

"An experiment. Just do it, okay?"

"Okay."

I slowly navigate the crowded room, weaving through the colonists. As I do, the dragons *follow* me, practically spilling over each other in their effort to keep pace. They're all now only a couple of feet away from where I've stopped by the window, with just the thickness of the transparent polymer between us.

"That's... new," someone else says.

"Do something!" Darcy calls to me in a harsh whisper.

I cleverly reply, "Huh?"

"Show them another trick," Kim tells me. Then, remembering herself, she adds, "A *small* one."

I pull a cloth napkin off the nearest table and, tossing it into the air, hit it with a concentrated shot of thermal energy. It doesn't so much catch fire as sort of ripple and then atomize. There isn't even much smoke; the reaction is too quick, and the heat too intense.

The dragons go nuts.

Their little bodies shake wildly, and they start slapping the viewport with their three-fingered hands. The sound is dull and faint through the thick polymer, as if coming from down a long tunnel.

Everyone gasps.

"They never get that excited about anything!" Kim says in wonderment. "Ever!"

"Oh, boss," Darcy says. "You *have* to let me take this guy swimming."

"I'm going with you!" another spacer declares.

"Me, too!" appends someone else.

I exclaim, "What a minute! What?"

"You up for it, Andy?" Kim asks.

"Up for what? For *swimming*? Like… out there swimming?" I point at the viewport, a gesture that the Europans find utterly fascinating.

Kim nods. "It's the primary way we study them, zoologically. We get out there, in their habitat, interact with them, and watch them interact with each other."

"The Dian Fossey method," Darcy adds. "Come on, Kim. Let's do it!"

I watch Kim consider the idea. "Okay. I'd be lying if I said that, after this display, I don't want to see how the dragons react to you in person."

Everybody applauds, which seems excessive. I suddenly feel like a rookie basketball player poised to make a game-winning free throw.

Except I suck at free throws.

I look at Kim, expecting to see a touch of Miranda's manipulative triumph, or at least some good old-fashioned guile. But it isn't there. She looks back at me with genuine excitement. Apparently, her annoyance at my "magic show" has been melted away—what can I say, I have a thing for puns—by the dragons' extreme reaction.

She and the rest of these colonists came to Europa to mine tantalum. Instead, they've ended up dedicating themselves to the study and preservation of the life they found here. That, by itself, says something positive about their collective character, doesn't it?

But here's what really convinces me. Yes, they've studied the dragons. But they haven't trapped them, imprisoned them, or used them. In other words, they haven't treated them as Miranda treated me.

I hear myself say, "I... guess so."

Kim grins. "Darcy? Jim? Carlos? Grab your gear and let's meet at the moon pool in twenty minutes." Then, when several people grumble that they want to come along, Kim adds in a gentle but surprisingly commanding tone. "You all know how the locals get if too many of us go out there at the same time. We'll keep it small for now. Five's plenty."

"Five?" I ask, counting names in my head.

"You didn't think *I* was going to pass this up, did you?" she replies. "Being the boss has its privileges!"

After that, things happen fast.

Kim hurries me down to a co-ed changing room on the Ops Deck that's filled with dive gear. "The water's warm," she explains while fishing through assorted piles of rubbery pants and shirts. "But water pressure's weird at sub-lunar gravity, so it's better if you wear a wetsuit. Dang, you're skinny!" she mutters, looking me over.

"Thanks," I reply.

She hands me a pair of diving pants. "Try these on while I find you a top. Fitting booth's over there."

Turns out, you don't just "put on" a pair of dive pants. They're not jeans. Instead, you roll them back and then kind of unfurl them up your legs. The hardest part is getting them past my briefs. But no way am I wearing these things commando.

Which makes me wonder if the *last* guy who wore them did.

I decide not to think about that.

A small fist juts through the curtain, clutching a blue rubbery top. "Try this," Kim says.

The top's even harder than the pants, from a putting-on perspective. But I finally step, barefoot but "rubberized," out of the fitting booth.

Kim has already donned a wet suit of her own and seems far more comfortable than I feel in mine. Seeing my face, she laughs. "You look like you're about to face a firing squad."

"Yeah, well, the Kind don't much like water."

Kim's smile vanishes. "Oh! That never occurred to me. Uh, you *do* know how to swim, right?"

"Yes."

"Do you want to call this off?" she asks, though I sense doing so would be like canceling Christmas.

"No. It'll be… fun." An absolute, utter lie.

Why am I suddenly so keen on not disappointing Kimberly Shelton?

Then, with something of a jolt, I realize it's not Kim I'm worried about disappointing.

"What about the others?" I ask.

"Who?"

"Darcy… and the other two." I've already forgotten their names.

"Jim and Carlos. They have their own personal gear. A lot of people do. I'm just not one of them. Here!" She hands me a rubber cowl.

I clumsily pull it over my head.

"Good," Kim says. "Now, the boots, mask, and breather."

This breathing gear looks nothing like the tank and regulator stuff you usually see on Earth. Instead, the clear mask covers the whole face, held in place by tight straps and fitted with a flexible hose running from under the chin and around to a kind of yoke that sits on the shoulders. "We call it a 'gill,'" Kim explains. "The system's almost self-sustaining. With every breath, it takes in water and uses an onboard fission reactor to break it down into hydrogen and oxygen. The oxygen it mixes with onboard gases and then passes to the wearer. The hydrogen is processed as fuel to keep the reactor going."

I blink. "So… I'm going to be wearing a nuclear reactor on my *face*?"

"Well, technically, the reactor's on your shoulders. Anyway, when you say it like that, it sounds dangerous."

"Isn't it?"

"Asked the man who blows up…"

"Point taken."

"Relax. The tech works flawlessly. Besides, I thought the Kind were impervious to any form of thermal energy, including nuclear?"

"That's the theory. But it doesn't mean I want to test it."

"Really? After your display in the Breakroom, I'd figured you'd embraced your nature." This shot is fired with oodles of snide.

I reply seriously, "All my life, I've been taught to hide what I am. Now, for the first time, I'm thinking maybe I don't need to hide anymore. So, tell me… big sister… is that such a crime?"

For a few pregnant seconds, she just looks at me.

Then, smiling ruefully, she marches toward the exit. "Come on then, little brother. Your namesakes await."

EIGHT – Day 21

The others have already gathered at the moon pool by the time we arrive. Darcy looks — well, amazing — in her skintight neoprene. Jim and Carlos, the former with a long frame and stringy hair and the latter with the huge mustache I mentioned before, less so. But all of them seem more at ease than I am.

"Listen up," Kim says. "Everyone set your dive watches for thirty minutes."

"I've got at least two hours of mixture," Darcy protests. The others nod in agreement.

"We all do. However, since this is Andy's first dive, we're keeping it to thirty minutes."

Darcy frowns. "But—"

"You can skip this dive if you want."

"Not a chance, boss."

"Then half-an-hour it is. Andy, we don't jump in. Sudden movements are a bad idea in Sublunar G. Instead, we sit ourselves down on the lip of the pool and slide into it. Jim, Carlos, and Darcy will go first. Then you and I will follow them in together. You good with that?"

I nod — though "good" might not be the right word.

Why am I doing this?

As the first three slip into the moon pool with practiced ease, more of my father's advice bubbles up to the surface of my memory. "The Kind have a tenuous treaty with water, son. We need it to survive, just as all living things do. We cook with it. We bathe in it. But it's our greatest enemy as well. Out there, under all that rain, our dragon is hampered if not completely drowned."

"It's our… kryptonite," I said at the time. I think I was nine.

"Close enough," he replied with a grin. "Now come on. Your mom's made mushroom ravioli for dinner, and as always, she boiled it in kryptonite!"

I love my mom's mushroom ravioli.

I *loved* it.

Another thought to push away.

"Ready?" Kim asks me.

I can't speak. So, I just nod.

Satisfied, she sits with her feet dangling in the water. Anxiously, I plop down beside her.

She tells me, "Don't worry about sinking. You're much more buoyant here than on Earth. In fact, we'll all be wearing weights to help us get around."

I nod again.

"On three. One. Two. Three."

We slide into the water.

I flashback on my childhood swimming lessons. My parents insisted on them, though they had to drag me to the community pool kicking and screaming. I disliked putting my face in the water and *hated* submerging completely. But, by the end of the eight-week course, I could do both without throwing up.

Now, the first thing I discover is that Kim was right. My body feels crazily buoyant. Bobbing there beside the others, I don't think I could drown if I tried.

"Masks on, everyone," Kim commands.

I fit the faceplate into position. It feels stifling, containing, just one more thing about this experience that I don't like. Then I draw a tentative breath and, a little to my surprise, the gill across my shoulders delivers air instantly. I take another breath, and there it is, right on command.

Easy peasy lemon squeezy.

Something my mom says.

Or… used to.

When next Kim speaks, I hear the words transmitted by speakers hidden somewhere inside the mask. *"Now the weight belts. Hold still, Andy, and I'll fasten yours. Don't want you dropping it."* Her voice sounds tinny but perfectly clear.

"Me, neither." I agree with a gulp, looking into the depths.

Jeez! That's a lot of water!

"How deep is it?" I ask.

Darcy replies, *"A hundred miles or so."*

Then Carlos adds, *"But Smokey's closer."*

Jim says, *"It's about eighty miles down, at least according to sonar sweeps."*

"Smokey's millennia-old," Darcy explains. *"It spews out tons of minerals and rare metals."*

"Including tantalum?" I ask.

"Yep," replies Carlos.

Kim says, *"We used to filter out the tantalum using molecular scrubbers. But we shut them all down about six months ago when we realized what they were doing to the dragons."*

"The ones who came close to the colony started getting ill, turning pale and sickly," says Darcy. *"I've never examined one hands-on, but their symptoms had all the signs of malnutrition. Then Ravi and some of the others started bringing…"* Her words trail off.

"Started showing us their dead," Jim finishes for her. *"They brought them right up to the viewport in Ops. No smiles this time. No greetings. Just 'look at what you're doing to us.'"*

"Jeez," I hear myself say.

"The only variable was the tantalum," Carlos explains.

"Right," says Kim. *"They need it, and without it, they were slowly starving."*

"By then, we'd all gotten tight with the little guys," Jim adds. *"So, Shelton called a vote. It was either keep mining the tantalum and watch the critters die or break our contract with Coffin and take what came."*

"Was it unanimous?" I ask. "To shut off the scrubbers, I mean."

"Just two dissenters," Darcy replies uncomfortably.

"Francis was one," Kim says. *"It's been months, and he's still pissed we went rogue."*

"Who was the other?"

Silence. Awkward, almost painful.

Finally, Darcy mutters, *"Me."*

"Oh."

The awkward silence drags on.

"Come on," Kim finally says. *"We don't have much time. When Shelton finds out we've taken Andy 'visiting,' he's going to pitch a fit."*

"Is he?" I ask.

"Sure. We're under siege, or soon will be. And my man's nothing if not practical. Let's go."

And, just like that, my heart starts hammering again. The idea of all that dragon-killing liquid completely enveloping me—well, it's scaring the furk out of me. Maybe that's why I've been asking so many questions, to postpone the moment of truth.

But, as moments of truth tend to do, this one's come at last.

The others slide beneath the surface of the warm ocean as if it's the most natural thing in the world. I try to steady myself and follow them. As I do, my "dragon brain" expects to plummet straight into alien liquid darkness. It's irrational since I've been treading water just fine. But when has logic ever beat terror?

"You okay, Andy?" Kim asks.

I reply, probably more loudly than necessary, "Sure! Um… don't we need fins or something?"

It's Darcy who says, *"We're higher tech than that. Do a Dorothy."*

"A what?"

She laughs, and Carlos asks, *"Didn't Kim explain it?"*

"Sorry," Kim replies. *"Forgot. Andy, click the heels of your boots together, like Dorothy in the Wizard of Oz."*

I do so, peering down at my feet.

Instantly, futurey fins snap out from the sides of each boot and lock together at its front.

Despite my anxiety, that's pretty furking cool, and I say as much.

"Better yet," Darcy explains. *"Once you're ready to get dry again, another click retracts them. Shelton designed them."*

Then the four of them turn downward and swim wordlessly into the abyss. For several seconds, I just hang there, my mouth ironically dry. Then, screwing up my courage, I bend at the waist and kick my feet.

Down I go.

Ever have a flying dream? You know, the kind where the world opens up and suddenly you're soaring? Swimming underwater on Europa feels like that. It's a sensation I've heard some people like. I'm not one of them.

The moon pool continues down for about fifty feet, with smooth circular metal walls all around me, before finally spilling into the open ocean. Here that feeling of flying through a vast nothingness only gets worse. The ocean goes from light blue near the surface to deep purple further down, and then to black. Suddenly, the only solid matter I can see is Marius's lit underbelly. Everything else is just—eternity.

"You still okay?" Darcy asks.

"Think so," I croak.

"We'll head up the north face of the colony," Kim explains. *"That's where the dragons are easiest to find."*

Jim remarks, *"More likely, they'll find us."*

Kim says, *"Andy, they're not big, but they're strong swimmers and can be a little… unnerving… if they close around you as a group. Just relax. I promise they won't hurt you."*

"Got it," I hear myself say.

"You sure you're up for this?" Darcy asks, sounding genuinely concerned.

"I'm sure," I tell her, tell them all, tell myself. "I'm good."

So. Much. Water!

We move out from beneath the colony and turn upward, the curving hull now filling one side of my field of vision. Overhead, the ice shelf is like an endless ceiling. And, everywhere else: ocean—the water around me rippling with Smokey's rising thermal currents.

"Stay close to the station," Kim warns. *"The water gets a lot colder away from Smokey's influence."*

"Okay," I reply, suppressing a shudder. It's bad enough to be completely immersed. The idea of drowning in dark, frigid water petrifies me.

Then Carlos exclaims, *"Here they come!"*

The Europans converge on us, rising like wraiths from the darkness. They cut the water with astonishing speed, blue-gray blurs, their muscular tails driving them like torpedoes.

I feel my heart, which is already pounding, leap into overdrive.

Kim says, *"They're curious and excited, but not dangerous."*

Two of them latch onto my arms.

Reflexively, I start to struggle. But then Darcy's calm face appears in front of my visor. *"It's all right. They do this a lot. They won't hurt you."*

I nod and try my best to calm down.

The pressure on my arms is firm but not painful. Their tiny hands seem to be kneading at me as if trying to figure out how my limbs work. Two more of them zip up to my face, peering at me through my mask, their big eyes wide with interest.

Then a smaller one—younger maybe?—takes my hand in its own. It explores my fingers with its own nimble digits, comparing them to its own with almost childlike wonder. Five fingers versus three. Large versus small.

"*They find us as interesting as we find them,*" Kim says, delight evident in her voice. "*They're more than sentient. They're intelligent and have no natural predators. That's why they don't fear us.*"

"So, they're at the top of the food chain?"

"*It's not much of a chain,*" Jim pipes in. "*Just the dragons feeding on the organic molecules spewing out of Smokey.*"

"*We've been able to identify some bacteria,*" Darcy adds. "*Almost sixty species so far. They probably make up some of the dragons' diet as well. But as to how a species like theirs evolved so far beyond the rest of the ecosystem...*"

"*Just one of their many mysteries,*" Kim says.

"*We don't even know for sure if they're warm- or cold-blooded,*" says Carlos. "*I mean, it's not like we capture and study them.*"

"*They're people,*" Darcy says. "*Not lab rats.*"

People, I think, as the dragons continue to examine me.

"*Darcy's right,*" says Kim. "*This is xenopology, not xenobiology. We're not going to dissect members of an intelligent race, not even in the name of science.*"

"*CSE would,*" Jim remarks.

"*If they cared,*" Carlos replies bitterly. "*But they don't. Marius is all about tantalum. Remember the message we got back when we first reported them?*"

They all nod.

I ask, "What did it say?"

It's Darcy who answers, sounding pissed. "*They reminded us of our fiduciary responsibilities. The 'indigenous obstacles' were to be ignored... or exterminated.*"

I look her way and think, *And yet you voted to keep the scrubbers going.*

Then I consider Miranda. *Does* she know about the dragons, as Kim suggested earlier? Or has her father, the 'great' Charles Coffin, kept that from her, maybe worried that her reaction might mirror the colonists?

I want to think it's the latter.

But, in my gut, I know better.

The dragon fiddling with my hand looks quizzically up at me as if expecting me to explain something. I have no idea how to respond. So, I just smile.

The dragon smiles back.

"They like you, Andy," Darcy says.

"They like everybody," Carlos remarks.

"Yeah, but look how they're circling him!"

It's true. There must be two dozen whizzing around me now. Their wake jostles me as I float in place, neutrally buoyant, and with the colony's outer hull thirty yards to my right and the ice shelf maybe twice that overhead. The others — Kim, Darcy, Jim, and Carlos — all stay close by, watching as more and more of the dragons settle on me. They aren't heavy. In fact, they seem to weigh almost nothing.

I suppose I should be unnerved, but there's something — welcoming — about their behavior. They want to understand me, yes. But they also want to befriend me. I'm not sure how I know that, but the feeling's strong.

"Andy?" Kim asks tentatively. *"Are you all right?"*

"Yeah!" I laugh. "It's amazing. I feel like —"

The ice shelf overhead *explodes*.

It happens so fast that I don't really register it, not until the shockwave hits me like a wall.

Suddenly, I'm blasted into the depths, tumbling head over heels. My entire body goes numb and, more terrifying still, my visor cracks.

Water begins spilling down my face.

I think, *I'm going to drown!* And suddenly, every water-related nightmare I had as a kid comes crashing back. I don't scream. I don't think I make any sound at all. I'm way, way too scared for that.

I have no idea where the others are. Hell, I don't even know where *I am.* I try kicking my feet in a desperate, instinctive bid for control. But the rushing water pushes me relentlessly downward. Both my ears close up, and an awful pressure clamps my chest, making it hard to breathe.

In blind panic now, I reach for my dragon.

And it's there. It's there, but it's trapped, useless, its heat overwhelmed by the sheer weight of water.

Kryptonite.

That's the last thing I remember.

NINE – Glimpse

"Mister Coffin, the coring unit has broken through the convection layer and has fastened onto the underside of the ice shelf."

"How close to MC-13?"

"Less than sixty yards."

"Well done, Spencer. How many of your people are on board?"

"Ten, sir. They're led by Sergeant Massey."

"He's a good man?"

"He's a she, and she has my absolute trust."

"What's the plan?"

"The coring unit will make its way to the colony's northern flank. Then they'll cut through the outer hull."

"Shelton knows we're there, I assume."

"It's likely."

"I don't want any deaths."

"Sir, that strategy may not be tenable."

"Make it tenable. These are miners, not soldiers. I want them subdued, not killed."

"And if we're fired upon?"

"Then you react appropriately, but with non-lethal ammunition. A few shots fired your way, if Shelton's people are so foolish, doesn't give you permission to slaughter the population."

"I understand, Mister Coffin."

"Good. Now, tell me about my daughter."

"Miss Coffin is… upset with the new command structure."

"Not surprising. What's she been doing? We haven't spoken."

"She keeps to her quarters."

"Sulking, or up to something?"

"Nothing that I've been able to determine, sir."

"Tell her to call me."

"Of course. But, with respect, your daughter's very… strong-willed. She's not going to accept her new circumstances."

"Do you have any children, Spencer?"

"An eight-year-old son. He lives with his mother. I haven't seen him in five years."

"Ah, yes. I remember. I'm sorry."

"No need, sir."

"Well, I've always found that a firm, but reasoned hand is most effective, no matter how strong-willed the child may be."

"If you say so, Mister Coffin."

"Indeed, I do. Her brother was less difficult. You know Miranda had a brother, don't you, Spencer?"

"Yes, sir. He passed away, didn't he?"

"Three years ago. He was twenty. Miranda, fifteen. Even then, she was the smarter of the two, but Charlie was more level-headed, easier to deal with. I lost him to heart failure. An undiagnosed congenital problem, the doctors surmised."

"I'm sorry for your loss."

"I'm not looking for sympathy. I just want to give you some perspective. Miranda's brilliant but, like many geniuses, struggles with… behavioral issues. Growing up, she required extensive professional counseling and continues to need medication to manage certain chronic psychological challenges. She's repeatedly promised me that she's been maintaining her treatment regimen. But some of her actions as adjunct have made me suspect otherwise. Just look at how attached she became to Brand."

"Yes, sir. Which brings me to the matter of the Dragon."

"Yes?"

"If we retake MC-13 and discover that he somehow survived the elevator blast, then does your no-kill policy apply to him as well?"

"Certainly not. As far as I'm concerned, Brand's every bit as alien… and unnecessary… as those creatures the colonists found in the Europan ocean. If the Dragon's alive, Spencer, I want you to end him. Do you understand?"

"Perfectly, Mister Coffin."

"But this time, do it smart."

"I'll instruct my blackbirds to take headshots, only."

"Good. You know what's at stake here, and I'm not just talking about the tantalum. Get it done, Spencer."

"Yes, sir."

TEN – Day 21

When I open my eyes, my first thought is, *Furk, I'm getting tired of always waking up in a strange place!*

I'm on my back on warm metal, looking blearily up at a conical ceiling. And there's a Europan on my face.

Gasping, I sit up and reflexively pull at it. The creature's four thin arms are hugging my head, and its thick muscular tail is curled around the back of my neck. Most of its torso is stretched over my mouth and nose, and its eyes—its big, lidless eyes—are staring sightlessly into mine.

There's a weird, almost serene smile on its face.

As I tug on it, the creature slides off. Its small body lands on my sternum, lifeless.

I gape at it, unable to comprehend.

My face tingles.

Finally, my sluggish brain starts working again, and I look around.

I'm in a small circular room, maybe eight feet in diameter. Tons of unmarked monitors and gadgets surround me, covering the walls and filling at least two-thirds of the floor space. The ceiling tapers to a point, like the coring unit's only smaller. The floor is a textured metal walkway encircling another moon pool. This one's only three feet across, its water as dark as ink.

The entire room lists slightly so that one side of the moon pool's water is closer to the lip than the other.

Then I spot Kim lying on its opposite side.

I struggle to my feet and lurch my way around to her. She's unconscious and, like me, has a Europan latched onto her face, covering her mouth and nose.

Kneeling, I pull the creature free. Its skin is astonishingly sticky, but it's every bit as dead as mine was.

"Kim?" I ask, my voice a croak.

She doesn't stir. Blood oozes from a tear in her wetsuit, just above her knee. The cut looks deep.

I touch her neck. There's a pulse, a strong one. That's good, at least.

"Kim!" I say sharply, shaking her.

She snaps awake so abruptly that, like a moron, I almost fall into the moon pool.

"Holy Moses on a popsicle stick!" she exclaims.

It may be the oddest curse I've ever heard.

She looks around with wide eyes. "Andy? Where are the others?"

"Not here. That's all I know. I'm not even sure what happened!"

"Something came through the ice. Something big." She rubs her cheeks. "My skin's a little numb."

"There was a dragon attached to your face."

"*What?*"

I nod to the dead creature on the floor between us. Kim stares at it in horror.

"There was one on my face too. It was covering my mouth and nose."

"Where is it?" Then, after I point it out to her, she says, "I don't understand."

"Well, if *you* don't understand… then I'm totally furked."

"How'd we get here?"

"Kim, I don't even know where 'here' is!"

She looks around again and, after several long moments, recognition dawns. "This… is Pod One!"

"It's what?"

"But it *can't* be!"

"Can't be what?"

"Pod One!"

"Kim, what the hell are you talking about?"

She swallows dryly. "I'm thirsty."

"Me, too."

She starts to stand, cries out in pain, and topples back down. Then she clutches her wounded leg and issues another string of wholly original curses.

"You're cut," I say uselessly, obviously. "But I don't know by what."

"A shard of ice," she replies through gritted teeth. "It caught me when that *thing* came through the shelf. I think it was the coring unit. It emerged with enough force to shoot pieces of ice every which way. One of them nailed me in the leg. I remember it happening. But after that…" She shakes her head. "I don't know. Where's my helmet?"

"Not here. The gills are gone, too."

"Are you sure?"

"It's not a big place," I reply.

She settles back down, taking a few slow, measured breaths. "Okay. First order of business: Stay calm."

"I'm trying."

"That's good, Andy. But I'm not talking to you."

"Oh."

"Second order of business: Confirm our location."

"Pod One, you said."

"So, it seems. Furk!"

"What *is* Pod One?" I ask.

"It's a probe that we dropped about a year after establishing Marius."

"Dropped where? To the bottom of the ocean?"

"Into Smokey."

"The *smoker?*"

"It's basically just a big pile of sensors, meant to provide data on the smoker's environment. Temperature. Water pressure. Salinity. Levels of organic and inorganic trace elements. But it stopped working almost immediately after deployment. The telemetry just never came. We figured it had landed badly and been damaged… or the heat inside Smokey was higher than expected and fried its electronics."

"And you're sure *this* is *that?*"

"I can't imagine where else we *could* be. But there's a way to be certain. There's a telemetry display over there. See that terminal? Hit the green button and try to wake it up."

When I do so, an adjacent screen lights up, almost blinding me as it begins displaying colorful diagnostics. "Got it," I say.

"In the upper right corner will be the local telemetry signature. What's it say?"

"P1."

"There's our confirmation. This is definitely Pod One. What's the internal temperature?"

It takes me a few moments to find it amidst the forest of numbers. "Um… it says it's two hundred and nine degrees in here!"

"Fahrenheit?"

"Yeah."

Such a temperature would kill a human instantly. But I'm Kind, and she's a Split, so aside from noticing it as being a bit warm, we haven't suffered at all.

I ask, "Shouldn't the water in the moon pool be close to boiling or something?"

"Pressure's probably too great," she replies.

"Are you sure we're in the smoker?"

"What's the external temp?"

I look. "Over a thousand!"

"And our depth?"

"Close to eighty miles."

"Oh, yes. We're in the smoker."

"How the furk did we get here?"

"I have no idea. And what about Darcy, Jim, and Carlos? Where are *they*? Are they even alive? That concussion was like a bomb going off!"

"I don't know. But *we* survived. So maybe they did, too. For all we know, they could have made it back to Marius."

"God, I hope so," she says.

I kneel back down at Kim's side and gently examine the dead dragon. As I do, I notice something I didn't before: a fifth appendage. It juts out of the creature's chest and now hangs limply against its body. It appears to be a flexible, translucent membrane tube, maybe eight inches long and open on the end, like a slack mouth.

I ask Kim, "What's that?"

She looks as bewildered as I feel. "No idea. We don't know much about Europan anatomy. Like Darcy told you, we don't capture and study them. Everything we've learned has been through observation, and I'm pretty sure I've never observed that before."

I tentatively touch the tubular appendage. "I think they saved us."

"How?" she asks.

"I don't know. But when that concussion hit, I had something like a dozen of them clinging to me. It seems pretty obvious that they brought us here."

Kim looks around the small circular room again. "But what happened to our helmets? I remember mine cracking… water leaking in."

"Mine, too."

"Even if they did carry us down here," she says. "We should have drowned on the way!"

"Good point. I wonder what killed these two, and where the rest of them are. The moon pool, maybe?"

"That's not a moon pool. It's the lower decks of the pod. They're flooded."

"Oh."

"Too many questions," Kim remarks, rubbing her face. "But even if we knew the answers, they wouldn't help us get out of here. What we need to do is get a signal to Marius. If we can let them know where we are, Shelton can send Pod Two."

"There's a Pod Two?"

"Space travel is all about redundancy. Besides, what would be the point of naming this one Pod One if there wasn't a Two?"

"Okay. Sure. But won't it get damaged coming down this deep?"

"The pods were designed to handle this depth."

"This one didn't!"

"This one *crashed*. Pod Two only needs to connect to Pod One, hatch to hatch. They're programmed to do that. Then, once we board it, it'll detach and bring us back up. It's much simpler than diving blindly into a smoker. Trust me, it'll work."

"If you say so. So how do we shoot up a flare?"

Kim tries changing position, only to cry out. "Jeez, this hurts and… worse… my toes are numb. I may have torn an artery, and it's only the pressure of my wetsuit that's keeping me from bleeding out."

"Then quit moving," I suggest helpfully. "Is there an emergency med kit?"

"It's an unmanned pod. The only time anyone's supposed to be in here is when it's in dry dock."

"So… that's a no?"

"That's a no. Check that display over there for our comms status."

I return to the console to look. "Comms are listed as 'Reset,' whatever that means."

"It means there's power but the system's off-line. It needs a reboot."

"How do we do that?"

"We can't. Not from here."

"Then where?"

Kim nods at the "moon pool."

"Oh, furk," I mutter.

"I'd go," she tells me. "But with this leg, I wouldn't get far. You'll have to do it."

"I don't have my helmet!"

"So, hold your breath."

"I'm… not really good at that."

"It's not far. The pod only has three levels. This is Level A. You swim straight down, through Level B and into Level C. Fifteen feet, tops. Comms is right there. It's marked."

"It's dark," I say, maybe a little desperately.

"See that panel on the left? The one marked, 'Maintenance.'"

"Yeah, I see it."

"Right now, the pod's functioning on low power. Hit the button marked FULL and it'll go into Maintenance Mode and lights will come on everywhere."

"You sure?"

"Yes."

"But what if it kills the battery or something?"

"My husband designed this thing," she explains patiently. "The batteries will last for fifty years."

"Unless they got damaged in the crash."

"If that happened, then the lights wouldn't be on at all. Now quit stalling."

Unhappily, I find and press the right button. Instantly, otherwise innocuous panels light up, chasing back the shadows. More than that, the "moon pool" starts eerily glowing. I tell myself its simple light refraction from panels in the flooded level. But I swear it looks like a Hellmouth.

"There," Kim announces cheerfully. "Now, you'll have no problem."

My stomach twists. "I… don't know if I can do this."

"It's okay. I get that the water's hot, but that's not going to bother either one of us, and you know it."

"It's… not the heat."

Kim eyes me. "Andy, are you hydrophobic?"

"No!" I exclaim.

She continues to eye me.

"Maybe," I say.

"But you went diving!"

"Well, you were all so jazzed about me meeting the dragons up close and personal. Everything happened so fast. I guess I just… powered through it."

"Andy! You should have said something!"

All I can do is shrug. No *way* am I telling her that I didn't want to look like a dweeb in front of Darcy.

Kim sighs. "Well, you *did* manage to dive and, from what I saw, faked it 'til you made it. Can't you do that here?"

"This is different."

"Why? Because there's no air supply?"

I nod. "The Kind have a… thing… about going completely underwater."

"I guess I can understand that. But we can't stay here. The pod wasn't designed to be inhabited. The only air is what was in here when the pod was dropped. That'll run out in a few hours."

"Furk," I mutter for the hundredth time.

"Andy, this is a survival situation. If you don't do this, we're both going to die down here." She says this with deliberate calm, though I can tell she's losing patience with me.

"Double furk," Then, standing on wobbly legs, I mutter, "Okay. Fine."

"It's not going to be that bad, I promise. Take my weight belt and add it to your own. It'll help you sink faster. Use your fins and swim straight down until you see another round opening like this one. Then go straight down through *that*. Then you'll be in Level C. The Comms System console is diamond-shaped and mounted on the wall on… let's see. If you keep your angle, it'll be on your left. The reboot control isn't marked, but it's easy to spot. It's a big white lever. Just pull the lever down and up again. Then drop the weights and swim straight back. Thirty seconds, tops."

"How long will the reboot take?" I ask.

"A couple of minutes, but you don't need to wait for that. Once comms is back online, it'll start sending telemetry back to Marius. Shelton will see it and put two and two together. There's your flare!"

I swallow.

"Got it?" she asks.

"Yeah."

"Keep your eyes open. The trace elements in the water might sting. But do your best to look where you're going."

I stare miserably down into the pool. At least now the water isn't completely black. Thanks to the defused light, I can make out some shapes. More gadgetry.

"Don't dive," Kim reminds me. "Just slide into the water."

I sit down on the edge, my legs dangling and my heart hammering. I'm sweating, but that's got nothing to do with the heat.

Kim says, "I know this seems scary, but you can do it."

I shudder and slide in, kicking my feet and bobbing in the center of the pool.

"Good. Take a few long slow breaths," she tells me. "Calm yourself. Steady your heart rate. Then, on the fourth breath, empty your lungs, and fill them way up. That's when you dive. Understand?"

I nod.

"Go save the day, little brother."

After preparing myself per instructions, I give Kim a final, terrified glance. She smiles in encouragement—then winces in fresh pain. Suddenly, I realize just how injured she is, and how guilty she must feel that I'm the one doing this and not her.

Time to grow a pair.

I empty my lungs and take as deep a breath as I can manage.

Then I slip beneath the surface.

Water envelopes me as it did back in Marius's moon pool, though this time it's much warmer and, with the lights turned on, a good deal brighter. As I start swimming downward, I notice that Level B looks pretty much the same as A, only with straight, curved walls without any tapering.

I swim harder. My lungs already feel tight, though I suppose most of that's psychological. Even so, I don't want to waste a second. I don't bother exploring or even looking around. Instead, I focus on the next open circular hatchway, this one in the floor.

The way to Level C, just like Kim said.

The water is far from clear. Little bits of *stuff* float in it. The particles are tiny, like grains of sugar, but all different colors. Gray, black, blue, green, and a kind of drab yellow.

My eyes begin stinging.

A fresh shudder runs through me at the thought of going blind, even temporarily. I'd never find my way back and would probably panic and drown down here.

I push the thought away—push it away *hard.*

The hatchway is only a few more feet down.

Suddenly, there's a dragon in my path.

It appears out of nowhere, filling most of my field of vision. Seeing it, I startle and let out a cry, a burst of bubbles that costs me precious air. I realize the dragon before me is Ravi—identified by its twin bracelets. It's waving its four arms energetically, even frantically.

Regardless, I need to get past the creature, and right now.

But when I try to skirt around, Ravi ducks in front of me again, blocking my way.

This isn't going to work. I'll have to turn back, tell Kim what happened. We'll figure something else out.

Then Ravi *moves.*

Remember the facehuggers from the old movie *Alien*? It's like that, lightning-quick, though maybe not quite as scary. The dragon suddenly bursts forward with terrific speed, spreading its arms wide. They clamp around my head, while its thick tail loops firmly around the back of my neck, and its entire body covers my mouth and nose.

An instant later, that weird fifth appendage juts out from the creature's chest — and *slithers* down my windpipe.

Instinctively, I recoil. But the little sucker's seriously strong; I can't budge him. Then, just as instinctively, my lungs spasm, trying to draw air that I know won't be there.

Except it is.

I don't know how, but warm oxygen-rich air fills my chest, clearing my head.

Almost immediately, my panic eases.

For several moments, I just float there in Level B with a dragon hugging my skull.

Ravi's face is right in front of mine, our eyes locked. It's hard to focus on them; he's just too close. But I can tell he's smiling.

Hold up. When did I start thinking of him as a "he?"

Four more dragons appear, rising up through the open hatchway. They latch onto my limbs, one each, and start pulling me downward with synchronized kicks of their strong tails.

Fresh fear burns in my chest. But then I focus on Ravi's serene, smiling face.

And, somehow, I know I'm okay.

The moment we enter Level C, I realize things are *very* different down here. Most of the hull has been crushed inward, probably when the pod crashed. Burnt orange stone juts through the ruptures, having destroyed much of the equipment. Alarmed, I look around for the Comms Systems — but don't see it. Then Ravi, as if sensing my anxiety, ducks his head to give me a better view.

And there it is.

Miraculously, the station that Kim described looks intact.

But that's not all that's down here, not by a long shot.

Eggs.

Thousands of them line every available surface, some mounted on the orange Europan stone, others stuck to what remains of the pod itself. There are adult dragons as well, dozens of them. They seem in constant motion, darting to and fro, tending the eggs.

Ravi and his "transport team" carry me deeper toward one cluster of eggs tucked in a corner between two mangled consoles. As we draw near, Ravi turns his head toward another dragon, who rushes forward as if commanded. In a surprisingly smooth transition, Ravi disconnects from me and swims away, and this new creature comes forward to take his place. The switch is so fast that I'm too surprised to protest. Besides, I need the air.

Afterward, with his replacement now at work keeping me from—well—drowning, Ravi hangs in the water, looking exhausted. Then he shakes himself, turns, and detaches one of the eggs from its cluster and holds it up for me to see. It's about half the size of my fist.

It's also clearly dead.

In fact, all the eggs share the same lackluster, lifeless gray.

Peering past the head of my new "air-bringer," I can now see that eighty percent of the eggs down here are dead. The remainder, a serious minority, have a more vibrant green color. Inside these, I can see young dragons shifting and twitching as they grow.

Things are looking bad for the next generation of Europans.

Is all this really from Marius scrubbing the tantalum out of the water?

But the dragons carry me deeper still.

In another niche amidst the jungle of stone and metal, I'm shown a cluster of eggs that are neither gray nor green, but somewhere in the middle. The fetuses inside move sluggishly, if at all. Ravi strokes these with particular care before looking up at me.

It's not easy to read his alien expression, but I'd have to be blind not to get what he's trying to communicate. While these particular eggs aren't dead, they soon will be. With the smoker plugged, there just isn't enough of the ambient warmth they need to survive.

And I guess that's where *I* come in.

I think of Kim. She's up there right now, breathing that stale, limited atmosphere, and probably half-convinced I've drowned. How long has it been? Two minutes?

But no way am I refusing this.

Waving Ravi aside, I reach out with one hand and summon my dragon. I'm afraid it might still be blocked by the surrounding ocean as it was earlier. But it comes easily enough, and I send it out through my palm. The intervening water ripples from the fresh thermal energy that kisses, rather than strikes, the dying eggs. Slowly, carefully, I turn up the thermostat.

The Europans all stop and watch, their bodies totally still and wearing looks of what I can only call a parent's terrified fascination. Watching so many of their children die must be torture for them.

I hope I can help.

I add a little more heat. Then a little more.

And, at last, the cluster of eggs turns green. The fetuses inside them begin to move.

Ravi smiles. They all do.

Then, almost all at once, the eggs under my dragon hatch.

They don't crack, like chicken eggs on Earth. Instead, they sort of tear and then deflate. Suddenly two dozen little dragons fill the water around me, each a fully-formed, miniature version of their already diminutive elders. At once, several adults rush forward and draw the hatchlings to their bosom. There, each hatchling attaches itself to one of those tubular chest appendages.

Is this how the babies breathe? Or maybe—eat?

Ravi is beaming ear-to-ear—not that he has ears.

After I pull back my dragon, I motion to Ravi to get his attention. Then I point toward where the Comms System Reboot lever is.

In answer, he gestures toward another group of half-dead eggs.

So, I nod and call my dragon again.

And again.

And again.

And again.

Not until Level C is crowded with tiny bodies that are either nursing, waiting to nurse, or whizzing about as if celebrating that they're alive at all, do I manage to make it over to the Comms System and do what Kim asked me to do.

ELEVEN – Glimpse

"My God, Kim!"

"Take it easy. I'm fine. Everybody's fine."

"Everybody almost *wasn't* fine. As it is, you came back needing twenty stitches, Carlos looks like he lost a fight with a bulldozer, and Jim's got two broken arms… *two*! He's going to need someone to wipe his butt for him for the next six weeks, assuming any of us live that long. For furk's sake, we've got armed soldiers closing in on us, and you decide to go on a dragon field trip?"

"Shelton, I get you're pissed. And maybe... *maybe...* going out the way we did was a stupid move. But think about what happened, what Andy and I found out!"

"You almost died!"

"But the dragons are smarter than we ever imagined! They brought Darcy, Jim, and Carlos back here. But they took Andy and me down to Pod One to show us the *real* damage we'd caused."

"There's no way we could have known what happened with Pod One."

"I agree with you, but that isn't my point. They picked Andy and me because they knew... somehow, they *knew*... that we were the only two who could survive Smokey's heat. What's more, they saw what Andy can do through the Breakroom viewport, and so they used him to save hundreds of their hatchlings."

"I get how they knew about Andy's abilities. But how did they figure out *you* were a Split?"

"I have no idea, but they clearly did."

"And if all they needed was Andy, why bring you along at all?"

"That's the part that really blows my mind! They brought me along because they grasped that Andy was a newcomer. They needed someone familiar enough with the pod to understand what we need to do."

"And what *do* we need to do?"

"Get Pod One out of Smokey!"

"We can't. Even if we didn't have CSE breathing down our necks, we don't have the means to pull it back up, not from that depth. You know that."

"But the dragons *didn't* know it, so they took a shot. They're far, far more advanced than we ever imagined!"

"Okay, I admit that's big news. But your timing still sucked. A lot's happened since you and Andy disappeared, none of it good. Coffin's thugs aren't 'coming' anymore. They're here... and right now, that coring unit of theirs is creeping toward us."

"Creeping?"

"As soon as it came through the ice, it immediately grew legs. Now it's crawling across the underside of the shelf toward us. Not fast, but steady."

"Liquid Bricks?"

"What else?"

"Well, we knew this day was coming."

"Yeah, Kim. And I *thought* we'd prepared. But with the Casimir Radio hack hosed and with the lift shot… well, we're in *big* trouble. I've got Francis working on shoring up our defenses. But the fact is that we can't keep them out, not for long."

"And once they're inside, they'll restart the scrubbers."

"It turns out that the scrubbers are only part of the problem and probably not the biggest part. Tantalum mining may have killed some of the adults, but Pod One being jammed inside the smoker is keeping whole new generations of dragons from hatching."

"Kim, are you telling me we could just switch the scrubbers back on?"

"No! Like we've all observed, stripping tantalum out of the water makes the locals sick, sometimes fatally. I'm saying that stopping the mining isn't enough to undo the damage we've done."

"Kim, I'm sorry as hell about Pod One. But right now, I'm more worried about our own lives. Remember Ramses and Vespa?"

"CSE won't go that far."

"Won't they? They know as well as we do what's really going on, what the stakes are."

"We all knew it when we voted."

"It's easy to be brave when the 'bad guys' are millions of miles away. Well, they're here now, they're pissed off, and they're going to want to make another example."

"What do you think Coffin'll do to *us*? The staff? You and me?"

"I don't know."

"But you can make a pretty good guess."

"I think Charles Coffin can't risk anyone spreading rumors about intelligent life on Europa."

"I was afraid you'd say that."

"Babe, I'm an engineer, not a revolutionary, and Marius is a mining colony, not a fortress. We've got few weapons, no training, and our backs are against a big wet deep proverbial 'wall.' If… when… CSE makes its assault, we don't have any long-term way to defend ourselves."

"We'll think of something. We always do."

"And, on top of all that… I thought you were dead."

"Well, I'm not. Um… you want a hug?"

"Wouldn't say no, but I'd rather have a weapon."

"Shelton…"

"Yeah, babe?"

"Maybe we *have* a weapon."

TWELVE – Day 22

"So far as I can tell," Darcy reports. *"They have only one gender."*

She's in her lab on — you guessed it — the Lab Deck. The space isn't large, but it's clean and seems well-equipped, and Darcy moves through it with competent familiarity. This is her turf and, dressed in her green scrubs, latex gloves, and surgical mask, she's all business.

The rest of us — Kim, Shelton, and me — are huddled outside the room, looking through the Biology Lab's single interior window, listening to Darcy's voice through the speakers as she autopsies her first Europan.

"The chest appendage seems connected to most of the primary systems, circulatory, respiratory, reproductive. From the look of things, I'd say they lay their eggs through this tube and also use it to feed their young."

"I saw the second part of that," I say.

Kim remarks, "Also, they somehow stuck them down our throats so they could breathe for us."

"Except," I add. "Doing that for too long… kills them."

The little guy Darcy's currently working on is the same dragon — not Ravi, but the *second* one — who latched onto my face in Level C.

Maybe I should catch you guys up.

Down in Pod One, after I fired off Kim's "flare," the Europans escorted me back up to Level A. Then, as I treaded water in the flooded hatchway with Kim looking on, the dragon who'd been breathing for me collapsed and slipped into the water. Dead.

Feeling sick, I pulled myself out of the "moon pool." Kim, meanwhile, had fashioned a crude tourniquet for her leg from a length of cable. She looked okay, though clearly in pain, and *very* relieved to see me.

Ravi and my escorts collected the dragon's floating corpse. Then Ravi motioned for us to put the other two, the ones who'd breathed for us when we were first brought into the pod, in the water so they could be taken, as well.

These creatures honored their dead.

We did as he asked. But, to our surprise, Ravi pushed the most recent guy over to the water's edge.

Kim and I exchanged looks.

"Take it," she whispered.

As I reached for the poor creature's body, Ravi nodded but didn't smile. The rest of them looked on solemnly.

The Europan weighed nothing and fit easily in one hand.

Afterward, Ravi and the others vanished beneath the surface.

Seated beside Kim on the deck of Level A, alone now, I held the body of the small being who'd guarded my life. Rescue came, just as Kim had predicted, a couple of hours later.

Being unmanned, both by design and necessity, Pod Two locked onto the telemetry Pod One was transmitting and navigated itself right to us, fastening onto our top port automatically. Once this was completed, I jumped up—bless low-G—opened the connecting hatchway, and helped a wincing Kim up and into Pod Two's Level C.

This was followed by a long, uncomfortable ride back up to the colony.

Once there, we found a greatly relieved Darcy and very pissed off Shelton waiting for us. Darcy had us take Kim straight to Sick Bay to be stitched up and treated for pain and swelling. Afterward, at Shelton's request, we left the two of them there to "debrief," while I followed Darcy up to the Lab Deck, carrying in my arms the dead dragon who, among others, had saved our lives.

Now the Sheltons, their "debrief" concluded, have joined me outside Darcy's lab to witness the Solar System's first practicing xenopologist do her medical examiner thing. Kim's leg is bandaged and she limps a little, but other than that she seems okay.

There. You're caught up.

"Did you ever name him?" I ask Kim.

"Who?"

"That dragon. The one she's… working on."

Kim shakes her head. "We only ever named Ravi. He's the only one we can easily identify. The others… look alike."

Her husband adds dryly, "They probably think the same thing about us."

"No, they don't," I remark. "They knew enough to take just me and Kim down to Pod One. They can recognize human faces." I look through the window again. "He should have a name."

"Then name him," Kim suggests.

I consider for maybe thirty seconds before declaring, "Albert, Isaac, and Charles."

They both look quizzically at me.

"Three Europans died to save us. The first two I'm naming for Albert Einstein and Isaac Newton. This one is Charles, for Charles Darwin."

"Then there's the three who brought Darcy, Jim, and Carlos back to Marius," Shelton points out. "They died as well, I'm sorry to say, and the rest of the dragons took their bodies away when they left."

"Why don't they take turns or something?" Kim wondered. "Why stick with us until they die?"

"I don't know," I reply miserably. "They switched with me back in Pod One, but I think that was because Ravi needed to be in charge."

Shelton suggests, "Maybe it's a cultural thing, a matter of personal honor."

"I wish we could ask them," Kim remarks.

"In the meantime," I say. "How about Stephen, Nikola, and Marie for the other three."

Kim considers. "Hawking, Tesla, and Curie? Why not?"

Through the speakers, Darcy reports, *"The level of oxygen in the subject's blood is practically zero. This little guy died of asphyxiation."*

"It died," I suppose, "because every bit of oxygen it could produce from the water it deliberately gave to me... and the effort eventually killed it."

"A pretty fair assessment," Darcy says. *"Man, there's some serious nobility there."*

"Yeah," I whispered. "There is."

"Why do you think Ravi gave us this specimen?" Shelton asks no one in particular. Then, seeing my face, he hastily amends, "Charles. I mean Charles."

"Maybe it was a thank you?" Kim replies. "To Andy, for saving their eggs."

"A weird thank you," I say.

"Not so weird," Shelton remarks. "They must know we're curious about them. Remember all those passive experiments Darcy conducted in the beginning?"

I look at him. "Passive experiments?"

Kim rolls her eyes. "As I've explained to my husband a million times, there are active experiments and passive observations, but not passive experiments."

"Nit-picking," Shelton grumbles.

She ignores him. "What he's talking about are noninvasive observations that Darcy and I made in the first months after we discovered the dragons… or, more accurately, after they discovered us. Back then, we still couldn't quite believe what we were seeing. I mean… there's been speculation about life on Europa for a century. But I never really believed that we'd…" Her words trailed off, her expression glassy with memory.

I catch Shelton's eye. He's smiling.

Kim continues, "Anyway, Darcy and I put together a series of tests meant to try to reveal aspects of their behavior. Visual stimuli mostly, since sound doesn't penetrate well through the viewports." She grins broadly. "And they seemed to *love* it. We showed them lights… white and colored, photographs of Earth, of Europa, of *themselves*. We even held up mirrors, and they couldn't get enough of that. After a while, Shelton set up a suggestion box for everyone to drop in further ideas."

Her husband adds, "Somewhere along the way, we stopped being miners and became zoologists."

"Xenopologists," Kim and I say at the same time.

He laughs.

Kim regards Darcy, still busy with her vivisection. "But this'll tell us more in an hour than we've learned the entire time we've been down here." Then, after a moment, she adds, a little bitterly, "It's fascinating but still awful."

Shelton says, "Let Darcy do her thing. Then let's put… everything… back as best we can and return the cadaver. Least we can do."

Kim nods.

"I'm glad I was able to help them," I remark. "It may be the first really good thing my dragon's ever done."

"You saved *Conquest*," Shelton points out. "That counts as a good thing, doesn't it?"

I think about the coring unit that's still crab walking toward us, no doubt loaded with blackbirds. "Does it?"

"If you hadn't, you'd be dead now," Kim points out. "That counts as a good thing in my book."

"Mine, too!" Darcy calls from inside the lab.

Shelton says. "I really wish we could do something more permanent to help them. The dragons, I mean. I had no idea Pod One had caused so much damage."

Kim nods. "It's plugging up Smokey, blocking most of the heat, and it's the heat that lets the dragon eggs hatch."

"Can't we get Pod One out of there somehow?" I ask.

Shelton shakes his head. "It's eighty miles down. The only thing we have that can reach that depth is Pod Two, and its engines weren't designed for towing something so big. I'm really sorry, but it's stuck down there."

Kim offers a crooked grin. "Don't suppose we could ask our arriving 'guests' to help out? We could tell them that having Smokey plugged is making it harder to get tantalum."

"No chance," Shelton mutters. "Even if we meekly roll over and turn the scrubbers back on, CSE's likely to bomb the smoker and wipe out the dragons just out of spite."

They both look my way as if expecting that I'll jump to Miranda's defense. I don't, though not because I believe she'd do something so callous and vindictive.

The truth is, I honestly don't know.

So, instead, I ask, "Where's the coring unit now?"

"Almost here," Shelton replies. "They managed to relaunch the damned thing sooner than we expected. I've already ordered the Ice Deck to be evacuated. Afterward, we'll seal it off from Lab and Ops. That'll buy us some time."

"But they'll get in?" I ask.

He nods.

Kim says, "We're hoping if we make it difficult enough, Coffin will decide to negotiate."

"Let me talk to them," I say. "To Miranda."

"That's a stupid idea!" This comes through the speakers. Darcy hasn't even looked up from her work, though I can see her scowl under the surgical mask.

"Darcy..." Shelton begins.

She straightens and angrily pulls off her gloves and mask before exiting the lab. "No, I mean it!" she exclaims, addressing Shelton. "That bitch played him! She played him like a fiddle!" Then she glances at me and adds, "No offense."

Cleverly, I reply, "Um…"

"She and her father shanghaied you, murdered your family, and manipulated you so that they could get down here to us. On top of all that, her security chief shot you in the back! Or am I missing something?"

"Sounds about right to me," Kim says.

I mutter, "Close enough."

"See?" Darcy declares. "A stupid idea!"

"Even so… I should talk to Miranda."

"She won't listen to you," Darcy insists sharply.

"She'll listen to me more than to any of you. Look, I'm not as blind as you think I am. I get what she did to me. The lies. The manipulation. But, for all that, there was… is… a connection between us. Besides, they're coming anyway. What have you got to lose by letting me try?"

Darcy says, "It's what *you've* got to lose! Your furking life!"

"Miranda's not going to —" But that's as far as I get before Kim beats me to the punch.

"I don't think so," she says.

Darcy glares at her. "You don't *think* so?"

"No, I don't," Kim replies calmly. "First of all, when Andy got shot topside, it was in response to the… accident… with the blackbird who tried to grab me."

I picture the man's grisly death and can't suppress a shudder.

Kim goes on. "Spencer's people may be thugs, but they're not stupid. They know the risks involved in shooting Andy. Even if Coffin doesn't care about *our* lives, she cares about getting our tantalum mining back online. And that won't happen if Marius… melts."

I don't bother explaining that shooting me wouldn't "melt" the colony; more likely, it would vaporize it.

Darcy says, "It's still stupid."

"Desperate, maybe," Kim replies. "But Andy's right. The blackbirds will be here soon, and making Andy our spokesman seems like a good play, maybe our *only* play."

Shelton considers. Then he turns my way. "You sure you're up for this?"

"It was *my* idea," I reply.

"Unfortunately, the blackbirds aren't responding to hails. So, we're going to have to be on hand to meet them when they attach and cut through the hull."

"Okay," I reply with more bravado than I feel.

"But not just you," he adds. "*I'll* be right beside you."

"And me," Kim says.

"No," her husband protests.

"And me," Darcy says.

"Listen to me, you two…" Shelton begins.

But from the way both women look at him, I know this is one battle of wills he's already lost. And from the expression on his face, *he* knows it too.

THIRTEEN – Day 22

The first time I stepped out of my room on Marius, the Ice Deck felt empty. Eerily so.

Was that *really* just two days ago?

Now, as Darcy, the Sheltons, and I climb the central staircase to Marius's top deck and seal the heavy flood door behind us, the place really *is* empty. An hour ago, everyone was evacuated to the lower decks to await Big Brother's visit.

To prepare to be boarded.

Shelton touches a comms unit affixed to his collar. No e-mans on Marius. "Francis, we're locked in. You got us?"

Saint Francis' sounds irritated, as usual. "*I've got you, boss. I'm registering four distinct heat signatures. Funny, I'd expect the Dragon to show up whiter… more heat.*"

When they all look at me, I shrug. "You want hotter? I can give you hotter."

"That's okay," Shelton tells me. Then, into the comms collar, he asks, "What about the coring unit?"

"*Sensors show it latching onto the hull now. Looks like a crazy-ass crab.*"

"Relative to us?"

"*Due north. When they cut through, it'll be into the fitness room.*"

"Got it." Shelton addresses the three of us, "This way."

Marius's fitness room occupies the end of one of the residential corridors. The machines inside look like alien torture devices, with padded clamps and rubberized bands to keep their health-conscious user firmly in place as well as physically challenged. This makes sense. Free weights aren't much good when they only weigh ten percent of what they would on Earth. By that yardstick, everyone on Europa is Superman. So instead, "isometric" and "isotonic" are the words of the day, with these specialized gadgets designed to offer resistance in a low-G environment. Of course, all my observations about exercise equipment are just to distract me from what's really going on.

The last time I was face-to-face with blackbirds, I killed one of them.

They're *not* going to be happy to see me.

"When will they come through?" Darcy asks Shelton.

"Any moment now."

"Get behind me," I tell them. "Stay bunched together in the doorway. Don't spread out."

"Andy—" Kim begins.

"They probably won't shoot me. But that guarantee doesn't apply to you guys."

Darcy exclaims, "You're not bulletproof!"

"Actually, I kind of am."

"You weren't topside!" Kim points out.

"Because I didn't see it coming. This time I will. I can even protect you guys… *if* I stay between you and the bullets."

"Okay," Shelton says. "We've got your back."

Kim and Darcy nod in agreement, and I'm both touched and unnerved by their faith in me. The three of them obligingly return to the fitness room threshold. A part of me wishes they'd shut the nice heavy metal door. But I know they won't.

And another part of me is very, very grateful to them for it.

Because I'm scared.

Okay, it's not exactly the first time I've been scared since all this started. But somehow, this "scared" feels different from those "scareds." Up until now, my fear's been personal. Even when I threw up that thermal shield in Engineering, I wasn't thinking of my shipmates' asses so much as my own.

I'm no hero.

This time, though, I'm not just scared for myself. It isn't for Shelton, or Darcy, or Kim either.

I keep picturing all those gray eggs in Pod One.

Two of the Europans died for me, literally gave their last breath. Yes, they did it for their own reasons, but they still did it, and the light of that selflessness is almost too bright to look at.

Darcy nailed it. The dragons, as a race, are—noble.

And I don't want to see them wiped out.

So, I'm scared.

Shelton's comms collar crackles to life. No surprise, it's Saint Francis. *"Boss, I've got a thermal spike coming from the coring unit. I think this is it."*

"Copy that," Shelton says. I look back and meet all their eyes.

Shelton and Kim both nod to me.

Darcy smiles.

But I can see that they're scared, too.

Abruptly, a jet of blue flame penetrates the metal of the fitness room's far wall. Spencer's people have apparently completed their seal, and now they're cutting their way inside with a laser torch.

"Andy?" Kim asks, sounding tentative.

Shelton responds before I can. "It's okay. He's got this."

Do I? Do I really?

It only takes a minute. Then a chunk of wall roughly six feet in diameter crashes to the floor. It's louder than I would have imagined, considering the low-G.

Blackbirds fill the space behind it. Blackbirds with guns.

I throw up my hand.

My dragon hits the circle of metal on the floor. I don't melt it. Instead, I concentrate on exciting the molecules in its first few millimeters of depth, supercharging them, and then supercharging the air above them.

A thermal wall.

It reaches the ceiling, softening the metal there. The air in between twists and writhes as bright streaks of static electricity run through it. A perfect shield, exactly where I want it, and as big as I want it. And, miraculously, here I am still wearing clothes. Whatever other miseries being in the coring unit visited on me and my life, it did teach me a level of control that I've never had before.

I wonder if my dad would be proud of me.

Three blackbirds emerge, followed by three more. They're gripping their rifles tightly, nervously.

I raise my other hand and widen the thermal wall between us.

The soldiers warily eye the shimmering curtain of superheated air. Their leader, a stone-faced woman, gestures to her troops. They fan out, moving carefully left and right and requiring me to widen my force field further. It's getting hard to maintain, not because I lack the power, but because directing it so precisely is exhausting. I don't know how long I can keep this up.

No one speaks.

Finally, I decide to break the silence. I say to the woman, "You in charge?"

Stone Face says something back. Except I can't hear her.

Shelton remarks from behind me, "Sound can't get through whatever you're doing."

"Oh," I say, feeling stupid. "Right." I think for a moment, trying to put aside my fear and instead weigh my options. Finally, I ask, "Um… do you guys trust me?"

"Yes," Kim replies at once.

"Darcy?"

"Yeah, I do."

"Shelton?"

Nothing.

"Shelton?"

"I trust you."

"Then close the door."

Shelton says, "Okay, but *I'm* staying in the room."

"It's liable to get really hot in here."

"I speak for Marius, Andy. I need to be here."

"*I'll* stay," Kim says.

Shelton shakes his head. "I get that would make the most sense from a Split point of view. But I'm the leader of this colony. It needs to be me."

Kim scowls. For a moment, husband and wife eye each other defiantly.

"Guys…" I say. Sweat's stinging my brow. That may sound weird, but it's happening. "Doing this isn't as easy as you might think…"

Finally, Kim sighs. "Let's go, Darcy." Then her gaze moves from me to her husband and back again. "Don't let him do anything stupid."

I honestly don't know which one of us she's talking to.

Kim and Darcy step back into the hallway, closing the heavy door behind them.

"Get in the corner," I tell Shelton.

He doesn't argue.

I turn back to the blackbirds and, with a sigh, drop the thermal wall. The instant it's gone, the soldiers raise their weapons. Some are pointed at me, some at Shelton.

I raise my hand toward them, not in a menacing way, but more with a "don't shoot!" vibe.

Shelton says, "Who's in charge?"

The woman in the middle steps forward. "I am."

"You're not Spencer," Shelton remarks.

"Sergeant Massey," she says. "I report to Mister Spencer and speak for the mission. You are Michael David Shelton?"

"Yeah."

"Michael David Shelton, I am placing you under arrest by order of Charles Coffin."

"Since when do billionaire businessmen get to write bench warrants?" Shelton asks, not as snarkily as you might think, either.

"You're under arrest," Massey says. "If you resist, you'll be fired upon. Marius is now under my direct command. Do you understand these orders?"

Shelton says nothing.

Massey raises her own rifle. "Do you understand these orders, Mister Shelton?"

Enough.

I call my dragon again.

This time, I don't try to direct it. I just let it out, the way I did back in my cell aboard *Conquest* before I had the slightest idea what the furk was going on. Back when Conceal and Protect still meant something.

My clothes vaporize. What little hair I've managed to grow back since exploding on the lift disappears. I see Shelton shield his face and drop down behind a bulky piece of exercise equipment. Elsewhere, the CSE guys stagger backward, their weapons now trained entirely on me.

Good.

"Nobody shoot!" I hear Massey order.

"This freak killed Hofmeister!"

I flash, once again, on those last terrible moments on the surface. So, now I know the man's name. If anything, it deepens my guilt. But I steel myself and say as callously as I can, "If you don't want to join him, lower your guns."

The hatred radiating off them seems as hot as any dragon. The kid in me—yeah, he's still there—wants to cringe away. But I don't. Instead, I regard them all through a heat haze that's still nowhere near enough to weaken the floor or ceiling. This isn't my cell, and the last thing I want to do is start melting walls.

"Do as he says," Massey tells the others. "Stand down. Now."

Her blackbirds obey, albeit reluctantly, resentfully. To them, I'm a monster and a murderer.

And maybe I am.

As Shelton rises from behind his makeshift shield, I draw back my dragon some more. With a nod to me, he looks at Massey and says, "Let's talk."

"My orders don't include negotiating."

"Then I suggest you get some *new* orders."

"You can't keep us out forever."

I say, "Sure, we can. All I have to do is melt that coring unit of yours."

"Liquid Bricks. We'll make another."

"And I'll melt that one, too," I tell her. "Liquid Bricks are cool, I'll grant you that. But they aren't a limitless resource. I, on the other hand, can do this forever."

Shelton says, "All of which points to talking instead of fighting."

Massey's face is red, either from consternation or heat. For a moment that's as tight as a guitar string, nobody speaks. Finally, the blackbird commander says, "I'll contact Mister Spencer and see what he wants to do. In the meantime, my men will stay right here."

"No," Shelton replies. "You and your men will withdraw, and we'll seal up the hull behind you. Then, when your negotiator comes, you can cut a new one… or you might consider coming in underwater, through the moon pool. You know, entering our colony like civilized guests."

"My men stay."

I take a step forward. "No, they don't."

Massey and every single other blackbird take an involuntary step back. A few raise their guns but then lower them again.

"Fine," Massey says. "I'll pass along your request."

"You do that," Shelton tells her.

The soldiers withdraw, moving much more slowly going out than they did coming in. When the last of them leave, I drop my dragon, and Shelton steps around his makeshift barrier to stand beside me. I'm stark naked, of course, but he offers no comment. I find myself liking him for that.

"Can you close the breach?" he asks me. "Or do I need to have Francis send up a metal-working staff?"

"I can do it," I reply. And I can. Maybe I couldn't back on *Conquest*, but the more I use my dragon, the better I'm getting at controlling it. Even my nakedness just now was more for effect than necessity. I'm not even all that tired. "But I'll need a couple of guys to help."

"Sure."

"In safety gear," I tell him.

"Copy that," he says with a grim smile.

"In the meantime, I'll stay here to make sure they don't try anything."

"Good idea. And I'll get you some new clothes."

"Thanks."

"No, Andy," he says, resting a hand on my bare shoulder. He does this tentatively as if afraid I might still be hot. Then, when he finds this isn't the case, he laughs a little and adds, "Thank *you*."

PART FIVE
THE DIPLOMAT

ONE – Glimpse

"Mister Coffin."

"*Spencer.*"

"Massey's reported in. Her blackbirds were able to penetrate the hull and enter MC-13."

"*Excellent work, though something in your tone suggests to me that things after that point were less successful.*"

"Yes, sir. They were met in the first chamber by Michael Shelton… and Andy Brand."

"*Brand's alive, then.*"

"He is. At first, he put up one of those force fields of his. But when he realized no one could speak through it, he lowered it again. Massey, as per my orders, then attempted to formally arrest Shelton, who resisted. However, before he could be compelled, Brand… he…"

"*Was anyone killed, Spencer?*"

"No, sir. Brand didn't attack; he simply… lit up, the way he did the first time he showed his abilities. Massey reports the heat was so great that nobody could approach or get around him."

"*I see.*"

"Shelton requested a negotiator. Massey refused. But then, judging the circumstances to be untenable, she opted to withdraw and forward Shelton's demand to me."

"*An interesting turn of events. But, given Brand's survival of the lift incident, his alliance with the colonists isn't surprising.*"

"Agreed. However, his presence there makes securing MC-13 without loss of life impractical, in my opinion."

"*I'm not convinced of that. MC-13 remains cut off from its supply lines. If need be, we can wait them out. Their stockpiles can't last forever.*"

"If you say so, sir."

"*I understand your objections. You want bold action to send a message to the broader spacer community. I know that was Miranda's thinking as well, and there was a time when I would have agreed. But right now, I'm less* concerned about making an example than in settling this matter as discreetly as possible. Please don't mistake reticence for weakness, Spencer. Political considerations have arisen since Conquest's launch that neither you nor Miranda are aware of."

"I understand, Mister Coffin."

"So, Shelton wants to negotiate?"

"Yes, sir."

"With me?"

"He didn't name anyone in particular."

"My daughter, perhaps?"

"With respect, I don't think that would be a good idea."

"I take it Miranda's still unhappy with her change of status. Did you convey my request to speak with her?"

"I did. But she refused to even acknowledge me. These days, she speaks to no one."

"She was always... willful. Even as a child, her boarding school-masters frequently reported errant behavior. She responds poorly to discipline and abhors having something taken from her once she's grown... accustomed to having it."

"I'm not following, sir."

"I'm speaking of power, Spencer. Authority. My daughter's self-possessed beyond her years, but it was wrong of me to burden her with the adjunct's role aboard Conquest, despite all her petitioning. Considering her reaction to the Dragon, my faith in her may have been... premature. In any event, I'm afraid I must agree with you. Miranda would make a poor negotiator. You'll have to take on that responsibility."

"Me? I—"

"Yes, I know. You've made it quite clear you're a soldier, not a diplomat. However, given the circumstances, you're the only option."

"What about Captain Wei?"

"Wei's a capable captain, but this situation calls for absolute loyalty to CSE, and his spacer sympathies make him an even poorer choice than Miranda. Sorry, Spencer. It has to be you."

"I understand, Mister Coffin."

"Look at it this way: Shelton's no fool. He must realize that, with the lift destroyed, the coring unit is the only hope his people have of long-term survival."

"I agree."

"*All right. Meet with him in good faith but inform him that no further supplies will be provided until control of MC-13 is surrendered. Bring armed men with you, but don't shoot unless fired upon.*"

"Yes, sir. And if Brand accompanies him?"

"*If an opportunity arises for you to do it safely, you are authorized to kill the Dragon. Then, with him out of the way, you can arrest Shelton and easily reclaim the colony.*"

"Yes, Mister Coffin."

TWO - Day 22

I'm back in the Ops Deck conference room, though this time, things are— different.

First, there are *lots* more people crammed in here, including Shelton, Kim, Darcy, Saint Francis, and about a dozen strangers. Kim introduced them as Marius's "department heads," but I've already forgotten their names.

Seventeen squeezed into a space meant for ten, tops.

I don't like tight spaces.

Second, Shelton, Kim, and Darcy all treat me like a rock star. In fact, Shelton's just finished recounting what happened in the fitness room, and with such enthusiasm that I'm reminded of Greenjeans. Unfortunately, his audience is less receptive than *Conquest's* crew. Most regard me with unease—a few, like Francis, with disapproval.

"So," Shelton announces. "It looks like the war's postponed, at least for now."

"When do you figure we'll hear back about this… negotiator?" Francis asks.

"Soon. But let's keep watching the scanners in case they try something."

"I don't like it," someone says. "CSE never negotiates fairly."

Darcy replies, "They will if it's their only option." Then she winks at me.

But Francis shakes his head. "Maybe they *have* other options. We just haven't considered them."

"Like what?" Kim asks.

Francis starts ticking off fingers. "From the outside, they could plug up the intake manifolds for our air makers."

"Air makers?" I ask.

Kim replies, "We get air by collecting water in special tanks and superheating it until the molecules split into oxygen and hydrogen. The hydrogen gets recycled into keeping the tanks hot, and the oxygen is mixed with inert gasses to make our air."

"Like the gills," I remark.

Shelton says, "Only on a much bigger scale."

Francis ignores us. "Then again, they could drop something in the manifolds that would either drug us or poison us. I can think of a half-dozen substances that would do the trick. Or, and this is the way *I'd* play it, they could do nothing."

"Nothing?" another someone says.

"Sure. We've got food stockpiled, but without fresh supplies, we'll run out eventually. We can manufacture drinking water, but there's not exactly much to eat on Europa… unless you count dragons, I guess."

"That's disgusting!" Darcy insists.

"Just making a point."

"CSE won't wait that long," Shelton says. "There's no way *Conquest* has fuel enough for a year's worth of orbits around Jupiter."

Francis shrugs. "All they have to do is set up a colony of their own on the surface. At minimum, they'd need a lander loaded with enough Liquid Bricks to build a semi-permanent shelter, with food and water to keep them going until the supply ships start up again. Six months, tops."

That thought shuts everyone down, even Shelton.

Finally, Kim mutters, "I didn't think of that."

Francis says, "It gets worse. Even if, by some miracle, we *do* get CSE to concede to all our demands, including restarting supply drops, we got no lift." He glares at me. "All thanks to our 'hero' here."

"Ease up, Francis," Kim warns.

"Somebody has to say it! You and the boss have been dancing around it for too long. Without the lift, our days are numbered. Granted, it's a big number. Two standard years, maybe. But unless we do something, we're all going to starve down here regardless of what the blackbirds do."

Kim shifts uncomfortably and suggests, "How about if we focus on one crisis at a time."

"No," Shelton replies. "Francis is right. The destruction of the lift wasn't anticipated, and it leaves us on a less than ideal footing." He doesn't look my way when he says this—though Francis and some of the others do. "But for now, let's focus on the more immediate threat. We knew it might come to this when we all voted to go down the Orpheus and Eurydice road. You all know that this is bigger than just Marius, bigger than just the dragons. Hell, it's bigger than just Europa."

That confuses me, but Francis speaks up before I can.

"Sure," he says. "The spacer cause is great, but I don't see any independent freighters showing up from Mars to defend us against CSE, do you?"

Darcy shoots back, "That's because nobody knows what we're doing!"

"A lot of spacers *must* know," Shelton says. "The supply ship crews would have spread word of what we've done, regardless of Coffin's news blackout."

"Yeah," Francis replies. "But they don't know the reason behind this half-baked rebellion. They don't know about the dragons!"

"That's because we didn't get the Casimir message out," Kim replies.

"And whose fault was that?" Francis asks, glaring at me again.

Kim and Darcy both look ready to launch themselves at the guy, something that might be doable in the low-G. But Shelton raises a hand. "Blame's useless at this point."

"That's right," Kim says, her eyes shooting daggers at Francis, who doesn't seem to give a crap. "But I still think getting our news to Earth should be our first priority."

Francis replies, "In *my* book, not dying should be our first priority."

"And the way to do that is by getting the message out," Kim insists. "Once the dragons' existence becomes system-wide public knowledge, CSE will have to back off."

"At least, that's the theory," Darcy remarks.

"Maybe there's another option," Francis says, crossing his arms like he knows his next words won't be popular. "We could tell Coffin that we'll restart the scrubbers."

He's right. It's not popular.

"We can't!" someone exclaims.

"Of course not!" someone else says at the same time.

"Are you nuts?" a third someone demands.

I *really* need to learn these people's names.

"That's not an option," Kim says darkly. "You *know* that!"

"Do I?" Francis presses. "What I know *now* is that it's hasn't been the tantalum mining that's been hurting the dragon population. It's Pod One plugging up Smokey."

"Not entirely," says Darcy. "The pod is crippling their breeding, but my autopsy of the dragon confirmed that their systems depend heavily on trace metals in the water. Stripping this part of the ocean of tantalum leaves them malnourished… on top of what Pod One has done."

Shelton turns to Francis. "Even if we *did* decide to resume harvesting, it'd take at least a week to bring the scrubbers back online and a month to reach our original production levels."

Darcy asks, "Can we keep the blackbirds out that long?"

"Not a chance," Francis replies.

"We don't have to," Shelton says. "Thanks to Andy, we've got a footing for negotiation. I say we tell them we'll resume mining, but that it'll take… three months… before we can provide them with a new tantalum shipment."

"We can't start mining again," Kim says. "You heard what Darcy just told us."

"And we're not going to. We're only going to *tell* them that."

Francis scowls. "You lost me."

Kim smiles at her husband. "You want to try the RCH again."

"Yep."

"What's an RCH?" I ask.

"It stands for 'Remote Comms Hack,'" Shelton explains. "It's a gadget we designed that taps into CSE's proprietary communication system when it's brought into close proximity."

"That's the thing that Kim had hidden in her suit," I surmise. "It would have let her send a pre-programmed message to Earth via the Casimir Radio."

"Not just Earth," Darcy says.

I look at her. "What?"

"The message wasn't just meant for Earth," Shelton explains. "The RCH was programmed to invade *Conquest's* comms system, request a wormhole, and then send the same data packet to two dozen different media outlets on Earth, Mars, the moon, and most of the larger colonies. Earth's too far away to help us quickly enough. But there are spacer communities in the asteroid belt and aboard merchant ships that *could* come to our aid."

Kim adds, "And even if nobody shows, the data packet includes incontrovertible proof that the dragons exist. That news won't just shake Coffin's applecart; it'll tip it over and stomp on his wares."

Nice metaphor.

Francis points at me. "Or that's what would have happened if this one hadn't screwed the pooch."

Not so nice a metaphor.

"Time to get over it, Saint Francis," Darcy tells him.

"I don't like being called that!" he shoots back.

"Kind of why I do it," Darcy replies sweetly.

"Enough," Shelton says. "The prototype RCH got cooked in the lift. But I've had another one assembled and tested. If we can get it onto their lander, it should interface with the onboard ship-to-surface comms, navigate their security, worm its way to the Casimir Radio, and execute its program."

"And our negotiator will wear it?" Francis asks.

"Exactly."

"What if CSE doesn't want to hold negotiations in the lander? What if they decide to keep things in the coring unit?"

"That's why we negotiate for three months," Shelton replies. "That'll give us ninety days to finagle a surface visit… once we're back to being good little CSE toadies."

"I hate pandering to those furkheads," Kim mutters.

"Me too," her husband admits. "But anybody got a better idea?"

No one does.

Kim says, "I'm assuming I just have to do the same thing with this RCH as I did with the last one?"

"Not you," Shelton replies. "This time, *I'm* going."

"No," his wife tells him.

"Yes," he says. "The last time you almost got killed."

She fixes him with the same kind of look that my mom musters… *used* to muster whenever she was pissed-off at Dad. "Oh, but it's okay for *you* to risk *your* life?"

Shelton says nothing.

"I'd volunteer," Francis remarks sourly. "But the way you're both selling it, I think I'll pass."

"This isn't open for debate," Shelton says. "I'm going."

"The hell you *are!*" Kim exclaims.

Something chirps.

Everyone goes quiet.

"What was that?" I ask Darcy.

"Intercom," she whispers back.

Shelton reaches forward and taps a button, one of many, set into the center of the crowded conference table. "Yeah?" he says, his tone impatient.

A woman's voice fills the cramped room. *"Boss, it's Sarah. We just got a message from Conquest."*

"Read it to us."

"It says, 'Charles Coffin is willing to negotiate. Negotiations will be held in good faith at 08:00 GMT tomorrow morning. The negotiator will present himself, alone, at today's point of entry. The negotiator's safety is guaranteed. The negotiator will be escorted into the coring unit to meet with Mister Coffin's representative. Upon completion of negotiations, regardless of the outcome, the negotiator will be returned to Marius if the negotiator so desires.'"

"'If the negotiator so desires?'" Francis says. "What the hell does *that* mean?"

"Uh oh," Kim mutters.

"What?" someone asks.

Shelton says into the intercom. "Is that all of it?"

"No, boss. There's this bit at the end, like a postscript."

"Read it."

"It says, 'Negotiator is to be Andy Brand. No one else will be accepted.'"

It takes me a few seconds to process this. When I look up, everyone at the table is staring at me.

Coffin's representative is going to be Miranda!

Well, of course, it is.

"That's just great," Francis mutters.

To my surprise, Darcy takes my hand under the table. It's the first time we've touched. The simple gesture hits me harder than I let on.

"Not a chance!" Kim says. "They're crazy!"

"It's a smart play," Shelton replies thoughtfully. "They know he's the only thing stopping them from retaking the colony. Capture him, and we're theirs."

"Or kill him," Darcy says.

Shelton slowly nods.

"Push back!" Kim exclaims. "Tell them we'll agree to everything except the negotiator. Tell them that's *our* call!"

"No," I say.

Once again, they all stare at me.

I clear my throat. "Up in the fitness room, the blackbird-in-charge wasted no time trying to arrest Shelton at gunpoint."

"And she would have," Shelton added, "if you hadn't been there."

"All the more reason *not* to hand him over to the blackbirds!" Francis insists.

"I didn't know you cared about him," Darcy chimes in.

"I care about *us*!" Francis replies sharply. "That freak's the best defense we've got! Furk, he's the *only* defense!"

"My *point*," I continue, ignoring the 'freak' remark, "is that Miranda's insisting on talking to nobody but me. That means anybody else who shows up is going to get arrested, period. Then they'll just make their demand again, only this time they'll have a hostage."

Francis smirks. "And what makes you think, once you're aboard the coring unit, they'll just let you make our case and leave?"

I meet his eyes. "What choice would they have?"

"They could arrest *you*!"

"Yeah? How?"

Francis stares at me. His mouth snaps shut. Small victories.

Kim and Shelton exchange a glance. Something passes between them in that weird "married-people" way.

Finally, Shelton says, "Andy's right."

Kim looks like she's eating an onion.

Darcy says, "So, your idea is to plant the RCH on Andy and then send him to see that… monster?"

"If he's up for it."

I look at Darcy. "I'm up for it."

She looks back at me. "This is crazy."

Kim mutters. "You bet it is. Got another idea?"

Darcy shuts her mouth and sits back, stewing.

I ask, "Will the RCH work from the coring unit?"

"No," Shelton replies. "It needs to be aboard the lander with close proximity access to its comms system."

"Then, I have to try to get Miranda to take me up to the lander."

Francis groans. "And if they do haul you up the ice shaft, how can you *force* them to bring you back?"

"I'll tell them I'll ground the lander if they don't."

Kim says, "This is risky as all get out."

"Yeah, it is," Shelton replies.

Under the table, Darcy squeezes my hand. "Can we put together some kind of discrete comms unit for him to wear?" she asks. "Maybe stay in touch with him while he's up there?"

Shelton considers. "Range will be a problem. But it's worth pursuing."

I swallow and remark, "If things go bad and I end up calling my dragon, won't the heat fry any gadget?"

It's Francis who replies, "Then don't call your damned dragon! Not everything can be fixed by throwing fire at it."

"That's enough, Francis," Shelton says.

Kim asks me, "Are you sure you're up for this?"

"I can do it."

"There's no guarantee we'll get you back."

"Maybe not," I tell her. "But if I *don't* do it, then there's a solid chance we're *all* dead, and that includes the Europans. Besides, if I can get up to the lander and the RCH *does* get the message out to the Solar System at large, it won't matter."

"It matters," Darcy mutters.

Shelton says, "Okay, people, we have our negotiator, and we're going to hedge every bet we can. Now we need to decide what Andy's going to say when he speaks for us. Thoughts, anyone?"

God help me, despite all the subsequent planning, despite all the tension and uncertainty, and even despite Darcy's small warm hand in mine the whole time—I still find myself thinking: *I'm going to see Miranda again!*

Yep, I'm an idiot.

THREE – Glimpse

"Hello, Mister Spencer."

"Ms. Coffin? This is… a surprise."

"I hope I'm not disturbing you. I know how you like to lunch alone here in your quarters."

"Not at all, Adjunct."

"You really shouldn't call me that. Not anymore."

"Of course. Habit. Um… what do you need?"

"A few minutes of your time. I want to bounce an idea off you."

"I'm not sure—"

"I promise I'll make it worth your while. Besides, I come bearing a gift."

"Is that whiskey?"

"It sure is."

"You managed to get alcohol on board when we left Earth?"

"Being… or rather, having been, my father's adjunct had its privileges. Look, Spencer. I know I've been wallowing in self-pity lately. Consider this an olive branch. Have a drink with me. Then hear my idea about tomorrow. That's all I ask."

"Yeah. Sure. Come on in."

"Thanks."

"Just one drink. I've got duties this afternoon."

"Of course."

"Can I see the bottle?"

"Certainly."

"Damn! This is a serious label!"

"Well, if you're going to break company policy, you might as well go all the way. In for a penny and all that."

"So, how do we drink this, given the microgravity?"

"I brought a Ballantine glass."

"Seriously? I've never seen one before."

"My father bought the patent some years ago. All you do is fasten it to the top of the bottle and it manages the whiskey so that microgravity isn't a problem. You can sip it more or less as if it were a crystal tumbler on Earth. The only problem is I just have the one, and you can't easily switch them out once they're connected anyway. Here, let me show you how it works…"

"Sure. Thanks."

"My pleasure. There. Care to take the first swallow?"

"Ladies first."

"No, Spencer. I insist."

"Thanks again. Ahh. Yeah, that's smooth. Haven't had a real drink in a month."

"It *is* one of the many things denied to astronauts. Wrongly, in my opinion."

"Couldn't agree more, Ms. Coffin."

"Why don't you call me, Miranda?"

"With respect, I don't think that would be appropriate."

"Ever the good soldier, Spencer."

"Your turn for a drink."

"Have one more. There's plenty."

"This Ballantine glass is amazing! I can see the whiskey floating inside it."

"Aesthetic yet functional. A pity they never caught on."

"Well, I appreciate the gesture, Ms. Coffin. But… maybe you shouldn't be drinking with me like this, given the circumstances?"

"What circumstances?"

"Well… your father told me about the medication you're on. Pretty serious stuff, if you'll forgive my saying so. Probably wouldn't mix well with alcohol."

"Oh, that. I stopped taking those last week."

"What?"

"After poor Doctor Okeke died, I didn't see the need. She was the one policing it, on my father's behalf."

"Ms. Coffin, I don't think—"

"No, you don't, and you probably shouldn't start now. Forget about the meds, Mister Spencer. They're not important. What is important is the idea I came to discuss."

"What idea?"

"I'm going to negotiate in your place."

"I don't think your father would approve."

"Oh, but it's already arranged. I've even taken the liberty of sending a communication to MC-13 informing them of my conditions."

"You did *what*? How—"

"After certain obstacles have been overcome, I'm going to have your blackbirds invade MC-13 and kill the Sheltons, along with anyone else who might remotely be a ringleader."

"*Furk*. Ms. Coffin, there's no—"

"Come on, Spencer. You know you prefer my plan to whatever my father's demanding."

"My personal wishes aren't the issue. Your father pays my salary."

"True. But then he's not here, is he?"

"I'm sorry, Ms. Coffin. I'm going to have to ask… wait… what's happening to me?"

"That'll be the tetrodioxin. I didn't think it would work so fast, but then I wasn't sure of your body weight or how to factor in the low gravity. No, I'm sorry, Mister Spencer. You're going to find it impossible to say anything. Tetrodioxin kills by blocking nerve responses.

By now, your body's completely paralyzed. In a few moments, your breathing will stop, and then your heart.

"When they find you, it'll look like cardiac failure. And with Okeke dead, there'll be no one to perform an autopsy that might indicate otherwise. There's the ship's medic, of course. But he's already in my camp. So is Captain Wei. You see, I haven't spent *all* of the last few days brooding.

"Are you gone yet, Spencer? Not quite? Well, for whatever it's worth, I'm sorry. I never thought much of your intellect, but you were good at your job. Unfortunately, you overreached when you and my father decided to… what's a good word for it? Depose me? Remove me? I suppose it doesn't matter.

"This is my mission. And I intend to see it through my way.

"Good-bye, Mister Spencer."

FOUR – Day 23

The remainder of the day passes in a blur of activity. By the time that long, cramped meeting ends, a script of sorts has been drafted. "Don't try to memorize it," Shelton tells me. "If all goes well, I'll be able to coach you remotely."

"Great," I tell him, and I hope I don't sound as anxious and conflicted as I feel.

The Sheltons and Darcy take me up to the Lab Deck. There I'm shown "Tech Central," where Jim and Carlos, along with a staff of maybe a dozen engineers, dream up, construct, and implement Shelton's gadgetry brainstorms.

Like this one.

"In addition to the RCH," Shelton explains to them. "Andy needs a specialized micro-comm. CSE'll scan him for one and jam it if they find it. So, I'm looking for something easily concealed on his person that'll transmit on frequencies less likely to raise any flags."

"Something voice-activated," Carlos suggests. He still wears the bandages from our shared swim, while poor Jim has both his arms in casts. "The rest of the time it'll stay on low power, so scans won't detect it… similar to the RCH, which doesn't activate until it passively detects the presence of a Casimir-compatible comms system."

"Voice-activated by *Andy*," Jim adds. Then he looks at me. "That way, if you don't want it detected, all you have to do is not talk while they're looking."

"Sure," I say, struggling to keep up. I turn to Jim. "Um… how are the arms?"

"Broke," Jim replies with a grin. "So, I guess Carlos here or one of our guys will have to do the detail work."

"And wipe your ass," Carlos mutters.

I expect this comment to piss Jim off; it would sure as furk piss *me* off. But the other man simply shrugs. "That's just for you, sweetie. Goes with the whole married gig."

I blink. "You two are married?"

Around me, the engineering staff abruptly starts laughing. Meanwhile, Carlos turns to Jim, his eyes sparkling. "Pay me."

Jim groans. "Later."

"Was I supposed to know that?" I ask no one in particular.

Kim rolls her eyes. "No, you weren't. How could you?"

Carlos explains, "Jim thinks we give off your standard gay vibe. I say there's no such thing. So, when we heard you were coming to Marius, he bet me that you'd get it just one day after meeting us. I won."

Jim shook his head. "Uh-huh. That just proves he didn't know we were married, not that he didn't know we were together."

"I didn't know you were together," I tell him.

"Furk," Jim says.

Carlos pumps his fist.

Jim adds with a grin, "Of course, it's going to be hard for me to give you a back rub for the foreseeable future." To punctuate this sentence, he waves his casted arms.

Carlo's own smile fades.

"Furk," he says. "Right now, back on Earth, some German lab is experimenting with cellular regenerators that would heal cuts and knit broken bones in hours instead of weeks. But good luck getting tech like that out here before the end of the next century!"

"Sorry, sweetie," Jim says. "Life of a spacer."

Then he laughs and, after a moment, everyone joins him. And it suddenly occurs to me that this is all nerves. These people are scared, and, when you're scared, it comes out in funny ways. Any opportunity you have to blow off a little steam, you take.

But the moment's over.

When the mirth finally melts, I say to Jim, "I really am sorry about your arms."

He shrugs, as least as well as he's able. "What for? *You* didn't break them."

I tell him sheepishly, "Maybe I'm just used to getting blamed for stuff."

Both Shelton and Kim laugh. Darcy doesn't.

"Glad *you're* okay, by the way," Carlos says. "You and Kim both."

"Yeah," Jim adds. "You gave us a scare. I'll say this for you, Andy, my friend, you've certainly livened this place up! Hasn't been a boring minute around here in days."

"Um… thank you?"

"Not to break up your sparkling repartee," Kim says. "But let's get back to the comms unit, okay?"

"She's right," her husband adds. "It has to be small enough that it won't be noticed if they search him. But, once it's active, Andy needs to be able to easily hear *us*."

Darcy suggests, "A micro-earbud maybe?"

"Ugh," Jim groans. "That *sooo* 2082. I think we can do better."

"I'll leave that up to you guys," Shelton says. "How long?"

"Give us the night," Carlos tells him.

With the Ice Deck now re-populated, we have dinner in the Breakroom. Afterward, Darcy takes off to run more tests on poor Charles. Before she does, she gives me a quick kiss on the cheek that I feel down to my toes.

Do I sound fickle, bouncing back and forth between Miranda and Darcy? Well, all I can say is, try spending the week *I* just had and see if your emotions aren't all over the place. Sometimes kindness, especially from a pretty woman, is like food when you're starving.

So, get over yourself.

"See you later?" I ask her, hoping I don't sound too needy.

She grins. "Natch!"

Kim and her husband take me to Shelton's office, which turns out to be a small room down the hall from the fitness center. It's windowless, with just a desk, a computer, and a handful of chairs. The only personal touch is a "Go Eagles! 10-Time Super Bowl Champs!" poster on the back wall.

"Sit," Kim tells me.

I sit. So, do they. There are only three of us in here and it feels crowded. "Cozy," I tell them.

"This is Shelton's inner sanctum," Kim says sardonically.

Giving her a pointed look, her husband adds, "My real workspace is down in Ops. I just need someplace to go where it's quiet, to think, from time to time. So, I had a storage room converted. Call it the boss's prerogative."

"Sure," I say.

"Are you worried about tomorrow?" asks Shelton.

I try to come up with an answer but finally just shrug.

"She's going to try to manipulate you," Kim tells me, her tone gentle.

This time, I reply. "I know." And I *do* know.

"We just want you to be prepared."

"I'm prepared," I say, thinking about the script and the transmitter.

"It's not just us at stake here," Shelton says.

"I get that. There's the dragons, too."

"Yeah."

"The first intelligent life ever discovered off Earth," Kim adds.

"That's huge!" I tell them, meaning it. "But… it's more than even *that*, isn't it?"

Shelton smiles thinly. "How much of it have you figured out?"

"Spacers versus CSE."

"Give the man a prize."

"Just how bad is it out here, really?" I ask. "When you watch the news vids at home… on Earth, I mean… it's all 'corporate leadership and miners and colonists working together."

"Neither one of us were born spacers," Kim says. "But it doesn't take working out here very long before you realize that most media coverage back on Earth is just Coffin's propaganda. The reality's very different."

"I saw some of it on *Conquest*. Tension between the crew and blackbirds."

"Crews on corporate ships have it better than most," Shelton explains. "Many colonies, particularly mining colonies, are run like workcamps. Long hours. Unsanitary conditions. Little or no medical care. Desperate spacers sign contracts to feed their families that end up indenturing them to CSE, pretty much for life. Blackbirds beating workers isn't officially sanctioned… but it happens anyway."

Kim says, "Once, on Ceres, a miner fell behind on her monthly quota. The foreman was a corp who called the blackbirds. They beat her half to death for no other reason than to send a message to the others. I happened to be there and saw the whole thing."

Shelton shakes his head. "We were meeting with CSE at the time, finalizing plans for the foundation of Marius. The meeting was in one of the ice factories. We'd taken a break, and Kim had simply gone for a walk." He took his wife's hand. "And she did what anyone would do… or *should* do. She put herself right in the middle of it. Got between the blackbirds and their 'example.'"

Kim touches her jaw. "One of the blackbirds fractured my cheekbone and cost me four teeth. But at least they stopped beating that poor woman."

"CSE was all apologies," Shelton explains. "Paid for Kim's care. Even so, we almost quit the deal. We really did. But the fact is, out here Charles Coffin is pretty much the only player in town. That's another thing you learn quick. Off-Earth, if you don't work for CSE, you don't work. We were already under contract. Abandoning the whole thing on principle would have ruined Shelton Mining… maybe permanently."

"Besides," his wife says. "If we hadn't come here, we wouldn't have found out about the dragons."

"But somebody else *would* have," Shelton adds. "Tantalum's simply too plentiful on Europa and too rare elsewhere to ignore. And maybe that other somebody wouldn't have shared our scruples about the fate of the natives."

I ask, "So, how do Orpheus and Eurydice fit in? Why would anything that happens on Marius matter to the rest of the spacers?"

"Good question," Shelton responds. "Let me reply with one of my own. "What would happen if intelligent life on Europa became public knowledge?"

I know the answer without having to think about it. Any science geek would. "People would go nuts. Everyone would want to know more. Scientists would be falling over each other, trying to get here and see for themselves."

He nods. "Universities throughout the Solar System would fund Europan expeditions. *Independent* expeditions. Charles Coffin wouldn't be able to do a thing to stop it. Suddenly, eggheads would be pouring onto every colony, all needing lodging, supplies, and chartered transport deeper into the system."

Kim says, "And the media would come with them."

I put it together. "Eventually, they'd see what *you* saw on Ceres, or things like it."

"It would shine a light in places that CSE needs to keep dark," Shelton explains.

"The dragons are more than just a miracle of life," Kim says. "They're the key to *everything*. They can help us change the rules and drastically improve the lives of hundreds of thousands of people… all by the simple fact of their existence."

"And let's face it," Shelton adds. "The fact that they're furking adorable doesn't hurt."

"Is this why you brought me here?" I ask. "To explain how it really is Off-Earth?"

"Partly," says Kim. "We figured it was time for you to finally know it all."

"Thanks," I reply.

Shelton adds, "But there's more."

"Okay…"

"Andy, we've spent most of the day trying to prep you for what's going to happen tomorrow."

"I know."

"And we'll be in your ear," Kim adds. "Helping all we can."

"I know that, too."

Shelton says, "And just now, I hope we've made clear to you how high the stakes really are."

"Yeah," I reply, maybe a little wearily.

"Then, there's just one more thing we want you to do for us."

I almost groan. "What?"

"We want you to forget all that and just do what you think is right."

"Huh?"

Kim grins, and Shelton laughs, albeit tiredly. "Yeah, I know. You haven't exactly been the grand marshal of the Marius Trust Parade. But that's changed since you and Kim came back from Pod One. Not for her…" He gestures at Kim, whose grin only widens. "*She's* trusted you from the get-go. But I was a harder sell."

"I understand," I say.

"But it wasn't fair of me. And, as of today, that's over. I trust you, Andy. I trust you with my life… with all our lives. You're the only real innocent in this whole furking mess. You didn't ask for this, and being involved has done nothing but hurt you in ways I don't like to think about, ways that are frankly the stuff of nightmares."

Or memory dreams.

Okay, I admit that sentiment hits me—hard.

My parents' faces, vivid and heartbreaking, fill my mind's eye. Almost without my noticing, tears well up. I don't want them to, and my first instinct is to get up and walk out, if only for the sake of my dignity.

Then Kim puts her arms around me.

It happens fast and without a word being spoken. She simply rises from her chair and kind of wraps me up. She's pretty short, so her doing this standing while I'm sitting isn't as awkward as you might think.

In fact, it isn't awkward at all.

It feels—good.

I can't remember the last time I was hugged, just hugged.

And, God help me, it gets the waterworks flowing.

The jag goes on for the better part of a minute. Kim holds me the whole time, squeezing hard. And Shelton, to his credit, stands and pretends to be interested in his Eagles poster.

Finally, and with no small effort, I manage to close the faucet.

As my shudders subside, Kim releases me. Then, in a gesture so much like my mom that it almost starts me off again, she kisses the top of my head.

"Sorry," I mutter as she sits back down.

"Don't be. You needed it."

And I did. I hadn't realized it, but I did.

Shelton faces us again.

"I'd suggest we call it a night," he says. "But tomorrow's coming, and we just can't afford to. You okay?"

"Yeah," I reply, though I feel like an idiot. "Sorry."

"Stop it," Kim says gently.

So, I do.

"Andy," Shelton explains. "There's one more thing you don't get. I don't blame you for not getting it because, until today up in the fitness room, I didn't get it either. Everything that's happening here, CSE, Marius, even the dragons… all of it is completely overshadowed by one thing."

"What's that?"

"You."

I choke back a laugh. "Me?"

He *doesn't* laugh. "Yes, you. Andy, you're a force of nature. I realize you don't like to look at it that way. You've been living your life like any normal kid, at least insofar as you could. Conceal and Protect, right?"

"Right."

"But, while that's who your people have tried to become, it's not who you are. You're *fire*, Andy. Not flesh."

"What's your point, Shelton?" his wife demands. From her tone, she's clearly unhappy with this turn in the conversation.

When Shelton answers, he directs it to me and not her. "Because now it's time to finally own it, really *own* who and what you are. Today, if you'd wanted to, you could have killed everyone in the fitness room, including me. You could have cooked us alive."

I don't deny it.

He goes on. "And tomorrow, when you step into that coring unit, you'll have the power to do the same to Miranda Coffin, and whoever else is there."

"I'm not going to—" I begin, speaking reflexively.

"I'm talking about capability, not intent. You're the most powerful person on Europa… and everybody around here knows it, except you."

Nagasaki…

New York…

I don't say anything.

Shelton does. "I'm going to confess something. After what happened in Pod One, I realized how… valuable… you could be. And, yes, I know how that sounds. You're a person, Andy, not a weapon. But that's an easy thing for people with even well-meaning agendas to forget. On the one hand, I refused you my trust, and on the other, I manipulated you into becoming the vanguard of our defense."

I stare at him, speechless.

Kim, no longer glaring, says in a small voice, "It was kind of my idea."

But Shelton shakes his head. "It was *my* call, period. And I'm truly sorry."

"Okay…" I'm trying to process this, not sure whether to be grateful for the dose of truth or pissed off at getting played again. Except, I don't feel particularly played. When it comes to manipulation, the Sheltons can't hold a candle to Miranda. When I agreed—or offered—to front them with the blackbirds in the fitness room, I knew exactly what they wanted from me.

"We're cool," I tell them both, and the relief in their faces surprises me. These are folks not used to lying.

"Thanks, Andy," Kim says.

Shelton blows out a long sigh. "Tomorrow, when you meet with Miranda Coffin, we'll be able to listen in and offer advice. But what you say and what you do is entirely up to *you.*"

"Yeah?"

"Yeah."

Kim nods in agreement.

So, I push it. "Even if I end up siding with Miranda again?" I don't mean this. I just want to get their reaction.

Kim pales but doesn't reply. Beside her, Shelton says, "Even if. Don't be a victim anymore. Don't hide who you are. Conceal and Protect means nothing out here. If you want to be a spacer, then *be* a spacer. If you want to be a blackbird, then be that. Either way, this time, choose it for yourself."

"Okay."

Kim clears her throat. "Tomorrow's a big day. Shelton and I are calling it a night. You might want to do the same."

"Yeah." Then I stand and look at them both. "Thanks again. Really."

They muster tired smiles.

I leave.

As I make my way back to my room, Shelton's words echo in my head.

Either way, this time, choose it for yourself.

It's the first time anyone has said such a thing since this whole miserable business started. I can't even imagine my parents, forever loyal to Conceal and Protect, offering such advice. All my life, the concept of "free will" has been—colored—by others' needs and wishes.

I honestly have no idea what to do with that kind of freedom.

Jeez. My head hurts.

I reach my bedroom door and, feeling exhausted to my very soul, spin the wheel, and step inside.

To my surprise, the lights are on.

To my somewhat *bigger* surprise, Darcy is stretched out on my bed.

"Hi," she says with a smile.

"Hi," I reply, my mouth drying up. "Um…"

"Why don't you shut the door?"

I gulp—yes, actually gulp. Then I shut the door.

"Sorry if I startled you," Darcy says, rising to her feet with a slow, feline grace that I can't stop looking at. She's wearing the same jeans and t-shirt as before. The t-shirt says, "BLINK IF YOU WANT ME." I noticed it earlier but didn't give it a second thought. Now I find myself suddenly both wanting and *not* wanting to blink.

"No locks on Marius," she explains, coming closer. There's a funny quality to her voice—a velvety aspect that, for some reason, sends an almost electric jolt through me. "So, there's this unwritten rule about not going into anyone's room uninvited."

"Yet… here you are," I stammer.

"Rules are made to be broken."

"Why?" I ask—croak really.

"Why what?"

"Why are you here?"

She looks slyly at me, as if she's going to dish up some clever comeback. But instead, she falters and says, "You want the honest truth?"

I nod.

"I want to take away her power."

"Who… who's power?" Still stammering.

Instead of answering, her arms snake around my neck, and she kisses me. Hard.

For a moment, the kiss steals my breath, and my heart leaps into turbo mode. It goes on for what seems like forever, though when it finally does end, it feels like it ended too soon. Weird.

Darcy pulls back, but not far, her arms still around me, and her face only inches from mine. "Do you want to do this, Andy?"

I gaze into her beautiful face. It's heart-shaped, not oval like Miranda's, her eyes brown instead of gray. But it's a more open face, less guarded, and a whole lot less cold. She's less self-possessed than Miranda, too. Or maybe it's fairer to say she's self-possessed in a different way.

Then I realize, with an almost painful jolt, that I'm making comparisons—measuring Darcy based on Miranda's yardstick.

And that's just *wrong*.

With another croak, I reply, "No."

For an instant, she blinks at me, uncomprehending. Then her sweet, coquettish smile just kind of withers. Her arms, still around my neck, go slack, and she starts to pull away.

I let her go. God help me, I do.

Quickly, maybe desperately, I add, "It's not because I don't want to."

She regards me with an expression I can't read.

So, like an idiot, I blunder on. "Darcy," I say, and realize with another jolt that it's the first time I've said her name aloud. "I'm messed up. I'm *so* messed up. I'm nowhere near able to wrap my head around everything that's happened to me. It wouldn't be fair to you, to either one of us, if I jumped into something right now. Furk, I can't believe I'm saying this."

She studies me, her head cocked at a thoughtful angle that's both intelligent and—well—hot. The tiniest of smiles plays on her full lips, fuller than Miranda's.

Stop doing that, will you!

"But later," I say quickly. "Down the road, after all this is over… if you still want to. Because I do, I really do." I sound like a tongue-tied schoolboy, which of course, I am.

For another long moment, she stays quiet.

Then, in a whisper, she says, "Good for you, Andy Brand."

Now it's my turn to blink. "What?"

Her smile brightens to about a million watts, way past anything Miranda ever—

You're a moron.

"I was all ready to give you this little speech," she tells me. "About how sex isn't love and how we can have fun together and how it would help you put away whatever feelings you're still harboring for… her. But now I get that maybe the whole thing would be just one more furking manipulation, and you deserve better than that."

My mouth feels dry. I swallow. It doesn't help.

"It's okay," she tells me. "In fact, it's better than okay. The thing is, I've found you attractive from the moment we met. I won't lie to you. Part of it's the Dragon thing. Power's sexy. But that's not all or even most of it. You're smart, and you're brave, and those two are even sexier."

I snort out a laugh. Yeah, *snort*. Smooth as always. "Brave?"

"Braver than you think. When we went diving, I knew you were terrified. The others didn't see it, not even Kim. But I did. You were scared out of your mind, and, given your… nature, I can guess why. Yet you did it, maybe partly because you were afraid you'd look foolish if you backed out. But mostly because you've got innate courage. You don't realize it, but you've been demonstrating it all along. *That's* what really appeals to me."

Jeez, it's warm in here.

Darcy says, "Besides, I find our height difference… intriguing."

She steps around me, moving toward the door. As she passes, and almost without thinking, I reach out and take her hand. She pauses and looks back at me, her eyebrows raised.

"When it's over?" I ask.

"You mean when we win?"

I nod.

She rises on her toes and gives me a devilish little kiss on the lips. "It's a date." Then she disappears through my bedroom door.

Standing there alone, I feel stupid, foolish, and frustrated.

But also *great*.

How strange is that?

FIVE – Day 23

The entire Solar System, Off-Earth, keeps Greenwich Mean Time, or GMT for short. It simplifies things tremendously if each ship and colony maintains the same clock as all the others. And guess who championed this thoroughly practical practice. Why, Charles Coffin, who else? The dude's everywhere. I guess that's what happens when your name's synonymous with space travel.

So, what's this mean to me? Only that, on Marius as elsewhere, 8:00 GMT is eight in the morning as I step into the Ice Deck fitness room. I'm accompanied by my usual escort, the three of them here to offer their collective support.

Kim's quieter than usual. She keeps looking askance at me, and then offering a smile whenever our eyes meet like we share a joke that I'm not in on. Conversely, Shelton is downright chatty. He's trying to play the supportive boss, maybe even the all-wise big brother.

Then there's Darcy.

I spent last night bouncing between a curious pride and self-recrimination. Somehow, I eventually managed to nod off. And, when I woke up this morning, my head felt—well, clear—perhaps clearer than it has since all this started.

Darcy said she wanted to take away Miranda's power.

Right now, I think maybe she did.

We say our "good lucks" in the fitness room threshold. Nobody says good-bye since, if all goes well, I'll be back here in an hour. Then, as I'm about to shut the door, Shelton shakes my hand, and Kim hugs me. "You got this, little brother," she whispers.

And, in that moment, I think maybe she's right.

How big an idiot am I?

Finally, I look at Darcy, uncertain of what to do. Should I hug her, too? Kiss her, maybe?

But she steps up, puts her hands on my chest, and unceremoniously shoves me back through the open doorway. Then, while pushing the heavy door closed between us, she offers me a quick, extremely suggestive wink.

And, just like that, I'm alone.

Taking a few deep breaths, I face the opposite wall, where the recent repair to Marius's hull is clearly visible. Any moment now, that repair's going to get un-repaired as Spencer's people burn their way into the colony for the second time in two days.

I wonder how long I'll have to wait.

Then a section of the metal begins to heat up.

Apparently, not long.

I say nothing, do nothing, as a newly sheared circle of metal crashes to the floor, loud as a church bell but not nearly as pitch-perfect. Beyond it, two blackbirds regard me apprehensively. One of them shuts down the laser-saw he's carrying. Neither raises his weapon.

"This way," one says.

I nod.

I follow them both through the hole in the colony wall.

Beyond it is a short umbilical corridor of Liquid Bricks linking the coring unit to Marius. Beyond that, I find myself in the coring unit's familiar round, tapering chamber, with some differences. Now, instead of a single seat in the center, there's a table and two matching chairs.

Miranda is seated in one of those chairs.

She's wearing her green dress, her hair tightly braided. The tear-drop shaped birthmark almost seems to glow reddish against her pale cheek.

She smiles. "Hello, Andy."

"Hi."

"I'm relieved to see you. Why don't you sit down?"

My mind churns. Seeing her hits me harder than I thought it would.

"Andy?" she repeats, her tone uber-friendly. "Do you want to sit?"

I glance back. The umbilical stands open, though my two-man escort now flanks it.

I return my gaze to Miranda. "His name was Hofmeister?"

"Who?"

"The man… I killed. His name was Hofmeister?"

"Honestly, I don't know." She addresses the escorts "Do either of you know who—"

One of them replies, cutting her off. "Mark Hofmeister, ma'am."

"Did you know him?"

"Just from this mission."

I face the guy. "I'm sorry. I didn't mean to hurt him."

"Like that makes a difference," he mutters. "Especially to his wife and kids."

A rock forms in my gut.

"I'm still sorry," I say again. It sounds lame.

I sit down across from Miranda.

"The situation was badly handled by everyone," she remarks. "The best thing we can do is put it behind us. Do you agree, Andy?"

"I guess so."

"Good. Now, you're here to negotiate on behalf of MC-13's colonists."

"Marius. And, yeah."

"Which means they've drafted a list of demands?"

I nod.

"I'm listening."

And she is; I know the posture. Back straight, delicate hands clasped, manner attentive, as if I'm the most interesting thing around. For the first time, I wonder how manufactured it is.

I say, "They want access to the Casimir Radio."

"Define access."

"Huh?"

"One transmission? Two? More?"

"Open-ended."

"And what do they want to say to my father?"

"Nothing," I tell her.

"Then, who?"

"Anyone they want."

"I see. I assume they're eager to reveal to the entire System how they've broken their contract with CSE." She says this without a trace of sarcasm. Impressive, really.

"They intend to tell everyone about the dragons."

"Dragons? *That's* what you call them?"

"That's what the miners call them."

"And that doesn't bother you?"

I blink at her. "Bother me?"

"You don't like being called a Dragon yourself, after all."

I suddenly realize that the epithet doesn't bug me the way it used to. Ravi and his people have lent it a kind of—honor.

But, for Miranda, all I do is shrug.

"And you've seen these… creatures?" she asks.

I nod.

"They're truly sentient?"

"Yeah."

"Intelligent?"

"Yeah."

"How can you be so sure?" she asks. No challenge. Just a question.

"Because they saved my life."

"Really? When?"

"When the coring unit first came through the bottom of the ice shelf yesterday, a few of us were in the water nearby wearing scuba gear. The concussion broke my faceplate and knocked me out. The dragons saved both Kim and me. Three of them gave their lives to do it."

Miranda studies me. "Kim. Kim… Shelton?"

I nod.

"So, she survived the lift explosion, too."

"Yeah."

"How?"

I don't reply. Shelton warned me this might come up. He doesn't want CSE to know that Kim's a Split.

Seconds pass.

Miranda doesn't take the hint. "Is Kimberly Shelton Kind, like you?"

The fact that she didn't use the term Dragon isn't lost on me. I answer truthfully, "No. She isn't Kind."

"Then how did she survive?"

I shake my head.

She says, "You don't know? Or won't say?"

"Take your pick."

Again, she studies me. This time it feels more like appraisal than soothsaying. "I've missed you."

I don't reply, 'I've missed you, too.' And it's not that I *haven't* missed her because, despite everything, I have. No, I don't say it because Shelton's micro-comm is attached to one of my back teeth. And missing Miranda Coffin doesn't seem like the kind of admission I'd like Darcy to hear.

Miranda eyes me, almost as if she's reading my mind. Now *there's* a furking scary thought.

"What else?" she asks.

"What else?"

"What are the colonists' other demands?"

"They want the supply runs to start up again."

"We couldn't do that if we wanted to," Miranda replies. "The lift's been destroyed."

I gesture around us. "You've kind of made a *new* lift."

She smiles slightly. "*You* made the lift shaft, Andy."

"Yeah, I did," I reply. "Because *you* told me there were hostages down here who needed rescuing."

Her amusement vanishes. "What else?"

"They want to be left alone."

"I see. So, Shelton expects us to lift the communications blackout, resume feeding them, and then go away. Does that about say it?"

"More or less."

"And in return?" she asks.

"In return, they'll restart limited tantalum production, with the first shipment to be delivered, again via the coring unit, three months from the date of the agreement." All this is right out of the script.

"Define 'limited.'"

"Sixty metric tons per standard year."

"Less than half their contracted quota," she points out.

"It allows for a scrubbing rate that minimizes risk to the indigenous population."

"The… dragons."

I nod.

Miranda sits back, regarding me again. More, I feel ogled at, as if I'm a favored possession. Did she always look at me that way? The more I think back, the surer I am that she did.

"I have to admit, it's bold," she finally remarks.

"What is?"

"Sending you in here, alone, to negotiate… only to offer terms so obviously slanted in the miners' favor. Bold. Especially given Mike and Kim Sheltons' lack of leverage. I'll be honest, when I demanded that *you* be the one to meet with me, I didn't think they'd go along with it."

I feel a thrill of alarm. Not for the first time, I sense that I'm missing something important.

"I insisted," I say.

"Did you?"

I nod.

"Why?"

"Because I watched your blackbirds try to arrest Shelton on sight yesterday."

"Spencer's blackbirds, not mine."

"Same thing."

"No, Andy. It really isn't. But never mind. Go on."

The missing-something feeling gets stronger. "Anyway, because of that, I figured you'd arrest whoever else showed up and hold them hostage or something. So, it made sense to send me."

"Really? How so?"

"Well…" I glance uneasily back at the stone-faced blackbirds. "Because we both know you can't keep me here against my will."

She nods. "Logical… if a bit naïve. Your fundamental problem is you're not a diplomat. Neither is Shelton, for that matter. He tends to look at the world in engineering terms. Black and white. Cause and effect. That's fine when you're solving a technical problem. But throw psychology in the mix, and that way of thinking falls short of the mark."

"What are you talking about?"

"Look at it from our perspective," Miranda explains. "We have the soldiers and the guns. We also have the literal high ground. We could easily starve them into submission. I'm sure they have stockpiles. But those stockpiles *must* be finite. So, unless we give them food, they'll have no choice but to surrender, sooner or later."

This is an argument I'm ready for. "But you don't know which one."

"What?"

"Sooner or later. You don't know which it would be, and, in the meantime, the tantalum isn't flowing."

"Point taken. And, as it happens, we realized the same thing. That's why we insisted on you as negotiator."

That missing-something feeling ratchets up to full-blown alarm. But it's just the three of them in here, and nobody's making a move toward me. They won't shoot me, and they can't restrain me.

So why am I suddenly — scared?

Miranda says, "You're putting it together, aren't you, Andy?"

And that's when I *do* put it together. I can almost hear the mental *thud* inside my head. It sounds like a coffin lid. "Vectors," I whisper.

"Vectors," she affirms.

Kim screams in my ear, *"Andy! Get out of there! Now!"*

The world tilts. I lash out instinctively, trying to call my dragon. But it's already too late.

I can't believe I forgot about the vectors.

Then everything goes black.

Again.

SIX – Day 24

When I wake up and find myself on my palette in my cell, my first conscious sensation is a mix of horror and divine relief.

Crazy as it sounds, for a few terrible, glorious seconds, I honestly believe everything that happened on Europa was just a dream. Of course, that means I'm still a captive, and that I've never met Kim, Shelton, Darcy, or even Miranda.

But it also means my parents are still alive.

Like I said: Horror and relief, together.

Obviously, it doesn't last.

First off, I realize that I'm *strapped* to my pallet. The straps run across my chest and both my legs but are easily unfastened and not meant to be restraints. In fact, they're loose enough to let me shift position, or even roll over. My bedroom aboard *Conquest* had them, too. They're for sleeping in zero-G.

Which means it was real, all of it.

And my mom and dad are gone, forever gone.

With a shuddering sigh, I undo the straps and let myself rise in a controlled float. Liquid Brick handholds jut out along the walls and ceiling. Using these, I pull myself upright and have a proper look around.

There is no exit, and, without an e-man, I can't make one. My pallet is fastened to the floor, and the toilet is a zero-G model with a hose instead of a bowl. Don't ask.

Bottom line: I'm a prisoner again.

Full circle.

The Voice says, *"I'm glad to see you're up."*

She doesn't bother disguising herself. What would be the point? And Miranda Coffin does nothing that anyone would call pointless.

"I'm an idiot," I say.

"Don't beat yourself up about the vectors. Whenever we're introduced to new technology, we tend to overlook its practical potential. I counted on that. It's only human."

I let the irony of that last sentence pass without comment. "What happens now?"

"Now Coffin Solar Exploration takes back what's ours."

Well, of course. They're going to invade Marius. And by letting myself get captured, I've removed the only sentry at the gates. Nice, Brand. Really nice.

"Why not just talk to them?" I ask, a little desperately.

"Because they're terrorists."

"But they're *not*! "They only stopped the mining when they discovered they were hurting the dragons."

"Oh, Andy… just a moment."

I float there like a moron, waiting. Several seconds later, a doorway appears. Miranda glides into my cell, looking beautiful and perfectly at ease. She's wearing a black CSE uniform, and behind her hover two armed blackbirds, different than the pair in the CU — but the same in manner and mood. Both eye me with genuine hatred.

"You deserve better than a disembodied voice," Miranda tells me. "I'm your friend, not your jailer."

"Glad to hear it. Can I go now?"

"Go where?"

"Back down to Marius."

"Why would you want to?"

"Because I have people down there who need me."

"Need you to what? Protect them?"

I don't reply.

She says, "The situation is more complicated than you realize."

"Oh, I'm pretty sure I've got a handle on it. Coffin Solar Exploration has had a stranglehold on spacer life for the past thirty years. They decide who works and who starves. They even arranged things so that they are the only police force, the only law. That means anyone who gets out of line is smacked down... hard. And CSE, namely your father, will do anything to protect that status quo. How am I doing so far?"

"Andy —" she says

But I keep talking right over her. "Now along comes Marius and its discovery of the dragons. The first sentient life ever found Off-Earth. That's the one thing that could throw you off trajectory, bring your whole totalitarian regime crashing down around your ears. This mission, *Conquest*, my kidnapping, my parents' murder... none of it was about rescuing miners. It wasn't even about the tantalum, not really. It was about maintaining CSE's iron control over the Solar System, about squashing the news that could take away that control."

As I hold Miranda's gaze, her face is unreadable.

"So?" I say bitterly. "How'd I do?"

After a few moments, she replies, "You did well. But then I've always been impressed by your intellect. You're underestimating the importance of Europa's tantalum, however. Humanity needs that metal."

"Don't you mean *CSE* needs it?"

"When it comes to space exploration and colonization, the two are interchangeable. Mankind is reaching for the stars, and tantalum will make it possible. Next to that, what do the lives of some local animals matter?"

"They're not animals, Miranda. They're intelligent, thinking beings."

"They're not human, so they don't count."

"I'm not human, either," I say. "Do *I* count?"

Her gaze softens. "Of course, you do. But there's a difference."

"Why? Because you took me to bed?" I know. Pretty hardcore. As soon as the words are out, I watch Miranda for a reaction. She offers nothing, though the guys with the guns share a fidgety kind of look.

"Let me talk to your father," I say.

"No."

"Why not?"

"Because he ordered your death, and I'm not ready to tell him that order isn't going to be carried out."

Okay, so it's apparently her turn to go hardcore. "Then let me talk to Spencer." I'm not sure what that'll accomplish. But speaking to Miranda seems a bit like speaking to a computer. I can't quite put my finger on it, but she's different—colder, even more calculating and deliberate. At least with Spencer, I'll know where I stand.

Miranda replies, "I'm afraid Mister Spencer was found dead in his quarters this morning. We suspect a heart attack."

Again, the men at her back fidget.

I absorb this news. Spencer's dead, and Charles Coffin is out of the loop. I'm not the only one who's had an eventful few days.

"Miranda, what's going on?" I ask.

"How do you mean?"

"Who's in charge around here?"

"The same person who always has been. Me."

"Okay, Person-in-Charge, if you don't care about the colonists or the dragons, then negotiate with *me*."

"For what?"

"For Marius."

"You don't speak for them."

"I'm their negotiator."

"You haven't any leverage, and, without leverage, you have no basis for negotiation. We're going to retake the colony in the next few hours. After that, tantalum production will be started back up."

"That'll take time. You'll need the colonists to cooperate."

Her manner, already cold, now ices over completely. "They'll cooperate... once they see their leaders executed."

"What?"

"I realize that may sound harsh, even cruel, but that's because you don't know what's happened. When we brought you up in the coring unit a few hours ago, unconscious, a device hidden in your clothes hacked into the lander's comms system and somehow transmitted itself up to *Conquest,* where it interfaced with the Casimir Radio."

I say nothing.

"Without anyone knowing, it requested a wormhole, got one, and proceeded to transmit a very unwise and destructive data packet to media outlets and government officials throughout the system. Andy… they've told *everyone* about these dragons of yours."

Still, I say nothing.

Miranda eyes me. "*Did* you know?"

I don't reply.

"Because, if you did, you're complicit."

"Complicit in what, telling the truth? Will you execute me, too?"

"I know I probably sound tyrannical. But it's simple, brutal practicality. CSE is the sole mechanism for law and order Off-Earth. And as the corporation's official representative, I'm required to enforce the law and dispense justice. What the Sheltons have done threatens the stability of the entire Solar System. Hundreds of thousands of lives are at risk on dozens of colonies. At this point, the only way to restore the system's health is to cut out the cancer that has threatened it. It's tragic but necessary."

"These are *people*, Miranda! Not tumors!"

She shrugs. She really does. "By sending out that data packet, they've put CSE at risk of losing control of the Solar System. And without us to fund, manage, and maintain it, the entire infrastructure will collapse."

Which is, of course, what Kim and Shelton are counting on. Spacer versus the CSE. Oppressed versus oppressors. An old song, I suppose.

"But how will killing them stop anything?" I protest. "It's too late!"

"Not quite. If I go down there, execute the ringleaders and cow the rest of the colonists, then I can take steps to make sure their 'new life' is never verified."

"You're going to wipe out the dragons!"

"I'm going to exterminate a threat to the future of civilization, Andy. Once MC-13 is mine, I'm going to have the blackbirds enter the water and hunt down every single Europan. We have months, maybe years, before the news sinks in and a government or academic expedition arrives in Jovian orbit. Plenty of time to make sure that Orpheus and Eurydice's claims of aliens under the ice are proven to be a hoax."

"The colonists will know!" I tell her desperately. "The ones you don't murder!"

"Without dragons to point to, no one will believe them. And, as survivors, they'll spread the word throughout the spacer community… a bitter reminder that CSE's authority will *not* be subverted. Sadly, it's a lesson that needs to be retaught to them every so often. It's been done before."

"It's genocide!"

"Yes, it is. But, as I said, it's necessary. The Sheltons created this situation. All I'm doing is cleaning up their mess."

"But, Miranda! This is insane!"

"It's anything but. Within the hour, I'll be returning to the Europan surface. Then a contingent of thirty blackbirds, under my direct command, will ride the coring unit down to MC-13 and launch our assault. By this evening, the worst will be over."

"No!"

I start toward her, reaching first for one handhold, then another. Reacting to me, the blackbirds draw their guns. I don't have a plan, really. I just know that I can't—won't—allow the curtain to go up on this horror show!

So, I call my dragon.

But it doesn't come.

I stop, clutching my latest handhold, confused. I call my dragon again. Nothing. Zilch. Where always before it's waited inside me, straining against its chains—now there's only a hard, blank barrier. Impenetrable. It's difficult to explain. The dragon's there; I'm sure of it. But there's something between us. A "wall."

Or, if that analogy's too fanciful, how about this?

My pilot light's out.

Miranda watches me impassively while her bodyguards flank her. I stare at them all, stunned into silence.

Finally, she asks, "Remember the tests Okeke ran on you?"

I do, of course. But I can't manage a reply.

She says, "One of the goals of those tests was to collect enough samples to map your genome, which was completed before Okeke's unfortunate death. Since then, I've had the rest of the medical staff working around the clock to identify the gene sequence that controls your… capabilities. While you slept, we administered an injection that blocks the brain's ability to trigger the extra organ in your body, your 'dragon.' It's temporary, but very effective, as I'm sure you've realized."

I still can't reply. I'm sick to my stomach, and the notion of Kim and Shelton's imminent murders is only a part of it. The rest is a horrific sense of violation. All my life, I've dreamed of being "normal" — living like a typical human teenager, able to date girls, play sports, fight if necessary, without worrying about setting everyone around me on fire.

A world without *Conceal and Protect*.

And now that world has been handed to me, and you know what? It feels empty.

"I was on your side," I hear myself say. "Why would you spend so much time to find a way to steal my dragon if it was already yours?"

She replies as if the answer should be obvious. "You can own a *gun*, Andy… but you still need to be able to unload it."

"So, I'm a gun?"

"The stakes are high. We… I… had to use the assets at hand. I never meant to hurt you."

Almost reflexively, I reach inside again, this time looking *deep*.

Nothing. Just that "wall."

"All this is transitory," Miranda says. "Once MC-13 is back online, and the native obstacles have been removed, we'll return to Earth. Then you and I will have plenty of time to… mend fences."

"In the meantime, I'm a prisoner… again."

"A special guest. You'll be treated well, fed well, and, once I'm back from Europa, you'll be given free rein to move about the ship again."

"Miranda," I say desperately. "Let me talk to Marius. Let me try to settle this without anybody else getting hurt!"

"It's too late for that. Get some rest. If you need anything, just ask it aloud and someone will respond."

"No! Wait! Please!"

But she turns and glides out the door, her escorts in tow, and looking as amazing and self-possessed as ever.

And colder than the surface of Europa.

SEVEN – Day 24

Her "special guest."

I find myself gripped by nervous energy, moving from handhold to handhold, back and forth across my cell — the zero-G version of pacing like a caged lion.

Could I possibly have furked this up any worse?

Again, I try to reach my dragon. And again after that. Each time I do, I hit that weird barrier in my mind, Miranda's anti-Kind shot.

Each failure only heightens my desperation.

After a while, I can't take it anymore.

"Hey!" I call out. Miranda said someone would answer. "Yo! Can anybody hear me?"

Zilch.

"Can I get something to eat?"

Finally, a disembodied voice replies tersely, *"What do you want?"*

"I want to talk to Miranda!" I exclaim.

"Ms. Coffin isn't available. Now, do you want something to eat or not?"

I think furiously. "Yeah."

"What do you want?"

I recall the zero-G pastes I "enjoyed" in the Mess. "The apple cinnamon's pretty good."

"Yeah, that one's not bad. Okay, I'll get something for you. Don't go anywhere." Was that last bit delivered with a healthy dose of snide? Maybe. Probably.

As silence ensues, I stop my weightless pacing. With whoever I just talked to gone, I suddenly wonder if anyone else is out there watching me?

I decide to take the chance.

I push myself over to the wall that opened earlier. Once there, I clutch a nearby handhold and ready myself. When the blackbird comes to deliver my food, I'll attack him, try to grab his gun. It's crazy and will probably get me killed. But at this point, even that would be better than doing nothing.

Abruptly, the Voice commands, *"Move away from the wall."*

So, they are *watching me.*

Cursing, I float across the room and wait there, frustrated.

Seconds later, the Liquid Bricks slide open. A blackbird floats there, wearing a scowl. In one hand, he holds an apple cinnamon food tube. In his other is a wicked-looking pistol. "There's no escape," he says.

"Corny. But I get it."

"If you'd attacked me, I'd have shot you."

"So what?"

His scowl deepens. But he tosses me the tube. I snatch it out of the air. "Thanks. Water?"

"There's a zero-G sink."

"You're a peach."

He steps back, his hand reaching for the e-man on his wrist.

Something hits him from behind, sending him hurling weightlessly forward. The blackbird's gun flies clear as he tumbles past me, hits the opposite wall, bounces off at an angle, still full of inertia, hits another wall, and slams down against the floor, only to ricochet up again. It's riveting to watch. Horrible, too. Throughout the first few impacts, the blackbird tries desperately to find a handhold. There are plenty, but he's disoriented and moving so fast that he keeps missing them.

Finally, his limp body stops trying.

When he comes to rest near the ceiling, red droplets run from gashes on his temple and chin. He's out cold.

That's when I look toward the doorway, where a figure in blue floats with easy familiarity.

"Damn! That guy took it hard! Hope I didn't kill him. Hey, how you doing, Draco?"

"Eric?"

Greenjeans winks at me. "You didn't think I was going to let the Ice Queen leave you in here, did you?"

"There's at least one more of them out there."

"No, there's not."

"But somebody warned me to move away from the door!"

"Yeah, that was me. After that blackbird left, I snuck into the guard-room down the hall to wait for an opening. I saw you on the vidscreen and, once I realized what you had in mind, I figured I'd keep you from getting shot."

"Oh. Thanks."

"Natch. Sorry the rescue took so long. My e-man doesn't work up here on Deck 1, so I had to wait for the jerk to get called away. Took forever."

"I… um… asked for food," I say, holding up the tube.

"Apple cinnamon. Good choice."

"Eric, do you know what's about to happen?"

"I know more than you think. But we'll get to that. Come on."

"Where are we going?"

"Your girlfriend and something like two-dozen blackbirds are about to leave for Europa. It won't be easy, but, with some good-old-fashioned spacer ingenuity, we might be able to sneak you onboard the lander."

I almost say, "She's not my girlfriend." But, really, what would be the point?

As he leads me down the corridor, I ask, "Where's the crew?"

"Keeping to the lower decks," he replies. "The Ice Queen's completely taken over. She's either bribed or intimidated the captain and most of the officers."

"But… aren't they all spacers?"

He laughs a little bitterly. "There's spacers, and there's *spacers*. Wei's one of us on paper, sure. But he's also a career CSE guy who's got a choice gig he doesn't want to lose. The same goes for most of his senior staff. All spacers, but none of them revolutionaries… like me." He gives me a rueful smile.

"And the Sheltons?" I say.

"Well, look who's been learning stuff. Yeah, like them. The bottom line is that, with Spencer dead, the blackbirds see your girlfriend as their best bet of getting paid, and so they're going along. And it doesn't hurt that most of them hate the hell out of you."

This time when he looks back at me, he isn't smiling.

"I didn't… mean it," I stammer.

"I know, Draco. And so do they, I'd bet. But they're pissed, and they've got guns."

Eric and I start down a pass-thru.

"Where are we going?" I ask.

"Engineering."

"Who's there?"

"The spacers who are on our side. Officially, Wei's restricted all non-essential personnel to quarters until the lander's left *Conquest*, I guess to avoid any last-minute attacks of conscience. But some of us, the *real* spacers, said 'furk that' and gathered down on Deck 15. Nobody knows we're there. Not the captain, not the blackbirds, and not your girlfriend."

"I wish you'd stop calling her my girlfriend."

"She was when you left."

"Not anymore."

"I guess stuff happened down there, huh? We stopped hearing a thing after the supply lift exploded."

"Yeah. Stuff happened."

"Like what?"

I shrug. "Stuff."

"This 'stuff' got a name?"

I don't answer.

Eric laughs. "Damn, Draco! For a skinny kid, women really seem to go for you! Okay, the Ice Queen ain't your significant other anymore. Noted. Let's keep going."

"Greenjeans?"

"What?"

"Are you the Sheltons' spy?"

To my surprise, he laughs. "You *have* learned a lot! Nope, not me."

"Then who?"

"You'll find out in a minute."

"I could do without the drama."

"Funny. I hear that a lot."

We reach Deck 15 and head straight through the Workshop where Exler and I ran into trouble back when *Conquest* hit the debris field. Neither of us speaks, and, in the silence, I find myself flashing back on my last visit to this place. Then, my only thought was to save Miranda.

Now, my only thought is to stop her.

I wonder if that's irony. Probably not.

"And here we are," Eric announces.

As we enter the Engine Room, I count maybe a dozen blue uniforms, their wearers grim-faced and agitated and talking amongst themselves. Behind them, the five remaining fission reactors churn.

We're noticed immediately, and all talking stops. As everyone looks our way, there's no mistaking the worry—maybe even fear—on their faces.

Somebody yells, "You got him!"

"Sure did!" Eric replies. He floats expertly over to one of the reactor railings. "Had to zip one of the blackbirds to do it, though." Then he beckons to me. "Come on over, Draco. You're among friends."

I launch myself toward Greenjeans, who smoothly catches my wrist and pulls me beside him. Then he says to the others, "Problem is, once the guy's relief shows up, we're blown."

"Great," someone says.

Others mutter low curses.

Then a gruff voice announces, "So, we'd better get this done."

Chief Tuttle floats smoothly over from deeper in the room. As usual, he's scowling. His skin is sallow, and his widow's peak pronounced—except now there's a familiarity to it.

And, just like *that*, another penny drops.

"It's *you*!" I exclaim, pointing a finger at him. "*You're* Shelton's spy!"

"It's impolite to point," Tuttle grumbles, and this time the irony positively glistens.

"You're Francis's brother! Tell me I'm right!"

"Give the man a trophy," Tuttle replies dryly.

Eric grins.

The other crewmen show no surprise. Apparently, this secret wasn't much of a secret, at least among the Engineering crew.

"But you two have different last names," I say.

"Tuttle's not my name. It's my handle. I was born Edwin Swift. But, when I got my first apprenticeship, one of the old guard noticed that Swift was the name of one of the two guys who discovered the Swift-Tuttle Comet back in 18-something. He started calling me Tuttle. At first, I hoped it wouldn't stick. But then somebody noticed that I was born on the same day as the comet's next perihelion in 2126. And that was it. I've been Tuttle ever since. These days, I don't go by anything else."

"So, nobody knows about your brother on Marius?"

"If they did, I probably wouldn't have gotten this job. I'm Tuttle in almost all the datacores. Good thing they never found out, since Francis has really needed me here."

"And you've been… spying for Marius all this time?"

"CSE tried hard to keep what Shelton's doing under wraps. But out here, at least some of the truth always leaks. A rebellion on Europa. Heavy-duty dangerous… and my kid brother right in the middle of it. We knew Coffin would send a ship out here PDQ, so me, Greenjeans, and a bunch of us signed on aboard *Conquest*. Then, once we got close enough to Europa, I got in touch with Frannie using short-range comms. He told me about all of it, the tantalum, the dragons, Orpheus and Eurydice. I told him I'd keep him and his boss informed on the goings-on up here because that's what *spacers* do for each other, never mind brothers."

It's the longest speech I've ever heard from this guy.

"Frannie?" I ask.

Tuttle's eyes narrow. "Yeah. You got a problem with 'Frannie?'"

Before I can muster a snarky reply, Greenjeans says, "The chief brought us all in. We'd been briefed about you. Wei called you our 'sleeping cargo' and said that at some point we'd be waking you up. He didn't come right out and announce you were dangerous, but he clearly didn't like having you aboard."

Tuttle adds sourly, "Then, of course, you *woke* up, went nuclear, and nearly melted the ship."

This time, I bring the snark proudly. "That wasn't me going nuclear. You haven't *seen* nuclear. And I didn't even come close to melting the ship." I meet each of their eyes. "But, I *could* have."

Everyone in Engineering, including Tuttle and Greenjeans, stare at me nervously. And, for the first time, I find myself weirdly, even scarily, gratified. Shelton was right. I've been muddling my way through this whole affair like I'm powerless.

Well, I'm *not*.

Except, of course, right now, I *am*.

"Anyway…" Greenjeans says after a moment. "Once things calmed down and you started popping up around the ship wearing the black uniform, the chief gave standing orders that nobody was supposed to talk to you."

Tuttle nods. "So, naturally, Greenjeans went ahead and introduced himself. Should've figured."

"Fish gotta swim," Eric replies with a grin. "Besides, I thought it might be a good idea for *somebody* to get to know you."

I look pointedly at him. "And that's why you became my friend?"

"Maybe in the beginning, and I told the chief as much. But later, I started… well… liking you."

"Nice to know," I remark dryly.

"Draco, you saved the ship, remember?"

"Yeah, you did," Tuttle says. "And it's why we just busted you out of the Ice Queen's cage. Right now, I have it on good authority that she intends to kill everybody even remotely in charge down there. That includes Frannie."

"Whose 'good authority?'" I ask.

"The captain's. He told me this morning. Turns out, he knows my brother's down there. Thing is, Wei and I go back twenty years. He's always been more of a corp than a true spacer, and he's sold his soul to the Ice Queen along with most of the officers. Despite that, he never told anybody about Frannie being my brother. If he had, they would've locked me up in the cell next to yours. So, I'll give Wei that much credit."

"Miranda told me she's assumed full command of the mission."

"Yeah," Eric replies. "And we're pretty sure she murdered Spencer to do it."

"She mentioned heart failure. Pretty convenient, I guess."

"Damn right, Draco," Tuttle says, the first time he's ever used my handle. "I talked to the ship's medic. His boss, Okeke, is gone, of course. But, even so, interplanetary law calls for a postmortem whenever a death occurs in space. The medic expected to perform one, but Miranda Coffin called him off. It doesn't take a genius to figure out she's hiding something. Now, I didn't like Spencer, not one bit. But the idea that Miranda murdered him in cold blood wipes away any hope I might have for the colonists on Marius."

"You okay, Draco?" Eric asks, reading my expression.

I just shake my head.

Tuttle floats over to me and does something bizarre. He pats my shoulder. "Don't take it too hard, kid. I'd lay heavy odds you're not the first guy she's scammed. If you ask me, she's even worse than her old man. Charles Coffin may be greedy and ruthless as hell, but his daughter's a furking sociopath."

I mutter, "And now she's heading down to Europa to kill a lot of people."

"All in the name of 'law and order,'" Greenjeans adds.

"Unless we stop her," Tuttle says.

"How many spacers do you have on your side?" I ask.

He gestures at the dozen men and women around us. "You're looking at it. No weapons to speak of. No training. And she's got a whole bunch of heavily-armed paid psychos at her disposal."

"But we've got you," Eric says, smiling broadly.

Quite suddenly, I understand. Tuttle wants me to save his brother. It's just like Shelton said. Everyone in this crapfest — absolutely every-one — has seen me as nothing but a weapon.

"Here's the thing," I tell them both. "I don't have my dragon."

They stare blankly at me.

"What's that mean?" Tuttle asks.

"It means that Miranda's done something to me, something that's somehow blocking me from… doing what I do."

"So, you can't make thermal energy, anymore," Greenjeans says.

"She told me it was temporary."

"How temporary?"

"She didn't say."

Tuttle throws up his hands. "Furk! What are we supposed to do now? Listen, no offense, kid. But we only busted you out because we counted on you leading the charge into the lander bay and preventing Coffin from making the next orbital window. Now we got nothing."

I have no answer.

But Eric does. "Maybe not *nothing*."

We all look at him.

"I know that face, Greenjeans," Tuttle says. "What're you cooking up now?"

Eric grins. "You're tall, Draco. But are you… flexible?"

"Why?" I ask, a little warily.

EIGHT – Day 24

The tool cart is large and bulky, though, of course, weightless while in Jovian orbit. The spare parts and diagnostic equipment it usually carries have all been removed to make room for yours truly.

"Just relax," Greenjeans tells me. "This should be over quick."

"I hope so," I groan. "Because this is really furking tight."

"Stop whining. Just close your eyes and keep breathing. And for furk's sake, keep quiet. You don't need to sneeze, do you?"

"No," I reply, hugging my knees. I'm already uncomfortable.

"Fart?"

"No."

"Good. Once we're inside the lander, we'll let you out and hide you. Got it?"

"Got it."

He shuts the doors

A *long* time passes. I can't see or hear anything, and in zero-G, even the sensation of movement is minimized. Soon, my limbs cramp, and my back starts aching. Worse, I still can't reach my dragon. The "wall" is as solid as ever; I can't so much as dent it.

Our plan relies heavily on my "Kind-ness" returning. If we reach Europa and that hasn't happened, getting onto the coring unit unseen and riding it down to Marius is a long shot, at best.

So, I keep trying.

And keep failing.

Two sharp raps startle me. We've reached the lander bay.

I steady my breathing. Then, to my horror, I realize that I may need to fart after all.

I hold it in.

Tuttle's muffled voice says, "Engineering detail."

"You making this ride yourself, Chief?" someone asks, presumably one of the blackbirds guarding the lander.

"Yeah? So?"

"So, shouldn't the chief engineer stay up here?"

"I've never been to Europa before. Wanted a look. Problem?"

"I guess not. What's the cart for?"

"It's an engineering cart. We're engineers. What do you *think* the cart is for?"

"Take it easy! In case you haven't heard, that damned Dragon got loose, and Ms. Coffin thinks he might be trying to get onto the lander."

"Yeah? Well, I haven't seen that freak and don't want to. Now, Greenjeans and me got some checks to run before this boat can go anywhere. You going to let us by, or would you rather miss the landing window?"

"Go ahead."

I let out the breath I've been holding.

A new voice says, "Open up the cart."

Another blackbird, female this time, and higher-ranked, by the tone.

"Sergeant!" the first guard barks.

"What'd you say?" Tuttle asks impatiently.

"I said open the cart."

"There's equipment in there," Eric remarks. He doesn't even sound particularly nervous.

I'm scared out of my mind.

"Is that right? Well, let me see, and we're good."

Tuttle replies, "No."

"What?"

"I said no. The diagnostic gear is precisely calibrated. If you so much as look at it funny, we'll have to spend the next hour re-calibrating it. So, no."

"Look, I'm ordering you—"

"I don't give a furk. I'm not wearing your snazzy black duds. I take my orders from Captain Wei, not you."

"Open it. I'm not going to tell you again."

"Come on, Greenjeans. We're on a schedule. Let's get this thing aboard."

I hear an ominous triple-click, like a rifle being readied. It sends a chill down my spine. "Stay where you are, Chief!" The sergeant commands. "Exler, open the cabinet. If either of these clowns twitches, shoot him."

"Shoot me then," Tuttle says.

"What?"

"You heard me. Pull your trigger. Kill me right here. Just make damned certain one of those bullets of yours doesn't hit something it shouldn't."

"These rounds can't pierce the ship's hull."

"No, but they can sure as hell pierce the *lander's* hull. Besides, Sarge, you ever fire a weapon in zero-G before? I'm guessing you idiots were at least preliminarily taught Newton's Laws of Motion. Remember the one about equal and opposite reaction?"

More silence. For a second, I think Tuttle's bluff might work.

Then the sergeant says coldly, "Enough. Shoot him."

"Stand down."

I recognize the voice immediately, and it makes my already nervous stomach clench like a fist.

"What's the delay?" Miranda asks. "Our landing window opens in fifteen minutes."

"Ms. Coffin," the sergeant says. "These men aren't willing to let us search their equipment cart."

I can almost *feel* her proximity. It makes me start to sweat. I silently curse myself.

"Search it for what?" she asks.

"For the Dragon," the sergeant replies.

"Andy's not hiding in there."

"How can you be sure, ma'am?"

"Because I'm not sure *I* could fit, and *he's* six-foot-four. Now, can we please let these men go about their business? We absolutely *can't* miss this landing window!"

"Yes, Ms. Coffin."

And just like that, it's over. As my cramped metal sarcophagus begins moving again, I try to work out what just happened.

Miranda dismissed the idea that I might be hiding in the very thing in which I'm hiding because she doesn't think I'd fit. Except I *do* fit, albeit uncomfortably.

Which means I just got seriously lucky.

So, why don't I *feel* like I just got seriously lucky?

Long minutes later, Greenjeans finally opens the cabinet doors. I spill out, floating weightless and trying to get the kinks out of my — well, everywhere. When I groan, Eric shushes me.

We're in a small cramped space with a low ceiling and little light. Around me are cables, piping, and more cables. The only exit is a large, closed hatch a few inches over our heads.

"Where are we?" I whisper.

"The lander bilges. The chief's topside, running command console diagnostics. I came down here with the cart supposedly to confirm the electrical and propulsion systems. All on the up and up. The Ice Queen and her troops are filing onboard right now. That means you stay here until I come to get you. Fair warning, it's going to get bumpy."

I remember my first ride to the Europan surface. Spending another like that down here doesn't sound fun.

Eric says, "I'm gonna suggest you wedge yourself behind that conduit." He points to a spot where a dozen or more cables converge. "They're flexible enough to give you some protection and secure enough that nothing you do will dislodge them. It'll be a tight fit, though. Just don't pass out and try hard not to vomit. Being in close quarters with vomit floating around your head… well, it sucks."

"Thanks for the advice," I mutter dryly.

"Hey, nobody ever said the hero thing was supposed to be easy. Anything happening yet… fire-wise, I mean?"

I try.

"No. Nothing."

"Well, there's still hope."

"What if it doesn't come back before we're on the surface?" I ask, trying to keep the desperation out of my voice.

"One problem at a time. Take it easy, Draco." He puts a hand on my shoulder. "Get settled in. Me and the cart need to go topside, and I don't want you in sight when I open the hatch."

I nod and, with some effort, tuck myself into the cable cranny. Eric's right. It's snug, but not too bad. Not too *good*, either.

He gives me a final nod. Then he opens the hatch and floats up and out with the equipment cart in tow. Moments later, the hatch slides closed with the finality of a coffin lid.

As things turn out, the ride down to Europa isn't as bad as I expected.

It's much, much worse.

The instant the lander departs *Conquest*, zero-G is replaced with the false gravity of acceleration. It takes me by surprise and slams me into the wall, where I manage to bash the back of my skull against the smooth metal. Then, as the dark bilge swims a little around me, the lander pilot—whoever the furker is—drops us hard into Europa's minuscule gravity well. This hurls my body sideways, yanking me out from my hiding place before I even know what's happened.

Instant living pinball.

When it finally ends, I know nothing about it, having ignored both of Greenjeans' suggestions: I've vomited *and* passed out.

Again.

NINE – Day 24

Seriously, I think as consciousness returns. *Can't I go anywhere without someone or something knocking me cold?*

My head pounds savagely, and the light shining in my face doesn't help. But when I start to gripe about it, a strong palm clamps over my mouth.

That wakes me up.

"Shut it, kid," Tuttle tells me.

I blink. Then I nod. He lets go and offers me a hand, pulling me to my feet. The bilges remain dark, the overhead hatch shut. But I can tell we're no longer in zero-G.

I meet Tuttle's eyes. "We landed."

"Yeah."

"Where's Greenjeans?"

"Topside. That smooth-talker has managed to convince the Ice Queen that she needs us to come along with her in the coring unit as she heads down to Marius… in case of technical glitches. Damn, I wish I could smile the way that kid does. There's power in smiles. You know what I mean?"

I think about Miranda, who seldom smiles, and about Darcy, who always does.

"Yeah," I say.

"Kid, you got anything… going on yet?"

At first, I don't know what he means. Chalk that up to the bump on my head. But then it clicks. Immediately, I reach for my dragon—only to find it still unreachable.

Except—

Except the wall seems a little bit *thinner* now. Whatever mental barrier Okeke's gene therapy erected, something's weakened it. Time, maybe? Is it simply starting to wear off?

"Well?" the chief asks impatiently.

"Not yet. Sorry."

He glowers. "You picked a hell of a time to turn normal, kid."

I don't bother objecting to his use of the word "normal." "I didn't exactly pick it."

"Yeah, I get that. Okay, you'll have to get into the cart again. Then I'm going to haul you both onboard the coring unit."

"How many of Spencer's men did Miranda bring?"

"Thirty. All armed to the teeth. She's going to kill a lot of people. And, unless you get your mojo back, we can't stop her."

I nod miserably.

"Put on a suit," Tuttle tells me, motioning to a heavy-duty footlocker labeled *Emergency Env Equip.* "We have to carry the cart across the moon's surface, and it's not pressurized."

I do so, aching every step of the way. Squeezing into the cart, however, is another matter. If it was a tight fit before, it's *crazy* tight with a spacesuit on. And the stiffness and bruises left behind by my game of "lander pinball" don't help.

But I manage.

While the cabinet and I are no longer completely weightless, gravity's still low enough that Tuttle doesn't have too much difficulty hauling us both up and out of the lander's bowels. That's not to say the trip to the coring unit is pleasant. It isn't. Within the first two minutes, my soreness ratchets up to full-blown pain.

Two minutes after that, I'm in agony.

Maybe a half-hour goes by, though it feels a lot longer. The only sound inside the spacesuit is my own ragged breathing. Finally, comes a series of hard bumps that send my already cramped muscles into screaming jags. By the time the bumps stop, and the cart goes blessedly still, I'm close to full-blown panic.

Suddenly, the cabinet doors swing open, and I tumble free, landing in an aching heap on the coring unit's smooth tile floor. The light's blinding, and I clamp my eyes shut reflexively.

Someone works my helmet's latches. Moments later, it comes free, and ample air fills my lungs.

With an effort, I open my eyes and gaze upward.

"I'm disappointed, Andy," Miranda says, kneeling beside me. "I thought you were smarter than this."

Dozens of blackbirds surround me, pointing rifles at my head. I struggle to comprehend, more confused than afraid. Then, I crane my neck and spot Greenjeans and Tuttle.

Both spacers are on their knees, their hands clasped behind them. Eric's trademark cock-sure smile is gone; he looks like a man on the gallows. That's bad enough, but it's Tuttle's sweat-soaked face that really drives home how utterly furked we are.

The chief looks terrified.

Miranda says, "On the other hand, I'm a little bit impressed." I look back to see her peering into the open cabinet. "I mean, I *knew* you were in there, or at least strongly suspected. But I didn't think you'd last as long as you did. It must have been awful. Clearly, you want to get to MC-13 as badly as I do."

With an effort, I manage to croak, "Please. You don't have to do this."

"I wish that were true. I really do." She straightens and faces Sergeant Massey. She's the same blackbird who tried to arrest Shelton and challenged Tuttle and Greenjeans back in the lander bay. "Restrain him and put him with the other two."

"Yes, Ms. Coffin. Should we... um... be concerned about his abilities?"

Miranda shakes her head. "While I imagine Tuttle and his apprentice were counting on exactly that, I promise you it won't happen."

As two blackbirds pull me to my feet, I shout hoarsely at Miranda, "You told me it was temporary!"

Her response is almost gentle. "Oh, it is. But temporary, in this case, is measured in weeks or even months, not hours. For the duration of this mission, you're just one of the boys." Then the soldiers drag me across the coring unit and force me to my knees beside Eric.

"Sorry," Greenjeans whispers.

"Shut up!" a blackbird snaps as he shackles my wrists behind my back with a plastic tie.

Eric obeys, but only until the two soldiers step away. Then, leaning toward me, he explains softly, "They were on us the minute the Chief and I came aboard the coring unit with the cart. Trussed us up and didn't even bother asking questions. The Ice Queen ordered everybody to keep quiet. She seemed to get off on waiting to see how long it took you to crack and come out. When you didn't, she got impatient and opened the cabinet herself. You okay?"

"No. You?"

"Not even a little bit. This was a piss-poor plan."

Beside him, the chief adds, "The plan was fine. That bitch is just too smart is all."

"Sergeant Massey," Miranda calls impatiently. "Please keep the prisoners quiet."

At Massey's nod, Tuttle gets slammed in the back of the head with the butt of a blackbird's rifle. He hits the floor—hard.

"Stop it!" I scream.

The same guard turns toward me, his rifle butt raised again.

"Enough," Miranda announces in a tone of utter command. The blackbird stands down, looking disappointed.

"Chief, you okay?" Eric asks urgently.

To my relief, Tuttle groans and then rises. His head is bloodied, and he wobbles as he regains his knees. "He hits like a girl."

The blackbird looming over him curses and makes as though to hit him again.

Massey snaps, "Ms. Coffin told you that's enough, Tepper!"

Tepper nods and steps back.

"Gag them," Miranda commands. Then, looking at me, she adds, "All three of them."

Tuttle doesn't struggle as duct tape is pulled tight across his mouth. Eric *does* but is easily restrained. When my turn comes, I consider yelling something out about innocent people and harmless, intelligent Europan life. But the blackbirds' collective expression tells me I'd be wasting my time.

So, I just kneel there as they tape my lips shut.

Meanwhile, Miranda stands amidst her personal army. "ETA to MC-13?"

One of the blackbirds replies, "One hour and fifty minutes, ma'am."

"Good." She addresses her entire contingent, "Sergeant Massey assures me that I can count on your absolute loyalty. I'll need that loyalty. This mission will be difficult, and, unfortunately, hard choices will have to be made. We are faced with a desperate, rebellious situation that can't be allowed to continue. If Spencer were still alive, he'd be saying this to you. But, as things are, the responsibility falls to me. You will take lives today. I don't know how many, but more than a few. Some of the orders I give you may seem extreme. But each one is absolutely necessary if we are to restore order, not only to this colony but to the System at large. This situation has become far more dangerous than any of us expected.

"When we began this rescue mission, we didn't yet understand the broader threat that was being posed. You're all soldiers. You know the dangers of living and working in deep space. And you understand that, for humankind to survive out here, there *must* be a clear chain of command. There must be authority.

"For decades, CSE has been that authority. Together we have established thriving colonies on dozens of worlds, moons, orbital stations, and asteroids. We have watched those colonies flourish and have brought discoveries and new science back to Mother Earth that have revolutionized civilization. Together, we have done so much good.

"I want you to *remember* all the good CSE has done. In fact, we came out here in the fastest and most cutting-edge spacecraft ever launched to do even more good.

"But since arriving at Europa, a terrible truth has made itself known. Orpheus and Eurydice are not, as we'd assumed, pirates or off-world criminals who arrived at MC-13 and seized control. Instead, they are the colonists themselves. They have declared themselves independent of CSE's authority and have, in just the last twelve hours, managed to hack into the Casimir Radio and broadcast dangerous and seditious messages throughout the Solar System. This isn't terrorism, people. It's treason."

Miranda pauses, letting that word hang in the air.

The soldiers around her listen in rapt attention, many of them nodding. They're buying every word—but then manipulation has always been Miranda's weapon of choice. I have to keep reminding myself that she is an eighteen-year-old girl, a teenager like me. Except she carries herself with the bearing and maturity of somebody twice her age — a *woman*, not a girl.

I suddenly wonder if Miranda Coffin was *ever* a "girl."

I wish I could tell them what really happened to Spencer. But I'm gagged and, of course, she knows that.

Two steps ahead, as always.

She continues, "Thanks to MC-13, as I speak, colonies throughout the system are beginning to question the very authority that has kept them alive for an entire generation. Soon, more rebellions will arise, more violence. And, if left unchecked, the entire infrastructure that holds humanity together Off-Earth may collapse. We can't allow that to happen."

She points at Tuttle and Greenjeans. "It has already started and in our very ranks. Today, two of our fellow shipmates conspired to break Andy Brand out of confinement and smuggle him to MC-13 with us, and in doing so, assaulted one of our own."

Dozens of eyes fix on the three of us. Hostile. Very hostile.

Miranda says darkly, "These men aren't soldiers, with a soldier's sense of honor. They're ignorant spacers who've sided with Orpheus and Eurydice to tear down the stability we've all worked so hard to build.

"Our only hope of avoiding the coming chaos is to end MC-13's revolt and make very clear the consequences of sedition. We do this today, not for our own sakes or for CSE's sake, but for the sake of all humanity.

"We need to retake MC-13 by force. But that won't be the worst of it. Once the colony is ours, we must identify the ringleaders, not just Orpheus and Eurydice, but *all* the key personnel who have supported them. Then we need to execute them. I know how that sounds. Believe me, I do. But this single, brutal act, once done and properly publicized, will send a message to the rest of the System… that this is what happens when the authority we all rely on is ignored."

She pauses again, reading her audience. Hard, emotionless faces meet her gaze. There are no fidgets, no looks askance, no equivocation at all.

"This horrible thing we do is to prevent larger, more horrible things. By taking twenty lives, we will be saving tens of thousands of others."

Another pause. Now there are nods.

She has them.

"But first, we have to clean our own house by dealing with the traitors in our midst. They've been secretly working against us all along, passing intel to MC-13. Their betrayal can't be excused nor allowed to pass. And, to show you that I stand with you, I'll take on this grim task myself."

Sergeant Massey steps forward. "Ms. Coffin! You don't need to. One of my blackbirds can—"

Miranda holds up a silencing hand. The whole thing smacks of contrivance, rehearsal even.

But the soldiers eat it up.

"This is on me, Massey," Miranda replies firmly. "Please give me your sidearm."

The sergeant hands the weapon over, butt first. Miranda thanks her. Then she makes a show of squaring her thin shoulders before heading toward where the three of us kneel, helpless.

Tuttle struggles frantically, but the blackbirds keep him in check. His eyes are wild, and he's making panicked sounds that the gag can't completely muffle.

Beside him, Greenjeans doesn't move. He simply watches Miranda's approach with resignation.

Oh, my God. She's going to do it!

As Miranda moves past me, I throw myself in her path without thinking. It's a useless gesture. With my wrists bound and my knees stiff from all the kneeling, all I manage to do is kind of sprawl awkwardly at her feet. But my desperate effort takes her by surprise and *almost* trips her. Startled, she stumbles, her freehand pinwheeling as she catches herself.

Our eyes meet and lock.

I put everything I have into that look.

Please! Don't do this! Don't be the person that can do this! Be Miranda Fiero, if only this one last time!

For an instant, I swear there's something there—a spark of regret, of humanity. And in that instant, I recognize another Miranda, a different one, one who *isn't* an Ice Queen, *isn't* a manipulator. She's simply a troubled girl, determined to do whatever it takes to earn her father's approval. His love.

And, for some reason, I think of her brother. Charlie, wasn't it?

Does all this seem like a lot to read into a single look? Trust me, it isn't. There's a reason they say eyes are the windows to the soul. The problem with windows, of course, is all you can do is see through them. You can't reach what's inside.

A moment later, all expression drains from Miranda's face, and the girl I knew, or thought I knew, or hoped I knew, falls away. Whatever remains steps over me and points her gun at Tuttle. The chief starts screaming behind the tape.

"For what it's worth," Miranda says. "Your brother will join you soon."

Then she shoots him.

I expect there to be a lot of blood, but there isn't. The bullet just turns him off, like a switch. Tuttle's lifeless body falls backward. The blackbirds step clear and let him hit the deck in the low-G.

With a long, shuddering sigh, Miranda moves on to Greenjeans.

As she raises her weapon, Eric's eyes find mine.

He offers me a little nod with a lot behind it.

Then Miranda shoots him too.

My friend — I realize with a shock that it's the first time I've thought of him that way — topples without a sound. He hits the floor beside Tuttle, his eyes still open but seeing nothing.

I hollow out. All my fear and desperation slip away, leaving behind a void without pain or hope. I've just watched a woman I cared for kill two men I knew. One I liked, and the other I could have come to like. But now, any future they might have has been snuffed out in an instant.

Miranda steps back, adroitly avoiding where I lay, still sprawled like an idiot. She hands the pistol back to Massey. The surrounding troops are almost funereally silent.

"What about Brand?" the sergeant asks.

"He's harmless," Miranda replies. "For now, put him in the airlock. Keep him bound and gagged, but conscious. I want to ask him a few questions about MC-13 — it's layout and such."

"We have the schematics, Ms. Coffin," Massey replies.

"Yes. But they may not tell us everything we need to know. Mike Shelton's an engineer, Sergeant. And engineers change things."

TEN – Day 24

They leave me in the airlock, trussed up like a lamb for slaughter.

That emotional void I experienced right after Eric's and Tuttle's murders has given way to a fresh wave of self-recrimination. No matter how much cold logic I throw at it, I can't shake the certainty that all this death should be laid at my feet.

None of it would have happened if I'd kept *Conceal and Protect.*

I know it doesn't make much sense. Kim would knock down my guilt like the narcissistic, self-indulgent house of cards it is. But Kim's not here at the moment, and she's likely to be dead in about an hour. I'm never going to see her again, or Darcy, or Shelton.

This is all my fault.

Anyway, that's where my head's at when Miranda pays a call.

Without warning, a bunch of tiles slide apart, and she steps through. Then, with the aperture closing behind her, she says, "If I remove your gag, will you promise not to yell your head off?"

I hesitate. Then I nod.

Miranda kneels and, with surprising tenderness, peels the duct tape off my face, wincing sympathetically as I flinch. Then she straightens and asks, "Are you all right?"

I don't reply. I'm desperately thirsty but don't say so.

She remarks, "You must hate me."

If only it were that simple.

Again, I don't reply.

"Terrible things are happening," she says.

This time, I *do* answer. "That much I agree with."

"I've had to make hard choices."

"Like killing Spencer?"

She looks flatly at me. "That one was fairly easy."

A cold chill runs up my spine.

"Does Massey know?" I ask sharply. "Or the rest of the blackbirds?"

"No."

"Maybe I should tell them."

She shrugs. "You could, but they won't believe you. I already warned them that killing Spencer was part of the chief's plan all along."

Of course, she did.

Miranda says quietly, "I know you think I'm a monster —"

"I think you're a murderer. And a liar."

" —but that's only because you've led a rather sheltered life."

"*What?*"

"Your parents kept you under their wing, never showing you the realities of the world. I grew up differently. From the time I could talk, my father taught me that only *results* are important. A person's worth isn't measured by their compassion or generosity. It's measured solely by what they accomplish. I know that sounds cynical. But he was right. We're not the sum of our parts; we're the sum of what we do with those parts.

"And here's another cruel truth for you, Andy. Civilization isn't split into Humanity and Kind. It isn't split into male and female either. Or Christian and Non-Christian, or Jewish and Gentile, or gay or straight, or any of the other cultural, political, or religious divides that most people hang so much weight on. There are really only two kinds of thinking beings: those who *matter*... and those who don't."

I gape at her. "Matter? What does that even mean?"

Her eyes flash with a fervor I've never seen there before. "It means standing on the side of progress, of science, of advancement! That's what my father has always done. That's what *I'm* doing!"

"By killing my friends?" I shoot back.

"If necessary, yes!"

"By killing my parents?"

"Yes, damn it! Don't you see? The future has no place for people without vision! Your parents died because they were *small*, Andy. I'm sorry, but it's true. Yes, we took you from them, but we *told* them it was for the greater good. They wouldn't listen. So, they stepped into the path of progress and died for it. What's worse, they took thousands of others with them!"

I can't believe what I'm hearing. "Your people... CSE people... shot them, knowing full well what would happen when they did. My family didn't destroy New York. CSE did."

Her eyebrows knit. "Maybe. But those people didn't matter, either. They were all small, like your parents. Twenty thousand nobodies. A hundred thousand. A million. What difference does it make?"

"You're insane!" I exclaim.

"Andy, you really should try to calm down."

"Or what? You'll vector me again?"

"If you force me to."

"Tell me something, Miranda," I demand. "Why am I still alive? You had no qualms about killing Eric and Tuttle in cold blood. Why not me, too? In your eyes, I have to be as 'guilty' as they were."

The question seems to annoy her. She looks askance. I get no reply.

I wait.

She chews her lip.

I wait some more.

She finally says, "My father wants you dead."

"So you've told me."

"He's always thought of you as nothing but an asset, and a dangerous one. He sees you as inhuman."

"Well, based on his definition, I am."

"I think you're the most human person I've ever met."

I'm not sure if that's supposed to be a compliment or not.

Miranda goes on, "You're smart, and you're noble. Your behavior in your cell aboard *Conquest* proves that."

"Most of that was me being a naïve boy."

"That's the way my father read it. Spencer, too. But they never saw what I saw."

Furk! I wish my insides wouldn't do what they're doing now when she says things like that. I don't want to care about this woman, not anymore. But maybe Kim was right. Feelings like this don't go away overnight, however much we might like them to.

Miranda says, "So, who was it?"

"Who was what?"

"The colonist girl on MC-13 who turned your head." She says this bitterly, as if I've betrayed her. The irony tastes like tin foil. I don't reply.

"Was it Kim Shelton?"

"No!" I exclaim.

"Why not? She's a Dragon, like you, isn't she?"

The words are out before I can stop them. "No, she's a Split."

"A… Split. What is that? A hybrid? Half-human, half-Kind?"

Again, I don't reply.

"I figured she had to be like you when we found out she didn't die in the lift. But it never occurred to me that the answer was more complicated than that. Okay, so it's not her. I suppose I knew that, having read her psych profile. Shelton's too, for that matter. He's not the kind of man to support such a dalliance. So, it must be someone else on Marius."

"Stop it," I tell her.

"Stop what?"

"This isn't about me hooking up with a girl. This is about me realizing, really realizing, what's at stake here."

"Andy, if you 'really realized' what's at stake, you'd be on my side."

"Miranda, there's life down there! Intelligent life!"

"I'm aware of that."

"And the tantalum mining was hurting that life."

"So, the Sheltons claim. They call them dragons. That's a sweet little coincidence, isn't it?"

Not really, given that Kim was the one who named them, but I don't say so. "I've seen them, communicated with them. They saved my life! They're smart, and they're noble, at least as noble as you think I am."

"It doesn't matter."

"Miranda!"

"Oh, I realize that, scientifically, the discovery of such life is... significant. But it pales beside the risk it poses. However 'smart and noble' these creatures are, this is *our* Solar System, not theirs. And if they are, indeed, the catalyst for Orpheus and Eurydice's rebellion, then they're as much a danger as the terrorists."

"There are no terrorists!"

"Semantics. Look, I know you think I've been lying from the beginning. But what I said about Orpheus and Eurydice taking hostages was, in a sense, true. By their actions, they've basically taken the entire colonized System hostage, and it's a situation that I can't allow to continue."

"Miranda, listen to me —"

But, of course, she doesn't. "While I'm certainly grateful to these... dragons... for saving your life, it doesn't change the fact that, like the miners themselves, they don't matter."

"Miranda," I say, stepping through my words as if through a minefield. "If you care about me like you say you do, then I'm *begging* you... don't do this. Let me talk to them. Let me see if maybe some kind of peace can be worked out. Please!"

"You think I enjoy this?" she asks me. She begins pacing back and forth, agitated. "These deaths will haunt me forever. But nobody, not even my father, is willing to do what *must* be done. I meant what I told the blackbirds. The stability of all occupied space is at stake. The Sheltons and their co-conspirators *need* to be put down."

The words cut like knives. "No!" I exclaim, fighting my bonds, trying to rise.

"I'm sorry, Andy."

"I'll stop you! Do you hear me? I'll stop you!"

"You can't. And, what's more, you shouldn't. All I can do is promise that you'll be safe… and hope that, someday, you'll see that I'm right."

Frantically, I hammer at the "wall" between my dragon and me. It's thinner than it was — I swear it is — but still as impregnable as iron. Beyond it, I can sense the dragon churning with barely contained power. It knows the wall's there, too — and it wants out.

It wants out badly.

Miranda summons a portal, pausing to look back at me one more time.

As we lock eyes, I say, venom in my every word, "If you do this, I'll burn you! Do you hear me? I'll turn you and everyone with you into ash!"

Miranda doesn't so much as blink. Instead, she treats me to a piteous look and replies, flatly, "How?"

And then she closes the portal and leaves me alone once more.

Alone with the dragon I can't reach.

Sometime later, they come for me.

I spend the intervening time struggling frantically against my cuffs but only succeed in slicing up the skin on my wrists and ankles and wrenching my shoulders. After that, defeated, I just lay there, bouncing between guilt and what's probably the blackest anger I've ever felt in my life. Every time I close my eyes, I see Eric's sweat-soaked face as he nodded to me the moment before he died.

And, with shame and horror, I keep remembering the way my pulse quickened when Miranda complimented me.

Love-sick idiot.

Ridiculous child.

You're crushing on a sociopath who thinks she's a savior.

A portal opens, and two blackbirds march in. Wordlessly, they pull me to my feet and drag me into the coring unit. As they do, two more blackbirds enter the airlock lugging a big tripod-mounted laser. No one says a word.

In the CU's center, Miranda is speaking with Massey, who's got the rest of her contingent lined up and ready to pour into Marius, once a fresh hole's been cut in its hull. Meanwhile, Eric and Tuttle's bodies have been wrapped in plastic and stacked up, like cordwood, against the wall.

I can't let this happen.

"Here's the plan," Miranda says, addressing everyone. "In a few minutes, we'll be inside the colony. Your orders are to secure the Operations Deck. If you encounter armed resistance, you are to use deadly force. Otherwise, waylay everyone you find and collect them on the Ops Deck by the moon pool. There should be enough room. If possible, I want the Sheltons and their department heads captured alive. Once you've secured the colony, Mister Brand and I will come down with our escort. Understood?"

There are nods of agreement. Then, just to put a period on the sentence, Massey adds, "Understood, Ms. Coffin."

"We should all prepare ourselves. These next few hours will be difficult. But I'm sure that—"

In the next instant, a loud *boom* fills the chamber, coming from the airlock.

ELEVEN - Day 24

"What the hell…" Massey exclaims. But that's as far as she gets as a piece of the wall suddenly juts outward like a tile fist and clocks her in the solar plexus. The blow slams her into a half-dozen blackbirds, and they all go down in a heap of flailing limbs. For an instant, nobody moves as the offending section of wall, about eight inches—four tiles— square, retracts and disappears.

Miranda's eyes find mine, her expression questioning.

But before either of us can speak, a barrier of Liquid Bricks blooms up between us. It extends the width of the coring unit from floor to ceiling, effectively cutting me, my two escorts, and the airlock off from the rest of the attack force.

"What's happening?" one of the blackbirds demands, raising his rifle.

Then Shelton's voice in my ear says, *"Andy, drop!"*

Blinking, I drop. It's not hard to do, trussed up as I am—painful, but not hard.

At the same instant, another Liquid Bricks "fist" lashes out from the wall and clubs one of my escorts from behind. An identical section simultaneously clips the other guy with enough force that I hear the *clunk* of tile against skull.

Both hit the floor like sacks of sand, leaving me lying there, bound and helpless between them.

"Andy?" Miranda calls from beyond the barrier. "Are you okay?"

Instead of replying, I glance back at the open airlock.

Mike Shelton is standing there, wielding a futurey gadget. He silences me with a wink and a gesture.

"Andy?" Miranda calls again. She sounds worried. It pisses me off.

Shelton's wearing the most cheerfully smug grin I think I've ever seen. Quietly, he kneels beside me, produces a short knife, and cuts the plastic cuffs holding my wrists and ankles. My hands tingle as the blood rushes back into them. My legs feel numb.

As he pulls me to my feet, I ask quietly, "How?"

"Later," he whispers. "Come on."

He leads me through the open airlock and into a short, freshly made umbilical corridor of Liquid Bricks. Just inside, lay the unconscious bodies of the two blackbirds with the laser drill. Beyond them, I see that there is, indeed, a fresh hole in Marius's outer hull. But this one wasn't burned. It was *blown*.

Shelton says, "We set incendiary charges as soon as we knew where they planned to latch on. Then we picked our moment and set them off."

"But the Liquid Bricks…"

He holds up the unfamiliar gadget. "I had this put together using the e-man access codes Francis got from his brother." Then he pauses. "Oh, I never got around to telling you that Francis and the guy who you know as Chief Tuttle are brothers."

The mention of Tuttle drains the blood from my face. The only response I can manage is a muttered, "Yeah, I know."

He reads my expression, and "smug" turns to "alarm."

He asks, "What happened, Andy?"

"Tuttle… Miranda killed him. His body's in the coring unit."

"Furk…"

"She shot him herself along with one of his apprentices. She declared them traitors to humanity or something and executed them right in front of me."

"Furk," Shelton says again. Then, as if trying to wrap his head around it, adds, "Okay. Okay."

We emerge into a pantry. A handful of colonists are there waiting for us.

"Seal it up," Shelton tells them. "But first grab the laser torch off those unconscious blackbirds. Maybe we'll get lucky and they won't be carrying a backup." Then, after some hesitation, he asks, "Where's Francis?"

"He went back down to Ops," one of the miners replies.

"And Kim?"

"I'm here!" Kim exclaims, running up and throwing her arms around my neck. I'm so exhausted that we both nearly topple over, but she doesn't seem to notice. "Andy! Thank God! We couldn't believe it when that bitch took you!"

"Let's go," Shelton says. "This isn't over. Not by a long shot."

As we hurry down to Ops Deck. I give them both a quick rundown of everything that happened after my "negotiator gig" went south. I explain about my captivity and rescue, about the gene therapy that put up a "wall" inside my head, about Spencer's "heart attack," and Tuttle and Eric smuggling me aboard the coring unit.

"But the RCH worked," I tell them, latching onto the one and only bright spot in this whole mess. "The message is out!"

"Andy!" Kim exclaims, and, suddenly, she's hugging me again. "You did it!"

"All I did was get myself captured. *You* guys did it."

Shelton remarks, "But we're still in hot water."

"Yeah," I say. "We are."

By now, exhaustion is hitting me hard. My knees wobble, and I sag against the staircase. Seeing this, Kim catches her husband's arm. "We're going too fast for Andy. Hold up."

Shelton holds up, though he looks impatient, and, given the circumstances, I don't blame him. His Liquid Bricks hack was genius, but we both know his impromptu barrier won't hold up for very long.

Even so, I drop down onto a step, shaking. Everything hurts, and I mean everything, body and soul. Kim watches me, concern on her face. Then, Shelton puts a hand on my shoulder. "It sucks, kid."

I smile weakly. "Which part?"

"All of it. But especially the you-getting-dragged-into-it part."

"Miranda claims that what you're all doing here, 'treason' is her word, is threatening the stability of the entire System."

"Does she?"

"Is it true?"

"God, I hope so."

I look at him.

Kim says, "Andy, out here, CSE is the only law and the only government. Whenever somebody like us has stepped out of line, they've been the judge, jury, and... on more than one occasion... the executioner."

"All this has happened before?"

"This or something like it," Shelton replies. "About fifteen years ago, a Martian colony got idealistic and declared independence. Not a word of the *real* story ever reached Earth but ask any spacer. That colony... Ramses it was called... was erased."

"I learned about it in school. But wasn't it a fuel station explosion that killed everybody?"

"No," Kim replies gently. "CSE wiped out a hundred and sixty-three scientists and engineers and their families as a warning to others."

"*Furk.*"

Shelton nods. "Big-time furk. Then, nine years ago, a mining colony on Vesta had a gas leak that poisoned thirty people."

"Same thing?" I ask.

"Same thing," he replies.

Vesta's the largest asteroid in the massive asteroid belt between Mars and Jupiter — well, the largest since Ceres, one-quarter the moon's size, got promoted to dwarf planet. Back when I was in grade school, the news reported an accident there that killed half the population. It was considered the second-worst space-based accident in human history... after Ramses. In both cases, there was a memorial, and the president gave the eulogy.

I say, "Miranda intends to collect all the 'ring leaders' and do to you what she did to Eric and Tuttle."

"Vesta and Ramses all over again," Kim mutters.

Shelton adds, "We figured that might be their play. CSE wants to set another 'example.'"

I say, "Not necessarily. I think Miranda's completely snapped. At first, I thought she was just doing what Daddy wants. But some things she said make me think maybe Charles Coffin doesn't know what's really going on here."

"Could be," Kim replies. "If Tuttle is… was… right, then maybe she killed Spencer to remove an obstacle."

"Or get rid of a rival," Shelton suggests.

"So, you think her father's *not* on board with what she's doing?" I say.

"Maybe not. Marius isn't Vesta. The work we do here is specialized, and most of our equipment and processes are homegrown and proprietary. If we're all killed, running the mining operations becomes problematic, maybe even impossible. Charles Coffin knows that."

Kim asks him, "But you think his daughter doesn't?"

"Or doesn't care. She probably figures she can remove management… us… and force the staff into stepping up. But, while our people can certainly run the machines, they don't have the knowledge or expertise to bring Ops back online. Without us, Marius'll be literally dead in the water."

"Maybe we can tell her that," I suggest. "It might… No, forget it. She's gone too far to stop."

Kim nods, looking miserable.

"Which is why we have to get to Ops," Shelton says. "You okay now?"

I'm not okay. I'm nothing like okay. But at least some of the exhaustion has ebbed. Call it adrenalin. "I'm good."

The mood in Ops is understandably tense. Everyone's busy. Everyone's talking. Every machine at every station is manned.

Seeing us, Francis hurries over, his scowl even deeper than usual. He looks so much like his brother that I wonder how I missed it. When he reaches us, Shelton, looking grim, starts to say something, but Francis beats him to it. "Miranda Coffin sent a message. Since you weren't here, I figured I'd speak for the colony."

"Of course," Shelton replies.

"When I told her who I was, she said… that my brother has been executed for treason. She told me I'm to be executed as well, along with you and Kim, and about twenty others. The psycho even has a list. She read it off to me. She told me the only way to avoid 'more than necessary bloodshed' is for all of us to surrender ourselves for punishment. She said, if we don't, then more will have to die."

"Jeez…" Kim breathes.

"After *that*," Francis says, with a twisted smile on his face that has nothing whatsoever to do with humor. "She offered me her condolences."

"You have the list of names?" Shelton asks.

Francis nods.

"Burn it."

"What?"

Shelton addresses the entire room, which has suddenly gone eerily quiet. "Listen up! We are not surrendering to these thugs! Anyone who isn't with me in fighting back, and I mean *fighting back,* people, should leave now. Lock yourselves in one of the labs up on Lab Deck, since Ice Deck's sealed off. Then, later, surrender yourselves to Coffin peacefully, and maybe she'll let you keep breathing. But I can't guarantee it.

"Our Liquid Bricks hack's got them trapped in their coring unit. But it won't last. As soon as they manually reboot the system, they'll regain control. But we're not done yet. Once they get into the colony, we have a few surprises planned. Again, no guarantees.

"So… who's staying, and who's going?"

Francis says, "We're with you, boss."

Other voices shout the same.

But then about a dozen colonists leave the room. They say nothing and make no eye contact.

Kim watches them, looking pained.

"Better than I thought," Shelton admits quietly. He turns to Francis. "Are the gas canisters hidden on Ice Deck?"

"Fifteen of them, all strategically placed. We can trigger them one at a time or all together."

"Good."

Francis looks at me, his expression a mix of grief and anger that I'm getting to know all too well. "What about you, Magic Fire Guy? What're *you* bringing to the fight?"

"Leave him alone!" Kim snaps protectively. "Andy's done enough."

"It's okay," I tell her. Then to Francis, I say, "Your brother came through for me. He didn't have to, and he died for it. I'm sorry about that."

To my surprise, his eyes moisten, and he replies, "Thanks."

"But Miranda did something to me aboard *Conquest,* some kind of gene therapy. And now I can't reach my dragon."

Francis considers. "So, you can't do the heat thing you do?"

I shake my head.

"So, you're basically worthless."

"Not entirely," I reply.

They all look at me.

I know how what I'm about to say will sound, but they need to hear it. "I'm the one person I'm pretty sure Miranda won't kill."

TWELVE – Day 24

"Just tell me you didn't tell her about *us*!" Darcy exclaims.

She's been treating my wrists and ankles, which bear bloody slices from the blackbirds' plastic cuffs. She's also smeared warm balm on my bare shoulders, shoulder blades, and quads to help ease my aching muscles. She's tending to me, and yet her manner is professional, even clinical. She's a medic right now.

I shift uncomfortably for a moment but don't answer.

"Andy," she says, eyeballing me.

"Um… not by name."

"But, you told her you've been kissing *someone*?"

"She guessed. I just didn't deny it."

Darcy groaned. "And you think she *doesn't* want to kill you?"

"Well… yeah." I blink. "No?"

"Guys…" she mutters.

"What?"

"Forget it. Tell me more about this gene therapy."

"I wasn't conscious for it," I reply, grateful for the subject change. "She mentioned a concoction that Okeke, *Conquest's* doctor, put together after she mapped my genome."

Darcy considers. "So, she compared your genetic map to a human baseline, identified the aberrant sequences, and then developed a serum to block the triggering of those sequences?"

For all my science-geekiness, I get about half of that. "Apparently, it's temporary… but might last days or weeks."

"You say it's like a wall between you and your dragon?"

I nod.

"So, I guess you've been mentally poking at this wall?"

"A lot."

"Like a dog trying to worry a bandage off its foot."

"Not sure I like the comparison, but yeah."

That earns me a somewhat begrudging laugh. Then the Biology Lab door opens, and Kim sweeps in. "So, how is he?"

"Banged up a little, that's all," Darcy replies. Then, with a mischievous smile, she adds, "Personally, I think the cuts and bruises make him sexier."

I *hate* the way that makes my face redden.

"I know what you mean," Kim says, making things much, much worse. "I always like it when Shelton shows up all sweaty from machine work. What is it about battle-weary men?"

"An evolutionary thing," Darcy replies.

They both laugh, and I wish I could crawl into a hole.

Then, more seriously, Kim asks, "What about this gene blocker?"

"I took some tissue samples, but I'll need more time than we have to analyze them. In the short term, Andy was about to tell me if he thinks he might be able to overcome the therapy on his own."

Was I?

I reply, "All I know for sure is that, after getting knocked stupid during the descent from *Conquest*, I noticed that the wall in my head felt… thinner."

"Thinner?" Darcy asks.

"Weaker? Not much. But a little bit."

"An environmental trigger?" Kim suggests. "Discomfort, maybe?"

"Physical distress," Darcy replies. "Heart rate and blood pressure elevate. It would make sense."

"The body releases adrenalin," Kim adds. "And cortisol. Andy, after what you saw happen to your friend and Francis' brother, you should try again now."

So I do, reaching inward.

"It's… even thinner," I tell them. "But still pretty furking strong."

"Adrenaline, maybe?" Kim suggests. "Could that jolt him enough to bring down this wall?"

"Possibly," Darcy replies. "I have some epinephrine auto-injectors in stock."

"And one of them could… fix me?" I ask.

"Impossible to say," Darcy replies. "Even if it does, its effects might not last long. It wouldn't reverse the therapy, but it might bypass it enough to let you activate the blocked sequences."

Which, I guess, is a sciencey way of saying I'd be able to reach my dragon. "Let's do it!"

Kim shakes her head. "Slow down. We don't have any idea what epinephrine does to Dragon… Kind… physiology. It might stop his heart!"

I look beseechingly at her. "We've got a crazy lady and her personal army banging on the door! It's worth the risk."

"I know you want to help. But Shelton has a plan."

"Kim—"

"Not a chance, Andy. We just got you back. I'm not ready to risk losing you again, not yet." She turns to Darcy. "Which brings me to the other reason I came by. Shelton wants everyone on Miranda Coffin's Top Twenty List down in Ops. That includes you, I'm sorry to say."

Darcy nods stoically. "When?"

"Ten minutes ago."

I rise from the exam table. "Has Miranda made it out of the coring unit?"

"Not yet, but we're reading power fluctuations that imply they've initiated a systems reboot, which will clear the hack."

"Let's go," Darcy says.

"I have to pee," I tell them.

Darcy points to a niche in the far wall. One of Marius's low-G toilets.

"Um… not a lot of privacy."

Darcy grins. "Shyness is sexy, too."

Once again, the women laugh. But then, thank God, they leave the room.

After they've gone, I do what needs doing. Then I follow them out.

Ops is more crowded than ever. Except for the dozen or so desertions, everybody has been evacuated from the Ice and Lab Decks. The entire remaining complement is down here now, all crammed into the most secure room on Marius.

The tension's thick. These people are scared. And they should be.

Shelton and Francis, among many others, are watching one of the big monitors, which shows the Ice Deck pantry, its wall freshly repaired. Almost as soon as Kim, Darcy, and I arrive, laser light begins to burn a new opening.

"They're cutting through," Francis reports unnecessarily.

Shelton replies, "It was inevitable."

Kim remarks, "Looks like they had a back-up laser cutter, after all."

"I would have," Shelton says.

Within a minute, a jagged oval of metal crashes to the pantry floor. Immediately, blackbirds emerge, their weapons drawn. They scan the pantry. Then one of them calls back, *"It's clear!"*

Massey comes next. After taking in the scene, she steps aside to let Miranda enter. The colonists collectively grumble at the sight of her. This is the woman who has come to subjugate most of them—and kill the rest.

One of the blackbirds points out the vidcam. Miranda steps forward. *"I'm assuming you can hear me, Mister Shelton."*

Shelton touches a button on his collar. "I hear you."

"I'm sorry it's come to this."

"So am I."

"Do you have Andy Brand with you?"

Shelton replies, "He's secure." It's an interesting choice of words.

Apparently, Miranda thinks so too. *"What's that mean?"*

Shelton doesn't reply.

"Is he unharmed?"

Shelton doesn't reply.

"Mister Shelton, is Andy Brand unharmed?"

He offers me a wink and replies, "Relatively."

I suppress a smile.

"It would be in your best interests if you release him to us."

Something about the way she says this chills me. Maybe it's genuine concern for my safety. To be fair, I'm pretty sure that's what *she* thinks it is. But it feels like something darker.

Shelton says, "Well, considering you've already slated me, my wife, and a number of our colleagues for execution, I'm not sure what you mean by my 'best interests.'"

Miranda's expression never changes. *"Give him back to me, or I'll kill a lot more."*

The words hit like hammer blows. The entire Ops Center falls into a collective, stunned silence. The thing is: it isn't the threat so much as the delivery. No malice. No anger. No pity. Just a statement of intent.

Ice Queen.

Miranda says, "*I assume this deck has already been evacuated and sealed off?*"

Shelton says nothing.

Undaunted, Miranda continues, "*I also assume that you've arranged some kind of 'surprise' for my CSE enforcement personnel?*"

"Of course not. Why don't you all just come on in?"

"*I have a better idea. Robotic probes have just finished attaching explosive charges to the claws fastening Marius to the ice shelf. Your Liquid Bricks hack was clever, but deploying the charges is what really delayed our entry.*"

Shelton mutes his mic and turns to Francis. "Check it out."

The other man hurries off as Marius holds its collective breath.

Shelton reactivates the comms. "Do that, and the current will carry us God-knows-where under the ice. CSE will lose its tantalum mining permanently."

"*There's more at stake here than tantalum production, or even CSE profits. I'm fighting for the political stability of the entire System.*"

'And you think killing us all will firm up your company's relationship with the spacer community?"

"*Accidents happen, Mister Shelton.*"

"Like Ramses and Vesta? You didn't fool anyone then, and you won't fool anyone now."

"*It'll fool the people it needs to fool and inform the rest. But let's not test it. Give me back Andy, unharmed, and surrender yourself and the other nineteen rebels named on my list. Once they've met proper justice, the rest of your staff can all live. I realize that such a self-sacrifice may seem harsh, but a true leader would recognize its necessity.*"

"And what about your father?" Shelton asks as Francis returns and offers only a grim nod. Apparently, Miranda's claw bombs are legit. Without breaking stride, Shelton continues, "Has Charles Coffin bought into this 'scorched earth' approach?"

"*My father put me in command. He trusts my judgment.*"

It's a lie. I can see it, and so can Shelton.

"Tell you what. Let me talk to him," Shelton suggests.

"*No.*"

"No? Why not?"

"*I'm not letting you, or anyone else on this treacherous colony, anywhere near a Casimir Radio. You've done enough damage already.*"

"Then I'll have to get back to you."

"I'll give you ten minutes, Mister Shelton. After that, we return to the coring unit and detach. Then we'll blow the charges and watch as every man and woman on this colony disappears into the Europan ocean."

"Including Andy?"

Miranda looks momentarily stricken. But then she squares her narrow shoulders. *"Yes. Including Andy. Now, let's see what kind of leader you really are."*

THIRTEEN – Day 24

After the comms link closes, Shelton pauses to give Francis another curt nod. Then, as the late Chief Tuttle's brother hurries off again, the head of Marius addresses the eighty or so people in the Ops Center. "Let's get this out of the way right off. Who wants to hand Andy here over to Coffin?"

There are murmurs and anxious glances, but nobody speaks up or raises their hand.

Shelton says, "Okay, next question. How many of you think Kim, me, and the other eighteen on Coffin's 'hit list' should surrender ourselves for summary execution?"

To my surprise, the anxiety in the room abruptly turns to anger. Eric once told me that spacers are a special breed, with an unofficial, largely unspoken, but iron-strong camaraderie among them.

Here it is.

"No way!" someone shouts.

"Let's kill the bitch!" someone else offers.

"You sure?" Shelton presses. "It might save all your lives if you just give us up."

"Not a chance in hell, boss!" Jim exclaims. He stands near the back of the room, his casted arms raised high.

And, just like that, everyone in the room starts applauding. Kim grins, tears in her eyes. Shelton only nods gratefully.

Kim, who's been watching the monitors, says, "We've got eight minutes left."

"Understood," Shelton says. Then he touches his collar. "Francis? Status?"

Francis's voice comes over the open channel. *"I'm in the water and in contact with Carlos. He says the Gatebuster's already past the first firewall. Looks like there are two more. I'm headed up there to help him."*

"How long do you need?"

"Fifteen minutes. Longer, if CSE's as smart as they think they are."

"Let me know the minute we're through. I'll go on mute but keep the channel open."

"Roger that."

Shelton mutes the connection and looks up to find everyone staring at him. With a grim smile, he explains, "We put together a gadget similar to the one I used to rescue Andy. It works by hacking its way through the coring unit's firewall. We figured, once Coffin realized what we'd done, she'd increase security. So, I had Carlos construct a second, more sophisticated box, which we're calling a 'Gatebuster.' Then I told Carlos to hit the water and wait for instructions.

"Francis just joined him out there where they can talk via short-range comms without any risk of CSE intercepting. The Gatebuster's fastened directly to the coring unit's outer hull right now. It's got enough mojo to penetrate any increased security but needs to be close by to work. With luck, we'll re-establish our remote control before too long."

Darcy asks, "And if the Gatebuster works. What then?"

"Then, we remotely detach the coring unit and crab walk it away from the colony."

"Won't that flood the deck?" I ask. "I mean… there's this hole in the wall."

"The flood doors will shut automatically," Kim replies. "Flooding will be minimal, and we can pump it out later."

Shelton explains, "In the meantime, Coffin and her goons will be stranded in here, with us. I'm guessing she'll think twice about blowing the station anchors then."

It's a cool plan. Just one problem. "But if it takes this Gatebuster fifteen minutes to do its thing," I point out. "And Miranda only gave us a ten-minute time limit—"

"Five-and-a-half now," Kim corrects.

"We bluff for more time," Shelton says.

"She won't buy it," I tell him. "She's a full-blown fanatic. She might even be willing to give her life to 'save the System.'"

"Maybe," Kim replies. "But the blackbirds are mercenaries, *not* fanatics. Self-sacrifice isn't in their job description."

Shelton adds, "And, once this is all over, we can use the coring unit to go topside for supplies."

I remark, "So we just stall Miranda long enough to steal the coring unit and then use it as leverage?"

"That's about it."

A good plan.

And, in the next instant, it goes the way of so many other good plans.

A shudder runs through the Ops Center. At the same time, Francis' voice squawks over the open comms link. *"Boss! We got company! They—"* Then nothing.

Shelton's hand shoots up to his collar. "Francis! Carlos! Status!"

Still nothing.

Without warning, the floor tilts sharply. If not for the low gravity, the dozens of people in the room would have dropped like bowling pins. As it is, everyone grabs onto either the nearest handhold or each other. Screams and horrified glances abound.

Shelton's face pales.

Kim, meanwhile, is still scanning the monitors. "They've blown two of our anchor claws! The other two are holding, but the current's hitting us pretty hard, and we're listing twenty-one degrees downstream."

Shelton asks, "What's the rate of current?"

"Only five knots, but it'll get worse. The next hard tidal surge might tear us free."

"Everyone, calm down!" Shelton calls, regaining his composure. "Flood the ballast tanks. Let's get a team out there to set up some temporary anchors. In the meantime, pump neon into the Ice Deck. Put that lunatic to sleep!"

Several colonists move to obey. As they do, Shelton opens a new comms channel. "Coffin! You said I had ten minutes!"

Miranda replies almost immediately. *"That was before we found two of your men trying to sabotage the coring unit."*

"Where are they?"

"Your men? My blackbirds killed them."

"Oh my God…" Darcy gasps. Around us, people utter cries of horror and anger. My eyes search for and find Jim, Carlos's husband. He no longer looks triumphant. Instead, he looks like he's been hit by a truck.

Miranda says blithely, *"Fortunately, I checked their faces against my list, and they were two of the twenty. So, really, there's nothing lost."*

The words are out before I can stop them. "Nothing lost? Are you insane?"

"Andy? Is that you? Are you all right?" Her coldness is gone, replaced by a concern that makes my skin crawl.

Shelton quiets me with a gesture. "That's him. And right now, I'm pointing a gun at his head. Have your troops stand down, or the next thing you hear will be a gunshot."

After several heartbeats, Miranda says with carefully controlled nonchalance, *"Shooting one of the Kind is dangerous. Just ask the good people of New York."*

The reference to my parents fuels my rage. Darcy touches her finger to my lips just in time.

"I know," she whispers. "But keep quiet."

She's right, of course.

And I *do* keep quiet, barely.

"Given your gene therapy," Shelton says. "I'm guessing he'll die pretty much as easily as Francis and Carlos did."

When Miranda replies, the coldness is back. *"Andy, if you can hear me, I'm sorry, but there's too much at stake. Mister Shelton, neither Andy's life nor mine means much beside the stability of the entire Solar System. If I have to, I will blow the remaining anchors and end us all."*

"How about your blackbirds? Are they also willing to die for your cause?"

"A few are. I've sent the rest back to the coring unit. They can detach and be safely out of danger in thirty seconds if need be."

Shelton mutes the link and calls out, "Where are we with the neon?"

"I've dropped the ratio way down," Kim replies, looking perplexed. "If she's still anywhere on the Ice Deck, she should be sleeping like a baby by now."

"Can you see anything on the monitors?"

Kim starts flipping through vid feeds. After a moment, she exclaims, "Oh no!" Then she taps a button and puts what she sees on the bigger monitor directly over Shelton's head.

Miranda and four blackbirds are visible. They're wearing masks and oxygen tanks.

"Mister Shelton. Are you still there?"

Shelton stares at the image with helpless dismay. Kim groans. Darcy has tears in her eyes. I don't blame any of them.

Shelton unmutes the link. "I'm here."

"You're out of tricks. My offer still stands. Surrender Andy Brand along with everyone on my list. In return, I'll guarantee the safety of the rest of Marius's complement. Otherwise, I'll blow the last two anchors. Either way, the System's stability will be maintained."

"I think you're bluffing," Shelton says.

"No, you don't. Not anymore. By now, you must have confirmed that all but four of my men are safely aboard the CU."

Shelton looks at Kim, who nods bleakly.

"Don't do it, boss!" someone yells. But I can't help noticing that it's the *only* protest at this point.

In an empty, defeated voice, Shelton says. "We're on our way up."

"Very sensible," Miranda replies. She doesn't sound smug, merely satisfied. *"You'll want to return the neon/oxygen to normal first."*

"Do it," Shelton orders.

"Your stock is rising, Mister Shelton."

"Furk you," Kim mutters.

Shelton says, "Can we have five minutes to say our goodbyes?"

Miranda's tone turns dangerous. *"No more games. No more warnings. Five minutes."*

This time, she's the one who breaks the link.

Shelton squares his shoulders and says, "When we voted to launch this crazy scheme, we all understood the risks. But folks, we're out of options, and I can't just do nothing and watch the rest of you die. Now, I won't speak for anyone else, but I'm going to surrender myself."

"Me, too," Kim announces.

"No!" I exclaim.

"And me," Darcy says.

"No!" I yell, even louder.

"And me," Jim says. With both his arms in slings, he's been somewhere in the back of the crowd instead of at one of the workstations. Now, however, he steps forward, his face pale but resolute.

Over the course of the next minute, fifteen other men and women step forward. I do the math and, with Francis and Carlos counted in, this is the twenty. Many are visibly crying. All of them, I know, are terrified.

But they do it.

So, this is what heroism looks like.

"Thank you," Shelton tells them.

"Thank you," Kim echoes. Incredibly, she's smiling.

And, in a flash, I know what has to be done.
Or, more specifically, I know what *I* have to do.

PART SIX
THE DRAGON

Nineteen of us say our good-byes to the rest.

I'm still an outsider here. This shouldn't hurt me — but it does, a little. It doesn't help that, of the "sacrificial lambs," I'm the only one not slated for slaughter. And, while the collective judgment seems to be that I'm not to blame, there remains an edge of resentment. I see it in their eyes as they embrace their friends and co-workers, almost certainly for the last time.

At some point, when my turn comes, Kim pulls me close. She doesn't cry. "You okay?"

"Nope," I reply. "This is *crazy*."

Her face crumples a little. Then she straightens up and replies, "If you've got a better idea, let's hear it."

I do. But I'm not going to share it with her, mainly because I know she'll never go along with it.

Then Kim says, "Listen, Andy. Shelton and I have been talking and, when we all go up to the Ice Deck, we think you should stay behind."

"No," I reply.

"Andy, you know what's going to happen. There's no reason for you to witness that."

"I'm going with you. Period."

"Andy, please —"

"Remember when I told you that each Kind is a brother and sister to every other Kind? Well, as far as I'm concerned, that makes you my family. And I'm not going to abandon you the way I abandoned my parents."

"Andy! You didn't 'abandon' them! CSE kidnapped you!"

And that's true. Except, it doesn't *feel* true.

I tell her, "I'm with you, come what may."

"Please. I don't want to cry."

I hug her again, feeling a thousand things all at once. Nearby, Darcy is talking with a tearful man in a lab coat. When I catch her eye, she gives me a smile of such courage that it hits me almost like a physical blow.

"It's going to be okay," I say to Kim.

"No, it's not," she whispers back.

A few minutes later, everyone on Miranda's list departs the Ops Center. Behind us, the rest of Marius's staff looks on in terror and grief.

As we reach the moon pool, I notice a half-dozen dragons bobbing in the dark water. They peer wordlessly up at us as we go past. Seeing them, Kim shudders and clings to Shelton. Darcy, walking beside me, chokes back a sob.

I know what they're all thinking.

Even if this sacrifice saves the rest of Marius, Miranda will hunt the Europans to extinction.

"Listen, everyone," Shelton says. "I know you're scared. Hell, *I'm* scared. But, once we're up there, I'm going to try to convince Miranda Coffin that the only one really at fault here is me."

"No!" Kim says sharply, but Shelton keeps right on talking.

"I can't promise anything. But I'm going to save as many of you as I can."

No one else protests though I get the feeling that Darcy wants to. For the first time, *I* take *her* hand.

Darcy whispers to me, "I kind of always figured things would probably go this way. Looking back, maybe that's why I voted against shutting down the scrubbers in the first place. Plain-furking-cowardice. It makes me feel like maybe I deserve this."

"Nobody deserves this," I tell her.

"Thanks for holding my hand," she says.

We all stop. Above us, the iris between Lab Deck and Ice Deck stands closed.

"I'll go first," Shelton announces. "Then Kim. After that, come up two at a time. Keep your hands in plain sight. Don't give these furkers any excuse to start shooting."

"Yet," someone mutters darkly.

Shelton ignores the remark. Touching his collar, he says, "Coffin, we're ready to board the Ice Deck. We're unarmed and surrendering freely. I'm opening the iris now."

"No tricks, Mister Shelton."

"No tricks."

He opens a wall panel and taps a code into a small, unlabeled keypad. With a final look at his wife, he presses ENTER.

The iris retracts, and new light fills the stairwell. Silhouettes surround the circular landing — blackbirds, all pointing their weapons down at us.

Shelton slowly raises his hands.

Miranda appears. Her gaze rakes across the faces in the stairwell until they find mine.

And it's not until that instant that I realize I'm still holding Darcy's hand.

I let go but can already see it's too late. Miranda stiffens and her eyes, if possible, go even colder. "Bring them up," she commands, turning away. "But watch them carefully."

We're ushered onto the Ice Deck and ordered to line up along one of the central chamber's curving walls. There are a dozen blackbirds here, not just the four that Miranda kept with her. After Shelton's surrender, she summoned back some of her troops. This colony, after all, is hers now.

With all nineteen of us corralled, Miranda walks the length of our ranks. When she reaches me, she stops and asks, "You okay?"

"No," I reply. "You're about to murder my friends."

For a moment, I think she might respond, but instead, she turns to Darcy, who still stands beside me. For several seconds, the two size each other up, and I find myself squirming uncomfortably — as if I don't have bigger things to worry about.

Finally, Miranda returns to the middle of the big round room and faces us. "I didn't create this situation. I didn't ask you all to conspire to unlawfully seize this colony and hold its mining product hostage with your ridiculous demand for 'independence.' *You* did that."

No one responds.

Miranda continues, "Despite my best efforts, you've managed to spread word of your uprising through the Solar System and have put at risk CSE's ability to govern its colonies. As such, I've no alternative but to send a message effective enough to offset the trouble you've caused. Remember, *you* all did this. Not me."

"How about if we skip the lecture," Shelton says flatly. "Unless you're just trying to assuage your conscience?"

"What I'm doing is necessary, though I understand that you're not in the right frame of mind to see that."

Shelton takes a step forward. As he does, several of the blackbirds raise their rifles. "Relax. I'm not going to try anything except an appeal to your… humanity." He motions back at the rest of us. Kim looks like she wants to say something but stifles herself.

Shelton continues, "*I'm* the owner of Shelton Mining and the leader of this colony. No one else bears any responsibility for my decisions. What we did here was done on my order… when it became clear that our mining efforts were killing Europa's intelligent life. I don't apologize and, if given a do-over, I'd handle things exactly the same way. But the rest of these people are underlings, not co-conspirators. Send your message with me, and only me. Let the rest of them go back to their lives."

When he's finished, a grim silence falls. The colonists, myself included, all look at Miranda—

—who says simply, "No."

"Please, listen—" Shelton begins.

But she cuts him off. "You're a brave man. But these people made the same choice you did. By rights, everyone aboard Marius should be paying the same price. I'm being generous as it is. You'll all be separated into groups of three and taken to specific rooms that we've already selected. It'll be as quick and painless as possible. But if you resist, the only thing you'll do is prolong your suffering. I'm truly sorry."

As the blackbirds advance, several of the colonists begin screaming. Shelton stands motionless. He looks—defeated. Kim takes his hand, a useless, loving gesture.

I look at Darcy. She looks back at me.

And now it's my turn to say simply, "No."

The soldiers glance my way. Behind them, Miranda meets my eyes. "Andy, I realize this is hard, but—"

"You're not going to kill these people!" I tell her, putting all of my outrage into those words.

"Massey, please escort Mister Brand to the coring unit. Restrain him if you have to." To me, she says, "I'm really hoping you'll come to understand—"

But I'm done with her furking rationalizations. "What I *understand* is that you're a heartless, murderous, sociopathic bitch who's lied to me from the day we met. I understand that you hide behind words like 'order' and 'greater good' to mask what's nothing more than an atrocity. I don't love you, Miranda Coffin. Maybe I loved Miranda Fiero, the first lie you told me. But since she wasn't real, I guess I'll never know. But *you*? All I feel for you is disgust!"

Miranda's staggers back a step as if my words have hit her like a slap.

"That's enough," Massey says. "You're finished, kid."

But I'm not finished, not quite yet. "Well, I'm no lovesick boy anymore. That idiot's gone. Now all that's left is what I really am, what I always have been!"

Then I pull from my pocket the auto-injector full of epinephrine that I swiped from the infirmary while using the zero-G toilet. And, as Massey lunges toward me, I drive it into the meat of my thigh.

TWO – Day 24

An almost electric jolt sends my heart into overdrive and drops me to my knees. My vision blurs. Somewhere nearby, a woman screams my name, though I'm not sure if it's Kim, Darcy, or Miranda.

I take several heaving breaths, struggling not to vomit.

A gloved hand closes around my upper arm, squeezing painfully. "Let's go, freak!" Massey barks.

I cry out, my heart beating even faster.

Then, quite suddenly, the wall between my ears comes crashing down.

Massey shrieks in pain and leaps back, clutching her smoldering hand. Its glove has partially melted into her skin.

I struggle to my feet to find everyone staring at me. Most are shielding their eyes as the air around me ripples with heat. My clothes, of course, are gone. I glance at Darcy and find her staring at me in slack-jawed wonder while, beside her, Shelton is partially shielding Kim with his body. This latter strikes me as a sweet, if pointless gesture, since my "sister" is the only person in the room I can't harm.

The rest of the colonists simply look terrified. We're a long way from thermally levitating forks in the Breakroom now.

Someone calls, "Andy!"

Miranda looks dismayed but not fearful, her beautiful face somewhat distorted through the heated air. Her blackbirds have rallied protectively around her, their guns all pointed at me.

"I'm not going to let you kill anyone else," I tell her.

"Please don't make me do this," she replies. It's not a plea, but a warning. Her finger is poised over her e-man, the threat obvious. Either

I turn off my dragon, or she blows the last two anchor clamps, and Marius gets swallowed up by the Europan sea.

That's when I recall the last thing my father ever taught me, something he called a "fire spear."

As a kid, I watched his dragon drill a perfectly round hole right through a Jersey pine. I thought at the time that I'd never have that much control, that much precision. In fact, I remember thinking that it was the coolest thing I'd never get to use.

But that was before this furk-show, before the stuff I've had to do to save myself and others. Before I learned—really learned—what I am.

So, feeling sick, I point my right index finger at Miranda.

And sear her *left* hand—the one with the e-man—off at the wrist.

Miranda screams and tumbles backward, the low-G preventing her from hitting the floor too hard. My fire spear has crudely cauterized the stump, so I'm pretty sure she won't bleed to death. But, while I expect the shock to make her pass out, it doesn't. Instead, she clutches her maimed, smoking wrist and wails, "*Shoot them! Shoot all of them!*"

The chamber erupts in pandemonium.

Shelton yells for the colonists to make for the stairwell. A few obey, but the rest just stand there, as helpless as deer in traffic. Meanwhile, the blackbirds follow Miranda's command and open fire.

Three of the colonists fall.

I don't aim. I don't plan. I just sweep my arm in a wide arc across the hemisphere of the room that's filled with soldiers. I wish I could say that I do this with some vague notion of throwing up a thermal wall. But I'm acting on a baser instinct than that.

Way baser.

A curtain of raw heat crosses the room in a millisecond. Most of the blackbirds' bullets vaporize an instant before their owners do. Twelve men and women, all soldiers, all intent on committing cold-blooded murder, die in a split second. Their blood boils. Their flesh melts away. Their bones desiccate and shatter. Even their rifles become nothing but puddles of cooling metal.

Miranda, however, still sprawled on the floor as the wave passes over her, is spared—sort of.

Her hair burns away as the right side of her face, the side turned upward, bubbles and blackens from the heat. This time she doesn't scream. This kind of injury goes way past screaming. But her one remaining eye finds mine and holds it tight, full of recrimination.

She can't *believe* that I betrayed her.

"Andy!"

It's Darcy. She's with Kim at the staircase. The rest of the colonists are already out of sight; even the wounded have been evacuated. Both of them gesture anxiously at me.

And I can't furking move.

My dragon has receded, though I only vaguely remember calling it back. Once again, I'm naked and hairless, like a newborn, in a room filled with death. The air reeks of burned hair and flesh — and worse, I know that most of the stench comes from Miranda, since the blackbirds, Massey included, have been atomized by heat so intense that it went way past burning them.

I've just killed a dozen people.

A dozen *more* people.

"Andy, come on!" Darcy catches my wrist and pulls me toward the staircase. I look at her, sick to my soul. There's blood on the wall behind her, colonists' blood.

So much violence.

And the worst offender is me.

I look toward Miranda.

She's a heap on the far side of the chamber, pressing the cauterized stump of her left arm against her body and clawing at the floor with her free hand. As I watch, she grasps something lying nearby — something charred and blackened.

"Andy... please," Darcy begs.

But I still can't move.

Miranda's head swivels my way. Half her face is a ruin of blistered skin. Most of her beautiful hair is gone. She marks me with her one remaining eye, her teardrop eye. "You did this to me," she rasps, the words like razors. "You... you... burned me!"

I don't move. I don't speak. I'm not even sure I'm breathing. The seconds drag on. Darcy stops pulling at me. Instead, she takes my hand again.

"You're *mine*!" Miranda screams, the sound harsh and wet and filled with rage. "I *made* you mine!"

"I'm not yours, Miranda," I whisper. "I never really was."

"You *are!*" she shrieks. "And that means you can't betray me, ever!"

That's when I finally realize what the grisly "something" she's holding actually *is*—and the shock clears the cobwebs of self-recrimination that are clogging my head.

It's her hand.

Her *left* hand, the one I burned off.

The one with the e-man on it.

In terror, I realize two fundamental truths.

First: Miranda Coffin doesn't stop. She never stops. She will keep going, and going, and going—to the brink of insanity and beyond—to get what she wants.

Second: I can't burn her, not because my conscience won't allow it. God help me, I'm beyond that. But because, at this moment, Darcy is still holding my hand. While my skin holds no residual heat with my dragon safely put away, that'll change if I let it out again.

Miranda dishes up a hideous, twisted parody of her dazzling smile, and her fingers—trembling, but resolute—reach for the e-man.

It's cooked. It must have been cooked by my fire spear. I'm not that precise! I can't be that furking precise!

But it seems I *have* improved with practice.

The room lurches violently. Darcy gasps and holds onto me more tightly as I stagger.

Elsewhere, Kim screams.

Miranda starts laughing, cackling, really, her eyes never leaving mine.

This time, when Darcy pulls me, I follow.

As we bolt for the stairwell, the floor rocks to and fro beneath our feet.

Marius has been cut free.

THREE – Day 24

Descending to the Lab Deck is an exercise in injury as Marius's violent shudders bounce us between the curving metal walls. Shelton has already gotten what remains of the Top Twenty to the middle level. Now he clutches a nearby bulkhead for support while he barks out orders. "Get into the inner labs! Just the *inner* labs. Keep away from rooms with viewports. Lay down on the floor, grab hold of something that's bolted down, and stay there! Nobody panic! We have protocols for this!"

Marius whirls around us, the floor rising and dipping like an insane version of an amusement park ride. As I stagger down the last step, things shift, and Darcy tumbles against me. I catch her, and she smiles gratefully.

I killed all those people!

But, somehow, Darcy's smile helps.

Meanwhile, Shelton touches his collar. "Shelton to Ops. Who's down there! Answer me!"

It takes a few pregnant seconds, but eventually, someone replies. I don't recognize the voice. *"Boss? My God! We've lost our last anchors!"*

"I'm aware! I want—"

Suddenly, Marius stops.

The cessation of motion is so abrupt that nearly everyone gets thrown to the floor. I land atop Darcy, who, amazingly, laughs as she looks up into my face. "Jeez, Brand. At least buy me dinner first," she whispers.

And I blush. Seriously, I furking *blush*!

"Damn it!" Shelton gasps as we all struggle to stand. Then he calls into his collar comms, "Grace! You still there?"

"Yeah... Yeah, boss. We're still here. Pretty banged up, though. We've got some injuries."

"Anyone who can't be moved?"

"Um… no, I don't think so."

"Good. Do we know what just happened?"

"I'm checking the scanners. Hold on…" Long seconds pass. *"The coring unit's torn free. It's gone. But somehow, the current has partially wedged us in the Ice Shaft. We're listing at thirty degrees."*

I look at the slanted floor. Yep, that's about right.

"Just blind, dumb luck," Grace adds.

"That's the best kind," Kim remarks.

"Wait a sec…"

"What is it, Grace?"

"Oh, my God…"

"Grace!"

"Boss, you're not going to believe this, but I just found out how we ended up wedged in the ice shaft."

"How?"

"The dragons..."

"What are you talking about?"

"Don't ask me how, but they... caught us."

"Caught us? That doesn't make any sense!"

"Well, 'caught us' isn't right. They're outside right now, hundreds of them, more than we've ever seen. They've latched onto the leeward side of the hull. I don't think they actually stopped us. There'd have to be a million of them out there to do that. But they somehow managed to redirect us into the ice shaft. And... they're keeping us there."

We all struggle to absorb this. Kim looks like she may burst into tears.

And these are the creatures that Miranda was ready to kill?

"We're not worthy," Darcy says.

I look at her. "What?"

"We're not worthy of them. We're really not."

"No, we're not," Shelton agrees.

"I'm so ashamed," Darcy whispers. I'm pretty sure I'm the only one who hears her.

Then Shelton curses, pounding his fist uselessly against the bulkhead. At first, I think he *did* hear, and that he's suddenly mad at Darcy for her earlier, admittedly selfish and short-sighted vote. But no. One look at his face, and I suddenly comprehend what he's thinking. We all do.

What the Europans have done is miraculous. Unfortunately, it also falls way short of salvation. The coring unit was our only hope of getting to the surface. Without it, Marius is at the bottom of a twenty-mile shaft, jammed in like an oversized cork in an undersized bottle. Sooner or later, despite whatever help we get from the locals, we're going to pop free.

We're completely screwed.

"Grace, listen," Shelton says, composing himself. "Get everyone up to the Lab Deck. Close down Ops completely. Try to keep everybody calm. I'm coming down."

"But, boss, without Ops, we won't be able to monitor —"

"At this point, it doesn't really matter if we're blind. Get everyone up here, and then we're going to flood the Ops Deck."

"We'll sink!"

"No, we won't. But the ballast should stabilize us until we can come up with something else. Do it."

"Okay. Yeah. On our way."

After Shelton breaks the link, Kim says to him, "We're just delaying the inevitable."

"I know," he replies.

Without warning, Darcy sidles up beside me, cups my face, and kisses me hard. It seems like a crazy move under the circumstances, but I'd be lying if I say I hate it.

Then she pulls back, takes my hand, and tells me, "Thank you."

I gape at her. "What the furk for?"

"For saving us all up there."

I feel my throat close up. "I killed all those people."

A hand touches my shoulder. I turn, expecting to see Kim, but it's Shelton. "Andy, if you hadn't done what you did, we'd all be dead. She's right. Thank you."

Fat lot of good it did. Miranda still managed to kill them. She managed to murder the whole lot of us.

Unless—

And, just like that, a terrible, terrifying resolve fills me.

Shelton says to Kim, Darcy, and myself, "You three stay up here. Head for the Biology Lab. I'll be along as soon as Ops Deck's been emptied."

"I'm coming with you," I say.

"No point."

I meet his eyes. "I'm not asking."

All three of them regard me with a look of apprehension that turns my insides to jelly. Gratitude aside, they're remembering, as I figured they would, what I did up on the Ice Deck just now. They're remembering what I am.

But Darcy doesn't let go of my hand.

"Andy?" Kim asks hesitantly.

I don't look at her. Instead, I keep my eyes locked on Shelton's. "I'm coming with you. Just the two of us."

His apprehension turns to appraisal. He says to Kim, "You and Darcy go get safe. Andy and I will head down to Ops."

Kim says, "Shelton…"

He touches her cheek with his hand, a tender, intimate gesture. It's the first time I've seen either of them engage in anything resembling PDA. "It's okay," he says.

Kim finally nods, looking none too happy about it. Her eyes flick over to me, and I can tell at once that she knows something's up. Fortunately, she doesn't know *what*, exactly. If she did, she'd be all over it, hell-bent on stopping me.

I meet her gaze and do my best to give her nothing.

"What's happening?" Darcy asks me.

"It's okay," I reply.

But it's not, and all of them know it. Gently but firmly, I extract my hand from Darcy's and, with what must be the phoniest smile ever, head down the spiral staircase. Moments later, Shelton follows me.

On the Ops Deck, the moon pool dances and churns. Not surprisingly, the dragons are gone, and seawater has pooled against the far wall, the low end of the list. Looking around, I try to recall the right corridor. At the time, I was exhausted and just plain glad to be alive. Standing here now, with everything going to hell around me, I can't remember which of the spokes is the correct one.

"Okay," Shelton says, impatiently. "We're alone, but not for long. Whatever this is about, now's the time to tell me."

"Exactly how much deuterium is there in the water?"

He looks at me like I've gone a little crazy. "What? Why?"

"Just tell me. Do you know?"

Something in my urgent tone makes him stop and really think it over. Then his eyes widen just enough to convince me that he's got it. "Yeah," he replies as some of the color drains from his face. "I know."

"Good. How much? Parts per million, I mean."

"One per 2500."

"On Earth, it's... what? One part per 6000?"

"Yeah," he says again. His eyes are locked on mine. "Andy—" he begins.

I cut him off. "Is it enough?"

For a moment, he doesn't answer. Then, in a small voice, he says, "It should be... if you can put enough into it."

I nod. My throat has gone suddenly dry.

"Andy... I don't know what to say."

"Just tell me the colony can survive it."

"We *might*. If nothing else, it'll give us a fighting chance."

"That'll have to be enough," I say, mustering my courage. "But I need you to tell me what I have to do."

So, he does, speaking quickly and without much eye contact, as if looking squarely at me will make it real.

Turns out, it's simple—maybe the simplest thing yet in this whole miserable mess.

When he's done, he asks me if I understand. I tell him I do. Then I add, "You're going to have to keep this from Kim and Darcy. They'd try to stop me."

"*I* should try to stop you."

"Even if you do, I'll just die with the rest of you."

"I know, which is why I'm *not* trying to stop you. But I should."

"Tell your wife you did. Tell her I threatened to cook you in your own juices."

"She'd never believe me. Kim says I'm a lousy liar."

"I envy you," I reply, meaning it. "I've been taught to lie my whole life. But I guess that's over now. Um… I should go before I chicken out."

"Andy… I'm at a furking loss here."

I stick out my hand. "Thanks."

"*You're* thanking *me*? What the hell *for*?" But he shakes my hand.

"For letting me be… well, me… for the first time in my life."

"It's been an honor, Mister Brand."

"Same here, Mister Shelton."

Then, as hurried footsteps sound along the Ops Center corridor, Shelton points me in the right direction. With a final nod to him, I head that way at a dead run.

Mom. Dad. I'm coming…

FOUR – Day 24

This entire wing of the Ops Deck is deserted—and in minutes, it'll be deliberately flooded. That thought makes me run all the faster. I reach the last door on the right, which is labeled "Pod Bay."

With hands that only shake a little, I turn its center wheel and step inside.

The chamber is filled with equipment mounted all around a second, smaller moon pool. And sticking partway out of the dark water of that moon pool is Pod Two. It hangs from a heavy black cable fastened to the tip of its tapered nose. Like everything else, it's listing sharply, with only its upper third visible above the surface.

Screwing up my courage, I approach it through the warm, sloshing, ankle-deep water and climb the steps. The pod's top hatch, like Marius's other doors, is wheel-operated.

This time my hands shake badly.

I've never been so scared in my life.

Lifting the hatch open, I climb down a low-G ladder to the pod's top deck. As in Pod One, there's a hole in the center of the floor allowing access below. But that's for later. Right now, I reseal the hatch and find the console Shelton described.

The pod, he explained, only ever has two coordinates programmed into its onboard navigation computer: a departure point and a destination point. The departure point is *here*, on Marius. The destination point is the same as it was the last time the pod was used.

Simple.

Shelton assured me that two buttons and a lever are all it takes. I find them easily enough.

Moment of truth time.

I take a deep breath.

"Andy? What are you doing?"

It's Kim's voice, coming through wall-mounted speakers.

Should I answer? What would be the point? I can't let her talk me out of this.

'Andy… can you hear me?"

I find the comms button. "I hear you."

"I want you to come up to the Lab Deck."

"Can't do it, Kim."

"Andy, this is suicide!"

"I know. But, if I do it right, it might save you."

"I don't want you to die for me!"

"I'm not doing anything you weren't prepared to do when you marched upstairs to be executed."

"That was different!"

"How?"

A pause. *"Andy, please…"*

"Kim," I say, my throat tightening. "I'm really glad I met you. You really are like a sister to me."

Silence.

"You still there?" I ask.

Then: *"Andy… I am your sister."*

For a second, I don't think I heard her right. "What…?"

"*It's true.*"

"It can't be…"

"*I ran a comparative genome analysis algorithm against a blood sample I took from you when you first came aboard. There's a 92% chance that we either had the same father or that our fathers were direct siblings. Did your father have any brothers?*"

I hear myself say, "No. But what? Why would you—"

"*You're the first Kind I've ever met. I had to know if we were related. I'm sorry I didn't tell you. I almost blurted it all out when you brought it up in Ops… but I couldn't, not then, not with what was about to happen.*"

"Sister?" I say, struggling to comprehend. "You're… my sister?"

"*Thirty-two years ago, before he met your mother, your dad and my mom…*" Her words trail away.

The idea's big—too big. "That's impossible."

"*No, it's not. Think it through. Only seven hundred Kind on Earth. That's a small gene pool. There were only so many of them at the right age at the right time to be both your father and mine. I've done the math a dozen times. Yes, it was a long shot, but not really so long as that.*"

"You're *really* my sister?"

"*Half-sister.*"

"Sister," I say again.

"*Andy… you were more right than you knew when you said you and I are family! I can't lose you, not now!*"

"Sister," I whisper.

"*Yes, Andy.*"

The next words are out before I even consciously think them. "I love you."

"*I love you, too.*"

I've gone blind. Tears have turned my vision into a watery blur.

Imagine it. After everything I've lost, here is something *gained*.

Something that must, at all costs, be protected.

"Kim," I say, impatiently wiping my eyes. "I'm not going to let you die."

"*Andy! No! Wait!*"

"My dad's in your veins. That means a part of him is still alive. Do me one favor. If… when… you and Shelton have kids, name one of them after him, okay?"

"*Andy, I… don't know our father's name.*"

"Oh. Right. It was Anthony. Tony."

"My father's name was Tony?"

"Yeah."

"Then I guess we'll have to have two kids. Two boys. One to name after him and one to name after you."

I try to think of something else to say, of anything else that *needs* saying, but there's nothing. "Goodbye, Sis."

When she responds, she's crying; I can hear it. *"Goodbye, little brother."*

I break the link.

Then, steeling myself, I press the two buttons and pull the lever.

Pod Two drops into Europa's cold, dark waters.

Eighty miles of ocean. Even with the pod's engines engaged, the trip will take almost two hours. Will Marius still be wedged in the ice shaft by then? Will the dragons be able to keep it in place that long? If not, then this trip will be for nothing.

As I sit down on the floor, I suddenly recall the time in my cell, back when I was scared but still blessedly ignorant of the tide of events that would so completely drown me; pun intended. Since abandoning Conceal and Protect, I've killed thirteen people. Miranda's body count, as far as I know, sits at three.

By that cold reckoning, I'm four times the murderer she is.

But is right and wrong that easy to calculate?

Life and death can't simply be a numbers game, can it?

Out loud, I say, "Mom and Dad, I'm sorry I let you down. I'm sorry I didn't hold on better to everything you taught me. I'm sorry for the lives I've taken, and I'm really, really sorry that you're both dead. Guess I'll be seeing you soon… assuming we go to the same place."

And, with that cheery thought, I settle myself down to wait.

Two hours later, wrapped in silence, grief, fear, and creeping despair, I feel the pod automatically slow its descent. Lateral jets fire, making micro-navigational adjustments. Then, with a jolt, it stops.

A console light Shelton told me to look for turns green. It means the two pods have successfully connected.

I'm here.

I climb to my feet and, moving stiffly, descend the ladder through the middle deck and then down to the lower one. Aside from the chirps and beeps of nameless equipment, the only noise is my own nervous breathing.

Once at Pod Two's tapered bottom, I open first one docking hatch and then another. Then I prepare to enter — or, rather, *re*-enter Pod One.

Deck A is now filled with water — but I expected that. It happened when Kim and I escaped up into Pod Two, thereby popping the air bubble that had been keeping us alive. As a result, Pod One flooded the rest of the way.

Time to go swimming.

I hold what I assume is going to be my last breath — ever.

It's a unique feeling, more about regret than fear. "Weird" doesn't begin to describe it.

I dive headfirst into the Europan water.

FIVE – Day 24

I swim straight down and with a bit more confidence than the first time, navigating Levels A and B easily and without incident. As I approach the open hatchway to Level C, I expect some dragons to greet me.

They don't.

The majority, I suppose, are still up near the ice shelf, trying to keep Marius from being swept away. But I figured at least some would've stayed behind to tend the eggs. So far, however, I'm alone.

I swim through the final hatchway.

And there they are.

I count a half-dozen of them way down at the pod's ruined bottom, where most of the egg clusters are attached. They're busy and haven't yet taken notice of me.

I swim closer.

One of them darts out of nowhere and fills my vision. I recognize the jewelry.

It's Ravi.

He looks me over apprehensively. Then, as if reaching a decision, he spreads his arms and comes toward me. Knowing what he's got in mind, I hold up a hand to stop him. He pauses, looking quizzical.

My lungs are starting to burn.

As the others take notice and begin circling me with curiosity, I lock eyes with Ravi. I wish I could talk to him. But all I can do is try to convey my intentions through action.

So, ignoring the tightness in my chest, I spread my arms. Then I reach inward and call my dragon.

It doesn't come.

Alarm sends my heart into overdrive, using up my lungful of air all the faster. Desperately, I try again, digging deep.

The wall's back up.

Oh, God!

Darcy told me that the effects of the epinephrine shot might only be temporary. But after everything that happened on the Ice Deck, somehow that little but oh-so-vital warning went right out of my head. I try once more, testing the wall. It feels as strong as ever, though I can sense my dragon on the far side of it, clawing and roaring in frustration.

My chest starts to heave. It's all I can do to keep myself from reflexively breathing in water. Even if I swim back up toward Pod Two, I'll never make it. I'm going to drown down here, having thrown away my life for nothing.

No, damn it! NO FURKING WAY!

Miranda's "blocker" was designed to separate me from my dragon. But maybe that was her mistake. She's treating me like a human being, one that just happens to be able to make fire. But the Kind *aren't* human. We never were. And we don't "make" fire.

We are *Fire.*

So, I stop trying to break the wall. Instead, I *burn* it. My dragon hits it full force, hurling flames that go beyond red hot, beyond white-hot.

I can feel the barrier buckle against the heat. It may just be a mental construct, but I now realize it's a construct that can *burn* or *melt*—just like everything else in the universe either burns or melts.

I give it everything I've got—and it's enough.

The wall doesn't collapse; it simply ceases to be.

And my dragon emerges, all fire and fury.

The water around me begins to boil.

The dragons, perhaps more surprised than alarmed, withdraw a bit. They're still circling but from further away. All but Ravi. He remains motionless in the water, watching me, his eyes on mine.

Suddenly, my need to breathe eases. I don't know why. I'm still a breathing creature. But somehow, my body in this state can feed my blood the oxygen it requires to keep going. Frankly, I wish I'd known about this the last time I went swimming, and the time before that.

As always, the dragon is my shield and my lifeline.

I meet Ravi's gaze and increase the heat, letting it roil the water around me. At the same time, I nod my head at the pod walls while looking pointedly at the little alien. Then I motion toward the eggs and make what I hope is a recognizable "get them out" gesture.

Ravi continues to stare at me.

Please, Ravi. Get it.

He does.

His eyes widen, and he begins frantically vibrating his tail, notifying the others. Moving with astonishing speed, they dive down, scooping huge armfuls of eggs before vanishing through one of the many cracks in the broken pod's hull. There are just enough of them to manage all the clusters, at least those that still show signs of life.

Within moments, the dragons are gone—again, except for Ravi.

I can't decipher his expression. All I know for sure is that he can't be here.

Go! I scream at him, if only in my head. *Swim as far as you can as fast as you can!*

But the Europan can't read my mind, right?

Then Ravi's eyes widen again, as if with a new realization, and he comes forward in a flash. But instead of trying again to breathe for me, he cups my face in all four of his hands. Then, apparently undaunted by the thermal output, he—well—kisses me on the nose.

I know. It sounds stupid. But it isn't. There's a lot behind that simple gesture: understanding, gratitude, admiration.

And friendship.

An instant later, he's gone, leaving me alone in Pod One's broken hull.

I give him as much time as I dare. But my body is pulsing now. Waves of superheated water, kept from becoming steam only by the ocean's immense pressure, hammer the pod walls. They twist. In moments, Pod One will collapse, and Pod Two will crush me flat.

If I'm going to do this, I need to do it now.

I can only pray that Ravi and his people are far enough away.

Mom.

Dad.

I love you.

This is my redemption.

Closing my eyes, I let my dragon out. All of it—and more.

Fusion.

This is one trick my father *didn't* teach me in the Jersey woods.

The difference between thermal and nuclear energy is more complicated than simply degrees of power, temperature, whatever. My force field, my fire spear, even my "naked fire guy thing," work using the everyday principles of conduction, convection, and radiation. Fusion, on the other hand, only happens when two small atoms slam together to make a bigger atom, with the particles left over being turned into energy.

All very sciencey. But bear with me.

Water doesn't work as fusionable fuel. However, something *in* water *can*. Deuterium is a stable isotope of hydrogen, and, unlike back home, Europa's ocean contains enough of it for me to use.

To *ignite*.

If you slam two atoms of D together, you get one helium atom… plus a remainder. And it's this remainder that packs the wallop.

So, as I send my dragon outward, giving it far more freedom than I've ever dared, the seawater immediately around me vaporizes, leaving a surrounding vacuum. As I feed it more and more energy, this bubble expands, filling the pod.

All that happens in the first instant.

In the second instant, my dragon finds the D atoms in the water and starts hurling them into one another. This releases more energy that then finds other D atoms and knocks *their* heads together, and so on.

Suddenly, I've ignited a fusion reaction.

In the third instant, both Pod One and Pod Two vaporize, consumed by the expanding sphere of energy.

In the fourth instant, Smokey explodes.

More precisely, the geothermal vent that forms the ancient smoker's foundations gets bigger—much bigger. In fact, the moon's mantle cracks like an eggshell, allowing its inner magma to burst through. By the fifth instant, a square mile of deep sea has begun to roil, with the subsequent, immense energy trapped by the mass of ocean overhead. So instead of turning to steam, the water temperature continues to rise. And rise. And rise.

In the sixth instant, my fusion bubble meets this wall of ultra-hot water, wherein more D's are found to feed the growing reaction. The scope of this reaction increases exponentially, becoming a kind of miniature sun beneath the sea with me at its center. The temperatures are off the chart, something nearing ten thousand degrees Fahrenheit.

And it keeps getting bigger, vaporizing a thousand tons of water and pushing the rest ahead of itself as a wave of superheated ocean.

I really hope the Europans got clear.

Meanwhile, I keep pouring out my dragon. I'm not even sure my body's still there anymore. It feels as if the dragon has completely taken over.

It's terrifying.

It's *liberating*.

And it's far from over.

In the next instant, I have one last memory dream. Only, this time, the dream is about *me*.

In it, I watch as my underwater sun continues to expand. In doing so, it carves a massive crater out of the seafloor before almost all of its incalculable energy bounces off the moon's mantle and heads in the direction that I really want it to go.

Up.

Eighty miles is a long way, but my sun's energy covers it in under a minute.

The shockwave of crazy furking-hot water strikes the ice shelf first. Except, by now, the water isn't water anymore. It's gone "supercritical," inhabiting a state somewhere between liquid and gas. It's moving at many times supersonic speed, and its temperature is nearly a thousand degrees Fahrenheit.

The ice shelf doesn't stand a chance.

It doesn't melt so much as vanish, barely slowing the rise of water.

The dragons have deserted the colony, no doubt at Ravi's instruction. I figured they would, and I'm wildly thankful. Because I don't care how "heat tolerant" you are, what I'm doing will kill any living thing in an instant.

They've left Marius wedged precariously in the mouth of the shaft I made, which is where the shockwave strikes it. The force would have crushed a less hardy structure like a beer can. But Michael Shelton is an engineer who knows the limits of his creation—and, as the ice above and around it melts, Marius rises. Withstanding the immense heat, the circular structure shoves its way violently up a chimney that, while still far too small for it, has walls that liquefy and fall aside with each new mile.

Convection.

Ascension.

As Marius penetrates the collapsing ice shelf, it spins like a top in the rising thermal energy. But it never upends. Flooding the Ops Deck gives it enough ballast to keep it upright. More or less. Mostly.

I try not to think about the people inside. I can only pray they're not cooking like potted lobsters. Shelton seemed certain the water temperature would be within Marius's tolerable limits. But he didn't know—couldn't know—how much fire my dragon contains.

After all, neither did I.

Finally, in an orgy of silent violence, the supercharged water, now greatly cooled by its battle with the ice, breaks through to Europa's airless surface. In doing so, it shoots a geyser thirty miles wide that reaches orbital heights.

Marius rises too, and, for one horrific moment, I'm afraid the colony will be blasted into space as though shot from a cannon. But instead, Marius tumbles free. It clears the geyser and strikes the adjacent ice, which has grown soft enough to catch it rather than shatter it.

There it settles, right side up, bobbing like a cork on a surface that, right now, bears the consistency of a piña colada.

As soon as I witness this, with an awareness that I barely understand but can't deny, I pull back my dragon.

Then I watch the rest of the reaction play itself out.

By now, a small sea has formed on the moon's surface. It exists on the knife's edge between the icy cold of space and the unhampered geothermal energy of Europa's core.

Without my dragon to fuel it, my undersea sun finally collapses. As it does, the surrounding ocean—still planetary and vast—rushes in to fill the vacuum left behind.

Rushes in on me.

The last thing I know is the unbearable pressure of a literal mountain of water hitting me from all sides. Then I'm gone, just one stupid kid dying alone in a worldwide ocean.

SIX – Day 24

I'm dead.

So why am I still naked?

I can tell I'm still naked because water rushes past parts of my body that water doesn't generally rush past. I've been naked a lot lately, and

I haven't enjoyed it much. So, it would be a big bummer to find out the afterlife is a big nudist colony.

I'm also moving—and moving fast. Except I'm not actually *doing* the moving. I'm being conveyed.

I open my eyes and realize, first, that I'm still underwater and, second, I'm staring into Ravi's face.

It takes me about two seconds to put it together.

Wait! No!

Since I can't talk, I start struggling. But my arms are gripped by other Europans, at least two dozen of them. My legs too. They're bearing me upward, their tails pounding the water furiously. Their effort is helped by the thermal current rising from an ocean floor that has become a webwork of massive, magma-lit fissures.

With Smokey gone and its hydrothermic vent turned into something that more closely resembles a lava canyon, the dragons' world just got a lot bigger.

If nothing else, I've managed to save them.

But any satisfaction I might feel is squashed by my understanding of what Ravi's doing and what it will mean.

I can't let another person die! I *won't*. Except, there's nothing I can do to stop it.

As the dragons bear me higher, Ravi's eyes lose focus, and his head sags. The sight is like an ice pick in my heart.

Around us, the water begins to cool appreciably. We must be nearing the surface, though the further we get from the magma fissures, the darker it becomes. Abruptly, I'm tugged to the left and into a section of half-frozen seawater that is brutally, savagely cold. My body begins shivering.

The dragons swim even faster.

Within a minute, I can no longer feel my body, and it's getting hard to think. Ravi seems to have lost consciousness—though I can no longer remember why that's a bad thing.

The next thing I know, I'm huddled on a level floor, curled up and shaking uncontrollably. With some effort, I summon just enough of my dragon to scare off the bitter chill.

Then, as I sit up, Ravi's lifeless body lands in my lap.

As understanding comes crashing back, I begin sobbing, uttering wails of bitter, aching grief. With tear-blinded eyes, I lift Ravi and hug him to my chest.

I don't know how long I sit there—naked, exhausted, and clutching the body of my friend. Finally, though, I lift my head and look around.

I'm beside Marius's moon pool—except I'm not. I'm on the Lab Deck, and the real moon pool is one level down, in the Ops Deck that's currently flooded. I'm looking at the central stairwell, filled all the way to this point with cold ocean.

That's when I notice the dragons.

Dozens of them are in the water, their tiny heads bobbing as they regard me. Of course, I know what it is they want.

Reverently, I pass Ravi's body down to them. Three swim close to collect it. One of them gently removes the bracelets from Ravi's arm. Then, with me looking on, he offers them to another of his comrades. This new Europan seems to briefly consider the whole situation before finally accepting one—just one. Then, with the other bracelet gripped in his tiny fist, he glides over to the edge of the moon pool and offers it to me.

"I don't deserve that," I say.

He doesn't move.

"He died to save me. That's enough."

He still doesn't move.

Finally, reluctantly, I accept. The bracelet is made of smooth black metal. It's way too small, of course, to fit around my wrist—so I slip it onto the ring finger of my right hand. It sits there comfortably enough, though I worry that it won't survive my next dragon incident. My mother never wore a wedding band. Gold melts too easily.

"Thanks," I say.

The dragon nods. Without thinking, I dub him, "Eric." Something tells me Greenjeans would approve.

Eric disappears beneath the water. A moment later, the rest follow, taking Ravi's body with them.

I sit there and stare at the dark water for a minute before climbing to my feet. Six corridors extend away from the central chamber. There's no one in sight. I pick the one that I know leads to Darcy's lab. I'm still naked, of course. But I'm way past worrying about it.

When I reach the lab, I find its door halfway open. I push inside.

"Darcy?"

The place is a wreck. Everything that wasn't nailed down has been tossed around as if by a tornado. There's no one here.

I try the next lab, and the next, but they're all the same. Running now, my exhaustion forgotten, I finally find a big library that occupies the corridor's end. Here, chairs and tables have been thrown every which way, sprinkled liberally with scattered books and upended and smashed computer terminals.

But still no colonists.

A viewport catches my eye. Through it, I can see Europa's frozen surface. Marius seems to be floating in a large, slushy lake. Some distance away, a massive plume of rising water vapor dominates the airless void. Much of this vapor freezes, only to settle down slowly — *so slowly* — in crystalline form.

It's snowing on Europa.

A dozen small monitors occupy one wall, all of them mounted securely enough to have survived the maelstrom. On each is a live feed that shows a different part of the colony. I scan them for some sign of movement.

I mean, where *is* everybody?

Then I spot the Ice Deck Breakroom, which, as far as I can figure, is positioned directly above me.

It looks as if Marius's entire complement is there, ninety-some people crowded together in one corner, near the viewports. Many appear injured, supporting themselves on crutches or wearing slings. Most are bloodied to some extent.

At least they're alive.

But then I count the twenty grim-faced blackbirds that guard them. Like the colonists, many appear injured, though it doesn't deter them. Each brandishes a rifle, its business end directed at the frightened crowd, corralling them like cattle.

Then, near the bottom of the frame, I spot Miranda.

I gasp. Somehow, I'd forgotten how hideously burned she was.

Her only remaining eye, with its teardrop birthmark, is wild with barely contained madness. She grips a pistol in her one remaining hand. Before her kneel Shelton, Kim, and Darcy. The familiar tableau almost makes me vomit.

Greenjeans. Tuttle.

The blood drains from my face.

Apparently, there's audio, too, because Miranda says, *"Michael and Kimberly Shelton, I find you both guilty of sedition."* Her words are slurred, either from pain or painkillers. *"Darcy Piatkowski, I find you guilty of theft. I sentence you all to death by public execution."*

"What did I steal?" Darcy demands. She looks frightened but defiant.

Miranda glares at her. *"You know what you took! Who you took!"* Her insane rage makes even the blackbirds seem uneasy.

She's talking about *me*.

"I'm responsible!" Shelton exclaims desperately. *"I get that you need to make an example, broadcast to the spacer community that CSE's still in charge. Fine. Use me! My name is the rallying cry! Killing Kim and Darcy won't send any message at all."*

"Maybe not," Miranda slurs, never taking her cycloptic gaze off Darcy. *"But it'll make me feel better."*

Kim pleads, *"My brother's dead. What does it matter now?"*

"He was mine!" Miranda screams.

A single soldier steps forward warily. I recognize him.

"Uh… Ms. Coffin?" Corporal Exler ventures.

Miranda pauses, turning toward him. *"I'm fine. Forgive my outburst, corporal."*

Exler looks about to say more. Instead, he just nods and steps back.

"Now then," Miranda continues, this time in a more level tone. *"Let's get this unpleasantness behind us as quickly as possible. Doctor Shelton, what say we start with you?"*

Kim visibly pales. I see it even on the vidcam.

Shouting in protest, Shelton tries to rise. But his wrists, ankles, and knees are all bound. All he can do is struggle like a landed fish as Miranda orders one of her blackbirds to drag Kim across the room. Miranda follows, gun in hand.

As this happens, I see Exler stiffen, his expression uncertain.

But he doesn't stop it.

And I think, *I'll never get there in time.*

Then I look at the ceiling two feet above my head.

Low-G.

I can do it. But I have to find the right spot, away from anyone. The last thing I need is another death on my conscience, accidental or not. So, turning in a circle, I run to a corner that's away from the view of Europa's surface, away from the section of the Breakroom where I *think* they're dragging Kim. Away from everyone up there.

Then, with one eye on the monitor as Miranda points her weapon at my sister's forehead, I call my dragon.

And jump.

SEVEN – Day 24

Honest to God, I'm not thinking about "dramatic entrances."

I just want to get there as fast as I can.

Leaping straight upward, I can tell immediately that my inertia's more than enough to slam me into the ceiling. Before it does, I throw my dragon—a lot of it—up at the riveted steel. The thermal wave is so intense that everything within ten feet of me either melts or turns to ash. The ceiling, which receives the brunt of it, all but vanishes.

Much of the steel goes straight from solid to a noxious gas. The rest liquefies, raining down around me in massive globs. As my body reaches the ceiling, or rather where the ceiling *used* to be, what's left parts like a misty veil.

Then I'm through, rising into the Breakroom above.

Two seconds. No more.

"What the furk?" someone yells. I never do find out who.

Clearing the hole I've made, I spread my legs and straddle it. Then, calling back my dragon, I look around and confirm that I didn't harm anybody.

For a change.

"Miranda!" I exclaim. "*Stop!*"

And stop she does, staring at me as if I'm a ghost.

"Andy?"

"Andy!" Kim and Darcy exclaim together.

In the Breakroom's far corner, every single blackbird points his rifle in my direction. Behind them, the remaining colonists gape at me, wide-eyed.

For several heartbeats, no one moves.

Well, at least I've got everyone's attention.

Then Miranda shrieks, "Look at me!" Real tears mix with the false one on her unblemished cheek. "Look at what you *did* to me!"

"It was… an accident," I stammer, wondering how true that is.

"You betrayed me! You picked these terrorists over me!"

Like flipping a switch, I go from guilt-ridden to pissed off. "You want to talk about betrayal? All you've ever done is lie to me and manipulate me. The only terrorist here is *you!*"

She keeps glaring but says nothing.

So, I press on. "Well, it's over now." I face the blackbirds. "Put down your guns. If you pull those triggers, I'll kill every single one of you, and I really... *really*... don't want to do that." I lock eyes with Exler. "I know you hate me. I've killed thirteen of your friends. I get that. The first was an accident, and the others died because they were firing on unarmed civilians. But it all stops now."

"Shoot them!" Miranda screams. "Shoot them all!"

It's probably the worst thing she could have said. She comes off as a raving nut job. I can see it in Exler's eyes, in all their eyes.

I say, "Put down your guns. *Now.*"

Exler places his rifle on the floor. After a few seconds, the other blackbirds follow suit. Within a half-minute, everyone is unarmed.

Almost everyone.

"Traitors!" Miranda exclaims, the "good" half of her face red with rage. Despite everything she's done, I can't help feeling a stab of pity.

She whirls on me, the gun still in her hand. "You're a monster!"

"I know."

"I've only taken four lives! You're worse than I ever was!"

I don't reply.

She sneers, the expression hideous on her ruined face. "You betrayed me for *them!*" She gestures with her pistol at Kim, who lies at her feet, helpless.

"These people are right."

"They're criminals!"

"This isn't our world, Miranda. It never was. It belongs to the Europans."

"This world... every world... belongs to Coffin Industries! To *me!*"

"No."

"*Yes!*" She levels the pistol at Kim's forehead, her finger exploring its trigger.

And I suddenly think: *Four?*

She said *four* lives.

Spencer. Tuttle. Greenjeans. Could she be talking about Francis or Carlos? But that makes five. And, if she counts *them*, then doesn't she have to include any other colonists who've died because of her invasion?

Or am I looking at this the wrong way?

And, just like that, the final penny drops.

"Miranda," I say quickly. "Answer me a question. Just one question!"

She hesitates. Kneeling before her, Kim's eyes are squeezed shut.

I make my guess. "What happened to Charlie?"

Her single eye blinks. "Wh — at?"

"Your older brother. The only true thing that Miranda Fiero told me. What happened to him?"

"He… died."

"How?"

I expect her to balk. I expect her to tell me to shut up or go furk myself. But instead, she just looks at me. The pistol's still pointed at Kim, but at least her finger has moved from the trigger. "I told you. Heart failure."

"Like Spencer?"

The gun wavers. "What?"

"Spencer died of a heart attack too."

Her only eye loses focus as if fixed on something in the past.

Around us, no one moves or speaks.

I say, "Miranda?"

She looks at me again. After a pile of uncomfortable moments go by, she says faintly, "I did what needed doing."

"What did you say?"

She raises her chin defiantly. "I did what needed doing."

"What's that mean?"

No answer.

So, I tell her what it means. "You killed your brother. You poisoned him with something, the same as Spencer. Something to make it look like a heart attack."

"They were in the way."

"In the way of what?" I ask.

"In *my* way!" she exclaims. "Charlie was Father's golden boy, the heir apparent! But I had twice his brains and ten times his nerve. Charlie was a dreamer, his head always in the clouds. He would have torn our family business down if I'd let him! I did us all a favor!"

"And Spencer?"

"He and Father stole this mission from me! After everything I did to get it, to get *here*, they just took it all away. I couldn't let it stand. I always keep what's mine!" Her scarred face twists into a grotesque snarl.

"Miranda. Please put down the gun."

She doesn't go that far, but she does lower the pistol from Kim's forehead, which feels like a major victory.

"You're mine," she says in a faraway, dreamy voice.

"No, I'm not. I never was."

Naïve as this probably sounds, right now, I really do think I have a handle on the situation. Sure, Miranda's unhinged, if not completely insane. But some part of me still clings to the desperate hope that, somewhere inside, there's enough of Miranda Fiero to get her to listen to me.

But I'm wrong.

Dead wrong.

"You're mine!" she suddenly screams, her single eye blazing. "And I keep what's mine!"

Then, to my utter astonishment, Miranda points her pistol at me.

I have a split second to think—and I blow it.

My first thought is a thermal wall, but I don't have time. My second thought is another fire spear, but the viewport is too close to risk it. I don't get a third thought. Instead, I just stand there like a dope and do nothing.

Unlike my sister, who bursts into flames.

It happens so *fast!* One instant, Kim's kneeling with her ankles, knees, and wrists cuffed; the next, every inch of her exposed skin is alive with fire. It's nothing like what I do, or any Kind I've ever known. This isn't about waves of heat. These are good old-fashioned flames.

Her plastic cuffs melt away in an instant. So, of course, do her clothes and what little hair she's grown back since the lift. What's left behind is a ball of roaring plasma, a Goddess of Fire whose sharp yellow minions are already heating up the crowded room and licking at the riveted ceiling.

Before anyone can react, Kim leaps to her feet and throws herself at Miranda in the instant before the pistol goes off.

The bullet whizzes past my ear, ricochets off the wall behind me, and strikes a blackbird in the shoulder. The man cries out, bleeding badly.

Miranda, in the meantime, *shrieks.*

Kim has her flaming arms around the other woman. As they crash to the floor in a tangle of limbs, my sister's fire engulfs Miranda, who thrashes like an animal in full panic. But Kim holds her, her eyes blazing—literally blazing—while her minions do their work.

Through it all, no one moves, not even the wounded man.

Thankfully, it doesn't take long.

Miranda's agonized cries rise in pitch. I hear Shelton calling his wife's name. I hear exclamations of horror from colonists and blackbirds alike.

I feel sick… in my stomach, in my heart, and in my soul.

But God forgive me, I think of Eric and feel some satisfaction, too.

Ten seconds later, Miranda Coffin dies by fire.

When it's over, Kim sits up, straddling what's left of the charred body, and glances around as if awakening from a trance. She looks down at her hands, which are still alight with flames, and wails, "What's… happening to me?"

Her fear gets me moving. Running up, I kneel beside her and pull her into my arms. The fact that we're both naked means nothing at this point. She's my friend. She's my sister.

And somehow, inexplicably, she's Kind.

"It's okay," I tell her. "It's just your dragon. It won't hurt you. It *is* you. Relax and call it back. That's all you have to do. Just take a slow, steady breath and pull it back in."

She trembles. But then she does what I tell her. And, almost at once, the flames recede, retreating into her skin.

Moments later, they're gone.

"Kim!" Shelton calls from where he still kneels, helplessly bound. "Kimmie! Babe!"

"I'm okay," she whispers, and I'm not sure if she's talking to herself, to Shelton, or to me.

"Hey, idiots!" Darcy yells at the blackbirds, who're watching Kim and me like we're the star attractions at a freak show—except for the shot guy whom Exler is attending. A few glance Darcy's way. "I'll make a deal with you," she says. "You cut us loose, and I'll keep your friend there from bleeding to death."

"Do it," Corporal Exler orders. Then, when none of the soldiers move, he barks, "Do it!"

Two blackbirds hurry forward and wordlessly snip Darcy's and Shelton's bonds. Shelton doesn't even bother standing. He crawls over to Kim and, without hesitation or apology, pulls her out of my arms and into his. Fortunately, as with my own dragon, there's no residual heat radiating off Kim's body.

When it's done, it's done.

In the meantime, Darcy stumbles stiffly over to the wounded man. As she moves past me, her hand strokes my face. It's a quick gesture, almost absent, but there's a lot behind it.

And it helps—a little.

As Darcy goes to work, Exler steps nervously over to where Shelton still holds his trembling, naked wife. "Mister Shelton," he says. "I'm Corporal Exler with the CSE. With the deaths of Commander Spencer, Sergeant Massey... and now Ms. Coffin..." He clears his throat. "Well, I'm now in command of Conquest's security contingent."

"Good for you," Shelton mutters.

"Mister Shelton, I want to... apologize."

Shelton looks up but says nothing.

So, Exler plows forward. "Ms. Coffin was acting irrationally when she ordered this assault on your colony. I regret the loss of life."

Shelton still says nothing.

"Under the circumstances... I'd like to place my people at your disposal."

"Yeah?" replies Shelton, his skepticism razor-sharp. "And why's that? Afraid either Andy or my wife might..." When Kim flinches in his arms, he tightens his embrace and reboots. "...afraid that what happened to some of your colleagues will happen to you?"

Exler glances at my sister and me. "Honestly, sir," he tells Shelton. "That's part of it. But it's not all of it."

"Then what's the rest?" Shelton asks.

"Andy Brand. He... um... saved my life."

Mike Shelton smiles without humor. "Well, there's a lot of that going around. Okay, Corporal Exler, you and your blackbirds want to switch sides? Fine by me. You can start by getting our heroes... both of them... something to wear."

"Yes, sir. Right away."

EIGHT – Day 27

So, you're probably wondering what happens now.

Furked if I know.

It's a few days later, and I find myself sitting alone in the Breakroom, looking out the viewport at the freshly scarred surface of the moon. Massive plumes of water vapor continue to rise from the slushy lake, filling the sky so completely that they partially obscure the massive shape of Jupiter. For its part, Marius still floats in the lake's center, steady and nicely level, though Ops Deck remains flooded. Shelton and his people — his surviving people — are still working on ways to pump it out, provided doing so won't destabilize us. At least, in the short term, we're safe enough. There's some risk that the surface temperature might drop and ice-lock the entire structure. But every analysis run so far indicates that the fissure I created in the moon's crust will keep this thermal pool at a more or less constant temperature, well, forever.

"*There* you are!"

Kim, my sister — I'm still getting used to thinking of her like that — appears in the doorway. She looks tired, her face a little pale, and her clothes disheveled. Her dark hair is stubby, like mine, five o'clock shadow of the scalp.

I've seen little of her since everything that happened — happened.

"Hey," I say, doing my best to muster a smile.

She comes over, grabs a chair, and joins me at the window. "You okay?" she asks.

I glance sideways at her. "Are you?"

"Yes and no."

"That sounds about right."

"I just got back from *Conquest*," she tells me. "I've been looking for you. You don't have a comms with you. Didn't think you'd be *here* of all places."

"There's never anybody in here these days," I tell her. "And sometimes I get tired of my room."

"Darcy tells me you've been keeping to yourself."

I shrug. "She's got an infirmary full of patients to worry about. In fact, *everybody's* busy, except me. You and Shelton have been up on *Conquest* with Exler and the blackbirds. And most of the rest of the colony…" My words trail off.

"They're afraid of you."

I nod.

"Me, too." Then, when I look at her, hurt, she adds hastily, "No! I mean, they're afraid of *me*, too."

"Oh. Yeah."

She shakes her head. "Friends. People I've known for years. Lived with. Worked with. They look at me now like I'm a ticking bomb. A lot of them won't even touch me."

"Shelton?"

She smiles. "Except him. He's been really wonderful."

"He's a good guy," I say. "A good… brother-in-law." It's the first time it's occurred to me to think of him in those terms.

"Furk," Kim mutters. It's not a word she uses very often. "All my life, I've had this… thing, this knack. Fire couldn't burn me. Not many people knew about it. But those who did accepted it, more or less. But now, it's totally different. As a psychologist, I suppose I get it. A passive ability has become an active one. A peculiarity has become a potential threat. I can see why they're scared." She shakes her head. "But as *me*, well, it really sucks."

"That's why we hide," I tell her. "Conceal and Protect."

"Conceal and Protect," she echoes. "Except that's not really practical, given where we are."

No argument there. Everybody on Marius knows. Everybody on *Conquest* knows. That's a lot of people, most of them spacers. And spacers, as I've learned, have a grapevine.

"Any more dragon stuff happen up there?" I ask her pointedly.

She shakes her head. "No. But I've been having really awful nightmares. It doesn't help that my husband and I have had to sleep in a strange Liquid Bricks bed these past few nights. Every time I startle awake, I half expect to find myself aflame again, to find that I've burned poor Shelton to death beside me."

As she says this, her eyes fill up.

I take her hand.

"That's not how it works," I tell her, making her look at me. "Your dragon'll only come when you call it."

"I didn't call it with Miranda."

"Didn't you?"

Her lip quivers. "She was about to kill you."

"I know. So… maybe, on some level, you *did* call it."

"Maybe."

She glances around the Breakroom, her gaze locking on a spot near one corner, where the floor is still scorched and a little misshapen from heat. A sign of violence. A sign of death.

The Breakroom hasn't been used much since that day. Lately, people have been eating in their private quarters, or their labs, or anywhere but here. The floor I melted through has been fixed, but most of the chairs and tables have been stacked against one wall and, for the time being at least, left forgotten.

Kim says, "I murdered somebody."

"Is it murder when you do it to save someone else?" I ask.

"I don't know."

Again, I shrug. "Welcome to the club."

For a half minute, we just sit there, looking at each other. Finally, in a small voice, Kim says, "Little brother?"

"Yes, big sister?"

"What should I do now?"

"About your dragon?"

She nods.

I've been expecting this. For the past few days, Kim's buried herself in the admittedly complicated business of the colony's new reality. She insisted on going up to *Conquest* with Shelton, insisted on staying there until she was sure everything would be sorted out. But, as important as all that was and still is, wasn't it also a kind of escape? Denial's like the sun. It can seem bright and warm and inviting. But it can also blind you.

Okay, it's a lousy simile. But give me a break. It's been a rough couple of weeks.

"Let me teach you how to use it," I suggest. "Like Dad taught me."

"He did?"

"Yeah. On camping trips way out in the Jersey Pine Barrens. Away from everyone."

Kim sighs. "Not really an option on Europa."

"No, but our precautions back then were more about Conceal and Protect than any accidental damage we might cause. Look, we're both off the scope here. I've never heard of a Split who can do what you do. There's nothing like it in the Chronicles. You're special, Kim. I don't know how special. I don't know what your limits are, if any. But, together, I think we can figure it out."

"Okay," she says, offering her first smile since walking into the room. "The best way to control something is to understand it."

"You sound like him."

"Like your dad?"

"Like *our* dad."

"Really?"

I nod, and she gives my hand a squeeze.

"What's been going on up there on *Conquest*?" I ask.

"Quite a lot. The blackbirds fell into line pretty much right away, once Ray... Corporal Exler... took command and told them all what happened down here."

"Did he mention me killing a dozen more of them?" I ask bitterly. "Or did he spin it so it sounded like Miranda's fault?"

"Andy, it *was* her fault."

I don't reply.

Kim continues, "Anyway, Shelton's in *de facto* command now. That Captain Wei... what a sycophantic jackass... pledged his immediate and total cooperation, once he saw all the blackbirds that Shelton had at his back. *Conquest* now belongs to us."

"Good to hear. Any news about the System at large?"

At that, she laughs. "Oh yeah! The genie's out of the bottle. Every media outlet is lit up about the dragons. Shelton's used the Casimir Radio to transmit vids of Miranda's crimes, and now CSE is getting put under a microscope. Almost every nation on Earth is demanding an investigation and full accounting. In the meantime, at least three scientific expeditions to Europa have been mounted. We're quite famous! I only wish it wasn't going to take them years to get here."

"So, go get them," I say.

"What?"

"*Conquest* can make the trip in two weeks, right? It's got space aboard for two hundred passengers. Miranda told me so. If Shelton's got Wei, the blackbirds, and the crew in his corner, what's to stop him from flying back to Earth, collecting some kind of big contingent of scientists and media types, refueling, stocking up on supplies, and getting back here within a month or so."

Kim grins. "Andy, I don't think that's occurred to anyone yet! It's genius!"

"Sometimes, I get lucky. I'll bet Charles Coffin is freaking out."

"Shelton talked to him."

"Yeah?"

She nods. "He called him on our first day up there and offered his condolences about Miranda. Then, when Coffin started spouting threats about armed ships dropping on us like hammers, Shelton patiently told him about the vid footage he sent to the media. By now, Coffin's too busy with lawyers to worry about us. At best, we think his board of directors will force him out. He'll be lucky if he stays out of jail."

Despite myself, despite everything, I feel a quick stab of pity. Charles Coffin has lost both his children and is about to lose his empire. But then I remember New York and my pity vanishes like smoke.

"What happens now?" I ask.

"To us?"

"To Marius."

Kim offers us a long sigh. "We sit tight, I guess. Wait for visitors. We're not a mining colony anymore. Now we're a research station." She looks hard at me. "But Andy, I don't think you and I are going to be able to hide from what's coming. What you did… what we all did… is going to shine a light on more than the Europans. The truth about the Kind is going to come out. It's going to go public. I don't think Conceal and Protect can stand up under that much scrutiny."

I give myself a minute to consider what she's saying. Finally, I reply, "Well, maybe it's time. We've been in the shadows for so long."

"I just hope people can… accept us."

"I guess we'll see."

Kim rubs her face with her hands. "Well, I'm exhausted. Shelton's going to be up there at least through tomorrow. I need to get something to eat and then go lay down for about ten hours. Are *you* okay? I'm sorry I left you alone for so long."

"I'm fine," I tell her, and it's pretty much true. I look down at my right hand, where Ravi's Ring, as I've come to think of it, is still around my finger. It survived my last dragon calling without breaking a sweat, so to speak. Whatever it's made of, it has to have a crazy-high melting point.

Watching me, Kim asks, "Seen any of the dragons today?"

"Eric and a few of the others keep popping up. I think it's hard for them to come this close to the surface. The water's probably too cold. But they do it anyway. That's partly why I come here, to look for them. This morning, I think I taught them how to wave. I did it to Eric, and he mimicked it, and now they're all doing it."

She laughs. "Good to know."

Then she stands up, stretches, and kisses me on the cheek. "I can't keep my eyes open."

"Get some rest," I tell her.

"You, too. You've earned it." Then, putting a gentle hand on my shoulder, she adds, "You did good, little brother."

"Did I?"

"Yes, you did. Your parents would be proud."

That hits me kind of hard, mainly because it's something that hasn't really occurred to me before. I've betrayed so much of their teachings that I guess I never considered that, in the end, they might look at what I did and call it "good."

"Do you really think so?" I ask, croak really.

"Andy, you've saved a lot of lives and helped change things on a scale that's bigger than either of us can really grasp. And you wouldn't have been able to do any of that if you weren't Kind. So yes, they'd be proud." Then, after a moment, she adds, "I know *I* am."

She leaves me alone then, alone with my thoughts, my regrets, my worries. After a few more minutes, I go as well, walking slowly back toward my bedroom. I'm not tired, but there aren't too many places on the colony where I feel particularly welcome right now.

"Andy?"

I look up.

Darcy's standing there at the far end of the hallway, having just come up the stairs from the Lab Deck.

"You busy?" she asks.

"Nope."

She comes closer, looking tired but fantastic. She's wearing her typical jeans and t-shirt combo, except the t-shirt reads "Team Dragon," and it occurs to me for the first time that Marius must have some means to silk-screen fabric.

"I was hoping to find you," she says. "I just got off shift. Want to grab something to eat?"

I stare at her. "You sure?"

She laughs. "Of course, I'm sure. I'm hungry!"

"No, I mean… aren't you afraid of me?"

Her manner sobers. "Of course not."

"The rest are."

"*Some* are, I guess. But most of them are just a little freaked out. The simple truth is that everyone on this colony knows what you are."

"A monster."

"A hero."

I almost tell her that I'm not a hero. I almost tell her that, right now, I don't know what I am. But she's got these eyes —

"Um… there aren't any tables set up in the Breakroom," I say.

She smiles. "I was thinking about something more private. Like my quarters."

"Oh."

She reaches one hand out toward me. Her expression seems to mix hope and concern, affection and entreaty. "Come with me?" she asks, a tentative note in her voice.

"I'm still messed up," I tell her.

"Me, too," she replies. "Let's be messed up together."

So, in gratitude, I take the offered hand. Her small fingers are warm as they close around mine.

"Here's the problem," Darcy says with a smile.

"Problem?"

"Nobody's been using the kitchen lately. So, I hope you like dried fruit and protein bars, Andy Brand."

I start to let her lead me back down the corridor, only to stop in my tracks. "No," I say suddenly.

She looks back at me. "No? You don't like dried fruit and protein bars?"

"I mean… no, my name's not Brand." Then, when she looks puzzled, I laugh a little uncertainly and explain. "My people… the Kind… Dragons, we change last names all the time. Brand isn't my 'family' name. It's just what my parents picked the last time they had to relocate. Well, they're gone now, and I want a *new* last name, something meaningful. Something… real."

Darcy seems to consider that. "I think it's a great idea," she finally tells me. "Got something in mind?"

"Yeah." Then, meeting her eyes and throwing back my shoulders, I say, "Draco. I'm Andy Draco."

When she smiles, the *way* she smiles — well, it has a heat all its own. Before I know what's happening, she pulls me close and kisses me, long and deep. Electricity jolts me from my toes to the top of my head, driving away, at least for now, my worries, my regrets, and my weary grief. Her body feels amazing pressed against mine, and somewhere inside, I feel a different dragon stir.

Finally, Darcy pulls back just enough to whisper in my ear, "It's nice to meet you… Andy Draco."

And then, together, we head toward whatever comes next.

About the Author

Ty Drago is a full-time writer and the author of nine published novels, including his five-book *Undertakers* series, the first of which has been optioned for a feature film. *Torq*, a dystopian YA superhero adventure, was released by Swallow's End Publishing in 2018. Add to these one novelette, myriad short stories and articles, and appearances in two anthologies. He's also the founder, publisher, and managing editor of ALLEGORY (www.allegoryezine.com), a highly successful online magazine that, for more than twenty years, has featured speculative fiction by new and established authors worldwide.

Ty's currently just completed *The New Americans*, a work of historical fiction and a collaborative effort with his father, who passed away in 1992. If that last sentence leaves you with questions, check out his podcast, "Legacy: The Novel Writing Experience," to get the whole story.

He lives in New Jersey with his wife Helene, plus one cat and one dog.

Team Dragon

Adam H Zerance	Dr Douglas Vaughan
Amanda Cavanagh	Ed Washburn
Anita Morris	Eric S. Schaefer
Anne Frates	Eric W. Stephenson
Annie Allen	Felicia Browell
Anonymous	Gary Phillips
Apotheosis Studios	Gav
April Walters	Gordon Horne
Ashley VanMeter	Greg Levick
Aysha Rehm	H Lynnea Johnson
Beth Sparks-Jacques	Howard J. Bampton
Beverly Bambury	IndolentCin
Bradon Jurn	Isaac 'Will It Work' Dansicker
Butch Howard	Jakub Narębski
C.A. Rowland	Jay Targaryen
Carol Jones	JC Kang
Cat Hunter	JDN
Charissa D. Jones	Jeanne Talbourdet
Chris Cooke	Jenn Whitworth
Christopher J. Burke	Jennifer Della'Zanna
Craig "Stevo" Stephenson	Jennifer L. Pierce
Curtis & Maryrita Steinhour	Jeremy Audet
Dale A Russell	Johanna Sachs
Dan Nolan	John Green
Daniel Lin	John Idlor
Danielle Ackley-McPhail	John L. French
David Perkins	John Monahan
David Sherman	Judith Waidlich
David Stolarz	Julian White
Debbie Cairo	Julie Giles Cooke
Debra Lieven	Keith R.A. DeCandido
Dee Sauerwein	Keith Rohrer
Dex Greenbright	Ken Brandt
Dino Hicks	Kierin Fox

L.E. Custodio
Lark Cunningham
Leokii
Leon W Fairley
Lewis Phillips
Lisa1200
Lori B.
Lorraine Anderson
maileguy
Marc W.
Margaret Bumby
Margaret St. John
Margie Martinson-Brezina
Maria T
Maria V. Arnold
Mark Lukens
Megan Mackie
Melissa Phelps
Mia Naeyaert
Michael Brooker
Mishee Kearney
Museworthy Inc.
Nanci Moy & Dave Bean
NIna Amaya
Oren Truitt (or The Legendary
W. Oren Truitt Historian, Gun-
smith, Scholar)
Otter Libris
Paul May
Paul van Oven
Pete Niedzielski
Peter D Engebos
pjk
Rich Riley
Richard Clark
Rick Heinz
Rob in AUS
Robert C Flipse
Robert Claney
Robin Lynn
Russell Ventimeglia
Ryan Harron
Sasquatch
Scherrix
Scott Elson
Scott Schaper
Shane "Asharon" Sylvia
Shell S.
Shervyn
Sheryl R. Hayes
STEAMPUNK Chef James
Stephen Ballentine
Stephen Lesnik
Steve Locke
Tad L. J. Pierson
Taia Hartman
Tasha Turner
The Creative Fund
Thomas Karwacki
Tim DuBois
Tina Noe Good
Tom B.
ToniAnn Marini
Tony C
V Hartman DiSanto
Wil Bastion
Yes